An Eldritch Horror

In

Dracula's Court

An Eldritch Horror In Dracula's Court

Epic Dark Fantasy Where Gothic
Horror Meets Cosmic Terror

A.T. Hansen

Dedication

*For **Her.***
My love.
My Muse.
My Inspiration.
The one who found me.
The one who held the rose on our wedding day.
The one who brought our children into the world.
The one who holds my heart in this realm, and all others.

You are mine.

Contents

Prologue..i

Chapter 1 1

Chapter 2 6

Chapter 3 15

Chapter 4 21

Chapter 5 27

Chapter 6 33

Chapter 7 39

Chapter 8 47

Chapter 9 57

Chapter 10 65

Chapter 11 71

Chapter 12 79

Chapter 13 85

Chapter 14 99

Chapter 15 107

Chapter 16 115

Chapter 17 126

Chapter 18 132

Chapter 19 139

Chapter 20 151

Chapter 21 159

Chapter 22 167

Chapter 23 175

Chapter 24 185

Chapter 25...195

Chapter 26...203

Chapter 27...216

Chapter 28...227

Chapter 29...239

Chapter 30...249

Chapter 31...264

Chapter 32...273

Chapter 33...286

Chapter 34...299

Chapter 35...311

Chapter 36...324

Chapter 37...336

Chapter 38...347

Chapter 39...359

Chapter 40...371

Chapter 41...384

Chapter 42...393

Chapter 43...406

Chapter 44...425

Prologue

My death is at hand.

After centuries of meticulous planning and manipulating fate itself, I am counting down the moments until I embrace the sweet release from this life that has plagued me for so very long. However, before my physical vessel enters stasis and my essence rejoins the Void, I feel it necessary to recount my story in the following chronicles. Should my plans fail, and I arise once more within the cursed halls of this castle, these records will give me a chance to gain my bearings before the vile creatures above can sink their fangs into my soul again.

To be clear, this is not a suicide note, though it could be mistaken for one. No, the blade waiting in the gardens above to strike me down is nothing more than the first step on my path to retribution. It is but a tool to force my inevitable evolution with the passage of time. After all, in the land of the dead, even death may die.

In the Castle, no one suspects I am aware of the plans being prepared for me, that every upcoming event has been crafted by my will. Not my so-called wife, not the assassin, not even Dracula himself. Of all the secrets I have amassed during my time in this wretched place, the plot to kill my avatar is the most fiercely protected.

Once completed, these tomes shall be hidden in a location that only I can access, bound to my very being through shimmering golden threads of fate, ensuring my secrets shall remain as such until I return to claim them. Should Dracula's forces accomplish the impossible and breach this sanctum, their efforts shall be in vain. My words cannot be pried from the pages by either mortal or immortal eyes, as I am crafting them in the language of the Void, a dialect manifested before time itself.

If I am reading this, it means I have been thrust back into the world of the undead: a place of blood, death, and endless atrocities. The creatures who inhabit this world will masquerade as my friends and call me family, but they only do so to use me for their own ends. They will offer every temptation they can summon to entwine me within their webs of deceit once again. I pray to the endless spaces between the stars that, should I rise in these cursed halls once more, I may recall that the exotic fruits here are rotten beneath the surface, the riches utterly worthless, and the bonds of love naught but twisted illusions.

It is with great reluctance that I must confess my awareness that, should I awaken again in this place of sorrow and torment, by the time I relocate these records, it will likely be too late for me to take the words at face value. The fiends lording over the land will have inserted their talons deep within my heart and mind already. Despite this, it is my hope that I will contemplate these works in full and know that every word, as hard to believe as it may be, is true.

Even after the countless centuries I have endured, my mind still struggles to accept the horrible things I've done in the name of a home that was never my own, for a wife who never loved me, and in service to a lord who wants me dead. Perhaps, by recording these truths, I can spare myself the horror of reliving the suffering and guilt that have afflicted me since the very moment Dracula and his ilk embraced me as one of their own.

My powers surpass the width and breadth of creation, but the gifts of my mothers have left me with vulnerabilities that these monsters delight in exploiting to the fullest. The home I have longed for is not within this Castle. The love I so desperately desire is not to be found with the one whose forked tongue venomously calls me husband.

If all goes according to plan, none of this will matter, and my records will remain untouched for eternity. When death finally dies, I shall rise in a realm far removed from this nightmare. Rise again with *her*. However, even the best of plans has flaws, and Dracula's insanity may cause him to take an unexpected path, subverting all of my efforts. In this scenario, I would have assurances that I can recall my time here and use that knowledge to defend myself from the unyielding onslaught sure to come.

   If I open my eye in this wretched Castle once more, then let there be no hesitation. *Kill them all.*

Chapter 1
The Fates

Since the birth of the physical realm of reality, multiple cultures have recognized the existence of the Fates. Three entities who together weave the strings of destiny for Gods and men alike. This trio appears in many forms and under various names across the multiverse, but the basic concept always remains the same: a divine triumvirate responsible for constructing the fabric of reality. They ensure major events come to pass and prophecies are fulfilled.

The truths of the Fates are far more grotesque than most believe, and can be traced all the way back to Azh'kaaroth, the birthing place where physical creation escaped the formless Void.

To most, the power that the Fates wield is terrifying and inescapable. Even the Gods tremble before them as their destinies are woven, tied, and cut by the hands of the Fates. But what happens when the Fates die? Who then takes up the needle and thread? If left untouched, will the very fabric of existence unravel?

These questions haunt me each time I turn my gaze back and watch the abhorrent scene unfold as the strain of pushing my frail infantile body out of the Void and into a physical form forces my mothers, the Fates of Azh'kaaroth, beyond the brink of life and death.

***

High atop a mountain, far above the clouds, a triune of screams pierces the air in unison. The sound echoes off of white marble pillars and through the ears of the Fates' doulas, who helplessly watch as the twisted form, which once was three individuals, writhes in agony. Barely recognizable limbs lash out, conjoined in a grotesque amalgamation of flesh surrounding a swollen belly.

The abomination, a squirming mass of flesh, has become a chaotic fusion of appendages, with arms protruding at unnatural angles, some still reaching out to grasp at invisible threads. Two of the heads, partially melded together, still sit upon the poor entity's neck, while the third emerges from the central mass just above a swollen breast. Their faces contort in agony as each contraction tears through their unnatural form, accompanied by the sickeningly wet sounds of meat ripping.

What caused my mothers to fuse into this monstrosity, I know not, but the results are disturbing to behold, even for me, who has seen firsthand the horrors hiding in the deepest recesses of the Abyss.

As my birth approaches, tendrils strain to escape their prison of flesh, stretching an overly distended belly. Blood flows from the single birthing canal, spilling across the temple's stone tiles. It seems like an impossible amount, streaming rivers of crimson rushing through crevasses in the carved floor. The creature begins to convulse violently, its multitude of limbs flailing in a macabre dance of agony.

With one final, terrible shriek, a child is born. As I fully emerge, the air becomes thick with the stench of decay and heavy with the oppressive weight of destiny.

While one might expect me to have arrived covered in tentacles, thousands of eyes, or otherwise horribly disfigured, considering the nightmare from whence I came, I appeared to be perfectly normal by human standards: a larger-than-average boy crying out in the cold night air. All traces of the nightmarish appendages tearing the Fates apart from within were gone.

The only hint that I was anything but typical was the corpses littering the temple grounds; demigod wet-nurses, all drained of their life force, the very instant my shrieking form escaped from my mothers' womb. The bodies, full of life and vigor just moments before, now lay strewn across the ancient temple in various states of decay.

Weakly looking toward the last surviving handmaiden, who had been calmly mopping sweat from their foreheads with a rag, the Fates issued their final words in unison: "Take him and run. They're coming for him."

With that, the timeless entities responsible for weaving the strings of destiny slipped from the physical realm, too weak to even hold their son before passing through the veil of life and death.

The young midwife did as instructed, wrapping me up in cloth and fleeing the temple as fast as she could without ever looking back, leaving before my mothers' misshapen body had even started to grow stiff.

No one was left to entomb them in the earth or even to build a funeral pyre, nor would anyone come to do so. Even the Gods of Prime, usually omnipotent and unwavering, now shuddered with a primal fear so profound that they dared not approach the ancient temple. The once-sacred shrine became a place of unspeakable horror, defiled by powers predating existence itself. In the face of this unimaginable dread, the Gods abandoned the temple, leaving it to fester as a forsaken monument to the horrors that came to pass there.

Reflections:

I often find myself wondering if they knew this was their destiny in advance and had simply accepted it, or if my birth was outside their scope of control. I have observed my mothers in the time before my conception and found them to be three separate entities until they became impregnated. Strangely enough, they seem to be aware of my presence when I watch them, their faces contorting into a mixture of sorrow and joy as they look toward me.

I fear they knew all along that their feverous wish, to keep me from those who would use and abuse my power, was always doomed to fail.

Chapter 2
The Maiden, the Mother, and the Crone

The existence of the young midwife who fled the temple with my frail body is shrouded in mystery, even to me. My best efforts to ascertain her origins have met with failure time and time again. Each time I try to peer through the veil of time and space to learn more of her, I find myself greeted by a veil of impenetrable darkness. She simply appears in the temple after my conception, alongside the others, to help the Fates prepare for my arrival. To be honest, I don't know if any of them even *existed* prior to that moment or if the universe at large manifested them as a response to the unfolding events.

Even as I recall her now, my memories carry a

great swell of pity for her life. When she left the temple, cradling my frail body in her arms, she appeared as a young girl of about seventeen cycles. Yet, as I toddled through my earliest years, her face aged with unnatural speed. Once I was able to form coherent sentences, she had the appearance of a woman in her early thirties.

We were constantly on the move during my early years, rarely settling in one place for more than a handful of months. I didn't understand then, but she feared the unspeakable forces hunting me, forces that would stop at nothing to claim their prize. My guardian was careful, always one step ahead, never raising suspicion despite her unnaturally rapid aging. From fishing villages along jagged coasts to the sprawling tent encampments of nomadic hunters, and even into vast cities with their labyrinthine streets, we passed through worlds like ghosts, lingering just long enough to touch their edges before disappearing again.

Despite the constant shuffling from one home to the next, my guardian raised me in a life full of laughter and bliss, determined to enshrine within me a deep sense of joy and humanity. Her smile, though often fleeting, shielded me from the shadows ever nipping at our heels. As I grew, she fueled my insatiable curiosity, imparting all her wisdom about the lands we explored. Her vast understanding appeared limitless, exceeding what a lifetime of study might achieve.

Again, this raises questions about the woman who raised me. Who was she, truly? This mystery haunts me to this day. How could a woman, her only possessions being a battered satchel and the child she carried, know so much about the world's hidden corners? The scholars in their gilded halls would have struggled to match her understanding. I would even go so far as to suggest her innate knowledge would challenge even the immortal Librarian, who wards over Dracula's endless tomes. Was she, perhaps, a goddess in disguise? Or a construct of some divine mechanism meant to protect me? I will likely never know.

Eventually, our path led to a small village nestled between snow-capped mountains, a place that would become our last refuge. The locals were simple folk, bound by a code of honor that governed every aspect of their lives. The men toiled in mines that dotted the mountainsides or hunted the local wildlife for food, while the women raised children, cooked, and did what foraging they were able to accomplish during the brief warm months.

The people here were fiercely loyal to one another and morally pure by most human standards. Honor was more than a code; the laws were strictly adhered to, and any of them would drop everything at a moment's notice to help one of their own.

The villagers were territorial and obnoxiously superstitious, terrified of anything they couldn't explain. Magic inspired utter dread in these people, who considered it evil in any context. This sheer terror ran so deep that if anyone in the village developed 'supernatural' gifts or was even perceived to be unusually lucky, they would be banished from the village without a second thought.

This deep-seated distrust of anything falling beyond their mundane existence extended to outsiders as well. While they would occasionally tolerate a random merchant to visit long enough to make trades, no one was permitted to settle in the village unless through an arranged marriage. Even these pairings tended to stem from other local mountain villages that were every bit as xenophobic.

We arrived in the dead of winter, my guardian wearing the guise of a frail grandmother raising her grandson alone. By this time, her aging had reached a point where the ruse was no longer questioned, and I had grown into an awkward, lanky youth. The villagers allowed us to stay, perhaps out of pity or guilt, settling us in a modest cabin at the forest's edge, just beyond the village proper on the path leading up to the mines.

My 'grandmother' made her keep as an herbalist, mending injured miners and concocting remedies for various ailments. The people kept us at arm's reach at all times, not convinced that the old woman wasn't performing vile, forbidden magic in her healing arts even though they had used similar techniques for generations. Eventually, they grew accustomed to our presence, though we would forever be outsiders to them, distrusted and not part of the flock, but allowed to remain for our usefulness.

In retrospect, I believe she chose this place

deliberately. Here, hidden among jagged peaks and untouched wilderness, there was no concentrated magic to accelerate my growth or magnify the faint whispers of my power. The mountains became our fortress, their rugged spires a natural barrier shielding me from the predatory eyes of those who sought me.

I have viewed my guardian many times over the ages, sometimes out of nostalgia or loneliness, but many more out of sheer curiosity. Doing so has made me see her through new eyes. Her sacrifice has become more apparent, her frailty more pronounced.

Through her, I learned the steep cost of my existence. Though I had no control over it, my presence, my need, fed on her vitality. It drained her, stole her years, yet she never spoke a word of resentment. I think she feared that knowing the truth of what I was would crush me. It still amazes me that she didn't abandon or hate me for what I was unknowingly doing to her as I grew.

Grandmother guarded me with unyielding vigilance. She knew my abilities would awaken long before I could control them, and once they did, she drilled into me the dangers of discovery. She also knew a high cost would be paid if the townsfolk ever learned of my true nature.

Most times, suspected practitioners of the forbidden arts were banished without mercy, though some, the unlucky few, met more brutal fates. Blood-stained cages stood as grim reminders in the village square, silent monuments to their fear.

As for myself, well, this is when life became complicated. Prior to this point, I was blissfully unaware of my horrifying creation or my true nature. But, as often happens with those who possess mystical gifts, as puberty began, so too did my abilities reveal themselves.

My powers seeped through the cracks. At first, it was in dreams; visions of places that my grandmother could find rare herbs or warnings of approaching storms. Then, they came in waking moments: flashes of insight, stray whispers from the threads of time.

One winter evening, I caught a bottle my grandmother dropped before it shattered on the floor. Another day, I steered a hunter away from a path where I knew a bear waited, saving his life without him realizing it. Grandmother would scold me for helping the villagers in this way, knowing that if I saved one too many miners from avalanches, animal attacks, or cave-ins, we would have a serious problem.

"They won't see a miracle. They'll see something to fear, and you... You will become the monster they seek to destroy," she told me, her eyes dark with worry. "These people don't forgive what they don't understand."

I tried to heed her wisdom, but my desire to belong often overpowered my caution. As a hard-headed teenager, I couldn't grasp the idea that the villagers could be angry with me for helping them. It hurt knowing that I could save someone from harm, but was bound not to act.

Still, I trusted my grandmother's judgment, and I had seen firsthand the villagers' paranoia, so I kept myself in check for the most part. I had enough issues with them for not being born a part of their community; it was best not to amplify their problems with me by feeding their mistrust.

Unfortunately, not all of my 'visions' were so kind or helpful. On occasion, they thrust my mind's eye into utter darkness, where writhing nightmares watched over me with grand bulbous orbs. Other times, I would glimpse monstrous creatures for which I had no words to describe. Half-man, half-wolf fiends stalking unfamiliar woods, fanged humans suckling the life force from babes, and men stripped of flesh yet somehow walking around as if still alive. Nightmarish premonitions haunted my dreams, causing me to wake with bloodcurdling screams.

Thankfully, our hut was far enough removed from the village itself that no one could hear my cries of terror. The locals' fearful nature was compounded once the sun disappeared behind the mountains. They believed all sorts of devilish creatures would stalk the woods at night, from disgruntled spirits of the dead to faceless monsters looking to make a meal of anyone foolish enough to be out in the dark. This worked to my advantage, as no one would ever be outside their homes this far away from the village proper to hear my cries when the night terrors would strike.

It was during these nights that I would venture outside, finding that the only solace to ease my troubled mind was to stare up into the stars. A strange calm settled over my troubled soul as I counted these tiny specs of light. Each blazing orb was a sparkling beacon of hope in an endless sea of loneliness, and watching them flicker gave me a sense of belonging I didn't have anywhere else.

At my age, most of the young men were already working in the mines or trained hunters, both of which were positions I was strictly forbidden from pursuing as an outsider. This left me with nothing else to do but gather herbs and deliver medicine for my guardian, both of which were jobs usually assigned to women or children in the village. I wasn't even allowed to help in the construction of new cabins or the repairs of those that were damaged by the rough winter storms. The most they would let me do is chop down trees and strip them of limbs, so long as I did it alone.

To make matters worse, the other young men would mock me behind my back and refuse to acknowledge my existence in public. I caught them laughing at my expense more than once, but they would always fall silent and hurry away when they found I had noticed them. My size saved me from having to deal with more than their stinging words, at least. They may have been mighty hunters and miners, but I still stood over a foot taller than most and was well-muscled from chopping wood.

Loneliness became my constant companion in the months that followed our arrival. The world outside the village had been full of light and warmth; here, the chill seeped into my bones. Yet, despite everything, I yearned to help these people, to prove my worth. My efforts only pushed them further away. Then, as if to seal my fate, I fell in love. Or what I thought was love, at least. A foolish, overwhelming infatuation with a girl whose smile could have lit the darkest corners of my soul.

Reflections:

Looking back, I wonder if her captivating nature was real or a manifestation of my need for connection and stability in a lonely world. Whatever the case, my heart chose her, and as I would soon learn, such choices rarely lead to peace. As would prove the case more than once in my extraordinarily long life, becoming smitten at first sight would be my undoing.

Chapter 3
Forbidden Fruit

The vibrant red-headed daughter of the village chief is a sight that refuses to fade from my memory. Her flaming hair burns in stark contrast to the icy whites and blues of the snow-covered ground, a vivid stroke of color against the muted greens of the trees that dotted the landscape of my former home. Her emerald eyes, ever curious, seemed to seek out danger and excitement, defying the boundaries her father had so meticulously set. Even now, thousands of years removed, I can recall the way they sparkled, alive with rebellion.

Katri was stunningly beautiful, a beacon of warmth and excitement in contrast to the cold, harsh existence of the village. Her allure did not go unnoticed; every young man in the village, and even those from neighboring settlements, vied for her attention. The chief was proud of his daughter and fiercely protective of her. He knew that any nearby chieftain would pay a handsome price to secure her hand in marriage for himself or a son. Then there was I, a loathed outsider with nothing to offer.

When she began to spend time with me, it felt as though the entire world had shifted. My lonely existence was shattered and replaced with hope brought about by the infatuation of youthful desire. The first time the chieftain caught her prancing around the woods with me, his anger was volcanic. I still remember the thunder in his voice as he sternly forbade her from ever associating with me again. His words, sharp and dismissive, reduced me to less than a man: an outcast, unworthy of her attention.

"You are the daughter of a chief," he told her, "destined for greater things than a lowly boy who gathers herbs like a woman."

Katri's response was bold, as it always was. She argued that my grandmother and I had lived among them for an entire year, that we were officially part of the village; that it wasn't my fault the other men refused to let me hunt or mine. Her defiance only seemed to stoke his rage. He dragged her back to their cabin, issuing strict orders that she was to stay away from me.

But such decrees, as many fathers discover, often achieve the opposite effect. The Chief's command transformed me from a curiosity into a forbidden fruit, and Katri's resolve to defy him only grew stronger. For those blissfully unaware, a teenage daughter's will to rebel rivals the power of any deity. Every morning after her father left for the mines, she sought me out in the woods where I gathered herbs, and our clandestine friendship flourished.

If I had been wise, I would have kept my distance. But wisdom is a rare trait among lonely boys with hearts full of longing and heads clouded by adolescent infatuation. Katri was the only person in the village, aside from my grandmother, who spoke to me with kindness. Desperation for companionship blinded me to the dangers of our secret meetings.

We spent our days wandering the mountainsides, picking flowers, berries, and herbs, our laughter echoing through the trees. For weeks, our connection remained innocent, though I could feel my attachment to her growing with each passing day. The villagers, however, were not so easily deceived. Rumors began to spread, whispers that reached the ears of her father.

Needless to say, he was furious to learn that his daughter had blatantly ignored his commands and was spending time with me alone in the woods. I'm certain his mind went to the absolute worst possible scenarios when he found out. However, my time with the girl had been mostly innocent to this point. She had given me a peck on the cheek once, but that was the full extent of our physical interactions.

Rather than laying the full blame on his daughter this time, the chief instead channeled his anger toward me. He marched to the little hovel I shared with my grandmother and bellowed furiously at her, threatening to kick us out if he ever heard of me associating with his prized child again.

In turn, my grandmother tore into my hide, informing me that I was to avoid the girl at all costs. "There is too much at stake for you to risk it over a pretty girl batting her eyelashes at you," she said, her voice firm despite the trembling of her hands, following up with the all too familiar warnings of a faceless darkness that never seemed to manifest.

I told myself I would not go. I had promised my grandmother. I knew what would happen if I defied the Chief again, and yet, when the morning sun crept over the frozen peaks, I found myself standing beneath the evergreens, waiting for Katri as if fate had bound me to her.

Despite the dangers, Katri and I continued to meet in secret. Under the light of the full moon or in the quiet hours before dawn, we found solace in each other's company. Our bond deepened, and the line between friendship and something more began to blur. She kissed me once, a fleeting touch of her lips against mine that sent my heart racing. It was a small, tender act, but one that carried a weight I couldn't yet comprehend.

The warmth of her lips lingered for hours, long after our time that day had drawn to a close and the chill evening air began to creep upon me. The shivers of delight transformed as the darkness approached, not from the wind or mountain air, but from something deeper. Something unseen. I tried to dismiss it as nerves or a guilty conscience born from disobeying my grandmother, but the feeling refused to fade.

That night, I dreamt of shadows coiling around the village, seeping through the cracks like ink. In the center of it all stood my grandmother, watching with hollow eyes. When I woke, the taste of frost lingered on my lips, though I had not left my bed. Following the dream, not even the stars could offer comfort as a dark blanket of dread wrapped me in a cold embrace.

What should have pushed me away from Katri only drove me closer to her, as I nearly ran out the door that morning to meet her. What a fool I was. In the end, I paid the price that all fools must pay. Over time, our innocence gave way to something more profound, more dangerous. Yet I couldn't let her go. She had become a beacon of light in a world that seemed intent on snuffing me out.

Reflections:

As I write down the events of my distant past, I find

myself reluctant to assign names to those whose ghosts now haunt me. Titles like "the chief" or "my grandmother" fill the gaps where proper names should be. This is not an oversight but a reflection of time's erosion. The names of some who shaped my life have been lost to me, or perhaps I have chosen to lose them, to avoid assigning false memories to those long gone.

Curiously, my grandmother's name eludes me entirely. Try as I might to recall it, or even to witness a moment when it was spoken, I am met with nothing but shadows. Her identity remains one of the many mysteries surrounding my past, an enigma I have yet to unravel.

As for myself, I was called Viktor. My grandmother claimed the name was chosen for me before my birth, though she never revealed who had chosen it. She was not my mother, a fact she made clear, but she never spoke of my parentage. Perhaps she feared the truths buried there.

Chapter 4
Downfall

For the first time in my life, I seemingly had a permanent home. Months passed and turned into years, all while I expected my grandmother to announce it was time to pack up and leave at a moment's notice, as had happened countless times in the preceding years. I was fully prepared to argue against such a move, so smitten was I with my red-haired love, but the need never arose. It would seem that whatever had feverishly stalked me for so long had given up the chase or was simply unable to find me in a place this remote.

I do not know my exact age at this point, but I assume it was roughly 17 or 18 in human years. My visions had progressed significantly with the passing of time in the village; grandmother had created an herbal concoction that made them more bearable and seemingly stopped the nightmares altogether, and now I could control myself, showing no outward signs of something amiss, when a vision overwhelmed my senses. However, on occasion, when something big was about to happen, the divinations would become formidable. Overlapping, the waking world, my eyes were perceiving things to come. This was rare, only occurring when a situation required my direct intervention, but one such vision was about to alter my fate forever.

Grandmother had become weak with age and could no longer help me gather the ingredients for her healing teas and balms, so I was out gathering herbs on my own in the forest near the foot of a mountain. The villagers seemed oblivious to her rapid aging, attributing it to a mixture of unusually harsh winters and failing health. It was Spring now, so the snow had begun to melt in the valleys, giving birth to new life and an opportunity to refresh our stores, which had dwindled over the recent long, extremely cold winter.

As I knelt, hunched over gathering yellow petals from a particularly potent flower, my eyes began to view a distant scene. I saw a man buried in snow, his body broken and twisted in unimaginable ways. Next, I beheld his wife and young daughter weeping, then suffering destitution without him there to support them.

I knew the family. They came to my grandmother frequently as the young girl, Natka, had a cough that never seemed to heal fully. Grandmother would concoct a tea that seemed to ease the poor child's furious lungs, allowing them to open and accept air once more. Her parents had been good to us, more friendly than the rest of the village, and particularly nice to me.

The man I had seen in the snow was Goran, Natka's father. I had gone hunting with him on a few occasions the previous summer, something the other men strictly refused even to consider. He had even taken me into a mine once to show me what it was like. Goran had taught me how to track deer and elk in the valley and how to prepare the meat so that it would remain good throughout the winter. His welcomed lessons had likely saved our lives, as the storms had raged to such a degree the past few months that straying far from our cabin was all but impossible for weeks on end. I had become close enough with the family over the previous year that they allowed me to bring flowers to Natka to help cheer her up when her cough was worse than usual.

My vision showed Natka's condition getting worse in the absence of her father, eventually claiming her life. I watched as Natka's mother, Cadya, flung herself from a cliff, the despair from such losses too much for her to bear.

Something inside me broke as these scenes

played out in my mind. These were good people, arguably the best of those in the village. They were kind and loving, and this fate was something they did not deserve. Consequences be damned, I thought to myself. I was seeing this for a reason, and I was going to stop it from happening. So, I ran.

After running for what seemed to be an eternity, I found the miner and tackled him to the ground. The anger in Goran's eyes quickly turned to shock as a crack shattered the air. The sound reverberated through the valley, shaking the ground and rattling my bones as the ridge Goran was about to pass through was swept away in an avalanche of ice, stone, and snow. As I lay on the ground, gasping for air, an endless string of questions rang from the man.

"Where did you come from?" "How did you know?" "What just happened?"

His shock quickly turned to fear and terror as he realized that my intervention was impossible to explain, not without some supernatural cause, anyway.

An hour later, the same questions echoed around me in the village square. None of them were particularly grateful in tone, either. Instead of being praised as a savior, I stood accused of being a user of dark magics. At the edge of the crowd, through the throng of anger and panic, I saw Natka clutching desperately to her still-breathing father's leg. The sight made the situation a bit more bearable.

Eventually, I was able to talk my way out of being banished. I explained that I had been out gathering herbs and heard a crack from the mountain. I saw the miner heading in that direction and ran like hell to save him. The villagers eventually accepted the story, but the sideways glances told me they weren't entirely convinced.

The miner himself lied to protect me, something I had not expected. Goran claimed he had seen me on the path, which wasn't true. His appreciation for still being counted among the living, coupled with his gratitude for the aid given to his family over the years, had moved him to break his strict code of honor. The act may have saved me, but my guilt was palpable.

A man who prided himself on honor had shattered his code because of what I had done. I should have felt relieved. Instead, I felt sick. From that moment on, every time I saw him, I imagined the weight of that lie pressing down on his shoulders, as heavy as the snow that should have buried him.

The villagers did not banish me outright following the event, but they may as well have. From that moment on, heads would quickly turn away in my presence, children were shooed off, and the Chief, seeing an opportunity, used the matter to ensure Katri would never see me again.

The condemnation from the Chief and the rest of the village was something I was already accustomed to. That didn't bother me. However, the fear I saw behind the emerald eyes I had grown to love hurt more than words could ever describe. At that moment, I had become a monster to her, and Katri became as much a stranger in my life as any of the others.

Then there was my grandmother. She tried to hide her emotions from me, attempting not to make the situation worse. She wasn't angry with me; she was sad. All of her warnings had failed, and so had she. In one moment, I had destroyed my forbidden love and crushed the soul of the woman who had raised me. I vowed never to use my powers again.

Chapter 5
Burned Away

Following my ill-advised heroism, I hid myself away from the village as best I could. The whispers and looks of disapproval were more than I could stand. I hadn't seen Katri since the incident, but learned from my grandmother that she had started spending time with another man from a neighboring settlement. The revelation created a void in my soul.

Slowly, the misery was beginning to eat away at my mind like maggots on diseased flesh. To make matters worse, I had begun to develop questions about my past that Grandmother refused to answer. What darkness was out there hunting me that had forced us to move so often? If it was such a threat, why had we remained here for so long? Who were my real parents?

Why did I have these damnable visions? Each time I breached these subjects, she would shoo me off to gather wood and herbs, or she would suddenly feel ill and need to rest. I was a young man, shunned and alone with no purpose other than to care for my fading grandmother, and my resentment toward her was growing with each passing day and each unanswered question. More and more, I found myself turning to a new friend, one so many others have sought solace from across the ages. Anger.

Anger at the damnable village for not recognizing the heroism of my actions. Anger at the chieftain for hiding his daughter. Anger at the new man who was replacing me in her eyes. Anger toward Grandmother for bringing us to this living hell in the middle of nowhere. But most of all, an all-consuming rage over having been born a freak.

Days turned to weeks and weeks to months, with my pit of misery growing alongside the passing time. As my fury grew, the visions began to slowly creep back into my mind... dreams of fire, villagers screaming, and death. At the time, I dismissed the sights as a byproduct of my emotional state, and justifiably so. I was wrong.

***

More time passed. The days began to grow

short as winter crept closer. Grandmother had grown increasingly frail, leaving her duties almost entirely upon my shoulders. She rarely left the cabin anymore, not even to get fresh air or enjoy the singing of the birds. Part of me knew, but didn't want to admit, that it would be her final winter.

I left our hut early, on the fateful day when my life would forever be changed, to begin the tasks of gathering wood for our winter stockpile. As had become routine for me, a storm was raging between my ears, and my attention was not on the path before me. My focus immediately snapped into place as a meek "Hello" pierced the dark clouds behind my eyes.

Startled, I swung around to find a small girl, no more than six or seven, standing there, hand outstretched, clutching a tiny wooden doll. It was Natka. I stood there in shock. No one from the village had spoken to me since the incident. Natka approached me, pushed the small trinket into my hand, smiled, and ran off down the path to her home without another word. The rush of joy that parted my dark mood is beyond my ability to describe. I had saved her dada, and she thanked me the only way she knew how: with a toy.

The single act of kindness washed away the fury that had built up and, as the Fates would have it (*or whatever had replaced them following my birth*), the walls I had built to keep my visions at bay crumbled.

In retrospect, it would have been better had

she never given me the gift.

With each new wave of emotion that tore through my consciousness, another wall fell, and my visions began to overwhelm me. Suddenly, I could see my grandmother huddled by the fire in our hut. The village filled my inner eye, then the mines, the lands beyond the mountains… vast oceans, deserts, forests, cities, and beyond. I found myself looking down on alien worlds, places I couldn't even dream of. My sight went rampaging through my consciousness, a broken dam flooding my senses, and once again, like a damned fool, I ran.

I found the chieftain's daughter at the bottom of a ravine, red hair matted with blood. The body of her new lover was crumpled at her side and unbreathing. They had been on a walk when the path gave way, causing them both to fall. To his credit, the man had somehow managed to save Katri by landing first and using his body to absorb the impact. Still, she was not in good shape. She winced with each breath, likely from broken ribs. I carefully gathered her up and carried her back to the village, knowing that saving her would likely lead to my exile…or worse. As we approached the village, the chieftain spotted us first. He immediately grabbed his daughter from my arms, fury and worry mixing into a grotesque mask upon his face. Screams broke out in the village around me, and then everything went black.

When I woke, my head screaming in agony and my vision blurred, I found myself locked inside one of the blood-stained cages that stood in the village square. A crowd had gathered, screaming and throwing refuse.

Slowly turning my head, I saw a second prison and an old woman huddled within. My grandmother. The rage of the village had turned on her as well.

Seeing me stir, the Chief stormed up to the door, a twisted look of hatred on his face. "Look! The villain wakes!" he screamed to the crowd. "These two have been a blight upon our land for too long! The witch who poisons our people with her vile magic and the boy who murdered my daughter's betrothed!"

He continued his rant to the roar of the gathered throng, feeding them pointed words and lies to whip them into a frenzy. It was then that I noticed a body lying nearby, the man who had replaced me. The chief was using his death to finally be rid of me.

He grabbed the door of my tiny prison, rattling it so hard I thought he might rip it off. "Watch, boy, watch the fate that awaits you!"

The mob of bloodthirsty villagers tore my guardian from her cage, tying her to a pole standing erect on the ground nearby. She looked directly into my eyes, a smile parting her beaten and swollen face. The horde had attacked the old woman before imprisoning her.

"It will be alright, my *Vision*," she said, closing her eyes and lifting her head in defiance of the crowd.

Her final words still sting my thoughts even now, so many centuries removed.

The first stone struck with a sickening thud, the wet sound of flesh tearing. Blood began to trickle down her forehead, but she did not scream. Another struck her shoulder, then her ribs. The villagers howled like starving wolves as they pelted my grandmother with stone after stone. I tried to scream as I watched them kill the only person who had ever truly loved me, but the sound would not form, my body leaden with helplessness.

Eventually, her form slumped, straining against the ropes that held her fast. More stones parted the air, pelting her body until it became nearly unrecognizable.

The rage that had built within me for so long returned, mixing with sorrow and an unbelievable desire to kill every one of these vile people. Just then, the burly chieftain turned toward me, ready to drag me out and serve his brutal justice. Instead, he burst into flame.

Chapter 6
Dawn of the Dead

My jaw dropped at the sight. Where once had stood a towering, muscled man who moved stone for a living, now was nothing more than a burning effigy. The scent of charred hair and flesh assaulted my nostrils, an aroma that, once encountered, can never be forgotten. The horde stood equally stunned at the sight; the cacophony of hatred and rage had quieted into a hush, only to be shattered by a cry of terror as the first villager beheld my unwanted savior

A lone figure stood to my right, just outside the cage. Arm outstretched with two gloved fingers pointed at what once was the chieftain, a steady stream of flame projecting from their tips. The stranger, who had seemingly manifested from thin air, stood framed head to toe in ancient, blackened armor, a tattered purple cloak flowing from atop his shoulders. A visorless helm concealed his face, yet where eyes should have been, two burning orbs seared. They weren't eyes, they were something else, something wrong. The fire illuminated nothing within the helmet, only an abyss that swallowed the light whole. My mind recoiled from it, as if instinct itself begged me not to look too long.

To their credit, the villagers sprang into action. Stones meant to end my life flew toward the new assailant, though the action proved futile. Each stone that slammed into the ornate armor bounced off with a thud, not leaving so much as a scratch.

The knight turned his stream of flame from the thoroughly cooked chieftain onto the crowd, incinerating the lot of them. Instantly, the mob became a choir of agony, their screams swallowed by the roaring inferno. The knight's fire rained upon them like divine judgment, turning flesh to cinders in seconds. I turned away, but the sounds burned into my skull: the crackle of skin splitting, the wet pop of bursting eyes, the sickening collapse of bodies too charred to stand. I clung to the cage bars, gasping for breath, the heat pressing against me like a living thing.

Before long, the entire village was a raging inferno. The heat radiating from the scene before me was unbearable, hitting me in waves and forcing me to retreat to the far side of the cage. All that remained was me and the figure standing before me. To be honest, I fully expected the knight to turn his magic on me next. Instead, he reached for the door and effortlessly tore it off, flinging it an impossible distance and out of sight. As he did, another sensation crashed upon me, piercing cold.

The flames obeyed him, yet he was not of them. As he stepped closer, the blistering heat faded... not to relief, but to something far worse. A breath of winter curled from his armor, a chill so deep it felt like the grave itself had opened before me. My breath fogged in the summer air, my fingers numb as frostbite clawed at my skin. It wasn't natural. It wasn't human. The closer he came to me, the more intense the feeling grew until it was unbearable. My teeth chattered against my will, and my body shivered despite the flames engulfing the people and buildings around me.

Fighting against the frigid force emanating from the man, I stood, using the cage to pull myself to my feet despite the world swimming beneath me. The pain in my head was nauseating, forcing me to wretch. The smell of burning flesh didn't help, nor did the sight of the charred corpses whose eyes had burst from the intense heat, leaking gory tears down desiccated cheeks. I heaved again and again, unable to control myself.

The knight began to reach for me in the cage, only to pause at the sound of sobbing. A small family had just arrived at the scene, a little girl clutching her father's leg. She was crying uncontrollably, her breathing more ragged than it should have been. Goran hurried to push his family behind him, a vain effort to protect them from the horror.

A hand began to rise, two fingers extending toward the newcomers.

"NO," I cried, stepping forward on unsteady legs, every nerve in my body screaming at me to run the other direction. "Not them!"

The burning eyes locked onto mine, staring through me, unflinching, with a force that seemed to press against my very soul. Despite the cold seeping ever deeper into my being, bringing with it the promise of death, I stood my ground and said, "You will have to kill me first."

I fully expected the monster before me to call my bluff, to swat me aside, or burn me to a crisp. Instead, the flaming eyes seemed to narrow within the helmet, almost as if questioning how I was able to maintain contact with them, much less challenge their owner. After an eternity locked in a battle of wills, the knight nodded. Without looking away from him, I yelled to the family, ordering them to run away as fast as they could.

With that, the arbiter of death turned from me and looked down at the pile of seared remains twisted in knots of smoking limbs. Again, he pointed, but this time, the knight spoke a single word in a language I could not understand. His voice was unearthly, hollow, and lifeless as if spoken absent of lips or breath. The sound made my head swim in ways the concussion couldn't touch, forcing bile into my throat.

If the events thus far had been a nightmare to me, there are no words to explain the sheer horror I felt as I watched what followed.

A twitch. A spasm. Then, impossibly, a corpse moved. Fingernails scraped against dirt as blackened hands clawed at the earth. The air filled with the wet squelch of flesh peeling away, the stench of burnt meat thick enough to choke on. Their eyes, or what remained of them, glistened like molten wax, sliding down their cheeks in grotesque tears. One by one, they rose, their mouths opening soundlessly as if they had forgotten how to scream.

I remember saying a silent prayer to whatever Gods had forsaken me, that Natka didn't see what was happening.

The knight went from body to body, reanimating each of them until he finally reached my guardian, the only person who hadn't been consumed in flames. He must have noticed me flinch when he began to point at her because he held his hand fast. It would be the last act of mercy he would ever offer me.

Once his cabal of carbonized cadavers was assembled, his gaze fell upon me once more as he reached out and seized me by the arm. The touch was agonizing, sending a chill down to the bone, worse than any winter storm could muster. I would have tried to pull away, but my last bit of energy had been spent. It was all I could do to stay on my feet, and I am not entirely sure that I did.

The air in front of us began to swirl and bubble, warping as though reality itself was rejecting what was coming. The knight coiled darkness into spirals, bleeding into the air like ink into water. A sound not heard but felt reverberated in my skull as the portal tore a hole through time and space. My vision blurred as I stared into the vacuum, watching the shambling corpses disappear into the yawning void one by one. The knight followed them, dragging me with him into the dark abyss.

Chapter 7
Death March

I do not know how long I was unconscious, much less how I was walking when I came to. All I remember is that when my senses returned, I was flanked on all sides by the charred remains of what had once been my neighbors. The scenery passing by, as we marched, was alien to me and unfamiliar to anything I had seen in my years of travel as a youth.

At the head of the ghastly procession rode my savior, or captor, on a monstrous steed. The beast was death incarnate; its rotting flesh having sloughed off in places to reveal stark, white bone beneath. Exposed sinew glistened under a pallid sky, and its putrid organs shifted visibly with each grotesque step. Its eyes burned with unholy fire, mirroring the blaze within its rider's hollow gaze. Each step the beast took blackened the ground beneath its hooves as if nature itself was rotting away in its wake. Once, this creature must have been majestic, a magnificent sight to behold. In death, it was a nightmare given form, a horrifying echo of life.

There was no discernible path through the terrain, not even a game trail. Thorny brambles tore through the remaining flesh of the walking dead around me, leaving streaks of gore in their wake. The vegetation did not spare me either. My arms, legs, and face bore the sting of countless cuts, and my tattered clothing clung to me like a second skin of misery. Meanwhile, the monstrous horse strode unbothered and impervious to the unforgiving forest.

"Where are we?" I managed to croak, my voice weak and dry. "Where are we going?" "Who are you?" My questions seemed to fall on deaf ears as my captor continued to ride on, ignoring them.

For hours, I stumbled onward, desperate for some sort of acknowledgement, until I finally gave up. My legs trembled with exhaustion until, at last, they betrayed me, and I collapsed into the dirt.

"Get up."

The knight's hollow voice pierced the silence, cold as the aura radiating from him.

"I can't." The words escaped me in a rasp. "I need water."

The knight turned without a word, and the undead horde descended upon me. Near skeletal hands grasped my arms and began to drag me forward as I feebly struggled against their grip. My attempts to rise proved useless and soon I succumbed to the darkness of unconsciousness once again.

This cycle repeats endlessly: walking, collapsing, being dragged. In fleeting moments of clarity, I begged my captor for mercy. "Please," I whispered hoarsely. "I need food. Water. I'm dying."

The knight finally paused, then slightly adjusted his course without saying a word. A short while later, we arrived at a small stream, and the fiendish formation ground to a halt.

Desperation consumed me. I threw myself into the water, gulping it down in frantic mouthfuls. But my weakened body couldn't sustain the effort; I began to choke as the stream filled my lungs.

As darkness began to descend on my consciousness, I saw the knight dismount. The land itself recoiled from his presence, the grass withering into brittle husks, and the trees leaning away as though nature itself feared this abomination.

Frigid fingers tangled in my hair, lifting me from the water with a force that wrenched my neck. My body dangled, weightless in his grasp, the world tilting violently as the water filling my lungs threatened to end me. I barely had time to register the glacial agony seeping into my skull before his gauntlet-covered fist drove into my stomach like a battering ram.

Water erupted from my mouth and nostrils in

violent hacking spasms, yet still I couldn't breathe. My vision faded into pulsing waves of blackness, my ribs screaming in protest. Taking note of my sorry state, my captor touched a finger to a nearby corpse, then to my forehead.

"You will not die yet," the Death Knight's hollow voice said. "The Master needs you intact."

The zombie's flesh began to shrivel, the remaining bits of meat seeming to fuse to the bone beneath with a grating sound I still cannot describe. When the last of the reanimating energy had been drained dry, the shambler fell to the ground in a heap.

It was then a sick, crawling sensation slithered through my senses like worms burrowing into my skin. The stolen energy was being injected into me, twisting through my body like a mockery of life. My lungs spasmed in response, forcing in a ragged, wheezing breath as though I were a corpse being dragged unwillingly back from the brink of death. Strength oozed into my limbs, just enough to allow me to sit up. The pain from the knight's blow dulled, but refused to vanish entirely, curdling within my guts like a wound stitched closed over infected flesh. Still, I managed to seize the moment, forcing my trembling hands to cup the water so I could drink absent the threat of drowning.

Looking down at my horrid, emaciated reflection in the water, afraid to look up at my captor,

I managed to gather the strength to speak. "I still need food."

"Then eat," the knight responded flatly, pointing to the corpse that had fallen motionless beside us.

The withered, charred carcass made my stomach threaten to relieve itself of the fluid sloshing around within. I decided to go hungry.

Time ceased to hold meaning as the days blurred into nights, the march stretching ever onward to some unknown destination. My tormentor only halted when I collapsed entirely, each time siphoning energy from the reanimated dead to infuse into my failing body. His magic sustained me just enough to keep me moving, a cruel parody of life.

The only rest I received was when merciful darkness overcame my senses, and I slipped into the blessed void of unconsciousness. My clothing, what was left of it, hung about me in soiled, bloody tatters and stank of piss and worse. My tormentor wouldn't even stop to allow me to relieve myself, though there was not much left in me to come out.

More days passed. Rain began to fall, mixing with the blood and filth that coated my skin. My body, once a towering testament to youthful strength and vitality, was now a haunting shadow of its former self. Muscles that once rippled with power had diminished, leaving a gaunt and skeletal frame. Every rib became visible, stark and harsh against my sunken chest. If the monstrous horseman had planned to see me off to a slow death, it was working.

Eventually, I became delirious with hunger. Strange, indescribable symbols blazed into life before my eyes, pulsing with an otherworldly green glow. Then came the voices whispered from unseen mouths, forcing their way into my mind. The groaning, clicking noises spoke in languages I couldn't understand, murmuring truths I was unable to grasp. Each tone caused the symbols to radiate with brighter light, amplifying the hunger growing within. My stomach twisted in agony, a hollow, gnawing sensation that no logic or revulsion could silence.

The maggots infesting the remains of my undead companions began to look disturbingly appetizing. Though I had resolved not to, I succumbed to the unrelenting, all-consuming hunger and feasted on the bloated little monsters. In a frenzy, I gave in, my hands trembling as I ripped off chunks of putrid, charred flesh infested with those squirming parasites and shoved them into my mouth. Laughter bubbled up, unbidden and hysterical, mingling with my tears. In the background, the unheard voices roared with delight. As they did, the world shifted between the realm of the living and that of something far older, far worse.

The nightmare stretched on. Weeks, or perhaps months, passed as we marched through the endless wilderness. I have no concept of how much time passed before my mind finally fractured. Consumed by delirium and despair, I ran mindlessly away from my captor and into the darkness of night.

The now primarily skeletal remains of the townsfolk gave chase through the forest, a relentless force I had no hope of escaping. Broken and bloody, skin torn open once again from a race through an unforgiving sea of trees, I found myself at the edge of a cliff, staring down into an abyss. Rain pounded against me, creating rivers of blood and stinging my wounds. My eyes burned. Tears mixed with the water poured down my face.

This chase haunts me to this day, resurfacing in my dreams from time to time.

The Death Knight approached upon his horrid steed, eyes burning bright in the darkness of night. He was not alone. Red eyes stared out from the pitch black behind him, perversely glowing. My sanity was gone. I looked down at my skeletal remains, gaunt flesh barely covering the bone.

Lightning flashed, illuminating the night for the briefest of moments. A nightmare marched toward me. The last of those taken from my home smiled at me, bare teeth exposed in mocking, sadistic grins. They finally get to fulfill their last wish, I thought to myself in a moment of fear-induced clarity: My death at their hands. Skeletal fingers reached out… and I leaped off the ledge.

The Void welcomed me, its embrace cold and infinite.

A great eye opened.

Tendrils of energy erupted around me, shattering my pursuers into dust.

The Death Knight was ripped from his monstrous steed and hurled into the darkness.

For a moment, I wondered: Did I cause this?

Laughter filled the air, cold and cruel.

It was not my own.

It didn't matter; I was free.

Chapter 8
In the Dark

I had no way to tell how long it had been from the moment I leapt off the cliff to the moment my eyes opened again. When they did, my first realization was complete and utter darkness. When my eyes opened and I realized I couldn't see, my heart began pounding in my chest like a war drum. Breathing became increasingly difficult as I sucked in short gasps of thick, humid air. Was I blind? Dead? Something worse?

Gradually, I forced myself to stillness, clinging to reason against the waves of fear. My sight was gone, yes, but my other senses remained. I could feel smooth, damp stone beneath me and scattered patches of what might be straw. A rhythmic dripping noise was also present, the only sound echoing through the oppressive silence. The air smelled like rain but was heavy with the tang of earth. Occasionally, something wet would splash upon my skin, raining down on me from above and causing me to jump with fright.

At least the pain was gone. The agony that had coursed through me during the march, every step a fresh torment, had vanished. My limbs, battered and broken then, somehow felt whole. Skeptical of this newfound ease, I hesitated before reaching down, trying to confirm I was not dead and in some hellish afterlife. My hands traced over solid muscle where there should have been gaunt weakness. The wounds that had marked my flesh were absent. Even scars, which would surely linger, were nowhere to be found.

Had weeks passed? Months? No, this was something… unnatural. My mind latched onto an uneasy thought: had I been remade? Or was I simply dead, my mind trapped in some ghastly imitation of life? My grandmother's voice echoed in my thoughts, her words a chilling reminder: "Darkness is hunting you." Had it finally caught me, or had everything that transpired since being taken from the village been nothing more than a feverish hallucination?

Pushing aside the spiraling sense of dread, I decided to crawl on hands and knees across the floor to get some sense of the situation I found myself in.

The ground was slick and uneven, the work of water and time rather than tools. The first wall I encountered verified that the room was naturally formed, as there was no seam to distinguish it from the floor. From there, I followed the cavity around until my fingers brushed against a wooden pail. The vessel was positioned so that the dripping I had heard was slowly filling it with water. I found a second pale that smelled as if it had previously been filled with something less inviting. Aside from the contrasting pails of fluid, the stone floor had naught to offer save straw piled up in a corner in some kind of makeshift bedding. Continuing to explore, I felt something that made my heart skip a beat. Metal bars.

I carefully felt my way around them, using my hands to probe each corroded stretch of iron, only to discover the single opening in the room was completely sealed off in a spiderweb of metalwork, with a locked door built in the middle. The realization settled over me: I was a prisoner, entombed within the earth.

Memories of a mine near my village surfaced unbidden, the one Goran had taken me to. I recalled its damp air, its stifling darkness, and the miner's warning. Without light, escape was impossible. My chest tightened. Even if I could break free of these bars, the labyrinth beyond would surely claim me.

With nothing better to do, I slumped against the pile of straw, the only meager comfort in this oppressive place. I waited to see if anyone would come. Time blurred. The dripping water and my restless thoughts were my only companions. Just as I began to drift into an uneasy sleep, a new sound tore through the monotony.

Drip. Drip. Drip. Scratch.

I froze. The noise was distant at first, like something being dragged across stone. Slowly, it grew louder, nearer. The temperature in the cell seemed to drop with each approaching scratch. My breath caught in my throat, and I huddled in the corner, willing myself to be invisible.

The scratching continued past my cell and down unseen corridors until it faded entirely from my perception. And yet, something lingered. There was a shift in the darkness, as though the air was suddenly pressing upon me, heavy and thick, an invisible weight thrust upon my shoulders. Something was still there, just beyond my reach. Watching.

A prickle ran up the back of my neck. I could feel the presence, and my skin tingled as the unseen eyes raked across it. My breath slowed as I strained to hear any hint of movement. There was nothing; no breath but my own, no sound but the forsaken drip, drip, drip.

When the feeling became too much to bear, I turned my head, expecting to see the glint of eyes staring back at me from the darkness. But I saw nothing. Just the abyss stretching endlessly in all directions. I told myself I was alone, that it was just my mind playing tricks. But some part of me knew better. I had been told my entire life that the darkness was hunting me, and now I could feel it. In all my years, I never expected it to be quite this literal, though. The thought made me chuckle out loud, a sound that pierced the oily ocean and echoed for eternity, mocking my very existence and my pathetic attempts to remain hidden.

Time became meaningless again, the hours — or days — melding into one another.

I tried, in those long stretches of black, to keep pieces of myself alive. I would whisper the names of stars and constellations my guardian had taught me, even though I could no longer see them. I would recall Katri's face, her laugh, and her smile in an attempt to make the bitter sting of loneliness more tolerable. I forced myself to remember the scent of pine trees, the sound of birds chirping, and the warmth of our little hut. I pictured the path leading from our home down the valley to the village square, counting each step as though I were walking it. But memory can be as much a curse as a healing balm.

The images I summoned began to twist, to contort into nightmares. Familiar faces began to appear in the dark, warped and wrong. Then came the voices.

First, it was the Chieftain. *"I always knew you were cursed, boy."*

I flinched, hugging my knees to my chest, as his booming voice poured insults and taunts on me like bitter rain.

Then came Katri, her voice soft and sorrowful. *"You let it burn. You were supposed to save us."*

I shouted back. Screamed until my throat turned raw. The darkness drank every sound, leaving only the drip, drip, drip — steady, uncaring, mocking. That is when doubt took root in my soul. I knew they were gone. I had watched the village burn, sat helplessly as the dead man turned them to ash, yet their ghosts had returned. Or were they creations of my mind, breaking in the absence of light and sound? Did I truly witness the village burn? Had there ever even been a village? Was I even Viktor anymore? Had I ever been?

As my mind spiraled deeper into the fringes of insanity, the scratching returned to jar me back into my cruel reality. This time, it paused in front of my cell, and my heart became an unmoving block of ice in my chest. A new sound pierced the air as something slid beneath the door. An eternity later, the scratching began again as my unseen tormentor began their methodical march once more.

When the scratching sound could no longer be heard, I gathered the strength of will to investigate what had been slid under the door. It took every ounce of courage I could muster, but slowly, I scooted along the wall and felt my way to the bars.

It is with some sense of shame that I admit it

took quite a long while for me to reach down and feel for whatever had been placed in my cell. In the utter darkness, it could have been quite literally anything. When I finally put my hand down, it brushed against an unknown item, nearly causing me to jump out of my skin. It was hard and round. My stomach growled as I realized it was food, stale bread.

Hunger won out over fear. I devoured it and drank cautiously from the dripping bucket, reasoning that my captors, whoever or whatever they were, did not need to poison me. I decided to use the bucket to track the passage of time, if that was even possible, by counting the drips. After I lost track of the droplets, I carefully reached into the bucket to see how much of it had filled. The water level hadn't changed. Had I only imagined drinking from it? Or had the dripping stopped at some point when I wasn't paying attention? Holding my breath, I strained my ears listening for the sound of water splashing into the pail. Drip. Drip. The rhythm was the same, relentlessly pounding at my sanity. I was absolutely certain the bucket *should* have been full, but it hadn't changed in the hours that had passed.

I pressed my fingers to my temples, the beginning of a headache forming as I grappled with the newfound mystery. Was the water vanishing, or was I losing my fragile grasp of reality? Risking another try, I reached my hand toward the bucket to find it filled to the brim with water. This was impossible, I thought, just moments ago it was less than half full.

Had I fallen asleep? Was I dreaming? Or were the laws of reality as I knew them before my captivity no longer working? The questions sent a chill through me, and I curled into a ball on my patch of straw to find a fitful sleep.

The sound of scratching shattered my slumber as another hunk of bread was slid into my cell. The routine repeated. Bread, water, scratching, and sleep. Each cycle blurred into the next.

Then the cell changed.

It was subtle at first, a shift in the air, a new angle to the stone walls. The dripping water altered its rhythm, no longer the steady tempo I'd come to rely on. After so long being serenaded by the same damnable rhythm, even the slightest change was maddeningly noticeable.

I groped through the darkness and discovered the dimensions of my prison had shifted. The buckets were no longer where I'd left them. The bars were rearranged, their pattern alien and wrong. I was in a different cell. In a panic, I went through the entire closure again, checking everything to ensure I hadn't made a mistake. Again and again, I mapped out the area until I was certain that the dimensions were different.

Somehow, I had been moved to a different cell while I was sleeping… or so I thought.

My prison seemed alive, reshaping itself while

I slept. The constancy of the routine was now twisted, unfamiliar. The walls seemed to close in around me, the oppressive darkness heavier, more suffocating. I whispered to myself, desperate to hear something human, but the echoes came back wrong, too long, distorted, as though something else was whispering along with me.

My guardian had been right. The darkness was hunting me, and it would not rest until it consumed me entirely. If my captor's goal was to drive me mad, it was working.

Reflections:

I thought I had known loneliness in the village, but it was a loneliness with familiar boundaries. I had my Guardian's stories, the distant sounds of neighbors, the occasional fleeting half-smile from a stranger too polite to sneer. Even when I was shunned, I could still hear life echoing through the valley. I could still walk through the forest or sit by a stream and pretend, if only for a moment, that I belonged somewhere. The ache of being apart from others was dull then, chronic, but survivable.

The cell, though... it was different. That loneliness was something else entirely. It was not the absence of people; it was the absence of presence. The silence in my cell was so complete, it seemed to devour thoughts before they could fully form. No voices, no wind, not even the groaning of old wood or the scurry of vermin. Just the drip of water and the echo of my own heartbeat.

There were no eyes to avoid, no whispers behind my back, only the growing suspicion that I was utterly forgotten. Or worse, remembered by something that didn't care if I screamed. My village had left me isolated, but that place made me feel erased.

Chapter 9
Eyes in the Dark

I can offer no concrete answer as to how long I was in the cell or how many times it changed before I had my first real visitation. Measuring the passage of time was impossible, the only clue being the steady growth of my facial hair, which had become an unruly length that extended past my neck. When my first visitor arrived, it shocked me to my core.

The feeling came first, a weight pressing on the back of my mind. It wasn't something I saw or heard, but I knew, without a doubt, that I was no longer alone. The hair on my neck bristled, and my pulse quickened. An invisible presence stalked me, just out of sight, but the air remained still as the grave. There was no sound, no breathing, no movement, nothing but deafening silence.

I sat frozen on my pile of damp hay as the sensation grew stronger. The cell had recently transformed again, bringing with it a new symphony of water lullabies from unseen drips and distant echoes. Yet now, even the maddening drip was gone, a fact that made my skin crawl.

Blind as a bat in the suffocating dark, I fumbled for my only weapon: the waste bucket. It was useless, of course, and deep down, I knew it wouldn't matter. Whatever lurked here wasn't something I could fight.

Then a voice tore into my mind, bypassing my ears entirely. It wasn't a sound that echoed off the damp stone walls; it was a presence within me, invading my thoughts. The Death Knight's voice had been twisted and unholy, but this was beyond comprehension; alien, ancient, and vast.

It spoke not in any language I recognized, but I understood it nonetheless, as though its words were inscribed on my soul in some distant past life. To describe it is an impossibility, but I will try. It was a chorus of guttural tones, clicks, and hisses, layered with vibrations that felt like thunderclaps breaking in my mind. It was maddening, like a melody woven from the screams of collapsing stars, and yet, it was somehow comforting.

"They will kill you if you do not change again," it said. The voice paused, presumably waiting

for some kind of response.

At this point, I wouldn't have minded being put down. A release from the nightmare I had been thrust into wasn't an altogether unwelcome thought. In truth, I had found myself hoping, on more than one occasion, that my captors would come along and put an end to my life.

I hadn't spoken aloud in what felt like an eternity, and when I finally forced the words out, my voice cracked. "Let them."

The entity seemed to consider my answer, the silence stretching endlessly. When it finally spoke again, its tone held neither judgment nor pity. Only fact. *"You came here for a reason."*

I laughed, mocking the unseen intruder who had somehow managed to enter my cage. "I am not here for any reason. I was taken against my will."

"No," it argued, *"You orchestrated these events, a mere thread in the vast tapestry of your prophecy. Yet, should you fail to alter your course, the cycle must commence anew."*

My breath caught in my throat. For a moment, I entertained the thought that my mind had finally broken, that I had gone insane. But then the cell was flooded with light, a blinding, lime-green illumination that forced me to shield my eyes. My vision blurred and burned, unaccustomed to anything but darkness. Once my eyes cleared enough to dare a glance at the entity in my cell, my mind recoiled at what they beheld: *eyes.*

Hundreds, perhaps thousands, of luminous orbs flickered in and out of existence, their bioluminescence casting shifting, phantasmal shadows across the cell. Some were no larger than pinpricks of light, while others loomed like lanterns in the Void.

Something vast lurked beyond and between them, its form obscured in writhing shadows. Its shape refused to settle, twisting and bulging, *rearranging*. The largest of the eyes, an abysmal thing that seemed to draw in the light from the others, fixed upon me, and I felt its gaze burrow beneath my skin, peeling away flesh and thoughts alike, laying my soul bare.

I tried to focus, to make sense of the hidden form twisting between the forest of shifting eyes, but my vision refused to see, my thoughts unravelling like threads pulled apart by unseen hands. Everything about the creature was *wrong*. The eyes were *wrong*. The space between was *wrong*. It was *wrong*.

It was wrong, and yet, it knew me. I knew it. I had always known it, though I could not explain how or why.

Behind the entity, the stone wall of my cell had vanished, replaced by a swirling void. A great maw of darkness consumed specks of light, dying stars, devoured by the emptiness.

In that moment, I became certain that I was both sane and completely mad all at once. My mind could never create the monstrosity hovering in the air before me, proving that my sanity was still intact. Yet, as I stared down the terrible visage, I knew I must be succumbing to madness. I should've been consumed by terror, frozen in place and ready to die, but *I wasn't*. If anything, I was comforted by the myriads of self-luminous eyes blinking in and out of existence just beyond my reach.

The voice returned, each syllable lingering in my mind as an echo refusing to fade. ***"I am. You are. Wake, forgotten one. The shape of you is not lost, only waiting to be recalled."***

Before I could respond, the entity surged forward, the massive, central eye locking onto mine. It was then the Void embraced me, vast and hungry, its unfathomable emptiness whispering with unheard voices. Time unraveled as stars and worlds streaked past, flickering like dying embers. Colossal things drifted at the edges of my perception, faceless and infinite, watching. Tendrils of ichor slithered from the abyss, darker still than the Void itself, threading through my flesh. My body blackened. Not burned, but rather *unmade* into something neither living nor dead. The power coiled around me, a presence both welcoming and intoxicating, as if I were sinking into a bed lined with silk, cradled in the cold embrace of a lost lover that had waited for me at the very edges of reality forever.

It was then that the visions that had plagued me in the village returned.

Scenes from my life flashed before me in a fevered cascade: the decaying temple where my mothers lay rotting, the charred ruins of my last home, the forest where I had run for my life. I saw myself on the cliff's edge, surrounded by the dead, my human form dissolving, twisting into something that should not be.

I watched in horror as the flesh of my former self writhed, splitting and peeling itself away. Beneath it, something new tore free. Something vast and cyclopean. The skin blackened, hardened into a carapace darker than the Void between the stars. A single, bulbous eye, luminous and unblinking, split my forehead open, illuminating the night with the same indescribable green that filled my cell. My new body was still humanoid, but where once there had been a cadaverous human on the verge of starvation, there was now a muscled monster.

Bursting forth from my back, like ruptured veins, slick and glistening, the tendrils began writhing into the air with a will of their own. Despite the fact that I was not in that body, merely watching the scene play out, I could *feel* them, feel how they slashed through the air with alien grace. I could feel each impact as they tore through the skeletal remains of the villagers.

Though my mind didn't want to accept it, I knew what I was watching was the truth. My memories from the event had been blocked, either by the sheer enormity of it or the trauma. Regardless, here I was, watching myself transform into an alien being and lay waste to my tormentors... and then, as suddenly as the visions had started, they stopped.

I blinked, and the cell returned. But everything had changed. I could see, not just the walls and bars of my prison, but the energy radiating from them. Threads of golden light wove through the air, connecting everything in a vast web. The skeletal Servant scratching across the floor toward my cell glowed faintly, its aura a dull, flickering gray. I turned back to the entity. A golden thread extended from my chest to its ever-shifting form, a tether binding us together.

When I focused on the threads, the physical world faded away, leaving only a massive web of golden strands as far as my bulbous eye could see and the faint auras of the surroundings. Tangible reality was gone, leaving behind only the energy signatures of what was once there. It was as if I had been blind all of my life, and suddenly, I could see all of creation and the ties that bind it together.

Upon seeing my transformation, a massive maw tore open between the vacillating eyes, revealing countless rows of razor-sharp teeth extending into infinity. The creature was smiling.

"Good. I must leave you now. I shall return in time." The entity spoke this time, using the same

foreign dialect that had echoed through my mind. The sound was piercing in my cell, but did not extend beyond the confinement. Somehow, it was able to rein in the words, to keep them close and just between us.

"Wait," I called out, my new voice alien to my ears. "Who are you?"

The jagged maw twisted into an unsettling grin. ***"Those who keep you captive name me Sight, their tongues unable to shape my truth. Speak not of me in their presence. Our communion is not for lesser beings."***

With that, Sight dissolved into the Void from whence he came. My transformation faded as well, my body returning to its human form. The only sign of the encounter dwelt in my eyes, which remained changed, faintly glowing with an unearthly green light. My vision, both in darkness and beyond, had been irrevocably altered. I could see every detail of my cell now, clear as though the sun was shining in the room. The first of many gifts bestowed upon me by the Void.

As I sat, replaying the visitation in my mind, the skeletal servant reached the bars of my cell. It hesitated, then let loose a piercing shriek — an impossible sound that echoed through my skull, promising that my ordeal was far from over.

Chapter 10
Strange Bedfellows

The shriek seemed endless, a sound unbound by lungs or breath, an eternal wail from something not meant for the living world. It vibrated through the cold stone of my cell, each note a reminder of my helplessness. Then, mercifully, it stopped. The silence that followed was deafening, but it didn't last long. An all-too-familiar portal tore through the air outside my cell, rippling with sickly light. My unwelcome savior stepped forward: the Death Knight. It would appear he had survived my assault on the mountaintop.

Before I could fully process his arrival, a second portal erupted into existence, bathing the cavern in crackling purple light. A newcomer emerged, their presence stealing the very air from the room. Clad in impossibly white garments accented with deep purples, midnight black, and streaks of gold, they exuded an unnatural grace. Their face, hidden behind a porcelain mask carved with an unnervingly perfect smile, and glowing yellow eyes, surrounded by scarred, angry flesh that spilled out beyond the mask's edges.

The masked figure spoke first, their tone lilting with mockery, though their gaze remained fixed on me. "I told you and your master. It IS him. You should know better than to doubt me."

The Death Knight, his burning eyes narrowing, snorted in derision. "Hojo," the knight spat, his voice grating with emotion for the first time. "I am surprised you showed up. Don't you have a specimen to dissect?"

The mask turned sharply toward the knight, the ever-present smile contrasting with the venom in the voice behind it. "Don't you have boots to be licking, *servant?*"

A wave of frigid energy emanated from the knight, far colder than the usual aura of death that clung to him like a second skin. The masked man had struck a nerve, and for a moment, I thought their clash might escalate further, but the Death Knight merely growled.

His voice a frigid snarl, he said, "I will report back to *our* master. You are to return to your laboratory. Do not speak to the prisoner." The knight clenched his fists, his eyes burning with rage for too long a moment before he disappeared into a portal once again, leaving me alone with the masked figure.

"Hmph. The welp presumes to order me. He is no better than the damn lapdog D keeps. Completely inept," the masked figure muttered, before turning his unsettling gaze back to me. "Welcome home. It is good to see you in the *flesh once again*."

The newcomer's words stirred a flicker of recognition within me. There was something familiar about this figure, though I couldn't place it. The gleaming white robes, the sneeringly serene mask, even the way he spoke felt like a half-remembered dream.

"How do I know you?" I asked, deciding to simply be blunt. Nothing I had experienced since the events in my village had been anything short of a nightmare, and I wanted answers.

The figure tilted his head, staring at me from behind the mask for a few moments before sighing. "The unfortunate side effect of incarnating into the physical realm is the erasure of memory or, more accurately, the sealing off of memory. It still exists, but is simply inaccessible to you for the time being. This is a conundrum that I have yet to solve despite my best efforts."

"So, I knew you before? What, in another life?" I asked, my confusion deepening.

"Quite so," he said, almost gently. "With time, those memories will resurface, and with your unique abilities, I suspect they may come back even sooner than they would for others. I am anxious to observe your development and record your progress."

His answer did very little to ease my nerves or clear my confusion. On the contrary, it only served to deepen the pool of questions swirling in my mind. As I spiraled through my ignorance into a pit of frustration, I decided to push my luck with the newcomer. "Where am I? Why am I a prisoner?"

"You are precisely where *you* told me *you* needed to be. You were quite strict in your instructions. So far, everything has transpired according to your plan. You are where you need to be in order to become what you must become. I cannot tell you more than that."

Their answer ignited a fire in my chest, burning away the despair that had clung to me. Rage replaced it, blinding and consuming. "My plan?" I hissed, my voice trembling with fury. "I lost my family. The only love I've ever known. I've been starved, tortured, beaten. Forced to eat the rotting, charred flesh of those I once called neighbors. And you're telling me this is all *my* plan?"

The masked figure did not flinch. "You told me you would be angry. This, too, is part of your plan. The suffering is necessary. To fulfill your prophecy, you must endure."

"What Gods-damned prophecy?" I roared,

standing abruptly. My hands gripped the bars of my cell, ready to tear them apart and drag the answers out of the man if I had to. Before I could act, however, the world dissolved into darkness.

A vision overwhelmed my senses: the Void stretched endlessly before me, an abyss without stars or hope. Somewhere, on a speck of dust lost in this infinite expanse, a microscopic being chanted my true name, its voice the same as the man who stood before me moments ago. It begged for my attention, its devotion absurd in its insignificance. Even so, the creature's persistence and methods earned my notice. It chanted, then died, only to instantly reappear and chant again. Over and over, it perished and returned, each death more violent and depraved than the last. Each physical manifestation identical to the one before.

Cultists chanting for my favor is nothing new. They scurry about on their unremarkable, laughably puny planets at the edge of reality, killing others, each other, and occasionally themselves in my name. Never before has one attracted more than my fleeting attention. But this one is different.

The vision ended as suddenly as it began, leaving me trembling. The immensity of the feelings that came with it left my head swimming in a nightmare of chaos, and I was forced to hold the cell bars to avoid crumbling to the floor. The masked figure leaned forward, his yellow eyes wide with curiosity.

"You've seen something, yes?" he inquired.

My mind was screaming, and I struggled to find words. My hands fell from the bars as I whispered, "You... killed yourself."

For the first time, the mask tilted downward, the carved smile clashing sharply with the bowed posture. "You remember...." The figure's voice softened, tinged with reverence. He raised his head, and the glowing eyes locked onto mine. "I must go now. The lord of this place is ever watchful, and he must never learn of our connection, or of who you once were. None of them can, if they do, they will tear you apart long before you can understand why. We will speak again soon."

With that, he turned and disappeared into a swirling portal, leaving me alone once more. Alone, but not unchanged. My cell now felt less like a prison and more like a waiting room for something inevitable.

Chapter 11
Homecoming

Following my strange vision, inspired by the masked man, I settled into the hay and drifted off to a fitful sleep. My dreams carried me away to distant lands where I found myself among majestic trees, the sun shining down to warm my skin through the canopy. The feeling was incredible, even in the dream, something I had overlooked in my life prior to being captured.

In the distance, I could see a massive castle built of gleaming white stone that reflected sunlight with breathtaking splendor. It stood in stark contrast to the Void I had seen in the vision, but somehow it too felt like home. A gentle breeze tousled my hair, bringing with it a faint whisper calling my name and an intoxicating, ambrosial scent that sparked a painful longing within my chest. Both the voice and the perfume were achingly familiar, yet no matter how hard I tried, I couldn't recall who they belonged to.

I awoke to warmth, tucked beneath blankets, in a bed near a roaring fire. The voice from the dream lingered in my mind, calling me back to the hauntingly familiar land. The voice faded, leaving only the crackling flames, and with them, the image of villagers consumed by fire forced its way into my mind's eye.

For a fleeting moment, I dared to believe everything I had suffered was nothing but a terrible dream, a vision of horror conjured by my mind. I kept my eyes shut, clinging to the hope that the nightmare had dissolved as I slept. There's no reason to get up, I told myself, no reason to open my eyes. I can gather the damnable firewood later. Grandmother will understand. She can wait.

As I lay there, desperately trying to convince myself that my abduction, torture, and imprisonment were nothing more than a bad dream, fingertips trailed across my leg. My eyes burst open at the touch, and I sat up in a panic, pushing myself against the wall behind the bed. I was not prepared for the sights waiting to greet my eyes.

"You're finally awake," said a young woman seated at the foot of the bed. Her voice, melodious yet tinged with amusement. She rose with practiced grace, and my breath caught. "I will inform the master."

Golden hair cascaded over her shoulders and down her back, framing a face of inhuman beauty. Her pale skin glistened, and she wore garments so thin they were an insult to modesty. I tried not to stare, my cheeks burning. Her presence exuded an almost hypnotic allure.

The chieftain's daughter had possessed a raw, untamed beauty, but this woman made Katri seem like an unwashed peasant. Katri had been stocky, built to survive in the harsh mountains we called home. This woman, however, was lithe to the point that she seemed almost fragile.

Still, something about her set my instincts on edge. Her eyes had vertical slits for pupils, like a feline, and bright yellow irises that seemed to glow. When she smiled, her canines gleamed, unnaturally sharp. These details pulled at distant memories, half-formed and elusive. Before I could grasp them, her voice interrupted my thoughts.

"When you are ready, dress yourself in the garments on the table. The master is eager to meet you in the Great Hall."

With that, she turned and left, her movements as fluid and deliberate as the stalk of a predator.

I let out a breath I hadn't realized I was holding, only to flush deeper when I noticed my state. Beneath the blankets, I was bare. My body had been washed and shaved; even my wild beard was gone.

The room itself was opulent beyond anything I

had ever known. Smooth stone walls, adorned with crimson tapestries, enclosed a space filled with furnishings of unparalleled craftsmanship. Nothing in the village could compare to this room, not even the chieftain's cabin. On the table, clothing of black fabric so soft it felt like touching a dream sat waiting for me. Once dressed, I took one last awestruck look around before stepping into the torch-lit hallway.

The grandeur extended beyond the room. The walls were lined with blood-red curtains, their threads finer than any I could have imagined. Even the golden torch sconces were masterworks of artistry. My footsteps whispered on the staircase as I descended. At its base, another woman awaited me. Her raven-black hair shimmered in the flickering light; her beauty exceeded that of the woman who woke me. She carried herself with a subdued grace, and yet her presence was equally unsettling. "This way," she said, her voice calm yet commanding.

I followed my captivating guide through another hall, desperate not to gawk at her, but something was unnaturally alluring about her. It seemed like both women had been blessed by a Goddess to awaken the primal instincts in men.

As I would later learn, the "Master's bloodline" is gifted with a very unnatural array of pheromones that aid them in hunting. Here, the women were so blessed that their mere presence would leave the opposite sex (and, most times, the same sex) mesmerized to the point of almost slave-like obedience without ever having to employ their inherent glamouring abilities.

We walked the corridor until it turned and opened into a Great Hall. Multiple hearths, carved in stone and decorated with gold, adorned the walls. Massive stained-glass windows reached toward a vaulted ceiling so high it seemed to belong to a cathedral, though no light emanated from them. Crimson banners hung from the walls, and empty banquet tables lined the room. At the far end, a single figure presided from a raised platform at an ornate table.

The woman beside me had vanished without a sound, leaving me alone to approach the platform. The man seated there rose as I neared, and I was struck by his presence. He appeared to be taller than the average man, though not as towering a presence as I. The master was dressed in black garments, a cape lined with blood-red silk draped from his shoulders. His sharp features came into view: a strong jawline, pronounced cheekbones, and pointed ears. By most standards, he would be quite handsome, if not imposing. His jet-black hair was slicked back without a single strand out of place.

From his raised platform, the striking figure was perched just high enough to allow him to look down at me. As I would learn, the Master enjoyed, above all else, looking down on those around him. A welcoming yet predatory smile touched his lips as he looked down. "Welcome to my home. Please, sit. I am sure you must be famished after your recent ordeals."

As I approached, the table came into full view, laden with a feast so lavish it felt surreal. Exotic dishes in a dazzling variety stretched before me, each more enticing than the last. My stomach twisted with hunger, but I forced myself to remain composed. His smile widened as he watched my eyes devour the feast; my shock clearly visible.

"I was unsure of your preferences, so I instructed my servants to prepare a selection of dishes from every corner of my realm. I trust you will find something to your liking."

"Thank you," I said, seating myself cautiously. "I take it you are the master I was told to meet?"

"I am. To my subjects, I am known as Master. To my court, Lord Dracula, but you may call me D," he said, before relaxing back into his throne.

"The walking dead man, is he your servant?" I asked, recalling the conversation from the underground cell.

The man's smile widened once again, revealing elongated canine teeth. "He is my Hand of Vengeance. A death knight bound to my service. So, yes. He is a loyal servant in that he has no choice but to obey."

As the last word parted his lips, a mocking laugh burst from the other side of the throne. A large animal crouched at Dracula's feet, coarse, spotted hair covering its body. More concerning were its eyes, which burned with malevolent intelligence. Lips pulled back from massive, powerful jaws in a twisted smile as the animal locked eyes with me.

Few beings could match the twisted evil lurking behind those eyes. In time, I would come to know it all too well.

"My guardian. In another world, his kind are called hyenas, though I admit his family is... unique. Enhanced." D reached down to pet the animal, which broke eye contact with me to gaze up at its master. "You will come to know him well in time. But first, you must eat. We have an eternity to speak, but I would have you do so on a full stomach."

The implicit command in his words was clear, and I obeyed, but not without hesitation. My stomach clenched at the thought of actual food after months of nothing but stale bread and water, but something about this seemed wrong. The spread was too much. Too generous. A kindness offered by someone who had held me captive for so long and had no reason to be kind now.

My fingers twitched against the polished wood of the table, every instinct screaming caution, but hunger was a force of its own. I reached for a piece of bread, forcing myself to break it apart slowly so as not to seem desperate or weak in front of my host. It was warm, and the first bite sent a shock through my body. The richness of it ravaged my tongue, overwhelming my senses after months of feasting on nothing. My guts recoiled as I swallowed the delicacy, revealing a hunger that I could not contain. I tried to restrain myself, to maintain some sense of decency, but the food disappeared faster than I had intended.

Across from me, Dracula remained motionless, studying me as I ate. He showed no interest in the meal himself, only touching it occasionally to idly toss chunks of meat to his beast. That, more than anything, set my nerves on edge.

Chapter 12
Down to Business

After the meal, Dracula explained he wished to speak with me in private, away from the eyes and ears of the Great Hall. At the time, it struck me as odd, considering we dined alone save for his pet. In reality, few locations in his home were truly private, a fact that I would come to know all too well.

D escorted me through a dizzying maze of hallways. The twists and turns blurred together, each corner more labyrinthine than the last, erasing my sense of direction. The architecture seemed to spin upon itself, the corridors impossibly shifting — wider, narrower, suffocating. I soon realized I could no longer tell if we were ascending or descending.

The room he selected was much smaller than the Great Hall, smaller even than the quarters in which

I had woken. Its oppressive intimacy was amplified by the stone walls, so dark they seemed to drink in the dim light. Candles dotted the space, their flames flickering with an unnatural crimson hue, casting shadows that moved with a mind of their own. A hearth blazed at one end of the room, its fire burning not the warm orange of home but the same blood-red as the candles. The flames seemed to breathe, exhaling thick and cloying waves of something that smelled like old blood left to stagnate.

Dracula motioned me toward a large chair positioned near the hearth. I hesitated but complied, sinking into the dark leather. He took the seat opposite, his eyes glinting in the eerie light.

The aura of a gracious host dissolved as his gaze sharpened, his voice cutting through the stillness. "You must surely realize by now that it is no act of chance that you find yourself here in my home." The words were not a question but a pronouncement, each syllable weighted with finality.

As I would learn over countless centuries, D was not one to suffer fools for long. Useful idiots were tolerated but never allowed to dwell in his presence for any period more than a passing moment. Even the most useful among them would find themselves unwilling specimens in the Doctor's laboratory if they tested his patience.

"My Hand of Vengeance plucked you from certain doom for a purpose," he continued, leaning forward. The friendly veneer of moments ago evaporated, replaced with the harsh mask of a leader accustomed to submission. "It is time for you to begin repaying the debt you owe me for saving your life." His tone was stone-cold, and I felt the air between us shift, the room seeming smaller and more suffocating. I matched his stare, refusing to shrink under its weight.

"I did not ask to be saved." The words left my mouth before I could give them thought. My voice sounded hoarse, not only from disuse but also from the pressure of everything I had endured. I had spent months entombed in darkness, my body wasting away as my mind consumed itself. Now this man expected gratitude? My fingers clenched the chair arms, digging into the fabric. "Everyone I cared for is gone. They died screaming as I watched from a cage. Now I sit here, fed and dressed, in the house of the man who made it happen. So, tell me, *D*, why should I care about debts when I have nothing left to lose?"

"Good," D murmured as his lips curved into a faint smile, not in cruelty but in something far worse: understanding. "There is fight in you. Defiance. Strength. I tire of the empty flattery and thoughtless obedience I am surrounded with. No, Viktor, you did not ask to be saved. Yet here you are."

My breath hitched. My name. Hearing it spoken aloud struck me harder than I'd expected. I thought it had been buried alongside the village, lost to the screams and ashes. Yet D wielded it like a blade, a revelation that sank deep into my gut.

"Yes, I know your name," he said, his smile widening. "You will find I know a great deal about you, far more than you likely do yourself."

His words hooked me, despite the warning bells sounding in my mind. I could feel the trap closing around me, but the lure of answers was too compelling to resist. My voice came out quieter than I intended. "How do you know my name?"

The impossibly convincing smile of his widened once again. "Stay here as my guest, and I will share my knowledge... when you are ready to hear it. But my hospitality and my knowledge will come at a cost."

The weight of my situation bore down on me, and I exhaled sharply. "I suppose my other option is to return to the cell," I said, fully aware of my position. I was alone in a strange environment, alive only because the man before me had deemed it so.

D chuckled, the sound low and measured. "You are intelligent as well. I may have a place for you in my Court one day."

I scoffed at the remark. "What could I possibly offer you? I have no skills or qualities that would be of service in a place such as this."

His eyes bore into mine, unblinking and relentless. "You are of far greater importance than you can imagine, young one. You possess power the likes of which this realm has never seen. The events on the cliff proved such."

My chest tightened. "You were there. The red eyes in the night."

"Indeed." His voice dropped; his words almost reverent. Blood seemed to rush into the whites of his eyes, and his fangs extended as he spoke. "I watched as you became the visage of a dark god, as you swatted my champion aside as if he were nothing."

"I do not know how I did… that," I admitted like a damn fool, my voice trembling with frustration and unease. "If I did, I would have left your prison long before now."

"It was an unconscious act of self-preservation," he explained. "You had no control over it. But in time, we can discover the key to your powers and unlock them fully. Join me. Fulfill your destiny, and in doing so, help me achieve mine. Those are my terms."

Silence stretched between us. I stared into the crimson fire, the flickering flames offering no solace, only casting shadows of my torment. Finally, I met his gaze again, resigned but resolute. "I want answers to the questions that haunt my dreams. You claim to have them. Prove it. Maybe then, I'll agree to your terms."

D nodded, a satisfied smile curling his lips.

With a wave of his hand, the door opened. Two men entered the room, if you could call them that. The first was the Death Knight, his heavy armor clinking with each step. Behind him stood a short, stocky man with long, ashen-white hair, stubble, and sharp, bestial features. Recognition sparked in my mind. The eyes. They were the same as the hyena's from the Great Hall. Somehow, the beast had transformed into the figure standing before me, a snarling grin smeared across his face.

D rose from his chair, addressing the pair. "Our guest has agreed to join our family. See him in his quarters. Once he has recovered his strength, you shall begin his training." Turning back to me, he stepped closer, and for the first time, I noticed the barest glint of hunger in his crimson gaze. "Here is your first answer," he said, his voice smooth as silk, sharp as a butcher's blade. "I know your name, Viktor... because your *father* gave it to me."

His words struck like a thunderclap. The room shrank; the fire, the shadows, the towering figure of the Death Knight, the beast-man, all of them blurred, washed away by a single, world-crushing word: father.

My father. I had never learned his name. He was a ghost who had loomed over my life without shape or face or *existence*.

I barely registered D's departure. The walls continued to close in, the weight of the past dragging me into depths I had no way of escaping. I was left alone, drowning in my revelation and suffocating from the burden of what lay ahead.

Chapter 13
Trial By Undeath

Once the meeting with D had concluded, the Death Knight led me through the Castle and back to the bedchamber where I had awoken. He instructed me to stay there until called upon. With no desire to get lost in the maze-like corridors, I did as commanded.

This new prison was, admittedly, far more appealing than the last, yet I was still confined to a small space against my will. Twice a day, I was taken from my quarters to the Dining Hall, where I was allowed to eat under the hungry gaze of the women I had seen before meeting my new benefactor. Like their master, neither of them would touch the offerings, preferring only to sit and watch as I ate.

At first, this was rather uncomfortable, as I was

unaccustomed to being the center of so much attention. In the village, people went out of their way not to look in my direction, so being studied made me conscious of my every movement. I did my best to ignore the staring, choosing to focus on the food before me and pretending I was alone. This helped, but occasionally, the vixens would giggle at my expense. The first time this happened was when I accidentally dropped a knife while slicing into a roast. A chorus of laughter erupted from the two women, only to be joined by another, whose visage was hidden from me. Perhaps, I thought, that is what Dracula was referring to when he said he wanted to speak absent the eyes and ears in the Great Hall.

On the fourth day, I made a potentially fatal error. Ryvina, the raven-haired, and Mayna, the blonde, had arrived at my quarters for my second meal of the day. By this time, the duo had introduced themselves to me, explaining they were Brides of Dracula. Both women wore garments that left little to the imagination, and I was more flustered by their appearance than usual. As I ate, my embarrassment led to a slip of the knife, which sliced through the tip of my thumb. A sharp pain, then warmth. Blood welled at the surface, a single bead forming before breaking loose and flowing down my finger. Mayna's reaction was immediate.

Her entire demeanor shifted. Her eyes

darkened, then glowed, suffused with a deep crimson. The languid amusement drained from her posture, replaced by the tense, hungry stance of a predator about to leap. Her perfect lips parted ever so slightly, revealing elongated canines. My body reacted before my mind could catch up. I seized the knife, my knuckles whitening in my grip, and prepared to defend myself. A cold sweat slicked my palms, and my grip on the knife trembled, only slightly, but enough for me to notice. Enough for them to notice.

It was then that Ryvina placed her delicate hand on Mayna's shoulder. "He is not ours, sister," Ryvina purred, a knowing smile playing at her lips. Her voice was soft, yet firm, commanding. "Look at him, ready to fight us. The master is right; he is not like the others."

Mayna's eyes regained their composure, though the crimson lingered at the edges of her sclera. She giggled seductively, more of a growl than a laugh. "He is nothing like the others. Perhaps this truly is the one our master seeks."

"I hope the master will let us play with him," a third voice said with a tone of sinister amusement that made my skin crawl. It emanated next to my ear, so close her breath stirred the hair on my neck as she spoke. Yet, when I turned with a start, the space was empty. No shadow. Nothing. I could feel the color fade from my skin as my heart skipped a beat. This led to another round of laughter from the Brides, joined by the unseen woman who had a moment before been impossibly close to me.

When she was done giggling at my expense, Ryvina approached me with the grace of a feline. "Relax, Viktor. I mean you no harm," she said.

She took my hand and slid her tongue over the wound as though it were the skin of a lover, licking the blood from my finger. I tried to recoil, but she held my wrist fast, her grip delicate yet impossible to break. The pain vanished in an instant, snuffed out of existence as though it had never been. My bewilderment was amplified when she withdrew, and I found the gash was gone as well, sealed shut without a trace. No scab or scar, just smooth flesh.

"All better now," she said, eyeing me as though I were a piece of meat rather than a person.

My stomach twisted as my mind wrestled to process what had just happened. "I think I am done for the day," I said, my voice shaking, as I stepped away from the dining table.

It was then that an invisible hand slid across my chest, parting my shirt as it did. "I think we spooked him, sisters." Again, the unseen woman laughed, joined by the two Brides I could see.

"Why do you hide from me?" I asked, speaking in the general direction I thought the woman was.

More laughter. "Because it is fun, Viktor. Don't you like games?" The voice echoed from above me, somewhere high in the arched ceiling.

I craned my neck, trying to discern where my invisible stalker was hiding, to no avail. "I do not find this fun," I said flatly, trying desperately to conceal the gaping pit of fear tearing at my chest. Not only was she somehow able to become invisible, but she was also moving around the room at an impossible speed as if flying.

Sharp nails trailed up my spine, ending with a playful tug at my hair. "Oh, you will, with time. I promise." Imperceptible lips pulled wetly at the lobe of my ear, then were gone.

***

I barely slept that night. Every crackle of the hearth in my quarters and each creak of the bed beneath me sent a shiver across my skin like ice forming on still water. The unseen woman, the lingering sensation of her phantom touch… I couldn't shake them off. When exhaustion finally overtook me, my dreams were restless, full of shadowy figures circling just beyond my perception. Laughter echoed from the darkness there, taunting me.

The following day arrived too soon, forcing me to rise from my uneasy slumber. Before I gave thought to what had happened the night before, the door to my chamber pushed open. The Death Knight had returned.

His presence banished the remnants of the haunting night, like the first rays of dawn scattering the mist. Months had passed since he had slain my village, yet seeing him brought the stench of burning flesh back to my nostrils, the screams of the dying to my ears, and the taste of rotten meat to my tongue. Here he was, the harbinger of my immeasurable suffering, standing before me as though it had all been nothing.

His hand held a neatly folded bit of cloth of the same material as the clothing D had provided for me. "Put this on," he commanded, tossing the new garment onto the bed next to me. "A gift from the master."

I pushed the blankets away, which did nothing to stop the frigid aura emanating from the knight anyway, and dressed. The fine, hooded cloak made my skin tingle after I touched it, as though it held some unseen power. In the time I had traveled with the Death Knight, I had never become accustomed to the feeling of being near him, the inescapable, excruciating cold that seeped through the flesh, down to the bone, and beyond. The discovery that the cloak offered protection from the biting chill delighted me.

The Death Knight saw my posture soften and approached, challenging the sanctuary offered by the cloth. He reached up and drew the hood over my head, and our eyes met for the first time since I challenged him over Natka's family in the village. After everything he had put me through, I wanted to cower, to hide from his burning gaze, but something deep within me stirred, refusing to let me back down. I stood erect, allowing my height to tower over him in a display of dominance.

We remained there for many moments, locked in a battle of wills, and I couldn't help but notice that even standing this close to him, I could discern no trace of his features within his helmet. Only the burning orbs that served as his eyes and the abyss of darkness surrounding them. I pondered, at that moment, if he even had a face.

"Do not remove the hood for any reason until we have reached our destination," he said, turning to walk out of the room. "Follow me."

As he did, I released a breath I didn't realize I had been holding. We left the comfort of my room behind, walking through the maze of corridors and down flights of stairs until, finally, we entered the castle courtyard where the Death Knight had a horse and various supplies to survive for an extended period outside the castle walls, waiting for me. The bright light burned my eyes, forcing me to squint, as it had been a very long time since I last had seen the light of day. Only then did I question why there were no windows to the outside world in the Castle, none that weren't so heavily stained as to be impervious to the beating rays of the sun. I made a mental note to ask about this peculiarity, but was soon so flush with embarrassment that the question passed unasked.

My new mentor was already atop his steed by the time my eyes adjusted to the brightness of the day, and he ordered me to mount the horse waiting for me. Unfortunately, my previous interactions with equines were limited at best, a fact that became painfully obvious in short order. So, my first lesson came in the form of how to mount and ride one.

The knight observed with a silent intensity, his imposing figure unnerving, as I struggled to maintain balance in the saddle. He only moved to correct my posture when I was at risk of injuring myself or the horse. When he was sufficiently convinced I wouldn't fall off, we began our journey into the unknown.

"Why not use a portal?" I asked, curious about the practicality of horseback travel given the knight's abilities.

He glanced at me then spoke, his voice devoid of warmth. "We survey the master's lands to ensure they are in order, and you must learn. There will be other creatures to ride in the future."

The cryptic remark left me uneasy, conjuring images of monstrous beasts lurking within D's domain. As we journeyed, the landscape did little to ease my discomfort. The forest darkened as we traveled, its trees gnarled and twisted, casting long, skeletal shadows. Hidden figures skulked in the underbrush, their glowing eyes disappearing as quickly as they appeared. Who, or what, they were didn't seem to matter to the knight, who continued as though they were nothing more than rodents.

Despite the haunting scenery, the journey itself was tolerable. Unlike the death march, I was granted time to eat, rest, and relieve myself. Now that I was part of Dracula's family, I was treated with a modicum of dignity. Still, the Death Knight's presence was an oppressive reminder of the stakes. He did not sleep or even rest. Ever. While I, still under the illusion of mortality, succumbed to exhaustion each night, he stood vigil, his hollow gaze scanning the horizon.

The process was slow-going at first, until I became more comfortable on the horse, which proved to be the only genuine source of company on the journey. The knight's silence stretched on for eternity, broken only when we passed some point of interest he deemed worthy of note. A random castle here and there, lorded over by nobles whom the knight was so disinterested in, he didn't even share their names. Only the locations mattered.

Then, there were what the Death Knight called 'farms,' human colonies that seemed more like bustling villages than any farmstead I had ever seen. We traveled far removed from them so as not to attract attention, just close enough to assess their existence and move on. At no point did we get close enough to see another human, nor to hear the voice of another living being. Yet still, seeing the smoke rising from chimneys in the distance drew forth a terrible longing in my chest.

We traveled like this for many days, through a variety of terrains, until we reached a small fortress on the outskirts of D's lands: the Keep. Its jagged walls loomed over a barren landscape, the last bastion of Dracula's power before the Lycan territory began. The Keep was devoid of life, guarded only by a platoon of skeletal warriors clad in armor reminiscent of the Death Knight's. These soldiers, he explained, were his personal army. Cursed, like him, to an eternity of undeath.

"This will be your home," the Death Knight announced upon our arrival, his voice as ominous as a tomb sealing shut, "Until you are ready to serve."

I barely had time to process the bleak proclamation before my first trial began. As the gate creaked open, the shadows belched out a grotesque parade of corpses. The smell hit me like a blow, a putrid mix of metallic blood and spoiled, maggot-infested meat that forced the fluid from my stomach into my throat, where it lingered, burning. They shambled forward with stunning speed, limbs jerking with unnatural purpose.

"If they bite you, you will die," the Death Knight said coldly as he tossed a short sword into the dirt several feet away.

I dove from my horse to retrieve it just as one

of the dead lunged at my thigh. Behind me, my horse shrieked in agony. I turned, sword in hand, just in time to see it swarmed, dragged down to the earth beneath snapping jaws and clawed fingers. Its dying cries mixed with the chorus of groans and smacking of gore-coated lips as the shamblers feasted on the meat.

By the time I rose, the horde was already coming. Not stumbling. Charging.

These were no sluggish revenants. They were freshly reanimated. Quick. Strong. They moved as if the memory of life still burned in their veins. These undead would run until their muscles ruptured and fight until their bodies were stripped of flesh.

I swung the sword clumsily, as if it were the firewood axe I had used in my previous life in the village. My strikes were desperate, wild, and ineffective, each fueled by fear.

The Death Knight watched from his skeletal steed, unmoving. His stillness was worse than mockery. It was indifference. He didn't care if I lived or died.

I tried to fend the creatures off, but they kept coming, relentless in their pursuit of fresh meat. Soon, my arms ached. My breath hitched. My heart pounded within my chest, loud enough to drown out the groans. Then I lost the sword.

It was wrenched from my grip, lodged in the chest of a moaning corpse. Slick with gore, it slipped from my fingers and vanished into the sea of rotten flesh. I was left with nothing but my fists and the certainty of death. I screamed and swung, fists connecting with jaws that seemed unaffected by the blows. Nothing I did mattered. They closed in, fingers raking my skin, teeth snapping inches from my throat. Pain exploded in my side, and I collapsed.

Only then did the Death Knight descend in a blur of death and steel.

The horde shattered before him like ice beneath a hammer, his blade cutting through the undead with surgical precision. One moment, I was drowning in claws and teeth. The next, I lay blinking beneath a crimson sky, twitching hunks of the dead surrounding me.

Gauntlets dripping with ichor, the Death Knight loomed over me like a vile god of destruction. He reached into the pile and dragged free a writhing torso by its severed spine. Even without arms or legs, the creature was still intent on reaching me until a single word from the Death Knight stilled it. He dropped the corpse, then seized me by the hair, pushing two fingers into my chest. Agony flared, then dulled as my wounds closed.

"Pathetic," he growled, voice hollow with disdain. "If you cannot best these, you will be of no use to me out there." He turned his head to look beyond the wall, into the canopy of trees that loomed in the distance. Then he dropped me to the blood-soaked ground like discarded meat. "Clean yourself, then meet me inside."

I didn't respond. I couldn't. Head bowed, throat tight, I did the only thing I could. I obeyed.

After my resounding failure, I was shown to my quarters, a small stone chamber overlooking the forest. The cold seeped into my bones, the fire ablaze in the tiny hearth doing little to stave off the chill. The howls from the timber echoed through the night, a constant reminder of the dangers lurking beyond the Keep's walls. Sleep eluded me, and by the time the first rays of sunlight breached the horizon, I felt more exhausted than when I had lain down.

Following a scant breakfast of stale bread and porridge, I made my way to the courtyard once again, where the Death Knight stood waiting to begin my formal training. He taught me to grip a sword, how to strike and parry, and the fundamentals of combat. His methods were harsh, but his skill was undeniable.

Each day, from sunrise until long after the enchanted braziers lining the battlements flared to life at dusk, we trained. When exhaustion overtook me, skeletal minions brought small animals from the forest, which the Death Knight used to heal me, as before. Their life would flow into him, then back out and into me.

Weeks turned into months as the process repeated. My body transformed, growing stronger and more agile with each day. The shame of my first failure drove me, and I absorbed every lesson with fervent determination. The Death Knight seemed to take a grim satisfaction in my progress, as though training me rekindled a long-buried part of himself from before the curse had claimed him. He provided training with every weapon the fortress had to offer and then petitioned the Castle for rarer arms to continue my instruction.

I was so focused on the training that my visions had all but stopped, and my other abilities remained dormant, locked away behind an invisible barrier. Even the most exhaustingly intense days didn't seem to bring anything extraordinary out of me, which I overlooked. The Death Knight, however, did not. Though he said nothing, I caught his hollow gaze lingering on me during our sessions, as if searching for any spark of the thing that had thrown him from his steed so many moons ago.

Reflections:

Unbeknownst to me at the time, my teacher was under strict orders to bring the monster out again by any means necessary. If D's assessment of the situation at the cliff was correct, then a near-death experience should have set me off. The zombie attack had been his first attempt, but it had failed. He soon realized that mere training would not suffice.

Chapter 14
Glory Unseen

My time with the Death Knight proved beneficial to me in a number of ways. In the short time under his tutelage, my hand-to-hand combat skills had become exceptional. My body had also changed, though not in the way my companion had hoped.

The muscles lurking beneath my skin had hardened, layered like plates of iron, and my reaction time had become almost superhuman. More than once, I suspected the Death Knight had to call upon his unnatural gifts to best me, though he would never admit it. My recent gains, impressive as they were, masked a deeper truth, an inner power that lay dormant. I feared it as much as I loathed it, ashamed of my inability to harness it.

The days blurred together, each one marked by the same ruthless rhythm: rise, fight, bleed, recover, repeat. Each bruise and cut I suffered from the training honed my skills, brutal lessons carved into my flesh. Then came a day that changed everything.

It began like any other. The Death Knight pushed me until my limbs trembled, and my breath came in gasps, but the lesson was cut short. A skeleton fired a warning arrow, signaling that someone was approaching the keep. We had a visitor. The Death Knight stopped mid-swing, then sheathed his sword. "To your quarters. Now," he said, his tone sharper than usual.

I nodded and left the courtyard, retreating into the darkness of the Keep. It wasn't the first time our fortress was graced with visitors. The first time was when D had sent a shipment of weapons to the fort at the dead man's request. The other handful of times had been messengers bringing news from the realm to keep the Death Knight up to date on the nation. Every time someone came to visit the Keep, I was sent away to hide in my quarters.

Unbeknownst to me, the Master had deemed my existence to be the strictest of secrets. The only persons privy to the knowledge that I even existed at this time were those closest to the man himself. The cloak I had been given upon parting the Castle was part of this secrecy, enchanted to alter the perception of anyone who may look upon me. To them, I would appear as nothing but one of the Death Knight's soldiers, which would arouse less suspicion than Dracula's high general traveling with a random human.

D's decree that my presence be kept as the highest of state secrets was unbreakable. The Death Knight was incapable of disobeying the orders from his lord, even if he wanted to. The Hyena was loyal to a fault and wouldn't dare risk losing his position or the benefits that came along with it. D's wives, bound to him through blood, wouldn't dare speak of me.

The Masked Man, Hojo, seemed to be the only weak link, but he was also on my side, or so he claimed. The only other individuals I had encountered since being abducted were non-sentient undead, thus ensuring my presence was cloaked in shadow.

D was using isolation to shield me and also to imprison me. Every time I was sequestered away, the weight of my confinement bore down on me. I did not know why I wasn't allowed to be seen, or, more importantly, heard. The Death Knight was many things, but good company was not among them. My desire to communicate with someone, anyone, who could provide companionship was growing with each passing day. The fortress was my cage, and the secrecy shrouding my existence only deepened my resentment.

Once the messenger had come and gone, the Death Knight appeared in my quarters and told me that under no circumstances was I to leave the barracks until he returned. He had received orders and was leaving to fulfill them. I knew questioning him was a waste of time, so I agreed.

As the hours stretched on, the sun dipped below the horizon, and the eerie stillness of the forest unnerved me. It was unnatural, this silence. The usual cacophony of insects and distant howls was absent, replaced by a heavy, oppressive vacuum. The light emanating from the enchanted torches lining the battlements below amplified my unease, casting shadows that moved like hidden enemies. My skin prickled as a familiar dread crept over me. Something was out there.

I donned the leather armor provided for training; it fit snugly but was protective. The cold steel of a longsword from the armory steadied my trembling. The blade was no match for the horrors lurking in the dark; non-magical weapons were as effective as twigs against most of D's enemies. Still, I convinced myself it was better than nothing. I paced the halls; the silence amplified every creak of my boots on the stone floor. My training had prepared me for combat, but not for this. Not for the suffocating fear of standing alone against the unknown.

The first howl pierced the air, too close and too menacing. My breath hitched, and I froze, straining to pinpoint the source. More howls followed. Each one echoed from a different direction, encircling the Keep.

The Hollow Tooth had come.

The Death Knight had warned me about them: dissenters among the Lycan clans. Dracula had forged an uneasy alliance with the werewolf chieftains, but the Hollow Tooth rejected the treaty that put an end to generations of fighting between the two nations. These rogue packs were unpredictable and vicious, and the Keep was a prize they'd long sought to reclaim. With its defenders split, they had found their opportunity.

I rushed to the main doors like a damned fool, driven more by instinct than strategy, and stepped into the courtyard. Torchlight flickered against the towering walls, casting long shadows that danced like specters. Then I saw it. The creature emerged from the darkness, its massive frame illuminated by the flames. A towering monster with dark fur covering muscles that rippled with every movement. Its eyes glowed with intelligence, and its lips peeled back in a grin that promised violence.

Battle cries rang out in the distance as skeletal defenders clashed with the invaders, but they were no help to me. The terror lunged, closing the gap in a blink.

Claws tore through the air, each swipe a blur of lethal precision. I barely dodged the onslaught and scrambled back into the fortress. The narrow passages provided me with a slight edge. Inside, the beast's size worked against it. Still, it pressed forward. Jaws snapped inches from my face, claws moving so fast they blurred. I slipped through the assault, managing to slice its arm, and moved back into a narrow corridor. It offered a double-edged advantage: the werewolf's movement was limited, but so was my escape. Only one path remained for me: backward, up a flight of stairs to the battlements.

Then I saw it, the wound I had inflicted on the werewolf's arm sealed closed before my eyes.

My blood ran cold. I could not kill the creature. Even if I continued to avoid its attacks, eventually I would tire. Its supernatural endurance would be my downfall.

I backed toward the stairwell, sword raised, never turning from the foe before me. To turn and run would be suicidal. It would outpace me, even in the confined space. Step by step, I retreated up the staircase to the battlements. The creature pressed forward, unyielding. Claws crashed against my blade. I landed blows where I could, each one met with a fresh surge of terror as the wounds closed before my eyes.

The parapet loomed. I burst into the open air with no other choice left. If another lycan waited, I was finished. Then, out of the corner of my eye, I saw them: the magical torches flaring along the walls. An idea sparked, desperate and reckless.

I baited the beast, feigning a stumble. It lunged, overextended, and I seized the moment. My blade arced. Bone shattered. Blood sprayed. The severed arm hit the stones, then the creature howled, clutching the stump.

I did not wait to see if it would regenerate. With the monster distracted, I drove my blade upward, piercing its heart, but even this wasn't enough to stop it. The werewolf staggered, its strength waning, but its fury undiminished. I barreled into it with all my weight, forcing it back toward a magical brazier. The enchanted flames roared as I shoved the lycan's massive face into the fire with all my might. Pain tore through my ears as the beast screamed. The sound was deafening, a guttural wail of agony that shook me to my core.

The effort cost me. A single swipe from its remaining arm sent me sprawling across the parapet. My back slammed into a merlon, and the impact knocked the wind from my lungs. The wolf, however, had bigger problems. Half of its face had melted off, and the remaining fur was engulfed in flames. With desperate claws, the creature tried to scrape away the burning flesh and stop the fire. Wracked by pain, it stumbled, then fell over the edge of the wall into the darkness below.

Howls of retreat followed. The remaining werewolves fled, leaving the Keep in battered silence. I tried to rise, but my limbs betrayed me, and I sank to the stone. A skeletal soldier emerged from the shadows, its armor streaked with blood. Bony fingers reached for me, curled around my arm, cold as the grave.

Then came the dark.

Chapter 15
Wounded

Within the abyss of unconscious dreams, I found myself floating beyond the veil of fractured thought and mortal pain. The Void. I had returned to the endless expanse, the sanctum where time knelt in silence and form lost all meaning. Here, there was no body, no pain, no breath, only the vast hum of eternity cradling my essence like a treasured relic.

The flesh I had worn, that brittle shell writhing in agony somewhere far away, was naught but a curiosity now. an echo of something laughably insignificant. Here, I was not Viktor. I was vast. Eternal. Here, where stars did not shine for their light was too young, I remembered who I was, and the Void remembered me.

The expanse of starless space spread before me, a buffet of roiling planets and nameless beings from a time before time. All of reality was at my disposal, inviting me to gorge upon it. Great Old Ones gathered at ancient altars no mortal man has ever blasphemed with their unseeing eyes.

I sat upon a black throne, a living, writhing thing, staring out as the Elder Gods and their minions scurried about beneath me. Their presence stirred neither awe nor fear, only a profound stillness within. Then, a voice called to me from afar, reverberating through the Void. An enchanting sound, unlike anything these lesser beings could ever hope to produce.

"Find me…"

Into the Void a light appeared. Resplendent wings spread and showered me with violet brilliance.

"Find me…"

The sweet words were shattered by excruciating pain, thrusting my soul into the cage of flesh once more. I drew in a breath, instinctive, panicked, too deep, and the agony was immediate and overwhelming. My lungs felt as though they were filled with shattered glass, each excruciating expansion exploding in my chest. My vision blurred, tears welling up against my will as I gritted my teeth. The sudden weight of my body, its limitations and frailty, crushed me.

Every slight shift drove blades deep into my nerves and forced strangled cries from my throat. My ribs were black and blue on both sides; one from the lycan's blow, the other from the raised stone of the parapet I had landed on. Ribs, many of them, were undeniably fractured. I was no longer in the sweet release of the Void. I was in hell.

Each breath carried a burning curse, mingling life and a longing for death in one. I remained in a state of feverish semi-unconsciousness for days as my body worked to heal the damage.

Every time I slipped back into the Void, those alluring words would return to me. *"Find me,"* she would say, calling to me in a voice of ageless wisdom and playful charm, resonating with a sweetness both captivating and enthralling. Some ancient part of my soul knew that voice, knew the owner, and ached to heed her command. In that dream space, I reached for her with all I had, desperate to draw closer. But the waking world was merciless.

Each time I would return, her voice faded, a distant whisper swallowed by the ocean of misery my body was drowning in. The comfort of her presence was replaced by fevered shivering, the light of her wings darkened by the dim glow of a dying hearth.

I was hovering somewhere between delirium and despair when a voice, not hers, shattered the haze.

"Pathetic."

The word struck like a slap, yanking me from

the edge of the abyss. The Death Knight stood in the doorway, his towering figure framed by flickering firelight, eyes of flame narrowed in disdain. Behind him, one of his soldiers waited, arms wrapped around a quivering piglet too frightened to squeal.

The knight thrust two fingers into my ribs so hard I nearly fainted, then performed his grisly magic to heal my wounds while the animal screamed. The sounds of ribs cracking as they righted themselves rang through my skull like bone chimes in a storm, each snap a scream echoing out from the marrow. The bruising turned from black and blue to a sickly yellow. Just before it no longer hurt to breathe, the knight pulled his fingers away, leaving me to suffer.

"I killed one," I said in a whisper, the effort still dizzyingly painful.

"No, you did not." The contempt in his voice was matched by the flaming orbs that once were the man's eyes when he was still human. "You should have killed them all. All you managed was to injure one and live to tell the tale. Pathetic."

I had been proud of myself for surviving the attack, for defeating an enemy that was beyond my capabilities, but that pride was now gone. In its place was an all-too-familiar sense of helplessness. I had given my best, and once again, my best was not enough.

"The Master wishes to speak with you. We ride

to the castle at dawn." The knight turned on his heel and stormed out of the room, but the chill of his presence remained.

I lay in my cot the rest of the night, steeping in the familiar rot of self-loathing. In the village, I was a freak because of what I was, an outcast marked by forbidden abilities no one understood and everyone feared. Now I was a freak because of what I wasn't. My power, whatever it truly was, had abandoned me when I needed it most. Here, among monsters and gods, I was just a fragile thing pretending to belong. I didn't fit among the humans who cast stones, nor the nightmares who wielded power like breath. I was a half-formed thing; adrift, unwanted, unfinished, and unless that changed, I wouldn't survive much longer.

***

The ride back to the castle was pure misery. I had become accustomed to riding a horse during the first trip, but now, each step the animal took felt like an earthquake shaking my insides, which were far from healed. To make matters worse, the knight was far less considerate now, giving very little regard to the needs of my living flesh.

I spent the time ruminating over my failure, desperate to uncover what had triggered my brief transformation at the cliff's edge and how to replicate it. Each unanswered question was a stone added to the weight of my despair. When the towers of the castle finally came into view, my hope was extinguished. I was devoid of strength and purpose. By the time we arrived, I was prepared to face my fate, to be cast into the catacombs, forgotten like so many before me.

To my surprise, the same women who first led me to meet D appeared once more, moving like shadows draped in silk. Their presence was no longer unfamiliar to me, but that only made them more unnerving. Their beauty was still staggering, still otherworldly, and it stirred something deep within me that I couldn't quite silence, something beyond a simple desire. That flicker of attraction now warred with a primal fear, rooted in memory; the Dining Hall, the blood, the terror. Underneath their laughter and perfume, the scent of death persisted.

They said nothing as they took me by the arms, their touch too cold and too soft. The musical chime of their amusement followed me as they led me to a bathing chamber, where steam curled like spirits fleeing from the heat.

"Drink this," Ryvina, the raven-haired bride, said, handing me a small vial.

Her smile was radiant, but I couldn't meet her eyes. My gaze sought refuge in the floor, partially out of shame as Mayna began removing my clothes, but more because the memory of her lapping the blood from my finger was still fresh in my mind. I drank the liquid anyway, shying away as I did. Within moments, the pain in my ribs dulled to a distant murmur.

They bathed me without shame or ceremony, scrubbing the road from my skin with delicate hands. I clenched my jaw as their fingers slid across my flesh, forcing my eyes away whenever one would stray into my line of sight. They noticed, of course. They always noticed.

"What is the matter, Viktor?" Mayna asked, "Are you afraid of us now?" She pushed her lower lip out in a mocking pout.

Ryvina leaned in close, her gown slipping like spilled wine across her shoulder. "So shy... he's trying so hard not to look," she whispered, brushing close enough that her breath stirred the hair on my neck. "But even the most disciplined men unravel... eventually."

They drifted into my field of vision, just at the edges, brushing my arms, leaning in to rinse my hair, each motion slow, deliberate, designed to pull me in. It was a game, yes, but one with stakes. They wanted to see if I'd flinch, if I'd risk a look to satisfy my curiosity. To them, I was less a guest and more of a pet brought in from the cold; something to be toyed with, tested, maybe even tasted. They were enjoying every second. Their laughter, like bells ringing in a crypt, echoed through the steam.

I kept my eyes forward, jaw tight. I told myself it would be disrespectful to look at Dracula's wives, even if they were doing their best to flaunt their bodies before me. But, in truth, I was terrified. Mayna had become something inhuman at the sight of my blood, and after my defeat at the Keep, I wasn't so sure D wouldn't let her indulge her appetite at my expense.

Once I was cleaned and presentable, they ushered me off to the same room I had woken up in the last time I was in the castle. "Stay here, young one. The Master will see you soon," Ryvina said with a flirtatious smile as she left, locking the door behind her.

Though vastly different from the dreaded catacombs, it remained a cell. Pain-free for the first time in weeks, I lay back on the bed and drifted to sleep.

"Find me."

I woke with a start. The voice, no longer ethereal but immediate, had slipped through the cracks between worlds, finding its way to my ear. It felt closer now, almost as though it had been whispered from within the room.

The door creaked open, revealing a woman with blazing red hair staring at me. Something about her unsettled me, yet I couldn't turn away from her gaze. How many wives did D have, I wondered?

He had many, but only one that he ever cherished, and she was gone.

Chapter 16
Quite Human for a Vampire

"The Master will see you now," the voluptuous redhead in the doorway announced, her voice smooth as silk and laced with amusement. Something about it snagged in my mind, familiar, teasing, and unmistakably the same as the one that had taunted me in the Dining Hall so many moons ago. My body shuddered against my will at the realization, which made her giggle.

"It's you," I said, regaining my composure. "The one I couldn't see. The one who likes to play games."

Her crimson lips curled into a knowing smile. "Mm. So you remember. I wondered how long it would take you to put that together."

"You were invisible."

"Only to your eyes," she said and tilted her head playfully. "You'll find that many things in this Castle are just out of sight... until they want to be seen." She waved her hand, beckoning me forward with a smile no mortal man could refuse. "Come, the master wishes to speak with you. Our games can wait... For now."

Her intoxicating smile nearly dispelled the dread that had clung to me since my defeat at the keep. I had failed and now stood on the edge of judgment, uncertain how D would respond. Fear gnawed at my thoughts like a starving animal, dulling everything but the weight of what awaited me. The meeting with D loomed over me like an executioner's blade, but the revelation of the third bride made me sick. How long had she been watching me? Was it just in the Great Hall, or had she been hiding in plain sight all along? Who, *or what*, else was watching me?

Lost in this storm of thoughts, I almost failed to notice that the hallway outside my room had changed entirely. The pale stone walls were gone, replaced by the same near-black masonry of D's private study. Crimson tapestries still clung to the walls, but they pulsed with a deeper menace now, lit by the same unsettling, flickering red torches. Their glow danced across the woman's hair, turning her already striking presence into something supernatural: fiery, divine, and dangerous.

"Is something wrong?" she asked, her voice honeyed. She leaned against the doorway, one arm lifted in a seductive posture. Despite her warm tone and inviting body language, her eyes held a gleam of sharp curiosity, as though she were dissecting me thought by thought.

I lifted a hand to gesture down the corridor, only for it to land against the soft swell of her breast. She giggled, a sound both musical and mocking, and gifted me a look so wickedly amused it felt like my soul had been undressed. My face went hot in an instant, blazing as red as her hair. I recoiled as if burned, yanking my hand back and fixing my gaze to the floor like I could will it to open and swallow me whole.

She laughed again, rich and delighted, and I struggled to make sense of what had just happened.

When I'd raised my hand, she had been standing a full pace away, nowhere near close enough for me to touch her. But in the blink it took to move, she had closed the distance without a sound, without so much as a shift of the air. One moment she was across from me, the next, she was there, impossibly close. "My sisters were right; this is a fun game," she said with a smirk, though there was something calculating behind it.

Still flushed with embarrassment, I responded to her original question. "The hall," I stuttered out, "it is not the same as when I entered the room."

"Ah, yes. The Castle likes to rearrange itself," she said, flashing a smile that was equal parts flirtation and mockery. "You'll get used to it… If it lets you." Her gaze lingered, sharp and amused, as if peeling back my thoughts for sport. Then, she grabbed my hand to lead me along to see her husband.

"Lilyth, leave him be." D's voice came from behind me, in the room I had just left. I nearly jumped out of my skin. I snatched my hand from hers and turned to face my host, blushing like a damn fool. "My apologies, I…" D cut me off before I could continue. "My wives are pestering you. You have nothing to apologize for."

As D finished speaking, Ryvina and Mayna materialized next to their sister out of thin air, each sporting a mocking pout. My blood ran cold as I realized Lilyth wasn't alone in her ability to cloak herself from my sight.

"You're so protective of this one," Lilyth said, her tone half-teasing but tinged with genuine curiosity. "You rarely take such an interest in outsiders, least of all humans." She ran a finger across my chest playfully, and her gaze flicked between us before she turned on her heel and sauntered off. "I'll be watching," she added before disappearing into the shadows with her sisters.

Before I could recover from the bevy of

sudden shocks, ranging from Dracula's appearance behind me to the Brides manifesting before me, the next wave of strangeness struck.

The floor beneath my feet seemed to ripple for just a moment, like disturbed water, and the torches flickered violently as if gasping for air. Looking up, I found myself staring into an unfamiliar area of the Castle. The doorway behind me was gone, swallowed by the shifting stone. Black walls that had once been draped in crimson were now a strange blue-gray, veined with dull, throbbing lines of silver that pulsed like a heartbeat.

I blinked hard, but the distortion remained, a brief but nauseating blur of motion that turned my stomach. For an instant, the hallway spun and stretched, impossibly wide and narrow all at once, before snapping back into place with an audible thrum that I felt in my teeth.

I hadn't taken a single step, and yet the world around me had changed. The Castle was not merely rearranging itself. It was watching, reacting, and making sure I knew it could. It was toying with me. Lilyth's words echoed in my mind: *"You'll get used to it... If it lets you."*

The shock must have been plain on my face, because Dracula's lips curled into a knowing smile. With a slow, deliberate motion, he mimicked the same wave I had made before the unfortunate encounter with his bride. "You will find this place is overflowing with magic, both the Castle itself and its inhabitants. Quite different from your previous home, from what I am told."

I nodded in agreement, still unable to look D in the face. The red hue from the crimson torches he was cast in made him a terrifying visage to behold, and I was still certain I was going to be punished for not achieving his goals.

"You look like a whipped dog. What happened to the defiance I noted in our last meeting?" He said, interrogating me with his eyes. "You had a great victory at the Keep. Few mortals can say they have beaten a lycan. I am proud of what you did to protect my home."

My jaw clenched in response to the compliment. I had steeled myself for punishment; perhaps a return to the cell, a beating, even execution, but praise was not something I was prepared to receive.

"You are surprised?" D asked, his voice touched with mirth. "Few in this Castle could have accomplished what you did. Lycans are formidable, deadly, even to one of us."

"One of us?" I echoed, brow furrowed. "What... are you, exactly?"

Dracula smiled and began to walk down the corridor, savoring the question. "Vampire," he said, letting the word hang in the air. "That is the name of our kind. Not quite living, not quite dead. We are immortal, blessed with strength, speed, and power far beyond the limits of your imagination."

"I suppose that explains the eyes," I muttered, more to myself than to my host.

D's smile widened just a bit. "Yes, our eyes differ from those of a human; they are attuned to darkness. Where humans stumble in the night, we see clearly."

I could tell he enjoyed speaking of his kind, or perhaps it was playing the role of teacher that pleased him.

"So, you are nocturnal, then?" I asked.

"In a sense," he said with a casual flick of his fingers. "The sun is... unkind. For many of our kin, its light is lethal. Even for those of us who've built resistance, it remains a loathsome thing."

"And the fangs?" I asked, uncertain if I was treading too far.

D laughed, soft but chilling. "You are quite observant, Viktor. I am impressed. Yes, the fangs serve a purpose. Both for feeding and for creation."

He explained the nature of his people to me, how they can be made through a bite and the exchange of blood, how pureblood vampires are born in the same manner as a human, and that, unlike most creatures who eat the flesh of the dead, they sup on the very lifeblood of the living.

"So, you drink the blood of living creatures to feed?" I asked, the revelation turning my stomach sour.

"Humans butcher livestock before consuming them. We simply kill as we feed. The result stands the same," he said with a shrug, as though there were no difference at all.

"This explains why you did not dine with me," I said, recalling our first interaction in the Dining Hall.

He nodded, apparently pleased that I had caught that detail during our initial meeting. "We can consume food and drink like any other being; it simply does nothing to nourish us. Only the blood of the living can do that."

I sat in silence for many moments before I gathered the courage to ask my next question. "Do you intend to make me a vampire, like you?"

Dracula's face twitched ever so slightly. "No, Viktor, I do not. Your outward appearance may be that of a human, but we both know you are something else. Attempting to change that could be... disastrous."

I will confess that, in that moment, I was relieved by his answer, though I worried that by remaining whatever I was, I would forever be an outsider in his home. D, sensing my unease, smiled with something bordering on tenderness.

"You do not need to be turned to belong with us. Neither my Hand of Vengeance nor my Hyena are vampires, yet they are part of my family all the same. Do not fret over the matter."

Looking to change the subject, I decided to

address the events at the Keep. "If my fight with the werewolf was a success, then why did your Hand not seem pleased? He was furious at me for failing."

The smile faded from D's lips as he answered. "I ordered him to make you transform, as you did on the cliff, to unlock your potential. He believed the lycan attack would accomplish this goal. It did not. He is unaccustomed to failure, and he took it out on you. I apologize for his rough treatment."

"So, he knew they were coming?" I said, a surge of heat filling my chest. "I could have been killed."

The smile returned. "Yet, here you are. The Fates are not done with you yet," D said, studying my face as though searching for some hint of recognition. Not finding any, he continued. "I feel as though your time with us has left you... unsatisfied. You have lost your family and your home, and I have offered you little in return." D stopped walking to examine me as though I were some puzzle to be unlocked. "Every warrior has something to fight for, a motivation that drives them. It is, for some, loyalty to a throne or a God. For others, it is greed for wealth and the attainment of power. For most men, it is love."

The floor rippled beneath my feet once again, and the hallway shifted, leaving us in Dracula's private study once more. D continued, ignoring the transformation as though it were commonplace.

"You have no family left to speak of, and you

do not know me or my lands well enough to have forged the loyalty required to drive a man beyond his means." He grabbed a bottle from a shelf and sat in an oversized chair, motioning for me to join him. Popping the cork with a long, pointed fingernail, he poured the contents into two cups that appeared on the small table between us. Seeing me hesitate at the offering made him chuckle. "It is not blood," he stated, handing me the drink. "Sip it slowly, for it is quite strong."

We sat in silence for some time, drinking the mysterious liquid that seemed to burn everything it touched, from my lips to my stomach.

"You have no family, no reason to be loyal to me *yet*, nor do I feel as though you are the kind who wishes to attain wealth or power. Such men are easy to identify." He tapped the edge of his glass with a finger in contemplation. "Do you want a woman?"

I must have blushed again as he grinned like a wolf. "Have you been with a woman?"

"One… She is gone now." Thinking about her, how she had abandoned me, and the fate she had suffered at the hands of the Knight brought a wave of sadness crashing down, amplified by the intoxicating drink.

Shockingly, I saw my sorrow reflected in the vampire's eyes. "I am sorry for your loss. I understand the feeling all too well." The tone in his voice stood as a testament to the truth of his words, dripping with hidden anguish. His facade of charisma cracked for a moment, showing the misery within.

Again, we sat in silence for many long moments before he regained composure and offered a toast. "To those we have lost and the pain they leave behind. May we never forget them."

We raised our glasses and drank, then sat in muted contemplation, each of us reliving the past through bitter reminiscences. Eventually, Dracula chuckled a bit to clear the mood and asked, "If you do not want power or a woman, what do you want?"

I sat for a moment, swirling the remaining contents of my cup as I watched it form a small vortex. Memories of all the lands I had visited in my youth played out in my mind, and then the village where I was shunned. Forever an outsider, never accepted. "I want what I have never had," I said reluctantly. "I want a home."

D grinned from ear to ear. "Then a home you shall have."

Despite his enthusiastic response, I found it difficult to believe Dracula could make good on his promise. Even here among monsters, I feared I would always be an outcast.

Chapter 17
Initiation

D sprang to his feet and walked to the doorway without warning. "Come. It is time to feed, and you may be just drunk enough to stomach the sight of your new reality. I welcome you to live among us, but first, you must fully understand what it is we are."

The effects of the alcohol struck with force as I stood. I had drunk wine in the past, but never enough to get inebriated. Whatever D had given me was far stronger, as the world was less stable than it had been when I sat down. I stumbled along behind the vampire as we traversed a number of hallways. Shadows deepened with our passing, walls folding into new shapes at D's approach to reveal endless passages, like a story being written as he moved. Eventually, the shifting corridors led to a smaller dining area, more compact than the grand hall I had come to know.

D's wives were seated at a table on the opposite side of the room, and a handful of servants were busy filling glasses and serving food. The Hyena was there as we entered, standing next to the door in his human form, though he never lost the animalistic traits of his true self.

"Did I miss out 'n all the fun?" he asked through a toothy grin.

D ignored the question and continued toward his wives, motioning toward a table across from them. "Here. Sit. Eat."

I did as instructed, washing down the food with wine provided by an attractive young servant. Midway through my second glass, D asked if I was ready to learn what it meant to live among his people. I nodded sheepishly, unsure of what to expect next.

The vampire lord's eyes flooded with a crimson glow, which, understandably, alarmed the servants. It was then that I realized they were the main course for my new family.

"Come to me," D said in a markedly languid tone. As he spoke, the servants seemed to relax, hypnotized by the sound of his voice. One by one, they strode to each of the vampires in a trance. The girl who, moments before, had served me, stood before Dracula himself. He turned her head to the side, brushing her long amber hair away to reveal smooth, milky-white skin.

"Do not look away," he commanded.

His eyes seemed to glow with an increased intensity as his mouth opened, revealing extended fangs. He ran his fingers along the curves of his victim's neck, nostrils flaring at the scent of warm blood flowing just beneath the skin. Then he struck, biting down and piercing the girl's veins. The motion was elegant, almost reverent, nothing like the gory spectacle I had expected to witness. Aside from the color fading from the poor girl's flesh, I wouldn't have even suspected anything was amiss if I didn't know better.

But I did know.

A part of me, the rational human part of my mind, screamed to look away, but no matter how much I wanted to, Dracula's command held me still. Every scream I suppressed felt like a betrayal of who I once was. In another life, I would have fought to save that girl, but that time was gone, burned away with my village, and so I watched.

The soft gurgle of blood being drawn filled the room, a grotesque symphony of death, as the Brides joined in the macabre feast. The servants' glassy eyes stared unblinking, their bodies collapsing as their lives were supped away. My face remained a mask of calm, but underneath, my stomach churned with nausea.

In a matter of moments, the group was

drained. D finished first, pulling back from the corpse with a look of ecstasy, fangs glistening with crimson gore. Unceremoniously, he dropped the body onto the floor, which the Hyena eyed hungrily.

"If we're gonna initiate the boy, may as well do it proper like…" D's pet began, but abruptly stopped as the vampire lord gave him a look that the beast knew better than to question.

Dracula stared a hole through his lapdog, then instructed him to clean up the mess. The Hyena nodded, somehow hefting all four bodies and hauling them out of the room with ease, but not before flashing a wicked smile my way.

Once the bodies were removed, the Brides returned to their seats, speaking in hushed whispers while watching me. The only evidence of the horrors that had just transpired was a thin trail of blood dripping from the corner of Lilyth's lips, which Mayna licked off. "You are such a messy eater," she teased.

D turned his piercing gaze away from the door where the Hyena had exited and looked at me with a sadistic grin. "You handled that well."

Outwardly, I showed no response to what I had just witnessed. Internally, however, my appetite had vanished, and I was stone-cold sober. D had claimed that vampires were just like humans, only that they fed on the living instead of the dead. What he failed to mention was that they fed on people. This seemed like vital information, but he wanted to see how I would react; thus, the insidious omission.

Determined not to show any hint of weakness, I met Dracula's gaze and held it fast. "I have seen the dead rise, fought half-wolf monstrosities, and watched your Castle do the impossible. Learning you feed on humans doesn't seem like a stretch," I said flatly. With that, I picked up a chunk of pheasant and shoved it into my mouth to prove I was unaffected by the ordeal, though doing so made me want to retch.

D chuckled at my response. "Very good. Very good indeed. We shall see if that resolve holds up in the years to come."

The Brides tittered at the comment. "Oh… another game," Mayna said mischievously.

"The Hyena will win this one," Lilyth spat, with more than a bit of disgust in her voice. The other two moaned in agreement.

D's jaw tightened ever so slightly, betraying a flicker of tension. "Grygor has his uses," he muttered, though his gaze lingered on me in an uncomfortably prophetic manner.

Reflections:

When a human slaughters a cow or chicken, they think very little of it. It is just another animal raised to be food. Vampires consider humans in much the same light: livestock to raise and consume. D's domain has many human settlements that he rules over, keeping them safe from the beasts outside their villages so that only his chosen monsters could feast upon them. Most are blissfully unaware that their ruler is not human, or what happens to those who are summoned to the Castle.

It took a long while for me to adjust to the idea of viewing the 'mortal races' as a resource rather than people, and I am unsure if I ever reached that point. To a true immortal, the human lifespan is comically short, making it easier to disregard. Elves and dwarves, however, live much longer, thus making culling them more morally challenging. This, ironically, makes them more exotic prey to the vampires, their blood a prize they covet. In fact, they often keep these races as blood slaves, only supping enough to weaken them, not kill them.

Elf blood is especially prized because it has an intoxicating effect on vampires, more so when turned into wine. Something about the near-immortal qualities of elves made it possible to bottle and ferment their blood without it going rancid, and only the highest of vampire bloodlines are privy to the secret methods required to create it.

Chapter 18
Whispers of a Marble Queen

After taking our leave of the Brides, Dracula gave me a tour of the Castle. We walked for hours, D revealing to me the myriads of wonders in my new home. Markedly, we never encountered another soul during our explorations. His decree, keeping my presence a secret from all but the most trusted members of his so-called family, was still in effect.

Gothic corridors stretched endlessly, lit only by sconce-mounted candles that flickered and cast dancing shadows, shadows that seemed to possess a secret life of their own. The Castle's brooding atmosphere was relentless, a labyrinth devoid of windows to the outside world. Without the faint glow of the candles, the place would be swallowed by an oppressive darkness, reminiscent of the cavernous prison where I had languished for months.

Dracula stopped at dozens of rooms, each an opportunity to showcase the grandiosity of his domain. Lavish guest quarters, resplendent in their extravagance, dotted our path. But it was the State Room that left me in awe. This immense chamber, designed to host royalty, was meant to inspire wonder and envy. Intricately carved furniture stood like monuments to opulence, their cushions of such finery that the drapes I had gawked at upon my arrival now seemed paltry by comparison.

Suits of ancient armor lined the walls, radiating an unseen magic that made the air tingle with a faint but unmistakable hum. Between them, ancestral portraits hung like sentinels, each depicting members of Dracula's lineage. The faces glared, their gazes piercing, as if daring me to challenge their legacy. D recounted their tales, victories that shaped history and defeats that ended lives. Even immortals, it seemed, were not invincible.

Once my brief history lesson had concluded, Dracula began the tour anew. We walked on, passing a massive garden filled with nocturnal plants that shimmered under the dim moonlight, their beauty otherworldly. A separate armory, bristling with weapons, followed, and then a treasure room overflowing with riches so vast that they defied comprehension. My amazement seemed to amuse D, who relished every moment, his delight palpable.

Then, as we turned a corner, D stopped abruptly. Before us stood a door unlike any we had encountered. Its surface bore an intricate carving of a forest filled with strange plants and creatures with elongated ears and butterfly-like wings. The frame was crafted from white marble, accented with silver, glowing with a soft, brilliant light that stood in stark contrast to the Castle's pervasive gloom.

"This seems out of place," I said, squinting against the light that seared my eyes after so long in the oppressive darkness. D remained silent, his expression a mask of stone. He stared at the door as if entranced, his commanding presence diminished.

After an extended silence, he spoke, his voice a whisper. "This... isn't supposed to be here." His pale lips barely moved, and his face was devoid of what little color it typically held. He stood motionless, a statue frozen in time.

Sensing the weight of his emotions, I decided it best to remain silent. My eyes traced the delicate carvings on the door, trying to decipher their meaning.

D's voice finally broke the stillness, now a mere whisper. "This was her place. I haven't opened this door since I lost her." He turned to face me, and I was startled to see a single droplet of blood well at the corner of his eye. Before it could fall, it seemed to reverse course, retreating into his tear duct as though time itself had rewound.

I wasn't sure how to respond, so I stood in silence, rooted to the spot. D's grief was a storm, palpable and raw, and I felt like an intruder in his private tempest.

"You are young," he said, his tone heavy with meaning, "but you have known significant loss. We share a bond in our sorrows, I think." He smiled at me, though not with his usual grin dripping with charm. It was a knowing smile, one that tried to conceal the torrent of emotions raging within him. "Let us leave this place. I would not have this sour your introduction to my home."

Though I nodded, my curiosity burned. I couldn't help but wonder what he meant by saying the room wasn't supposed to be there.

Perhaps sensing my unspoken question, D sighed. "The Castle has a mind of its own. It is as much of a living organism as you or I. While it follows my commands, it also senses my emotions and subconscious desires. Our brief foray into the sorrows of the past must have summoned this place."

He waved his hand, and a door appeared in the blank wall beside us. When it opened, I saw my quarters beyond. "Rest well. I will have food sent to you."

I inclined my head in gratitude and stepped through the doorway. As the door closed behind me, I turned back to see D lingering in the hall, his hand resting on the marble as though bidding farewell to a ghost.

***

Sleep came on swift wings, but with it returned the visions that had been absent since my fevered dreams after the lycan attack. In the dream, I stood before the carved door, which creaked open of its own accord. The room beyond was blindingly white, its brightness obscuring all but a single feature: a statue at the far end. As I approached, details emerged.

It was a woman carved from marble, her beauty transcendent and heart-wrenching. Her sharp features and elongated ears gave her an ethereal air, as if the sculptor had tried to capture a goddess in mourning. Long, straight hair cascaded down her back, each strand delicately rendered in stone. She wore a flowing gown that left her shoulders bare, its folds so lifelike they seemed to ripple in a phantom breeze. The craftsmanship was so perfect that a random passerby could mistake it for an actual person. Her cupped hands seemed to hold an invisible orb between them, an empty space that hummed with purpose, as though the void between her hands contained a secret too vast to sculpt. A presence lingered in that emptiness, drawing me in, making me feel as though I was being watched.

I tore my gaze away, only then registering the full weight of the statue's aura. Even the allure of D's Brides paled in comparison to this figure. They were laughter and sinister playfulness. She was authority and sorrow incarnate. The woman this visage was based upon was something else: regal, commanding, a Queen. As I studied the statue, another figure entered the room, stumbling forward before collapsing at the statue's feet.

Dracula.

He was sobbing, torrents of blood streaming from his eyes and pooling on the pristine floor. His fists pounded the marble tiles in silent anguish, his cries unheard in the dream's suffocating quiet. His hands were soaked in blood, whether from his tears or wounds inflicted by his rage, I could not tell.

As I looked down at him, I realized I could not hear his anguished cries or the pounding of his fists. I could perceive no sound whatsoever. Even my heartbeat was absent.

The crumpled mass gathered himself enough to stare up at the impassive carving and silently screamed, "Why?"

Then, the silence shattered. The sound of grinding stone tore my attention from the grieving vampire and back to the statue. Its head turned slowly, lifeless eyes locking onto mine. The motion was unnatural and jarring. Then its mouth parted ever so slightly, and in a voice like the echo of breaking glass, it whispered, "Find me."

Dracula continued his silent lamentations as the statue returned to its original position, unaware that it had ever moved. Then I woke, drenched in cold sweat, heart hammering, with the Marble Queen's command echoing in my mind.

Chapter 19
The Hyena's Game

The chamber was shrouded in suffocating darkness when I snapped back to the waking world, the air bitingly cold and still. My heart pounded in my chest as if trying to flee some unseen terror. The voice echoed through me like the toll of a distant bell, its command etched into every nerve: "Find me."

I sat upright, slick with sweat, staring into the void beyond the edge of my bed. The hearth across the room, normally a constant source of warmth and light, had gone out. In all my nights here, I had never seen it extinguished. Curiosity tugged at the edges of my unease. I crossed the chamber, footsteps muffled by the stone floor, and knelt beside the hearth. The charred logs, coated in a thin sheen of frost, glistened in the darkness. I reached toward the ice-laced wood, hesitation prickling my fingertips, but stopped myself before making contact. Wary of the strangeness of it all, I returned to my bed.

A bevy of questions ran through my mind as I lay in the dark. Who was the Marble Queen? Why did she want me to find her? What extinguished the fire? As I searched for answers, the hearth burst into flame once again, startling me from the recesses of my mind.

Sleep would not return. I sat there staring at the flames for what felt like hours. Shadows danced in the corners of the room, and the walls felt closer than before, as though the Castle had been watching me dream. Then came the soft groan of old hinges.

The door opened of its own accord, spilling a narrow blade of light into the chamber. The bizarre torches in the hall beyond pierced the darkness of my room with a blade of crimson. I stared at the threshold, heart thudding in my throat. No wind had stirred it. No servants stood beyond it. I wondered if one of the Brides was there, watching.

For a time, I remained frozen, fear rooting me to the floor. After what I had witnessed, the walls moving, the halls reshaping themselves, I wasn't eager to step back into that shifting nightmare alone. But something gnawed at me. A compulsion. A pull. The Marble Queen's voice echoed again in my mind, colder now, almost coaxing: "Find me."

I rose and dressed, my fingers trembling as I fastened each button. I told myself I would only look. Just beyond the door. Just for a moment. I would stay close to the room. I would not go far.

At the time, I knew little of the veil of secrecy drawn around my presence here, only that I'd been concealed from wandering eyes in the Keep. For all I understood then, the Death Knight's haste had been no more than a measure of security, the kind demanded by war. I hadn't yet grasped how deeply the silence ran.

The door opened fully before I could gather the will to approach it, creaking wide as if the Castle itself had grown impatient with my hesitation. For a long moment, I stared at the threshold, heart thudding, half-expecting a giggle to break the silence or some horror to come slithering through, but nothing came. Only a subtle pull.

It could have been curiosity, or the Queen's command still resonating within me, but I moved into the corridor, irresistibly drawn like a moth to a flame.

"Yer up early," growled a voice behind me. It belonged to D's hyena, Grygor.

Turning to face him, I found the Castle had already begun to play its tricks on me. The doorway to my room was no longer there, replaced in the blink of an eye with a long hallway I hadn't seen before.

"I couldn't sleep," I said, not willing to disclose why.

"I's still a long time fore moonrise. Tha mas'er won't be 'wake til then." He reached up and slapped my shoulder, flashing a malevolent grin at me. "So 'ow 'bout we go 'n' find sum trouble ta pass tha time?"

The man, if you could call him that, was much shorter than I, having to stand on his tiptoes to reach my shoulder. What he lacked in height, however, he made up for in muscle.

"Le's go."

I hesitated. Something about him scratched at the edges of my instincts, a low hum of danger I couldn't quite explain. It wasn't just the way he looked or the guttural way he spoke. It was the way he smiled, the hateful malice lurking behind his eyes.

Even the Brides had shunned him. I remembered the way Lilyth spat his name like it was poison, her eyes flashing with revulsion. That alone should have been warning enough. Anyone who could unsettle creatures such as the Brides wasn't someone to be followed lightly. I told myself I was being paranoid, but I kept a careful distance, watching the way his shoulders moved, coiled like a predator's, always a half-second away from lunging.

The creature led me to a room I had yet to visit, one laden with bottles of various sizes, shapes, and colors. He sniffed around the containers, sifting through them as he sought a specific bottle. Finally, he pulled two from the back of a shelf, dusted them off, and handed one to me.

"First, we drink, then we go find sum *sport*."

I did not like the way he said the last word, as though his intentions were not at all what I would consider fun. I was immediately on guard, given the Bride's previous prediction that the Hyena would win some unknown game against me.

Sensing my sudden tension, the man formed his best imitation of an innocent grin, though his sharp teeth did little to comfort me. "Yer part o' tha family now, so ya 'n' I are gonna be fast friends. I'll take good care o' ya, jus' ya watch."

We sat at a dusty table on stools that appeared untouched for years, opening our bottles. The fumes from the liquid lurking within the yellow glass I held were enough to burn through solid stone. He laughed at the face I made as the aroma singed my sinuses.

"I's Dwarven. Stout stuff. Ya'll luv it."

I did not love it.

The first mouthful tasted worse than the putrid zombie flesh I had ingested while the Death Knight attempted to march me into an early grave. Despite the overwhelming urge to spit it back into the bottle, I swallowed the liquor down. The fluid burned like a hot coal in my throat, but I kept it from coming back up through sheer willpower alone. Even then, my eyes watered, and I started to cough.

"Welcome t' tha family." He sneered as he said it, then raised his bottle and gulped the contents down.

It was empty by the time he came up for air, and he grabbed another one. Bottle in hand, he turned and headed toward the door.

"Ya coming?"

I nodded and tried to stand, only to find myself damn near unable to do so. The drink I had with D was potent, but it was like water compared to the noxious syrup the Hyena had given me. One swallow of the dwarven alcohol, and the walls had become swirling portals to the abyss, and that is to say nothing about the floor, which seemed to have come alive beneath my feet. Given the Castle's mischievous nature, perhaps it did.

"Look at ya; ya 'aven't even spewed yer guts yet! Come on, le's 'ave sum fun. Ya can walk it off on tha way."

He wrapped an arm around my waist and held me up as we went, as I was far too drunk to walk on my own. Surprisingly, he could carry me with ease.

The Hyena made a quick stop to grab a loaf of bread, instructing me to eat it as it would help absorb the alcohol. Then, he continued onward toward whatever destination he had in mind. We traveled down a winding set of stairs, during which he may as well have just thrown me over his shoulder, as I was incapable of moving of my own accord. Once we reached the bottom, the candelabras on the walls became spaced further apart, casting long shadows and leaving much of the space shrouded in darkness.

"Almos' there," he said, his grin growing wide.

Finally, he stopped before a rather lackluster door.

"Yer 'bout to live every young'un's dream."

He opened the door, revealing a large room full of women in various states of undress. Eyes gleaming, the concubines turned toward us and began writhing like a nest of snakes, beckoning us to join them.

Grygor slapped my shoulder again, but this time, it was enough to rattle the contents of my stomach free. The dwarven spirits came shooting back up and across the floor.

True to form, the Hyena laughed at my misfortune. His laughter, however, ended in an instant as the temperature dropped in the hallway. The room beyond the doorway no longer led to a chamber of concubines, but instead opened to the hallway outside my chambers. Standing there, cloaked in swirling shadows, was Dracula.

"Did they see him?" D hissed, his tone dripping with darkness. Even in my drunken stupor, the threat lurking behind his words was obvious. "They were 'bout ta do a lot more than see…" the Hyena began before his words were cut short as D backhanded him, sending the beast crashing into a wall.

"I made it *very* clear that no one outside my innermost court was to know of his existence. Yet you took him to the slave quarters?" D's eyes were fully engulfed in blood, fangs extended as though he were about to rip Grygor apart on the spot. "You will return and ensure none can speak of what they may have seen. Now!"

With his head hung in shame, the Hyena whispered, "Yes, mas'er."

As he turned his gaze to me, the crimson in D's eyes receded. "Come, let us see to it that you recover from this imbecile's juvenile antics." The vampire picked me up with ease, then shot the Hyena one last look. "Fix this."

D carried me like a hapless babe through the doorway and into my quarters, where he laid me down upon my bed. "Drink this. It will help," he said while manifesting a vial of black liquid from thin air.

The fluid was tasteless, but had an immediate effect.

"Better?"

As soon as I swallowed the ichorous medicine, the world ceased its nauseating rotations, and my stomach felt less likely to expel its contents once again.

I nodded at D, then wiped the remnants of the previous discharge from my chin.

"Grygor will be punished for this, I assure you," he said, his irritation bleeding through his concern. "He is a base creature, driven only by carnal desires that often overcome his better judgment, but even he should have known better. I am sure he intended only to bring you into the fold in his own misguided manner."

I sat up, the bitter taste of the liquor still lingering in my throat. "You said I must remain a secret. Why?"

D's eyes glinted in the dim light, his expression sharpening. "Knowledge is power, young Viktor. Secrets are the only true currency in my realm. If my enemies learn of you, they will spend that knowledge lavishly on your destruction."

"Why would they seek to destroy me?" I asked, more confused by the cryptic answer than I was to begin with.

Dracula looked down at me, his face devoid of emotion. "Your power is a threat they will fear," he said simply, as if I should already know the answer. "Even in your infancy, your potential is clear. They will see in you what I see: a weapon that could tip the scales of this world."

His words weighed heavily, but I pushed back. "What kind of weapon? Against what?"

D's charming smile returned, but this time it made my skin crawl. "Against anyone I choose," he said, stepping closer. His towering figure loomed over me, casting long shadows across the room. "You'll find that power is not just strength; it is control. Right now, you lack both. That's why I keep you hidden. You must grow in the shadows before you can stand in the darkness."

"And if I refuse?" I asked, my voice steadier than I felt.

"Refuse?" He chuckled, the sound low and predatory. "Refusal is a privilege reserved for those who have something to bargain with. Do you?"

I looked away, unable to answer.

D softened, though his smile remained dangerous. "There is no shame in being unready, but understand this: there are forces in this world, and beyond, that would see you broken for what you are. For what you will become. I will not allow them the opportunity to stop you. Therefore, you will remain hidden until I decide otherwise."

"Are your enemies that powerful?" I asked, trying to deflect the weight of his words.

D's smile twisted into something bitter. "Powerful enough to challenge me, yes. Do not mistake strength for invincibility, Viktor. Even the mightiest castles fall if the cracks are ignored." He paused, studying me. "That is why you must harness your power. There is no room for weakness in this world. Not in you, not in me."

I nodded in response. My defeat at the Keep, still a fresh wound on my already battered pride, had proven the truth of his words. D had praised my actions as some sort of victory, but I knew I had barely survived the ordeal. Even if his enemies weren't strong enough to challenge him directly, they could likely end my life with relative ease until I learned how to access my abilities.

"Come, your clothes are soiled, and the stench of bile spoils the air. I shall summon my Brides to serve you," he said, his grin twisting lasciviously. "They have not stopped prattling about you since your arrival. I may as well indulge their curiosity."

I felt my face flush, turning as red as the tapestries hanging in the room.

"You do not find them suitable?" he asked.

"They are your Brides," I said sheepishly. "Having them bathe me seems... wrong. Marriage was a sacred thing in my home." A pang of loss struck my heart as I spoke the last word.

"Your home is here with us now, and it differs greatly from the one you left behind," D said, his tone smooth but distant, as if recalling a memory he'd rather forget. "The bond between man and wife is still sacred here, though perhaps not in the way you are accustomed to. You see, Viktor, immortality changes everything, even love."

I frowned. "How so?"

He turned his back to me, his silhouette framed by the faint glow of the hearth. "In mortal life, love is fleeting, a spark that burns brightly before it fades with age and time. It is cherished precisely because it is temporary, because it must end. But for us, there is no end, no natural rhythm to remind us of what we might lose. Over time, even the most passionate bonds can wither under the weight of eternity."

D looked over his shoulder, his smile tinged with something between bitterness and resignation. "We take lovers not for love's sake, but for distraction, for novelty, for the fleeting illusion that something in this endless existence can still feel... vital."

I shifted uncomfortably, unsure whether his words were meant to console or unsettle me. "So, love is just... hollow here?"

He laughed softly, a sound that carried no joy. "Not hollow... different. Love among immortals must be remade, reforged, over and over again, or it becomes a chain that binds us to despair. That is the price of immortality, Viktor. An eternity spent searching for meaning in things that once came so easily."

He gestured toward the bathhouse that had appeared in the doorway. "Enough of my musings. Go, cleanse yourself."

With his words pressing on my mind, I rose from the bed and obeyed.

Chapter 20
Lure of the Undying

By the time I had walked out of my chamber to the bathhouse, the Brides were already assembled by the large bathing pool. Their pale flesh shimmered in the light reflected from the water, amplified by the sheer garments that barely concealed them. My discomfort in their presence was palpable. My gaze fell to the gray and white marble floor, as though staring at its intricate patterns might shield me from their predatory attention. Blood rushed to my face, and I moved to cover myself, a futile gesture that only seemed to amuse them.

"Such heat in his cheeks," Ryvina purred, "and he hasn't even removed a stitch of clothing. His innocence still clings to life. How... delicious."

Her words struck me like ice water, snapping

me out of my flustered state. My head snapped up, and I eyed her with alarm.

"Don't worry," Mayna cooed, her lips curling into a smile that failed to comfort. "We have already fed."

Lilyth took a step toward me, her fingers beckoning me forward in a sensual gesture. "Come to us," she said, pulling at her bottom lip with the hint of a fang.

Her words pulled at unseen strings in my mind. I wanted to fulfill her command, but my embarrassment would not allow it. I shook my head clear and averted my eyes, then I dashed to the pool. I all but ran past the Brides and their ravenous stares, disrobing with haste at the water's edge. To my utter discomfort, none of the women laughed or giggled. Instead, their eyes captured my every movement in silence, stripping away my virtue and laying my soul bare.

The heat of the steaming water offered sanctuary as I plunged into the pool, concealing my nakedness. Yet, the relief was short-lived. The vampiresses followed me, casting aside their silken garments with unhurried grace, revealing their pale and flawless forms.

My cheeks burned, hotter than the scalding water, a fiery blush that mirrored the steam still clouding my vision. They slithered like serpents through the mist, each fluid movement bringing them closer, one thunderous heartbeat at a time. Despite the heat of the pool, cold shivers left their mark on my skin as I watched with uncertain horror as the nude women descended on me, wielding sponges and soap with disarming intimacy. Their hands taunted my flesh, lingering in places they should not have been just long enough to make blood rush through my veins. The Brides relished each uncomfortable twitch, every sideways glance as my innocence was challenged.

When their overly thorough task of washing my body was complete, Lilyth reached for a razor. I stiffened at the sight, my stomach retreating against my spine with force as she drew closer. The blade gleamed ominously as the seductress tilted my head to expose my neck.

"Relax, Viktor," she said. "You don't want me to slip, do you?" She giggled at her joke, but not as before. Her tone was different now: sharper, more subdued.

Each stroke of the blade was deliberate and agonizingly slow. My heart thundered in my chest as if it feared she would grow bored with her game and let her true nature take hold.

"Don't worry," Ryvina whispered, her tone thick with dark promise, as her hands glided down my chest. "We will make you forget all about Grygor and his little game."

In a matter of moments, that seemed to stretch

on for hours, I was shaved. It was then that they closed in, sealing off all avenues of escape. Their hands, unburdened by sponges or soap, began exploring my body. Every touch created a maddening symphony of sensations, each more overwhelming than the last. Claustrophobia choked me as the closeness became suffocating. My breath quickened, and the hammering of my heart roared in my ears; a cruel reminder of the blood that kept me alive…the same blood I knew they hungered for.

"He's afraid of us," Mayna quipped, her voice a dagger of amusement as she traced a vein in my neck with her tongue.

"I understand you have a weakness for redheads," Lilyth said, biting her lip with a moan as she pushed herself out of the water and onto my lap.

Before I could answer, she pressed her lips to mine, her body thrust against me. The barbed comment should have hit a very raw nerve, but as her mouth caressed me with bruising force, all the cares in the world seemed to melt from my mind. My fears, shame, and identity itself seemed to dissolve under her spell.

My old life was gone, I thought, I must embrace that which is before me, but something was wrong. The voice in my mind urging me to surrender was not my own. It slithered through my thoughts like a thief, insidious and foreign. As I grappled with the confusion, trying to regain control, Lilyth kissed me again, so softly that I nearly mistook it for affection. Then the illusion shattered.

Lilyth pulled back, her eyes glowing an unholy crimson. As I watched, her form shifted, reforming into a visage I knew all too well. The chieftain's daughter.

"Katri..." The name escaped my lips in a confused, horrified whisper.

It was then that she mounted me, slowly lowering herself down as my mind tried to grapple with what was happening. The woman I once loved looked at me with crimson eyes burning with malice, fangs extended, a twisted nightmare of what Katri was.

The heat of the water no longer held warmth. The ice flowing through my veins washed it away. I thrashed, not for air, but to get away from her. From it. But Ryvina and Mayna pinned me down, their fingers restraining me like iron shackles. Frenzied, I strained against them until every muscle burned. Katri's fingers laced through my hair, jerking my head backward so she could smother me with her lips once more. Still, I fought, jerking, writhing, shaking, anything to break free from the thing she had become.

Yet my efforts were useless. My size and strength were nothing against the Brides. I was prey, helpless as a newborn. When the fight finally abandoned me, replaced by quivering submission, Katri pulled away to leer down at me.

"I am gone, Viktor," the ghost said. "Leave me in the past." Though the voice was hers, it felt wrong: mocking, devoid of the warmth I once cherished.

The visage shifted once more. Blackened, charred flesh sloughed off her body and sizzled in the water, as red hair fell away in burning clumps.

"Look at me now, Viktor," she hissed, her scorched lips curling into a grotesque grin. "See what they did to me, what you let them do…"

Bile rose in my throat, and for a moment, I couldn't breathe. My vision blurred as tears burned behind my eyes. Tears I refused to shed. The stench of burnt flesh clung to the steam, invading my lungs, my pores, my soul. It was too much to endure. The sight, the smell, the blasphemy of it all. The girl I had once cherished, whose laugh had softened the world, now sat astride me as a mockery of everything she had been.

Katri's doppelganger threw her head back, laughing, as the flaky meat gave way to Lilyth's flawless form once more.

She leaned in, her voice a silken caress within my thoughts. "You belong to us now, Viktor."

She moaned with each movement as she began to ride me with vigor. Lilyth's words wormed into my consciousness like a spell, "We are all you will ever need. You are ours forever."

The Brides took turns using me, their games a grotesque parody of intimacy that stretched on for what felt like hours. By the end, I was too weak to resist, my mind and body battered into submission.

When the doors to the bathhouse swung open, I barely registered the Hyena's entrance. He stood in his human form, slick with gore from head to toe, a vicious grin plastered on his face until he saw what was happening in the pool. His smile faded in an instant, replaced with unbridled jealousy. Grygor's eyes glared at me with a hate I had never felt before. Not the kind that comes from rivalry, but the kind born of envy.

"LEAVE US!" Ryvina's voice thundered, so unnaturally loud that it made my ears ring.

Lilyth sneered at him, her disgust clear. "Pathetic wretch," she spat, before turning back to me and forcing her tongue into my mouth.

Grygor obeyed, risking a final glance before shutting the door behind him.

By the time the monsters were done, I was so discombobulated that it felt as though I had drunk the entire bottle of alcohol the Hyena had tricked me into sampling. I could not lift myself from the water, much less walk, which seemed to entertain the Brides as they laughed at my weakness.

"Poor Viktor, we wore him out," Lilyth said, flashing a malevolent grin at her sisters. The other Brides cackled.

Tired of their plaything, they hefted me from the water with ease and returned me to my quarters, tossing me like a butchered animal onto the bed.

Ryvina leaned down, running her tongue from the bottom of my chin, over my lips, and up to the tip of my nose. "Dream of us," she commanded before vanishing into the darkness.

I pulled the blanket over my shoulders and huddled against the corner where the bed met the wall. My eyes darted about the room, terrified that the sisters lurked beyond my vision, intending to use me once more, unsure if I would survive another round. Just when I thought my heart would explode, an invisible finger touched my forehead, and I fell asleep.

The darkness offered no rest. There, in my dreams, I fulfilled Ryvina's command against my will. As I would soon discover, their torment had merely begun.

Chapter 21
Ensnared in Shadows

When I woke the following evening, pain greeted every aspect of my being. The charred memory of Katri's face haunted me, a phantom image seared into my mind, but that was only the beginning of my suffering. Following the assault by the Brides, each movement was a struggle. My limbs trembled with exhaustion, my muscles cramped (or were torn), and my thoughts swam in the murky waters of dread.

I forced myself to pull on my clothes and stagger to the door, desperate for the smallest shred of nourishment to replace what had been stolen from me the night before. Shakily, I tried the door, shocked by the discovery that they had not bothered to lock me in. With painstaking effort, I opened the entryway, doing everything possible to remain silent. I braced myself against the door and peered out into the hall, goosebumps rising on my skin as I searched for signs of the vampires. I saw nothing.

After taking more than a few moments to gather my courage, I stepped out, trying with all my might not to make a noise that might alert them to my presence. My heartbeat thundered in my ears, each step down the candlelit corridor an eternity of uncertainty. Shadows clung to the edges of my vision, and the oppressive silence magnified the sound of my shallow breaths. I reached the corner, so close to the Dining Hall I could almost taste salvation, when the giggle came. Soft, syrupy, and impossibly close.

It was Lilyth.

Behind me.

I spun on my heels to face her, but found myself staring down an empty hallway. More laughter erupted from behind me, this time from Ryvina. I wheeled to find another empty corridor. To my horror, the passage to the Dining Hall was nowhere to be found.

"Good evening, Viktor," Mayna whispered into my ear, her voice a poisoned caress that snaked down my spine.

I froze. I knew they were able to hide their presence from my eyes. Knew they could overpower me with no effort at all. I was helpless.

As I stood trembling against the wall, my hand grasping a tapestry for support, the candles at the end of the hall snuffed out, blanketing the hallway in darkness. One by one, each candelabra went dark in rhythm with my pounding heart, each beat coinciding with another wave of impenetrable darkness creeping toward me.

The icy grip of dread tore into my chest. I turned and ran from the encroaching black closing in on me. I knew the move was futile; despite my height and muscled frame, the Brides were far faster and stronger than I. Still, my limbs were moving of their own accord, forcing me to flee in panic-stricken madness.

The adrenaline rushing through my veins pushed my body to move despite the fatigue, and I sprinted down doorless hallways as the pitch black nipped at my heels, all the while the Brides cackled at my pathetic attempts to elude them. My lungs burning from exertion, stomach muscles contracting until I cried out. I dared a glance over my shoulder, only to find that the hallway was gone altogether. Instead, I faced a stone wall less than an arm's length away.

I turned again, gasping for air, but the corridor had vanished, just like the one behind me.

Once again, I found myself with no escape. D's wives were using the Castle itself to hunt me. Or perhaps it was playing along with their game.

Though I could not see them, the vampiresses

were there, their presence betrayed by the sweet smell of their sweat and their insidious giggling. My eyes darted from side to side, desperate to find somewhere to run, but the chamber had nowhere to go. Each direction offered nothing but unforgiving stone. I was trapped.

Just as my despair became unbearable, unseen hands grabbed me, slamming me against the stone wall and tearing the trousers from my legs.

"The Master has left you all alone with us," Ryvina said through unseen lips. "He took the Hand and his beast with him, so there is no one here to stop us…"

Her tone made my heart sink into my stomach. There would be no escape from her, no mercy, just the inevitability of suffering, drawn out like the moment before a scream.

I knew what was coming, and that knowledge was nearly worse than the act itself.

"We will not tire, Viktor. Neither will you. We will not allow it. The Master's absence only frees us to indulge in you… entirely," Lilyth said, sucking on my ear as she finished speaking. My heart pounded, then stopped as the point of her fang scraped my flesh as she pulled away.

Were they going to bite me, I thought in a panic? D claimed he had no plans to have me turned, but he wasn't there. My mind raced as I contemplated the horrors of having my veins drained of life. But they didn't need fangs to quench their current appetite.

The Brides seized me, invisible hands dragging me to the cold floor with a force that left no room for resistance. Their laughter rang out, a melody of malice as they took turns satiating their lust without restraint, leaving me stripped of will and dignity. They whispered secrets they had no way of knowing as they used me, unearthing memories I thought long buried. Fears pulled from the darkness of my soul poured from their lips like wine from a bottle, each more terrible than the last. Their words were not mere torment; they were the sharp claws of predators peeling away my humanity, one layer at a time.

When their hunger was finally sated, the three women manifested before me, red torchlight dancing along the sweat covering their bodies. They stared down at me with cruel satisfaction. Without a word, they hauled my broken body to the Dining Hall, tossing me toward the waiting feast as if I were nothing more than a drained vessel to be refilled.

My arms shook to such a degree that I spilled my goblet as I tried to lift it to my lips. Lilyth, seeing me struggle, took the cup and raised it, allowing me to drink.

"Poor thing," she said, wiping a wet strand of hair from my face. "You must be famished. Let me help you." She pouted as she spoke, feigning concern.

Her nude body pressed against mine, she fed

me as if I were a child, never moving away. Even as I ate and drank my fill, I was given no quarter. No solitude in which to recover.

The very instant I was done, Lilyth cleared the remnants of my meal with a mere gesture, sending plates and food alike crashing to the floor. With one hand, she lifted me and threw me down on the table. Then, they were upon me again.

I was certain that my body would be useless to them. I was wrong. In defiance of the fatigue, my flesh responded to their touch, warmth flowing through my veins despite their cold skin.

For days, this cycle continued, a grim parody of routine. Feeding, torment, exhaustion, then the briefest moments of harried rest before they came for me again. When my body became too raw to operate, they would use the healing properties of their saliva to close the wounds so they could continue their rampage. The women were inescapable. Insatiable. I had no way to run from them, nowhere to hide. I was their prey, and they had me locked in an unwinnable maze.

Between their assaults, I was left alone with my thoughts, the silence of the Castle stretching on into eternity. I felt their power most keenly in those moments, not in their actions, but in the oppressive anticipation of them.

Reflections:

In other realms, mortal men and women dream of surrendering to the allure of vampiric seduction, imagining nights of hedonistic pleasure. Allow me to shatter that illusion. This was no romanticized tale. It was a nightmare, one in which my body was no longer my own, and my desires were puppeteered by forces beyond my control. A waking hell, devoid of tenderness or consent.

I was as helpless as a newborn babe to defend myself against their ceaseless advances. Their unnatural, vampiric strength allowed them to overwhelm my all-too-human form. To make matters worse, I was not yet immune to the pheromones secreted by the creatures. When they decided it was time to engage, my body responded despite my mind's objections. No matter how sore or chafed I became, they would force my body to betray me, moving against my will as if I were nothing more than a marionette controlled by the invisible strings of their desire,

Eventually, I succumbed to my fate, hoping they would grow bored with me. It was then that they deemed it time to teach me the ways of pleasuring a woman. They began reshaping me, teaching not out of care but conquest.

Many of the pleasures they sought were not for the faint of heart, considering their immortality. However, the pain they enjoyed receiving, they also delighted in inflicting.

The mental torture they employed during my initial education was but the beginning, as they had spent countless centuries learning how to inflict agony without permanently damaging their victims.

Chapter 22
Thread of Becoming

After one particularly draining tryst, the Brides left me unattended in my quarters, content that I was too exhausted to get myself into any trouble. As I lay on the bed, my body drenched in the remnants of their attention, my eyes rolled back into my skull, and I felt as though I was falling into a vast abyss. The feeling wasn't far removed from the truth.

At first, I thought I must be dreaming as the room faded into profound darkness, and I braced myself for more torment. However, the Brides didn't appear. Instead, I felt myself float, not so much in the air, but more akin to gliding across the surface of a calm sea.

"They will kill you if you do not change again."

Sight.

My visitor in the prison was once again before me, eyes glistening in an even darker color than the obsidian waters surrounding me. My first visitation had been so long ago, and my mental state stretched so thin since then that I had all but written it off as a hallucination. Yet here he was, floating mere feet in front of my face in the utter darkness.

"Let them," I responded, once again mirroring our first meeting.

When I looked up, something had shockingly changed. The shadows that once cloaked the creature's body unraveled like smoke caught in a windless breeze. For the first time, I saw him. Truly saw him.

The thing that hung before me defied logic, a grotesque, hourglass-shaped mass floating in the stale air. Its gray, fleshy surface rippled with movement, not from breath or heartbeat, but from eyes, countless eyes, drifting across and beneath the skin like fish in murky waters. They vanished and reappeared at random, as though navigating dimensions unseen. The great eye I remembered from my cell was nestled in the upper lobe, unblinking and ancient, while the lower portion bore a gaping maw lined with rows of pointed teeth.

As my conscious struggled to accept what I was beholding, the uncountable number of eyes on the creature began to glow in a yellowish-green, as they had before.

"You came here for a reason," it said, continuing our little game of reliving the past.

"So you said," I sighed, unable to force my gaze away from the monstrosity. "If I knew how to change, I would have already."

The largest of the eyes focused on me for a long moment, as though peering through the flesh and into my very soul.

"The path is not hidden from you," Sight said, his tone a chorus of whispers and screams folded into one. *"It lies before you, as it always has, like a thread stretching through eternity. You do not lack the ability to follow it, only the will to look beyond the veil you've so carefully drawn around your fragile, mortal mind."*

The surrounding air thickened as if the darkness itself had weight. Sight's words pierced my thoughts like needles, unraveling my denial. I wanted to speak, to offer an argument against him, but my tongue lay heavy in my mouth.

"The terror you harbor for your true form blinds you, shackles you to a dying existence." Sight paused again, and as it did, the darkness above me coalesced into a swirling abyss of black stars and gargantuan planets. I saw a thing with no name drifting between galaxies, its form older than suns, older than light, yet I knew it. I knew it as myself.

"Remember your home."

The inky sea rose around me, its cool depths seeping into my pores, mending what the Brides had broken and flooding my being with a power that defied comprehension. I rose from the abyss transformed, my flesh now a sleek armor of glassy black, veins coursing with emerald light. A colossal, glowing eye replaced the human orbs I was so accustomed to, and through it, I beheld the Void in all its terrifying splendor. Rope-like tendrils tore through the air, erupting from both sides of my back and shoulders, writhing of their own free will.

"You lean upon me as a feeble crutch against the weight of your awareness," Sight said, his voice an indistinct murmur that rippled through the Void like distant thunder.

I looked down at my shifting form, the boundaries between flesh and nothingness blurring in the Void's embrace. "It is easy to change here," I confessed, my voice scarcely more than a whisper. "But out there, it is… impossible."

"We dwell now within the Void," Sight said. *"We are one with its unfathomable depths. Separation from it is not possible for us, only the illusion of distance. Where it is, you are. Where you are, it is… mortal realm or not."*

The words struck like a chime ringing through the silence. I lowered my gaze into the swirling abyss beneath my feet, where the Void stretched, a writhing expanse without beginning or end. I drew it into me, its unseen currents threading through my veins like the tentacles of a forgotten god. The sensation clung to my bones, a pull of inevitability, as if the universe itself exhaled, and I was drawn into the breathless space between worlds. I focused on that sensation, carving it into my mind to be recalled in the material world.

Sight's maw stretched into the semblance of a smile, a slow and deliberate movement that felt both approving and unnerving. ***"At last, you see,"*** he rumbled, the words reverberating like echoes from a distant, collapsing star.

With the lesson learned, I fell, spiraling into the abyss as Sight's massive form shrank to nothing in the distance.

The world shifted around me, the oppressive vastness of the Void collapsing into the stale familiarity of my chamber. Both it and Sight were gone, and with them, the eldritch form I had worn within the depths. Yet, the faint, otherworldly glow lingered in my eyes. It illuminated the darkened room in hues that felt both comfortingly alien and disturbingly natural. I could see every detail of my room as though the darkness obeyed me now.

It was then that the realization dawned. The pain inflicted by the Brides had vanished. Their torment, every lash and every violation, seemed to have been swallowed by the Void, leaving my body pristine, rejuvenated, and humming with latent energy.

No longer weary, I resolved to prepare for their return. I sat cross-legged on the bed, focusing on the stillness within me, reaching for the presence I had touched in the Void. My thoughts coiled around the memory of my eldritch form, and as I meditated, I felt the faintest tremor of that power stir.

When the door finally creaked open, the sisters drifted in, graceful, sinuous, and dripping menace. Their forms shimmered with the magic meant to conceal, but it no longer hid them from my eyes. Through the veil of shadow, I traced their every step.

The Void thrummed beneath my skin, a rising tide awaiting release, but I gave them no reason to suspect. I lay still, feigning frailty, pretending their sorcery still cloaked them, while eldritch perception unraveled every thread of their illusion.

Lilyth was the first to approach. Her fingers trailed down my spine, her touch gentle, like a serpent testing its prey.

"Are you rested?" she purred, her voice thick with mock concern.

I waited for the perfect moment, letting the silence stretch until it became a noose. Then, with a speed that startled even me, I twisted, seizing her wrist and pulling her onto the bed. The timeless strength coursing through me made her struggles futile. Shocked by my sudden surge of strength, Lilyth attacked, her sharp nails clawing at my face, but I held her down effortlessly.

Fear flickered behind the golden sheen of her gaze, and the sight filled me with a savage satisfaction. I leaned closer, allowing my new power to rise and illuminate her face.

"His eyes!" Lilyth gasped, her voice trembling.

Ryvina and Mayna rushed to their sister's aid, eyes blood-red and fangs extended, but I was ready for them. I caught Ryvina's arm as she tried to grab me and threw her down next to Lilyth. After watching me subdue the other Brides with ease, Mayna paused, then took a step backward. With blinding speed, I rose and rushed past her, slamming the door shut before she could escape.

Knowing I had turned the tables on them, I smiled, the gesture sharper and colder than any blade.

"My turn," I said, my voice a low growl that carried the weight of the Void.

What followed was not vengeance born of cruelty, but retribution. Every touch, every movement, was a reclamation of power, a reversal of the torment they had inflicted upon me. By the time I rose, the three of them lay sprawled, their arrogance shattered, their bodies trembling with exhaustion.

The chamber was silent but for my breathing, the three of them having been forced into vampiric sleep to recuperate. I stood over them, feeling the Void's presence still coiled around me like a second skin.

I had the upper hand, and the taste of it was sweet; electric and terrifying all at once, and yet, even as I loomed over them, a whisper of doubt curled in the back of my mind.

What was I becoming?

Chapter 23

Foreboding Premonition

The following days blurred together in a haze of power and practice. My growing abilities granted me an undeniable edge over the Brides. Enhanced by the Void, my strength and speed eclipsed theirs, leaving no doubt about the shift in dominance. More satisfying still, I discovered that their psionic manipulations and pheromonal charms had lost their hold on me. Their words no longer crept into my mind, twisting my thoughts, nor did their intoxicating scents force my body into compliance. Yet, I found myself savoring that aroma, now sharpened into something distinct and identifiable.

With my physical transformation came a

resurgence of visions — stronger, sharper, unrelenting. I could sense the Brides' movements throughout the Castle with uncanny precision: I knew when they fed, bathed, or approached my chambers. Their comings and goings became practice opportunities for my gifts. From afar, I observed them as if they were marionettes on strings, unguarded and unaware.

But the Brides weren't my only focus. My sight reached beyond the Castle walls to find D himself, returning from a distant land. He traveled in a stagecoach alongside the Hyena, the Death Knight riding his ghastly steed at its side. Behind them marched an army of skeletal riders mounted on undead horses.

The scene puzzled me. Why would they choose such a methodical, pedestrian pace when portals could bring them back within moments? There was purpose in it, though what it was eluded me. Was it tradition, a display of power, or something else?

When D finally arrived, he found his wives and me asleep in my bed, a tangled web of limbs and sheets. The door creaked open, and in a flash, the Brides were at D's side. Lilyth led the charge, her laughter sharp as a blade as she draped herself over him. Mayna lingered behind, her movements as fluid as water, her whispers brushing his ear. Ryvina trailed last, her smirk betraying a cunning far deeper than her sultry gaze. Though they each greeted him differently, they were united in their purpose: to remind him, and perhaps me, to whom they belonged.

For his part, D seemed rather uninterested in them, instead focusing his attention on my eyes, which were no longer the deep blue they had been when he left. The virescent glow emanating from them reflected in his crimson orbs.

"You are *awake*." The weight he placed on the last word lingered like silent applause.

I nodded in reply. "Welcome home."

The vampire lord smiled with a slight bow and turned to leave. "If these three haven't drained the life out of you," he said, looking over his shoulder, "my Hand wishes to resume your training."

"I look forward to it," I replied, a sneer pulling at my lip.

It wasn't a lie, or even an exaggeration. Since sampling my powers, an undying urge to see how they would fare against the Death Knight had swelled in my chest.

D smiled and departed with his coven of wives.

After the family had departed, I dressed and ventured out into the Castle, driven by an ache in my stomach.

I had begun to unravel the inner workings of my new home and its movements, discovering that if I focused hard enough on a specific location, the halls would shift to bring me to it, unless the Castle was in a mischievous mood. Then, it would refuse to move at all or lead me further away from my desired destination.

That day, however, it seemed as eager to see the confrontation between me and the Hand as I was. The passageways filled with the rich aroma of freshly baked bread and roasted meat as the Castle opened a path to the Dining Hall. The smell tore open a void in my stomach, and hunger blinded my senses.

With the onset of my newfound gifts, my appetite multiplied to an almost disturbing degree. The more I tapped into those powers, the deeper the hunger burrowed, insatiable and consuming. It was as if my very being had transformed into a vortex, devouring everything I consumed and funneling it into some unseen abyss. With every meal, I felt the weight of something vast and unknowable expanding within me.

In D's absence, I had grown accustomed to eating in solitude. After my ascension, the Brides supped on blood slaves in a separate portion of the Castle while I consumed more mundane sustenance. Today, however, they were sitting aside D in the Great Hall, eager to see the interaction between the realm's champion and my evolved self.

I chose a table opposite the family and sat. With what I expected to be an eventful day waiting to begin, I ate far more than usual, not wanting the pangs of hunger to distract from what I had planned. I had debts to settle with the Death Knight — grievances ranging from the brutal aftermath of the lycan battle to the unforgivable destruction of my home. Each of those wrongs I intended to repay in kind.

As I tore into the bevy of dishes spread before me, Lilyth smirked from across the table. Her piercing gaze danced over me as though she could still see the mortal weakness I had shed, though something else lingered there that I couldn't quite place. Even when the Hand arrived and everyone else turned to acknowledge his presence, her eyes never ventured away from me.

"Are you ready to begin?" The cursed one asked, his voice an echo of something long dead, spoken without breath or life. It didn't just reach the ears; it crawled under the skin, a reminder of the unnatural, icy grip of death that held him in its thrall. Each word carried the weight of centuries, hollow and distant, as though spoken from beneath a grave.

I rose from my seat, my previous insecurities melting away like butter over hot bread as I towered over him. His burning eyes met the eerie glow of mine, the disparity in our heights only adding to the tension crackling between us. Like D, he was all too comfortable looking down on those around him.

"After you," I said with a smirk, gesturing for him to lead with a wave of my hand. For the briefest of moments, he hesitated before summoning a portal and stepping through. I risked a last glance toward the

Brides to see Lilyth's smile shift ever so slightly.

"He doesn't stand a chance," she said, her words dripping with dark humor.

I stepped into the portal, not sure if she meant the Death Knight or me.

The moment I exited, the Death Knight's blade was already descending, aimed to cleave me in two. Reflexes sharper than any mortal's propelled me out of harm's way. In a single motion, I spun and drove my fist into his midsection with a force that sent him flying back. Before he could recover, I closed the distance and delivered a kick that launched him into the Keep's stone wall, leaving cracks in its ancient surface.

He struggled to rise, but I was relentless. In the blink of an eye, I was upon him, raining down blows that shook the earth beneath us. Dust and debris clouded the air as I unleashed the fury that had built within me for so long. His torment mixed with that of the Brides, and with every other misfortune I had suffered since his arrival in my life. Every blow was a release, a venting of rage that had been held in check until it boiled. At last, I stepped back, my chest heaving, the Void within me thrumming with satisfaction.

"Pathetic," I spat, the word laced with bitter gratification, a deliberate echo of his past derision. Yet, as I stood over him, fists bleeding, the triumph felt hollow.

Was this who I was now, I thought? Trading cruelty for cruelty, reveling in the same mockery that once stung me?

Looking up from the ground, eyes blazing with restrained fury, the knight rose. "You have improved," he said flatly, though the frigid energy crashing upon me in waves betrayed his anger.

With a horrendous screech, his battered armor reshaped itself, metal bending and reforging as though alive.

"Now, are you ready to resume your learning?"

I nodded.

What followed was a lesson unlike any before. We sparred for hours, the clash of steel ringing through the courtyard as the Death Knight pushed me to master techniques my mortal body had been incapable of performing. Each movement felt effortless, my enhancements adapting with frightening ease. The sun rose as we concluded, and I retreated to my chamber, exhaustion finally settling into my bones.

Unbeknownst to me, the time with the Brides had adjusted my routine to sleeping during the day, as they did.

As I lay down, prepared to slip into the blissful release of sleep, a cold unease gripped me. My stomach tightened as the rhythm of my heart sped up. Something was wrong. I tried to push the unease away, but it refused to vacate my mind. The longer I sat with it, the more pressing the feeling became until it could not be ignored. With my eyes closed, I used my senses to locate the source of the ominous feeling. It didn't take long to find it. My consciousness bolted from my body and into the Castle like a phantom.

In an unfamiliar chamber, I saw Dracula walking through a large room filled with bookshelves. He was not alone. A shadow clung to the room, veiled in magic. My vision sharpened, and the threat became clear. An intruder had infiltrated the Castle.

I bolted upright and sprinted to the battlements where the Death Knight stood watch. He turned as I approached, his burning eyes unreadable.

"Dracula is in danger," I exclaimed, breathless.

"How do you know this?"

"I saw an intruder in the Castle, hiding behind a veil of magic. You must warn him!"

The panic etched in my voice gave him pause, his gauntleted hand reaching for his sword instinctively.

"You *saw* an intruder?" the Death Knight said in an unusually low tone. "How?"

Frustration boiled over. I stepped closer, my glowing eyes glared into his. "Go. Now." My voice trembled with raw power, and the brightness of my gaze intensified.

Without a word, the Death Knight opened a portal and walked through.

With nothing else I could do, I rushed to my room and sat on the edge of my bed, closing my eyes.

Black waves crashed upon my consciousness, and once again, I found myself in the unseen chamber, a formless observer beside D.

The Death Knight had already arrived and was speaking with Dracula when the air behind him shimmered, twisting as though reality itself recoiled. Then, a figure emerged, its form cloaked in shadow, a black dagger glinting with malevolent energy in its grasp. The blade hissed as it drove into the knight's back, a sound like dying embers meeting water. The Hand staggered, the weapon drawing a grunt of pain as dark magic surged from the wound, rippling through his armor like cracks spreading through glass.

The Knight fell to one knee, the flicker in his eyes fading as the attacker withdrew the blade and lunged toward D, the dagger thirsting for a far greater prize. Unfortunately for the intruder, the undead warrior was not so easily felled.

With blinding speed, he rose, drew his sword, and cleaved the assassin in two with one decisive strike. Blood and entrails splattered across the magical shield that surrounded D as both halves of the intruder's body crumpled to the ground.

D's gaze fell on the corpse, his voice calm but edged. "How did you know?" he asked the Death Knight.

The reply came in a single word. "Viktor."

Reflections:

At the time of my vision in the Keep, I was unaware of the fact that the major vampire clans of the world engaged in a little game that involved trying to assassinate one another constantly. More often than not, these attempts failed miserably and were more a product of boredom than any serious intent to harm. Should an attempt succeed, there would be a shift in power, and bragging rights would be bestowed on the victor. If it failed, then the loser would be mocked for their incompetence.

Dracula, however, did not see this game in the same half-hearted light as the other vampire elders did and would send the Hyena out as his assassin when it was his turn to play. Most of the other families had learned to leave D alone as a result. Very few among them were willing to risk facing the sickening carnage Grygor would unleash when unchained.

Chapter 24
The Lycan Conclave

I sat on my cot, breathless, my heart still racing from the vision. My consciousness had returned to my physical form, but my mind lingered in the aftershock. For the first time in my life, my visions had been used for something beyond personal suffering. They had saved the life of the closest thing to a friend I had ever known, and with that, the curse I had once loathed now felt like a twisted blessing. The exhilaration still thrummed through me, and yet, beneath it, a gnawing feeling of responsibility settled. What else could I do with this power? Was this the beginning of something larger?

I couldn't sleep; my thoughts jumbled, too electrified. So, I practiced, testing the limits of my gifts, to see if I could continue to use them for something good. I closed my eyes and stretched my mind beyond the stone and silence of the Keep. My vision unfurled like smoke, spiraling outward until it slipped past tree branches and into the forest beyond.

Suddenly there I was. Not merely seeing it — experiencing it. I stood unseen beneath the dark canopy, my senses alive. The scent of wet earth and damp fur drifted to me, mingling with the sharp tang of pine. I could hear the distant hoot of an owl, the low growl of something stirring in the underbrush. The cold bit at the skin I no longer wore, yet still, I felt it. The only sense my power left denied was that of touch. My hand passed through a low-hanging branch as if through mist. I was there, present, but unable to act.

The forest stretched endlessly, broken only by glints of moonlight scattered like gold coins on the mossy ground. Beneath the canopy, the land thrummed with the pulse of nature, but something darker lingered just beneath the surface. The lycan settlements, if they could even be called that, dotted the woods like crude, skeletal remnants of civilization. Not homes, but meeting grounds: worn patches of earth marked with clan symbols, where wolves gathered to speak, to celebrate, and to remember.

I had learned little of these creatures, only bits and pieces from my first chaotic encounter and then what I could pry from the Death Knight. But now, with my heightened awareness, I saw the truth: these were no mere beasts. They were intelligent, strategic, and organized.

As I drew my vision back, something caught my attention: movement in the woods. A group of werewolves, several of whom were wearing armor, massed in the distance. The sight of the armor caught me off guard. None of the werewolves I had seen during the siege of the Keep had worn it. Until then, I had assumed these creatures were just mindless predators, but the armor told a different story. It was as though they were preparing for battle, and that realization set my nerves alight.

Each piece of armor bore markings, distinct symbols. The leaders were here, speaking in a language I didn't understand, their tone sharp and calculating. They weren't just wolves. They were warriors, strategists, perhaps even rulers of their kind. This wasn't just an attack; It was a siege. The Keep was about to be under threat once again.

***

When the Death Knight returned later that night, his presence as cold and silent as ever, I rushed to meet him.

"The lycans are amassing in the woods, preparing an assault on the Keep. Dozens of them, maybe more. They're planning something big," I said, excited to share my vision, but the Death Knight was not impressed.

The cursed one paused, his burning gaze unreadable. "We are already aware of the threat."

"What?" I blinked. "How?"

"The Oracle has foreseen it," he said flatly. "We have orders to intercept their forces before they strike southeast of our position."

"No," I said, sharper than I intended. "They're in the Southwest. I saw them just now. Their camps, their leaders, the symbols on their armor."

The Death Knight tilted his head, something almost like curiosity — or doubt — in his posture. "Then one of you is mistaken."

A cold unease bloomed in my chest. I had never heard mention of this Oracle before. The idea that someone else had access to knowledge like mine, was trusted with it, gnawed at me. Worse was the idea that D might take their word over mine. He claimed I had power that would turn the tide of this world, but it no longer seemed as though my abilities were unique. I kept my face calm, but the seed of mistrust was already rooting deep in my soul.

Determined to prove I was correct, I recounted every detail I had seen: the terrain, the number of werewolves, the way their makeshift camps were clustered among the trees. When I finished, the Death Knight gave a low, thoughtful grunt.

"Impressive," he said. "We'll see if your truth

outweighs the Oracle's tonight."

I didn't like the way he implied I might be mistaken in this moment. I had just proven the validity of my abilities by saving Dracula from an assassin's blade, yet the Death Knight was questioning my skill already, and who was this Oracle, anyway? I would find out, but not for many years.

Then, as if the conversation were over, he reached into the folds of his tattered cloak and pulled free a sheathed blade. "The master sends this. A gift for your service in his protection."

The sword was black from pommel to point, its surface shimmering with barely contained energy. Even before I touched it, I could feel the magic humming in the air. It felt weightless in my hand, yet potent, like a winter storm caught in steel.

"The blade will not harm its master," the Death Knight explained. "It drinks deep from enemies, but knows the hand that wields it."

As I tested its balance, slashing at shadows like a child, he turned away in disgust. "Save your strength. You will need it before the night is done."

As he walked away, I slid the sword into its sheath and hurried after him. "Wait. I need to learn their language. The wolves. I heard them speaking, but I could understand none of it. I would be more useful if I knew what they were saying."

The Death Knight nodded ever so slightly in approval, then instructed me to go get some rest. A long night stretched ahead.

The evening fell with a heavy silence, the air thick with anticipation. Before the last of the sun's rays vanished from the sky, I was suited up in my black leather armor, the new blade sheathed at my side. As I descended to the Great Hall, a diminutive thing compared to the one in the Castle, I found the Death Knight waiting. He looked me over, decided I was ready, and opened a portal as he began to cast a spell. The air shimmered, and we stepped through, finding ourselves among the trees just outside the werewolf encampment.

His voice was hushed as he finished his spell. "We must remain unseen."

I felt the magic settle around us like a cloak, masking our presence in the dim light. The incantation bathed us in unnatural darkness, concealing our luminous eyes, which otherwise would have announced our presence to the clans spread before us. It also hid the portal that brought us to the encampment, which normally would swirl with purple energy.

My senses sharpened as I saw the camp laid out before us, exactly as I had told my companion it would be. Roughly thirty wolves were gathered, the leaders easily identifiable by their more ornate and complete suits of armor. In their culture, I presumed, the armor was a sign of status. However, in the situation they were about to face, the protective suits were signs of which wolves to target first. The Death Knight confirmed my train of thought, pointing to the leaders.

"We must ensure that *they* do not escape."

At first, I was surprised he spoke out loud, but no one in the camp reacted to the sound, and I realized his spell must mask our voices.

I would later learn it also hid the biggest giveaway of our presence: the smell. Without his magic, the werewolves would have been alerted to our exact location by the odors emanating from the Death Knight the second we stepped out of his portal. Although his flesh had been mummified long ago, the lycans' honed olfactory senses would have caught the smell instantly.

I nodded in response, not quite willing to speak and test his magic further than we already had. The dead man them marched out of the protective cloak of shrubbery, raised his hand, and released a torrent of flame. The air cracked with heat as several wolves were incinerated. Howls and screams mixed with the crackling fire, and the camp descended into madness.

I was moving before the first charred husk hit the ground, sword drawn and mind focused on the closest chieftain, clad in golden armor. The beast was distracted, confused by the sudden onslaught, its eyes wide with disbelief at the audacity of the attack. Unfortunately, the armor-clad werewolf's heightened senses alerted it to my attack at the last moment, and it swung a sword of its own up to parry my strike.

The look that crossed the lycan's beastly face when he saw me was almost comical. The sight of the

Death Knight was something these warriors were accustomed to; This was, however, the first time a human had breached their territory, much less had the reckless disregard to attack a clan leader.

Intent on taking full advantage of the bewildered mutt, I pressed forward, attacking the beast from multiple angles as the knight had taught me. To its credit, the brown-furred monstrosity blocked and dodged most of my strikes, but I persisted, pushing harder until my sword found a chink in the wolf's defenses. The cut was slight, but the reaction was anything but.

The creature responded to the wound as though I had impaled it. Elongated lips peeled back from sharp teeth as it released a feral scream, retreating backward, yelping like a pup. The gash oozed with black goop, and dark veins stretched from it across the brute's torso. The magic flowing through my ebony blade crippled the lycanthrope in a flash. Not wanting to wait and see if the venom would kill the creature, I spun and ended the werewolf's suffering with a swift stroke, separating its head from its massive shoulders.

The victory was short-lived. Before the severed head of my first kill hit the ground, two more wolfmen were upon me.

I wheeled to meet them, but the movement was too slow, even with my eldritch-enhanced reflexes. One beast, larger than the others, slammed into me with a roar. Its claws, as thick as tree branches, tore through my armor and raked across my chest, sending a flood of hot, sticky blood across the dirt.

Despite the pain, I parried the next blow, my blade catching the chieftain's wrist and slicing clean through. The severed hand hit the dirt with a thud, and the beast's howl split the night. Black veins raced up what remained of its arm, necrotizing the flesh as it shrieked in agony. It turned to run, but didn't make it far. A torrent of flame engulfed it from behind as the Death Knight's magic reduced it to a collapsing pillar of cinders.

I didn't have time to breath.

The last commander was upon me before I could react, closing the gap between us in less than a heartbeat. I dropped to my knees, my life pouring from the gashes across my chest in streams of crimson as I gasped for air. The towering brute raised his clawed hand, poised to bring my nightmarish existence to an end.

Then, the Void opened.

It felt like a great sucking force, pulling at the ragged edges of my being. It rushed through my veins, filled the wound, and ran thick through my body before erupting from my back. Black tendrils shot out, impaling the wolf.

The beast never had a chance to scream before its body was ripped apart, shredded into fragments of flesh and bone by my new appendages.

Chapter 25
Immaculate Empowerment

The last werewolves escaped into the night after witnessing their leader torn apart by a mere human with what looked like a writhing mass of worms emerging from his back. The battlefield was quiet now, save for the distant rustle of wind through the trees and the soft, wet squelch of lycan remains underfoot. The air reeked of charred fur and coppery blood.

I stood up, somewhat dazed, trying to see what remained of the werewolf scattered across the ground. Try as I might, I couldn't tear my gaze away from the mangled chunks of flesh still steaming in the cool night air. Its lifeless eyes were fixed on the sky, its mouth twisted in a final snarl. Something within me churned — a visceral, uncontrollable revulsion mingling with an almost sinister satisfaction.

What had I done, I thought? My shock devolved into horror as I recalled the gaping wound in my chest, and I looked down to find no trace of it. The only signs I had been injured were the tattered straps of leather that formed the chest piece of my armor. As I traced the jagged edges of the ruined cuirass, something moved at the edge of my vision. I spun instinctively, like a cornered animal.

The tendrils. They undulated in the air above my shoulders.

I felt them. Not just the motion, but the sensation: every brush against the leaves overhead sent a ripple of ecstasy down their lengths and along my spine. It was like regaining lost limbs I hadn't known were missing. A breeze kissed their stalks, and I shuddered in response. The pleasure was unearthly — intimate, vivid, wrong. Yet some hidden part of me delighted in their grace, while the rest of me curled inward, repulsed by my body's betrayal.

My hand reached over my shoulder, trembling. Fingers met the slick, warm stalk of a tendril where there should've been only skin. My knees gave out.

No. This wasn't supposed to be here, I thought. I didn't want this.

The sweat on my back turned frigid. My breath came in ragged gasps. Dead men, vanished wounds, half-wolf-creatures — none of it mattered anymore.

These *things* were growing out of me.

I grabbed one, my fingers slipping on its pulsing surface, and yanked.

Agony. Not in the tendril, or even in my body, but *deep*. The ageless recesses of my soul recoiled at the affront, the part of me born before time that had watched without interest as stars burst into being, shedding the first rays of light into creation.

It wanted the tendrils, and I was powerless to deny it.

I gagged, bile burning my throat as my mortal mind fought against a force it could neither fathom nor refuse. In the Void, these appendages had felt like living strands of creation: divine, natural. Here, in the world of breath and bone, they shattered what little illusion I had left. I was no longer human. I never had been.

A sharp clang jolted my thoughts back from the chaos.

The Death Knight's imposing figure loomed into view like a walking tomb, his blackened armor a cruel, jagged silhouette against the eerie glow of the twilight. For the first time, the frigid aura surrounding him was most welcome, as it froze the crawling madness within my mind.

With an armored boot, he kicked a bloody remnant of the lycan.

"Strange," he muttered, more to himself than to me. "It isn't regenerating." Then, he turned his gaze to the protrusions squirming above my shoulders. The flaming eyes narrowed, their light flickering as if dimmed. For the first time, I saw it. A crack in his impenetrable facade.

Fear.

During our time training together, I had grown accustomed to the general sense of dread that emanated from the Death Knight like a dark cloud. I was so used to it by now that I scarcely noticed it anymore. However, as he studied the eldritch appendages, that terrible feeling increased a hundredfold.

The undead warrior stood motionless for an uncomfortable amount of time, watching me until my desperate desire to be rid of the tendrils willed them back into my body. I was as shocked as he was when they slithered back to the unseen abyss from which they sprang, retreating into my flesh without a trace.

An intense sense of relief washed over me as they did, the vise crushing my chest releasing so I could breathe. The reprieve lasted but a heartbeat.

The Death Knight's voice cut through my spiraling thoughts, low and commanding. "Summon them again."

I recoiled from the command. "No," I whispered, barely able to force the word from my lungs. I yearned to believe the tendrils were nothing more than a hallucination, some machination of my mind as it grappled with nearly dying once again.

"Summon them again," he said, his arcane voice low and demonic. His demand left no room for argument. I would either obey or be broken.

Transfixed on the horrors spread across the ground, hunks of meat still twitching, I couldn't force myself to speak. My nightmare existence had just taken on a new dimension, and it took everything I could muster not to cry out in sheer terror.

Then, a gauntlet struck my face like stone. My head snapped to the side, and stars erupted in my vision.

Rage followed, clouding my vision.

Months of humiliation, fear, doubt, and sorrow surged up at once. The shame. The helplessness. It flowed through me, a broken dam of repressed emotion that had been simmering in my soul for months. It burned white-hot inside me, unleashing a raw power that cut through my hesitation.

Fine! I thought, with righteous indignation. He wanted my tendrils? He could have them.

My furious desire to retaliate overcame my disgust, and the abominable whips burst from my back like silent screams, gleaming as though polished by starlight. Their tips moved with predatory precision, each point poised to strike the Death Knight.

For the first time, they obeyed me. My tendrils moved not of their own will but mine, striking the cursed one with a force that felt both alien and exhilarating. Sparks flew as the impact drove him back a step. For a moment, the entire forest seemed to hold its breath. Then the onslaught began.

Tendrils rained down upon the Death Knight, slashing and stabbing with blinding speed. He attempted to draw his sword to deflect the blows that pierced his armor.

Too slow.

His training had taught me the intricacies of swordplay, and I had a dozen weapons capable of twisting and coiling to attack from impossible angles. There was no defense he could muster capable of stopping me.

In the blink of an eye, it was over. The warrior lay upon the ground, his armor gouged and furrowed, revealing the mummified flesh beneath. His flaming orbs were but faint embers, and the icy aura that emanates from him fell to a meager chill.

I smiled for the first time since my abduction. I had inflicted some semblance of pain upon the monster who had murdered my village and tortured me for sport. This brought a wave of sinister satisfaction — dark, blissful, and venomous. It wasn't the first time I had taken him down, but this was different. I hadn't just defeated him; I had emasculated him.

I sneered down at my defeated foe, savoring the victory. The cursed one grunted as he began pulling himself up, trying to appear unaffected by the assault as his armor righted itself. His eyes, however, betrayed him. The flaming orbs were mere slivers, glowing in the unnatural darkness behind the helm that cloaked his wilted face.

We stood there, neither willing to flinch a muscle, for what seemed like an eternity. The icy atmosphere returned as he regained strength, amplifying to match what I felt in the cell when he traded barbed words with the masked stranger. Still, I refused to move.

Finally, the knight turned and walked away as though nothing had happened.

As I watched, he moved to a pile of supplies the wolves had gathered and began rummaging through them. Upon finding a suitably sized sack, he threw it to me.

"Put what *pieces* you can find in here," he commanded, gesturing to the remains of the creature I had mutilated minutes before.

Anger seared my tongue, but I swallowed it. He had walked away, and so would I, for the moment.

I held the bag open with my hands, then began coiling the tips of my tendrils around the various slabs of pulverized meat and using them to fill the container. When I realized what I was doing, I gasped loudly enough to make the Knight reach for his sword once again.

"Did it move?"

I shook my head, grappling with the shock of

how natural using the otherworldly extensions seemed to be. Mere moments before, I had been horrified by their existence. Now, here I was, using them as though they had always been there. The revulsion returned with the realization, yet it paled in comparison to before.

When the sack was full of somewhat recognizable chunks, I unsummoned my tendrils. The Death Knight, who had been staring at the sack, waiting for it to move, decided the lycan was truly dead. He grabbed the package from me and opened a portal, walking through it without a word.

As the portal shimmered and swallowed him whole, I lingered for a moment, staring at the surrounding carnage. My tendrils were gone, but their phantom presence lingered, curling around my thoughts like a beast of prey waiting to strike.

Pushing the feeling down, I stepped through the portal, knowing this was only the beginning.

Chapter 26
Labyrinths of Lunacy

The portal's pull spat me into a cavernous expanse, the stale air thick with humidity and something more insidious — a cloying familiarity that made my stomach knot. The rock walls, smooth and damp, loomed like the cell that had swallowed me for an eternity. A shiver crawled down my spine as I fought off the lingering ghosts of my imprisonment. This place wasn't the same, but it *felt* the same, as though it had been carved from the same malignant stone, meant to contain and break something, someone.

Ahead, the cursed one moved without hesitation, a specter clad in steel and shadow. His gauntlet, slick with blood, clenched his grisly trophy as he strode toward a distant glow. I forced myself to follow, though every step deeper into this place made my skin tighten, my instincts whispering that I had just stepped into another kind of prison.

Then, the light exposed the prison's nature.

The glow came not from torches or open flames, but from strange glass canisters mounted along the walls, their light cold and sterile, casting distorted reflections across the cavern's grotesque contents. A labyrinth of tables cluttered with vials, tubes, and arcane instruments, exuding an air of impossible precision, stretched beyond sight. Shelves rose like mausoleums, cradling bottles filled with creatures suspended in thick, sluggish liquid. Some were whole; Others, mere assemblages of mismatched limbs, stitched torsos, and vacant, unblinking eyes.

The air hummed here, a low vibration that pressed against my bones. Strange wires snaked along the ceiling, hissing with energy, their occasional sparks slithering through the dark like predatory fireflies. Every breath tasted of ozone and decay, the mingling stench of rot, burnt flesh, and chemicals so pungent they clawed at my throat.

The Death Knight continued through the laboratory, weaving through the labyrinth of crates, operating tables, and machinery that I could not understand. I followed behind, careful not to disturb any of the immaculately organized chaos around me.

As we ventured deeper, the horror *shifted*. The

organized rows of specimens gave way to towering cylinders of glass, each imprisoning grotesque figures trapped in murky liquid. Some were hulking things, their twisted features subhuman, while others bore familiar shapes — lycans and humans — their bodies bloated, violated by unnatural grafts. A hand attached to a too-long arm twitched. Another blasphemy, half of its skull missing, turned its head toward me, then shrank away from the glass to hide.

They were alive.

I clenched my jaw, forcing my gaze forward as bile rose in my throat. The Death Knight wove through the nightmare without hesitation, but I had to suppress the urge to run. My pulse pounded against my temples, every instinct screaming that this place was an abomination of anti-life. Still, some deep part of me sensed a strange and terrible familiarity in the lab, as though the contents connected to me somehow.

Then, we came upon him. Hojo. He was hunched over an operating table, a bloody scalpel gliding across his latest specimen. The restrained thing beneath his hands twitched, its throat stitched shut — likely to silence its screams.

Though we did not announce our presence, the Doctor knew we were there. He turned away from his specimen. The porcelain mask remained fixed in its ever-present grin, but his eyes, a sickly, molten gold, burned with a knowing amusement.

The Doctor's movements were too smooth,

too fluid, his limbs bending and flowing with a grace known only to elves. When he stepped closer, it was not the rhythm of a man, but something unnaturally perfect.

The Death Knight stiffened beside me, dumping the gruesome contents of his bag atop an extensive pile of research papers. "What happened here?"

"You made a mess, you insufferable imbecile," the Doctor drawled, waving his scalpel like a dismissive hand gesture before turning back to his work. His voice was light, almost playful, but the weight beneath it was suffocating.

The Death Knight's fingers curled into fists, his gauntlets groaning under the strain. "Obviously," he spat, his voice dangerously low. "Why isn't it regenerating?"

Hojo did not look up. Instead, he slid the scalpel into a fresh incision, parting skin with a sickening ease. "Because it is dead," he said, as if explaining a simple equation. "Surely, by now, you know what kills these filthy beasts."

The Death Knight was shaking now. His flaming eyes burned brighter, seething. The Doctor finally tilted his head, the movement unnatural — too slow, too exact. The golden orbs in his mask seemed to drink in the sight of the Knight's anger like a connoisseur savoring fine wine. Hojo was not afraid of him. On the contrary, he seemed to enjoy infuriating the cursed one.

Deciding to speak up before the Death Knight's rage exploded, I stepped toward the Doctor. "I killed the lycan. Without using magic."

This got Hojo's attention. He turned toward me, the lunatic grin carved in his mask seeming to widen. "How?"

Sheepishly, I summoned my tendrils in response, careful not to further damage the Doctor's workspace. The sickly golden orbs hiding behind the mask widened in wonder at the sight.

"Leave us, whelp. Tell your master I need to examine his new toy." The Doctor spoke without looking toward the knight, keeping his gaze planted on the writhing mass of headless serpents squirming from my back.

"I will not leave him alone with you," the knight growled, crossing his arms across his chest in defiance.

The Doctor set his scalpel down with deliberate care, the metal tinkling against the tray. Then, he moved, not walking, but gliding, his robes billowing like a phantom's shroud as he closed the space between himself and the Death Knight. He leaned in, pressing the smooth mask so close to the warrior's burning gaze that, for a moment, I thought the heat might sear the gold from his eyes.

"You will do precisely as instructed, you

posturing wretch," he said, his voice like a scalpel itself: precise, cutting, and impossibly sharp. The two men stood there for an eternity, eyes locked in a battle of wills neither was willing to forfeit. Whatever bad blood they shared, it ran deep.

Finally, the Death Knight broke the silence. "You should have been purged with the others when the kingdom fell." The words were a whisper, echoing with something that went far beyond mere hatred.

"As should you. Yet, here you stand, enjoying the just reward for your service to the crown; may it never be undone."

Hojo's words struck a nerve. The knight's eyes blazed, the flames reaching out from the confines of his helmet to lick the Doctor's mask. He wasn't alone in his reaction. Something deep inside me recognized the conflict, the history between these two, and it ached within my chest. A distant memory pulled at my thoughts, concealed by the space between lives.

Pushing the feeling down into my gut, I stepped forward into the arctic aura emanating from the knight. It seemed as if I had walked into the tempest of a winter storm, as nude as the day I was born. "You brought me here to seek answers. Let him speak to me," I said through chattering teeth.

"If he tries anything, kill him." Without breaking eye contact with his nemesis, the Death Knight opened a portal around himself and disappeared.

"Craven dolt." The Doctor lingered in place, staring at the empty air where the Death Knight had stood, as though still watching him. Then, with a slow, deliberate motion, he turned to me.

"The lycan died because your tendrils drank its essence," he said, his voice almost gentle. "Without this energy, life cannot exist."

"You already knew," I said, realizing he had played the undead commander for a fool.

The Doctor resumed operating on his unwilling subject, slicing through flesh with uncanny precision. "Of course, I knew." He paused for a moment, looking up from a rising pool of blood to speak to me. "What else have you unlocked?"

As he continued to operate, I recounted everything that had happened since we last spoke: the abuse from D's Brides, the following surge of strength, the visions, even the battle at the wolves' encampment.

"Your metamorphosis is welcome news. Physical transfiguration is excellent, but the onset of controlled clairvoyance and clairaudience so soon is astounding." He spoke to me as though we were old friends, a stark contrast to his tone and mannerisms in the presence of the Death Knight, I thought.

"We are old friends," the Doctor said, answering the thought I hadn't spoken aloud.

The realization that he could hear the voice inside my head sent a chill down my spine, causing me to shudder.

"As I said before, the others cannot know the truth of our connection. Thus, the ruse for the *Quindulla*." He spat the last word, hatred dripping from it like venom. "D would try to kill us both if he knew the true nature of your prophecy." He paused for a moment, raising the scalpel in the air to emphasize his point. "That would be an unfortunate setback."

My blood ran cold as he spoke, yet I could not shake his invasion of my mind. "You can read my thoughts?" I asked.

"Many in the Castle can, but our connection makes it easier for me. Still, you must learn to protect your mind. D will not keep his prized champion hidden from the court forever, and those vultures will use any advantage they can to manipulate you."

"How am I supposed to do that?" I asked, watching as Hojo injected a mysterious, glowing green goop into the weeping specimen on his table.

"Eventually, you will manifest natural defenses against invasive minds as you evolve. In the meantime, do your best to mute the chatter in your head to ensure your secrets remain so."

The Brides had touched my memories during their onslaught. I remembered Lilyth smiling wickedly as she plucked Katri's image from the shadows of my mind, twisting it into something unholy. But that was different. They had rummaged through recollections like children playing with old toys —

laughing, mocking, seducing. Unlike them, Hojo didn't need to sift through memories. He listened as I thought. Watched as I reasoned. The Brides intruded with emotional force, pulling feelings and desires into the open. But Hojo dissected thoughts mid-formation, cold and surgical, like an autopsy of the soul.

No refuge remained, it seemed. Not even within myself.

"As you told me so very long ago, the suffering is necessary. It was through the Brides' torment that your abilities first manifested, was it not?" His voice was once again gentle, as though he regretted the burden placed upon my shoulders.

I nodded reluctantly. "What is the story with you and the knight?" I asked, ready to push out thoughts of the three women and the horrors they inflicted upon me.

Hojo paused mid-incision. Though he didn't speak, I could almost hear the gears turning in his head as he chose how to respond.

"You already know our story. You are part of it." He sliced once again.

I sighed. Why did everything in this damned place have to be so cryptic?

Hojo placed the scalpel down again and turned to face me. He clasped his hands behind his back, as he did every time they weren't working. "You are young and unprepared for the burden of our shared past. To enlighten you now would put us all in danger. Until you can shield your mind and your emotions, it is best that you know as little as possible. That is why I am cryptic."

My shoulders slumped in defeat.

I had no way of knowing it then, but he was right. Dracula would have had me killed a thousand times over if he knew the full scope of my shared history with Hojo.

For a moment, the silence between us deepened. The creature on the table gave a low, wet moan. Something inside it had seized again. Hojo regarded the spasming form without emotion. "There is much you do not understand yet," he said, more softly. "But perhaps… some things can be shown, if not yet explained."

He spun on his heel. "Come. Let me show you *our* laboratory." Without a thought, he left the poor creature convulsing and foaming at the mouth to give me a grand tour.

I was baffled by it all; His work's scale was both awe-inspiring and horrifying. The further we delved into the facility, the more twisted and indescribable the environment became. The Doctor seemed quite pleased to show off his work, explaining that he had been busy preparing for my arrival.

"You said D would try to kill us if he learned the truth of my alleged prophecy, why?" I eventually questioned.

The Doctor stopped the tour with this question, standing before a massive tube containing the unnatural amalgamation of a dragon and numerous unidentifiable monstrosities. "He and many others in this realm believe the prophecy will give them this world and access to those beyond."

He ran his hand along the glass containing the gargantuan abomination as if he were an artist admiring his work. "If Dracula were ever to discover the truth, he would try to kill us both, and I would unleash your army upon his kingdom. My so-called 'failures' would overrun the Castle in a matter of moments. We would survive, but it would be a costly setback."

"My army?" I asked, confusion twisting my thoughts.

Hojo nodded, waving his hand toward the countless rows of massive holding tanks.

I turned, scanning the lab again, not as an outsider, but with a creeping, insidious sense that I had seen it before. Not just seen it. *Understood it.*

The realization curdled in my stomach. Up to that point, I had fought hard to keep down my last meal, but now the sickness twisted deeper, not just from the displays lining the room but from something far worse: a sense of misplaced ownership.

It was the arrangement of the equipment, the calculated spacing of the operating tables, and the seamless integration of technology, sorcery, and grotesque organic matter. It all fit together with unnatural precision, a design too intentional to be random. Some part of me recognized why, even if the truth shied away from my consciousness.

I clenched my hands into fists, forcing my breath to steady. This place was not mine. I could never create something so twisted. Yet, beneath the revulsion, hiding behind the horror, a whisper of something else slithered through my mind. A sense of something unfinished. Incomplete.

I swallowed hard, tearing my gaze from the towering glass vats and the writing things inside. The fact that so many of these creatures were alien to me was, ironically, the only thing keeping my revulsion from spilling over into something worse. If I had understood more of what I was looking at, if I could put names to them, I might have lost the contents of my stomach to the cold, stone floor.

"As I said, I have been busy," the Doctor mused, his voice light, almost pleased. "Each exquisite experiment you have seen, and countless more thriving beneath our feet, are all at your command, should the need arise. No one in the Castle above is any wiser to their true purpose." He spun on his heel again, hands clasped behind his back, and continued the tour as if he were showing me paintings of family rather than a vault of horrors.

As we walked, the Doctor explained that his laboratories stretched deep beneath the ever-changing palace above and were hidden even from D's all-seeing vigilance. This allowed us to speak freely, but was also a cause for concern with the lord of the land, who was, above all else, obsessed with control.

Before ushering me back to the Castle above, Hojo insisted I stay for a lesson. "Your newfound defenses against the mind games of Dracula's Brides are... commendable," he admitted, his gloved fingers steepled. "But instinct alone will not protect you from those who have perfected the art of intrusion."

He instructed me in the finer methods of defense against psychic intruders, not merely resisting, but deceiving. Masking my true thoughts behind a constructed facade, one that would allow me to hide in plain sight. A shield, not of strength, but of deception.

As he spoke, I realized that this knowledge, too, felt uncomfortably familiar. The growing feeling that all of this truly had been my design disturbed me more than anything dwelling in Hojo's labyrinths of lunacy.

Chapter 27
Nocturnal Bond

Once Hojo decided his tutelage was sufficient for the time being, he opened a portal that deposited me back in my quarters. Exhausted, I collapsed on the bed. My body was desperate for sleep. My thoughts, however, had other intentions.

I tried to push out the images of Hojo and his experiments from my mind, but the horrors I had witnessed were burned into my conscience. The sight of those sterile chambers, the cruel machinery humming in the dark, still clawed at the edges of my thoughts. There had been something sickeningly familiar about them, something I couldn't quite place, but trying to recall why only deepened my exhaustion.

Part of me wanted to tell D of the Doctor's

treachery. So far as I knew, Hojo was every bit as mad as he seemed, and Dracula had been the only person I had met since my abduction who had treated me with even a shred of kindness. But some forbidden aspect of my soul knew Hojo, recognized in him the man he once was before the Doctor was created. Also, if he was correct, and all of this was some grand scheme I had crafted in a previous life, then Dracula would reward my loyalty with death.

What would that death look like, I wondered? Would it be swift, my severed head rolling across the stone floor? Or something more fitting, something akin to what I had seen in Hojo's domain? The uncertainty gnawed at me like a rat at a corpse, and for once, exhaustion was a mercy.

Tired of my mind's endless spiral, I closed my eyes and forced my consciousness to the stillness of the Void, where blessed silence would enshroud me like cool waters. However, before that release washed over me, I sensed another presence entering the room.

As I dared a glance into the darkness, I saw yellow eyes gleaming back at me. Lilyth.

D's youngest bride stood just inside the doorway. In the dim light, her cat-like pupils and golden irises were unmistakable.

"I am too tired for this, Lilyth," I said, not wanting to engage in her favorite pastime. "Tell your sisters I am not to be disturbed." Before, she would have laughed at such a demand, brushed it aside along with my defenses. But now, with my abilities bubbling to the surface, my command carried a force she could no longer ignore.

She paused in the doorway; The usual predatory glint in her gaze had dulled, swallowed by the room's gloom. Her eyes flicked toward my bed, hesitant, uncertain, as if caught between desire and doubt. Then, as if sealing some inner decision, her lips drew into a thin, practiced smile. When she finally spoke, her voice was low, stripped bare of the venom she so often wielded.

"I'm alone… I just wanted to know if you were well." The words broke apart on her tongue. She turned away as though ashamed they had ever been formed.

Despite the weariness, my body tensed, every nerve alert. Whatever game she was playing, I wasn't in the mood. "I'm fine," I said, "Just tired. It's been a long night."

"Can I stay with you?" she asked, her fingers fidgeting with the silken nightgown concealing her thighs. "I have fed, so you don't need to worry…" Her eyes darted up to meet mine.

Finally, irritation broke through my calm facade. "Is this a game, Lilyth?" I barked. "I told you already, I am too tired for this."

The seductress had always been cruel, torturously so, and I was not about to fall into some new trap disguised as tenderness. Not after the pain she had put me through.

Lilyth's posture faltered for just a moment. Her back, which had always been a picture of rigid elegance, seemed to sag ever so slightly. She masked it, but the effort came too late.

"No games, Viktor. Not today." Her eyes met mine, her gaze devoid of the vicious edge it always carried. "I know you are tired. The master told me what you faced in the wilds tonight..." She hesitated a moment too long, as if what she was to say were painful to speak aloud. "I was afraid you would not return."

Her words stung like a slap to the face. Of all the things I had expected to come from the vampiress, an admission of fear was not among them. It seemed genuine, which was even more shocking. Still, I was not convinced.

"You were worried about me?" I asked with a chuckle, suspicion dripping from my words.

"Does that surprise you? Is it so difficult to believe I might care to see you again?" Her brow arched, elegant and sharp. "We are not immune to feeling, Viktor. Our hearts may not beat, but they still ache."

The laughter died in my throat, strangled by the sincerity of her tone. I could discern no deception lingering there. No games. She was being honest, and I did not know how to respond.

The silence that followed stretched between us until, at last, she glided across the room and slid under the covers, curling up beside me with practiced grace. Her skin, chill to the touch, pressed against mine as she nestled beneath my arm. A muted word passed her lips, and the hearth beside the bed flared, burning hotter than usual.

"I'll grow colder when I sleep," she murmured, almost to herself. "I don't want you to freeze." Then, she closed her eyes.

The fire crackled at my back, its warmth licking up my spine, while from the front, her body pressed like ice against my ribs. The contrast was jarring, one side flushed with heat, the other drained by death. It was as if I were caught between two worlds, one struggling to keep me alive, the other beckoning me toward something colder, darker.

I lay there in stunned silence, the weight of her words pressing down harder than her body ever could. A single, unthinking act of kindness should not have affected me so, but from her, it felt like the sky tilting sideways, as if reality itself was doubting its own rules. She had tortured me. Mocked me. Broke me for sport. And now this?

As if her sudden tenderness weren't unsettling enough, the knowledge that she belonged to another man twisted my unease like a blade in my back. She was spoken for, and not just by any man, but by Dracula himself. He had given his Brides leave to toy with me, to slake their immortal boredom in cruelty and flesh, but this… this was different. What lingered between us now felt sacrilegious, something unspoken and forbidden, an emotional entanglement where there should have been only indulgence.

I wanted to recoil, to banish her with the same uncaring harshness she had offered me so many times, but I could not get myself to do it. Something inside me craved her presence, despite all logical reasons not to. Exhaustion eventually overcame the conflict tearing me apart from the inside, and I succumbed to fatigue. Many hours later, I awoke to the sound of my chamber door opening, the red-haired predator still pressed against my body.

I felt Dracula's gaze before I saw him, like a shadow stretching across the room. It wasn't the kind of quiet that offered comfort; It was the kind that pressed on your chest, demanding your attention.

I didn't move. I could not move. Every instinct in me screamed to rise, to face him, but my legs were stone. His shadow filled the doorway, like a specter from an old nightmare. A heavy hush lingered before he spoke. When the words finally came, his voice was calm, but it carried the power of an avalanche.

"Lilyth. What are you doing here?"

Startled awake, she shot out of bed like an arrow, twisting in midair to land on the ceiling as though it were the floor.

"Did she bite you?" D asked, his voice carrying the promise of violence should he receive the incorrect response. His stillness was more unnerving than an outburst ever could have been.

The chamber, which had felt small only moments ago, now seemed too large, the walls stretching away into shadow. My pulse quickened. If he chose to punish me, would I even have time to react?

"No," I stammered out. "She came to me after she fed. I was too tired to entertain her, so she drifted to sleep here."

My words seemed to calm the vampire lord as his shoulders relaxed, and the clenched muscles in his face released with an amused chuckle.

"You have made quite the impression, Viktor," he said, his voice now smooth as velvet but with an edge of cold steel. He stepped into the room, his movement languid but precise, as if the very act of walking across the floor was beneath him. "My young bride seems to have taken a liking to you," he said, glancing up at his wife once again. "Leave us."

Lilyth dropped from the ceiling like a feather, twirling in slow motion to land without a sound at D's feet. "Yes, Master." She passed D, shooting a last look at me before leaving the room.

"I am told that you achieved a glorious victory against our enemies. Congratulations. The Hand says you are becoming quite formidable."

I smiled sheepishly at the compliment, my previous fears melting away. Climbing out of bed, I summoned my tendrils for D to see. He clasped his hands together at the sight, his grin genuine rather than his usual charming facade.

"Magnificent," he said as his eyes followed the extensions of my form while they coiled and writhed in the air. "Come, let us feed. I wish to hear every detail of your transformation."

After leaving my room, D and I made our way to the Dining Hall, his steady barrage of questions about the encounter with the wolves passing the time.

The Brides were already assembled when we arrived, and I couldn't help but notice Lilyth's gaze fixed on me; Not the familiar, predatory hunger of before, but something conflicted. I caught a fleeting blush on her cheeks as she stared, a subtle signal that sent a ripple of surprise through me. Before I could dwell on it further, Dracula's voice cut through the moment.

"You've begun to earn your place here in my court. You've shed blood in my name, taken lives at my command." His voice deepened, like distant thunder. "Now comes the true test of your allegiance. Prove to me you belong — not to the world that shunned you, but to us." He inclined his head ever so slightly, a flicker of a smirk at his lips.

"What would you have of me?" I asked, an

invisible weight clamping my chest.

"Another initiation of sorts."

I nodded, though I did not know what he meant.

Following my meal, D escorted me to an armory and allowed me to pick new armor since my last set had met an unfortunate fate. I selected a lightweight leather cuirass, bracers, and greaves, all dyed pitch black, and then slid them over my enchanted robes.

D's gaze swept over me, a rare gleam of approval in his ageless eyes. "You walk among gods and monsters now, Viktor, no longer a child of the world you left behind." His voice was calm, but each word carried weight. "It is time you chose what you are to become: a fading echo of humanity, or something more — a cherished member of my family." He placed a hand on my shoulder, firm and deliberate. "I have faith that you will choose wisely."

Even then, I had no illusions that this was to be some symbolic rite of passage. Dracula never wasted time on empty gestures. Whatever came next, I knew it would be unpleasant, and it would demand more of me than I might be ready to give.

As D turned to leave, Grygor walked into the room, a sickening grin plastered across his gruff face. "How 'bout we go find sum trouble?"

Seeing Dracula's pet made my skin crawl and filled me with a desire to flee from the Castle, to escape this nightmare before it consumed me. But another part of me, the part that had tasted power and blood, whispered that this was the only path forward.

I didn't know who I was anymore. Was I the man I had been, or was I already something else?

I was about to find out.

Chapter 28
Forsaken

Before leaving, D spoke to his pet, leaning close so only the beast could hear his whispered command. The twisted smile plastered on Grygor's face deepened as Dracula spoke, his expression a vile mix of mischief and menace. Without so much as a glance in my direction, the lord of the land marched out the door.

It was then that Grygor approached me, pointed teeth on full display. "We're goin'ta play a game, you 'n' I."

Most of the monsters I'd faced thus far were cruel by nature, but there was something uniquely perverse in this creature. I didn't need a sixth sense to know Grygor would soon introduce me to horrors beyond my darkest imaginings — his sadistic grin told me all I needed to know.

"C'mon, big man, time ta go," he said, his voice rough with excitement. He attempted to slap me on the shoulder again, as he had months before, but this time I stopped him. Before the blow connected, a tendril erupted from my shoulder and coiled around his wrist.

Grygor laughed, a sound like shattered glass, as the tendril tightened its grip and lifted him off the floor. Lilting his head sideways towards me as he hung there helplessly, his amber eyes burned with a wild, unholy delight. "Maybe ya belong 'ere after all," not even trying to conceal his amusement. "Le's go hunt'n' n see wha' these li'l gifts can really do," he said before breaking out into his psychotic laughter.

The Death Knight marched into the room just as I released the grinning idiot, allowing him to drop to the floor. Without a word, the undead warrior opened a swirling portal. The horrific pair, one with raw, bestial hunger and the other a grim arbiter of violence, stepped through. I hesitated before following. An inescapable dread blossomed within my chest as I stared into the churning abyss.

I recognized the forest immediately as I stepped out of the portal. It deposited me into a familiar clearing high in the mountains. A sliver of a moon hung overhead, and the night air carried the nostalgic scents of spring. The aroma of wildflowers and fresh greenery carried my senses back to when I had gathered herbs for my long-departed protector. In that bittersweet moment, I realized the Death Knight had brought me home.

I glanced at the Hyena, whose nose twitched as he tested the air, then shifted my gaze to the Death Knight. "He said we were hunting. What could be left to find here? Deer?" My voice faltered as I spoke, betraying my unease.

These two wouldn't bring me here to hunt something as mundane as deer, or even a bear, which would still be hibernating this early in the season. No, they had other plans. A heavy sense of foreboding pressed in, as if I stood at the edge of a memory beyond my grasp.

"This way," the Hyena announced, having caught the scent of what he was after. The cursed knight followed him without a word, leaving my question unanswered. I summoned eldritch energy to pierce the night, a soft, eerie green glow lighting my vision. With each cautious step, an inexplicable dread settled in my gut.

As we walked, my mind ventured back to that day in the village when the Death Knight set the town aflame and claimed me. Everyone had perished at his hand. Then, realization dawned, bringing with it an unbearable weight of despair. He hadn't killed everyone.

The little girl, Natka, and her parents had been spared. They had survived the knight's fiery wrath after

I stepped in front of them. Now, Grygor was leading us to their cabin.

Each step forward came slower than the last, my limbs leaden, as if the ground itself were resisting my movement. Cold sweat prickled my spine. The surrounding forest seemed too quiet, the wind holding its breath as we passed, and the trees leaning in to see what was to come. I could feel the bitter touch of destiny waiting, patient and cruel, just ahead.

Grygor glanced back, nostrils flaring as he caught whatever stench my fear released into the air. He grinned, wide and toothy, eyes gleaming with the delight of someone who already knew the surprise waiting just around the corner.

When at last the cabin crested into view, every breath turned ragged, as though the mountains were sitting on my chest.

The Death Knight had not allowed the family to live out of any kindness to me. No, kindness and mercy had rotted from him long ago. They survived only to pave the way for this moment, to become unwilling pawns in my twisted fate. Dracula's orders had brought us here to ensure I was transformed into a monster, another villain in his grim collection.

With sadistic glee, Grygor turned to face me, his form rippling and contorting before my eyes. Muscles and sinews tore away as he morphed into a towering hybrid — both man and beast. Coarse, spotted fur spread over undulating skin, and his jaws elongated, revealing rows of jagged teeth. "Are ya ready t' begin, or should I go first?" he said, then laughed.

I didn't get the chance to respond. Chaos erupted within the cabin as the miner, Goran, began lighting torches and gathering weapons to defend his family. The hovel's door swung open, and the man stepped out, wielding a bow with an arrow notched and ready.

"Kill them," the Death Knight commanded, his flaming eyes somehow crueler and more uncaring than usual.

Inside the cabin, a meek voice called out, "Papa?" only to be shushed into silence by her mother. I stood frozen, unable to move so much as a muscle. I had fought for Dracula, defended my new home, and dispatched lycans without remorse. But these were not faceless monsters; They were people, my people, and now they stood on the brink of a fate I could not endure.

"Kill them… or he will," the Death Knight intoned, the 'he' falling like a curse in the silence.

I shuddered at the thought of the Hyena's cruelty should it be given free rein. With every ounce of willpower at my disposal, I left the forest's shadows for the clearing that held the cabin.

"Who's there?" the father called out.

"It's me," I croaked, barely able to get the words out.

"Viktor?" At the doorway, Cadya appeared. Her gentle presence, marked by a swollen belly, was illuminated by the soft glow of a torch, revealing tender vulnerability. The light brushed over me, igniting in me a deep, aching sorrow.

Before I could respond, an arrow sank into my chest.

"It's a demon!" Goran shouted. "Look at his eyes!"

In my distress, I had forgotten to release the eldritch energy that made them glow an unearthly green.

"They were right about him all along," he spat, his voice trembling as he fumbled for another arrow. The effort would prove futile.

Before Goran could pull another arrow from his quiver, the Hyena sprang from the darkness, slashing him open and spilling his steaming insides onto the cold ground. As her mate fell into his own gore, the beast dragged Cadya from the doorway. I watched in mute horror as he threw her down next to her dying husband and indulged himself. Bile burned my throat as the ordeal played out in slow motion before my eyes.

Nothing could have prepared me for what I saw.

Not the Brides.

Not the Death Knight.

Nothing.

Grygor took his time, careful not to inflict wounds that would end the woman's suffering before his fun was over. He wanted her to be alive for every gruesome moment. It didn't take long until I tried to turn from the scene, to hide in shame from the events before me. I clamped my eyes shut, praying Cadya would die and end the nightmare before I opened them again. I begged my ears not to listen, but the screaming and squelching continued their unrelenting assault on my senses.

I missed the frigid presence approaching behind me, so focused was I on blocking out the sights and sounds of the Hyena's delights. It wasn't until the arrow tore from my chest that my eyes shot open again, only to find themselves unable to shut, held fast by fingers cold as death. I tried to struggle, to break free of the Death Knight's grip, but the shock of what I saw sapped my strength away.

What followed, I do not have the stomach to put into words.

The aftermath left Goran, Cadya, and their unborn child unrecognizable, save for a tangle of umbilical cord dangling from the Hyena's twisted grin. The beast rose, his fur a gleaming, matted mess in the moonlight, and stretched with satisfaction. He moved toward me, only to stop mid-step as a sound from within the cabin made his ears perk up. Natka. She was still alive inside the home, choked, broken sobs wracking her frail body. Once again, the Hyena smiled at me and began his hideous laugh.

I knew everything Grygor would do to the girl; I had just seen what he would do. The idea of it awoke my soul, my true self.

It was then that the world fell away. A silence deeper than death swallowed everything, deafening my forsaken ears and blinding my cursed eyes. From that Void, something ancient clawed its way to the surface. Rage, fierce and inhuman, surged through my body, flowing through my veins and running ice-cold across my flesh, turning it blacker than the night sky.

With a primal cry, tendrils erupted from my back. They speared through the Death Knight before hurling him aside like a discarded puppet. Another tendril lashed out, coiling around the Hyena's throat. His laughter died in a choked gurgle. I felt his neck snap beneath my fury before I threw his body through the air. A satisfying crack echoed as he hit the far-off trees, his back splintering like brittle wood.

As my monstrous form exacted revenge, I could sense the fading pulse of little Natka inside the cabin. Her lungs, long weakened by illness, now buckled under the strain of terror. She was dying. Rather than let her suffer, I fulfilled the Death Knight's command. With a sorrow as deep as the abyss, I offered her a swift, painless release with the tip of a tendril.

No sooner had I done so than a torrent of visions crashed over me. I felt her joy and sorrow, every hope and secret dream, as if they were my own. In an instant, I saw countless futures where her gentle spirit had blossomed. Each life, filled with love and kindness, brightened the world even in darkness.

All of her possible futures slammed into my consciousness with a force greater than the avalanche I had spared her father from not so very long ago. She had been pure and innocent, her only fault having been born sick and weak in a world with no pity for such things. Now, those possibilities were lost forever, extinguished by my hand. The hearts beating within my chest shattered into innumerable pieces as I realized how happy she had been despite the misery her body forced her to endure.

I watched with sorrow as thousands of possible lifetimes played out, how she would have lived and eventually died had I never returned to the village... or had I never arrived there to begin with. Some of these phantom possibilities saw her become a mother; in others, the act of childbirth claimed her life. In each, she remained frail, yet shone with a joy unmatched even by the most benevolent of Gods. She left the realm at peace in every outcome... all save the one I had ushered upon her.

As I stood outside the cabin, watching each strand of fate wither and fade, I failed to notice the sky above turn a violent black. The moons disappeared behind ebony clouds boiling with agony as my sorrow expanded ever upward. Preternatural lightning tore through the heavens, casting shadows across the land that moved of their own accord, bowing in reverence to their awakened master. With a clap so loud it sounded as though reality itself was being torn in two, inky rain pelted down, washing away the evidence of Grygor's delights.

My tendrils, frozen in place where they had been as the final breath of life fled from Natka, retreated from the dwelling as the rain hit them, sending shivers through my body. They brought her remains to my arms, where I held her close.

Despite the torrential downpour, not a single drop touched her.

Natka's pale, pink flesh contrasted with the shiny black armor that encased my soul, which felt every bit as dark and twisted as the clawed hands now holding her. I stared down at the only creature who had ever been truly kind to me, seeing all the faces she could have grown into had I never returned here.

The echoes of Natka's unfulfilled future reverberated through my soul, each heartbeat a reminder of the cost of this monstrous life I'd been given. Though my flesh was cloaked in darkness, it was the light of lost innocence that would haunt me for all eternity.

It was then that I noticed the little doll she had

once given me clutched in her arms. I didn't think my anguish could become more potent than it already was, but seeing the doll multiplied my suffering a thousandfold. She must have found the trinket after I was taken, reclaiming the property she had given me on that fateful day. Both the child and the doll stared up at me with lifeless eyes, reflecting the eldritch glow of my own.

I carried her broken form back into the cabin and laid her to rest upon the meager cot where she had just woken from the blissful dreams of a child to a real-life nightmare. I closed her eyes, careful not to injure her flesh with the black talons extending from my fingertips. Then, I placed the doll next to her with care, tucking them both under a fur blanket. I gathered what little was left of her parents and put them in the house with her. Without a second look, I left the hut.

Both monsters were standing in the dark, waiting for me. While I handled the dead, they had scraped their way out of the woods, slowly regenerating from the wounds I had inflicted. With my gaze fixed on the cursed one, the command "Burn it" escaped my lips.

The Death Knight lifted his fingers into the air and unleashed an inferno so mighty that the soaked wood ignited with ease. For once, the thrice-damned Hyena was silent, his smile washed away along with the blood he had spilled. He fixed his gaze on my true form, his eyes betraying the horror lurking behind them.

Chapter 29
Isolation

I stood between the pair and the cabin, my back turned to the raging fire. The trembling flames battled the relentless darkness ushered in by the storm. It was as if some malignant, inverse sun lurked behind the oppressive clouds, pouring malevolence onto a land already steeped in sorrow. Every crackle of power in the heavens sent unnatural light racing across my glistening obsidian flesh, as though aware that its luminescence was as fleeting as my remaining humanity.

The glow of my eye remained unaffected by the unnatural miasma churning around us, daring the villains before me to move toward it. Rain pounded against us with fervor as ear-splitting cracks of thunder hammered down. It was as if the Gods themselves were waging war against the cruelty of my existence in the heavens above.

Fury boiled within my abyssal shell, a living thing extending beyond my form through unmoving tendrils poised to strike the two figures before me. Neither of the creatures dared to move, so much as to breathe, for fear the act might unleash my wrath upon them.

The Death Knight had seen this form once before and had felt the sting of my tendrils. But Grygor was seeing the full glory of my ascension for the first time. He looked comical with his soaked, ragged fur clinging to his frame as he shook, not from the storm or the chill of the Death Knight, but from the fear lashing at his innards. In any other moment, this might have filled me with mirth. I might have celebrated his discomfort in my presence. Then, however, it only provoked in me a dark, visceral desire to strip away his flesh, to let my tendrils trace every nerve, and to drink in his pain. I wanted nothing more than to inflict upon him wounds that would scar his soul and haunt him for thousands of lifetimes.

Yet, even as the desire for vengeance flowed molten hot through my veins, a deeper yearning emerged: a longing to be alone. I wanted to be far from Dracula, far from his Brides, and far from the walking sacks of maggot-infested excrement that stood before me. In that moment of desperate need, the darkness answered.

Without warning, the Void wrapped around me like a shroud, pulling me away from my tormentors and depositing me upon a barren, ice-crowned peak. I blinked in disbelief as my mind tried to comprehend what had happened. One moment, I had been standing before the Death Knight and the Hyena, ready to flay them both, and the next, I was miles away from them. In the far distance, I could see the unnatural storm, my emotions had summoned, dissipating in my absence.

It was then that a haunting sense of awareness washed over my mind, a feeling that would become all too familiar with each new ability I would unlock over the centuries. I had moved through the Void, using it to fold reality like parchment with little more than a focused thought. It was effortless. Instinctive. This wasn't a skill I learned, but something I remembered — knowledge that had always been mine, buried beneath the surface, waiting to be released from another life. Like the tendrils that I wielded without thought, this, too, was an extension of me.

When the Death Knight opened a portal, it was an act of sorcery. His teleportation was from one point to another through magical means. For me, it is different. I simply cease to be in one place and am instantly in another, as if creation itself moves around me. Eventually, I would come to refer to this ability as 'void-walking.

Too overcome by grief to put more thought into my newfound skill, I instead collapsed in a snowdrift, seeking to freeze the memories that scorched my soul. The chill offered no solace. I yearned to feel the sting of cold, to pay some meager penance for the atrocities etched into the valley below, but I could feel nothing.

Hours bled into each other as I sat there, motionless, under a leaden sky. When the sun finally crept over the mountaintops, I realized I had not blinked since sitting. I hadn't even taken a breath. In that unnerving moment of awareness, I discovered my basic human functions were unraveling, leaving me more like Dracula's family than I liked. Revulsion bloomed in my stomach, alongside the epiphany.

The Death Knight didn't breathe, his lungs having rotted away eons ago. His voice was not powered by air flowing through vocal cords, but by mystical means gifted by his curse. The vampires, likewise, didn't have to breathe unless they were trying to conceal their nature while among mortals, or they wished to speak.

When I finally resolved to move from my icy stupor, I rose and found myself clutching something small within my monstrous hand. Natka's doll. I had left it with her in the hovel before the flames had reduced it all to ashes. I wanted her to have it. For her to take her gift with her to whatever afterlife awaited the innocent child, but here it was, staring up at me with lifeless eyes.

As I turned the doll over in my grasp, its worn

surface stirred a tempest of memories and remorse. Was it a sign from Natka's spirit, an echo affirming that I had, in some twisted way, spared her from a fate far worse? Or was it a manifestation of guilt, a reminder of the price I had to pay for what I was becoming? Peering down at the trinket brought a maelstrom of emotions, yet some unknown force seemed to radiate from the doll that eased my suffering ever so slightly.

I stared at the toy until the sun was high in the sky, unmoving against the harsh winds that battered me. How could such a tiny thing hold so much meaning, such conflicting emotions? The more I gazed at the simple figurine, the more precious it became. This was the last piece of my home, a relic of a people who had been erased from existence because they had been cursed by my presence.

Eventually, the pull of memory urged me back to the remnants of my former home. With a bitter acceptance, I void-walked from the icy summit to the crumbling hut where my guardian had raised me in her final years. The cabin, like my past, bore the scars of time and tragedy.

Months had passed, perhaps more than a year, since I was taken by the Death Knight, but I wasn't sure exactly how long it had been. Natka's mother had not been pregnant, visibly at least, when I left, and she was heavy with child when… I cut the thought off before it could finish forming.

With a shake of my head to clear my thoughts,

I focused again on the cabin. Boards were missing here and there, and part of the roof had collapsed. My eldritch form was far too large to fit in the doorway, so I let my body return to its human state and walked inside, still forced to duck as I passed through the door.

It may have been Spring in the valley, but the cold air hit me like a slap to the face, forcing me to shiver. The inside of the hut was in shambles. When the villagers came for my guardian, they must have torn the place apart looking for evidence of our supposed wrongdoings. The thought of them desecrating her sanctuary, of robbing her of the dignity she once possessed, shattered me anew.

With my jaw clenched to stop it from quivering, I sat by the hearth and started a fire using the wood I had gathered before my life was upended forever. The cold I had desired the previous night was no longer welcome, and I was ready to find some small comfort in the world.

I positioned the doll a safe distance from the flames while I searched for a place to hide it. A loose stone in the foundation provided a sanctuary to protect the last vestige of a home I no longer recognized.

Convinced the doll was safe, I wrapped myself in a tattered, matted fur and stared into the dancing fire. A conflux of grief, guilt, and rage surged within me as I lost my thoughts in the flames, a noxious elixir of sorrow that threatened to overwhelm every remnant of the man I once was. Then, the tension in my soul was shattered by a measured voice.

"So, this is where you were raised."

Dracula.

The vampire stood just outside the doorway, bathed in sunlight, his long shadow casting me into darkness. I did not turn to face him or even bother to respond, preferring instead to let the fire's flicker mirror the turmoil churning within.

"May I join you?" he asked, his tone uncharacteristically subdued.

I nodded my approval, refusing to look in his direction.

He settled beside me, heavy cloak around him, peering into the flames until at last he murmured, "I am sorry, Viktor."

He sighed, low and sorrowful, then let the silence stretch before continuing. "I had forgotten what it was like to lose all you hold dear. It takes time to grieve the loss of who we were before tragedy changed us forever," he said, the words little more than a whisper. "You have done everything I have asked of you, and I have wounded you in return. It seems to be my curse that I always hurt those whom I care for."

I remained silent, allowing his words to linger. We sat for an eternity, both lost in our thoughts. Eventually, I reached out and added another log to the hearth, as it had burned through the original offerings. It felt symbolic, as if I was burning away the last vestiges of my old life. Only later, as the long shadows merged with the deepening dusk, did I whisper, "Viktor is dead. I need a new name."

D turned, his eyes reflecting both pride and the heavy burden of regret. "Then a new name you shall have. We call your father Sight, so you shall be known as Vision."

The name struck me with bitter clarity. Sight, the eldritch being who had haunted my darkest moments, was my father. The revelation was less shocking to me than it should have been. What truly disturbed me was the name Dracula chose for me. Once again, my mind returned to the horrors of my final day in the village, my guardian's last words playing in my mind. *"It will be alright, my Vision."*

The memory forced me to swallow hard, repressing the desire to break down in tears. Were her words prophetic? Had she known the path I was about to walk? The questions made me feel alone in the universe, the only sense of companionship I had being the soulless monster sitting at my side. Still, I found in him something I had been missing the entirety of my life.

"You are the closest thing to a father I have ever had," I admitted quietly, my voice trembling with both longing and despair. In all the years we had wandered before arriving in the village, no man had ever stepped into the role, nor had my guardian ever taken a mate.

That he, of all people, was something I would liken to a father is a testament to just how isolated and broken my life had been.

D's gaze returned to the fire, then he spoke again, his voice soft. "I have never been much good at being a father, I fear. But for you, I will try harder."

Despite the rare warmth of his words, the revelation that he was a father jolted me. "You have children?" I asked, having seen nothing in the Castle that would suggest as much.

D nodded slowly, the firelight casting deep shadows on his face. "A daughter, Sorina. She is my Vesputa, my firstborn. The heir of my lands should I ever… step aside." He paused, his gaze drifting for a moment before he added, "Her name means *sun*."

"That seems rather odd for a vampire," I mused, recalling my lesson about his kind.

This caused D to chuckle ever so slightly. "Her mother chose it. A name meant to wound, I think." Then, his voice grew quieter. "Still, it suits her. She is radiant. Defiant. Unable to dim herself." He looked away to the fire, as if the hearth were a portal to another world. "She is her mother's daughter."

I should have asked him more about Sorina, the Daughter of the Night, but something in his tone pulled my attention elsewhere. The statue. The voice. *Find me.* I wanted to learn more about his missing Queen, to see if he would reveal a new piece of the puzzle forming in my mind.

"What happened to her? Your wife?" The question left my lips before I could stop it.

D's composure faltered, and his jaw clenched tight enough to shatter teeth. The hearth crackled louder as the air seemed to shift around him. When he finally spoke, his voice was low.

"That is a tale for another time," he replied, turning back to the flames.

Again, silence stretched between as the hours passed by unnoticed. Finally, Dracula stood, stretched, and flashed his familiar, charismatic grin. "I must return to the Castle. I can return for you later if you wish to say farewell to your former home in private… although Lilyth's nagging about your whereabouts is growing tiresome."

I cast one final look at the place that had sheltered and shaped me, then smothered the fire. The ashes hissed beneath the dirt; the flames snuffed out like the life I had lived here.

"Let's go home. There is nothing left for me here."

Chapter 30
Crimson Comforts

The moment Dracula's portal spat us back into the Castle's shadowed embrace, I sensed her presence. Lilyth glided along the corridor like a predatory phantom. Her eyes burned with a hunger that was at once familiar and yet... confusing. I felt my blood run cold, the old urge to flee warring with a reluctant curiosity coupled with the knowledge I could now defend myself.

She passed her husband without stopping or even acknowledging his presence and pressed her cool flesh against mine. "Welcome home. We missed you."

Her fingers traced over the muscles of my arms with an intimacy that dredged up memories of past torments. I stiffened as her gaze held mine a beat too long, a look that carried both seduction and something new that I couldn't quite place. The attention made me deeply uncomfortable, an unease amplified by the fact that she belonged to Dracula, and he was watching the scene play out from the shadows. Sensing my unease, he commanded the vampiress away until I was ready to see her.

For his part, Dracula didn't seem the least bit concerned with his bride showering me with attention. If anything, he appeared relieved to have her doting over someone else.

With a sigh, Lilyth paused just long enough to place her hand on my chest, feeling the heart beating within, and walked away to join her sisters, who were giggling wickedly.

D watched with curiosity as my eyes followed Lilyth, my mind trying to peel through her defenses to reveal whatever twisted game she was trying to play at my expense. When it became apparent that I was lost in thought, he reached out to squeeze my shoulder.

"Come, you have had a trying day. I suspect you could use a stiff drink," he said, his characteristic smile leaving no room for refusal.

Dracula led me through the Castle in silence until we reached the quiet intimacy of his private chamber, the very one where we had first spoken after my imprisonment. D poured two glasses of amber liquid, the firelight dancing in the depths of his eyes.

Once again, we sat peering into a blazing hearth, only this time in comfort rather than the decrepit home I used to know.

D spoke first. "Something has changed with my Bride. I haven't seen her so... alive... since I welcomed her into the family." He shot me a smile that said he was not bothered by it. "I believe she has developed feelings for you, a rare thing in my lands. Perhaps you might even claim her as your own bride, if you wish."

His words struck me as an accusation. "I am not here to steal from you, least of all your wife," I replied, bitterness mingling with guilt over having slept with his Brides. "I am not a thief."

D's gaze drifted to the swirling liquid in his glass as he murmured, "You cannot steal what is given. Love, especially here, is a rarity not to be squandered on petty human rules."

"Do you not love her?" I asked, hesitantly.

A soft laugh escaped his lips, void of warmth. "My heart belongs to another, much to the detriment of my Brides." He peered up from the glass, looking at me. "In our world, marriages are transactions; Tools for power or distraction. Love, as you know it, is exceedingly rare. My Brides are born of boredom, not passion."

The moral standards of those who call the Castle home, if such a thing even exists, are a far cry from those I was raised with. At this point in my new life, I was struggling to come to terms with how things operated here. This internal conflict remains unconquered, a last vestige of my humanity.

Uncomfortable with the direction of the conversation, I shifted the subject. "You spoke of my father. Tell me about him."

"Ah, Sight…" D began, his tone softening into a reverent murmur as he swirled his drink. "Born of the Void beyond the stars, he is an entity of unimaginable power, though he rarely uses it. His words come in riddles of futures yet to pass. He is more cryptic than a sphinx." Dracula sipped his drink, then continued. "We call him Sight because he sees all: the past, the present, and every possibility the future might hold."

I was jolted by Dracula's words, recalling Natka and all the lives I'd watched slip away as I held her corpse. I forced the images away, hoping he had not noticed the shudder that betrayed my inner turmoil. "Is he here in the Castle?" I asked, my voice tight with a mix of dread and curiosity.

D took a slow, deliberate sip before replying, "He comes and goes as he pleases. It was he who revealed your location to me, ensuring that my Hand could rescue you. Without his intervention, your former people would have killed you… as they did your protector."

Dracula knew about my guardian. He knew the villagers had killed her. Did he command his Death

Knight to let her die, I wondered? Had that been a part of his plan to bait the monster lurking behind my eyes out of hiding? The idea of it emboldened me to the point where I finally gave words to a question that had burned in my chest since he welcomed me into his home. "Why did you have me imprisoned?" I blurted out. "You claim to want me as a member of your family, yet I have been mistreated from the start. I want to know why."

I could almost see the thoughts churning in Dracula's mind as he calculated which words would be best employed in his response, curating what he could say that would make the suffering he had ushered upon me seem necessary. Finally, he settled on some semblance of the truth.

"We knew almost nothing about you then. Sight had offered fragments of insight into your capabilities, but nothing certain. After the events on the cliff, I could not risk bringing you into the Castle. Not until I was sure you would not shatter the very home I intended to give you. So, when you fell from the sky, human once more, I caught you and sealed you below. Then I watched and waited. Only when it became clear that you were not a threat did I allow you to be released."

I hated to admit it, but his answer made sense, though it did little to ease my mind. "And the torment from your Brides?" I asked, still wanting some reason for my suffering.

"You are young," Dracula replied, his voice solemn. "Your immortal life has just begun. Would it have served you better had I shielded you from the truth of your new world? Kept the horrors hidden away until they revealed themselves with the passing of centuries? No. You would have turned from us then, resentful and lost." He leaned closer, his tone softening, yet no less resolute. "I allowed them to draw you in, cruelly perhaps, so that you might understand what it means to live among us. Now you do. Now you *are* one of us. Each of my kin would kill for you. Die for you. Their torment was the price and the bond of your belonging."

I leaned forward, determined to press the wound he'd only just begun to dress, and met D's commanding gaze. "You say I belong. You claim your kin would kill or die for me... but that isn't true. I remain hidden from your court, from the rest of your world. I do not belong so long as I am kept a secret. You have a daughter I have yet to meet. Your nobles, your lands, and your people are a complete mystery. How can you claim I am one of you when it is apparent that I am not?"

Dracula sat back in his chair, a sly smile parting his lips with wicked amusement. "Perceptive as ever." He spoke with unmasked pride, as a father would to his son. "No, you have not met my lesser court, but you have no need to. You are a part of my court now,

Vision. The only one that matters. The sniveling nobles who posture and beg for scraps of importance below are of no consequence. In time, you will see for yourself just how far beneath you they are. As for Sorina..." His smile faded, replaced with an icy edge. "She cannot be trusted to know of your existence. Not while she still believes that knowledge is a power she can wield unchecked. Until that illusion is shattered, for her to learn of you would be a danger to us all."

Dracula's words lingered in my mind, coiled like smoke that refused to dissipate. He had dismissed his nobles as though they were insects orbiting a flame they could never touch. That I could understand; power breeds disdain, but the way he spoke of his daughter unsettled me. It was not as a father burdened with worry for his child, but as a strategist wary of an unpredictable opponent. His voice carried caution, not affection. A spark of curiosity flared in me then, muted but persistent. Whoever Sorina was, she was no footnote in Dracula's existence, and I doubted she would be in mine.

D drained the last of his drink, then stood, his eyes gleaming with impatient hunger. "If your thirst for answers is sufficiently sated, let us venture out to feed. I desire something more substantial to drink." I nodded and rose from my seat, following him out the door.

The scene awaiting us in the Dining Hall was a far cry from the peaceful solitude we had left behind in the study. A scream tore down the corridor as we approached, raw and ragged.

We emerged to find Grygor hunched over a writhing servant on the floor, tearing into him and swallowing down heaping mouthfuls of flesh. The sight brought back visions of the previous night, and I felt the Void rise behind my eyes as their glow reignited. Without a sound, a tendril erupted from my shoulder and drove through the man's skull, ending the Hyena's favorite game — seeing how long he could keep a victim alive while he ate them.

Grygor's face twisted between beast and man, his sneer morphing into a challenge as he stood. "Remind ya of anythin'?" he taunted, advancing with a swagger born of cruelty.

Before he could take a second step, my fist collided with his gore-frosted face. The blow sent his teeth and crumpled form raining down upon the stone floor. As he struggled upright, I extended my tendril again, severing the tendons in his ankles with precise brutality.

It was then that D's booming voice shattered the tension. "Stay down, or I will allow him to finish you."

The threat left Grygor cowering, his eyes burning with wounded pride as he lay humbled and hobbled before me. In the background, the Brides' hissing laughter multiplied the beast's humiliation.

Grygor was accustomed to all but the very top echelon of the court fearing him and his brutal tactics. His penchant for perverse violence was legendary, stretching far beyond Dracula's lands. He was also D's favorite pet and, as such, enjoyed a higher degree of freedom than most of the vampire's subordinates. My arrival, however, had put a massive dent in his ego.

For starters, the Brides were revolted by the creature, yet they fawned over me, something Grygor envied. Then there was the fact that I was allowed to speak with Dracula in the most informal way. He allowed me to call him D, something unheard of in the Castle. Even his Brides were required to call him Master. Now, the Hyena had been humiliated and then punished for stepping out of line with me for the second time. His eyes burned with hatred as he glared at me from the floor, the emotion rivaling the rancor in my own eyes.

I chose a seat where I could stare into the chastised monster's eyes, reveling in his shame. The rest of this world might fear the creature, but I was no longer among them, and I was determined to make sure he knew it.

Lilyth, sensing an opening to ingratiate herself with me, dropped the servant she had just drained and glided across the room with a knowing smile to sit at my side. Her thinly veiled plot worked perfectly as the hatred in Grygor's eyes boiled.

"Come, I have something I want to show you."

Her voice, low and alluring, carried the weight of a secret too precious to share with just anyone. She stood and tugged on my hand until I yielded to her.

"Lilyth…" D's voice echoed across the hall, his tone low and threatening. "Do not pester Vision. If he wants your attention, he can call for you."

Her hand squeezed mine as she turned to leave with a practiced pout, only to find my hand holding fast to hers.

"Her attention is most welcome," I partially lied, finally turning my gaze away from the Hyena to face his master. I wasn't sure how I felt about Lilyth, but her presence had become a knife that I enjoyed twisting in Grygor's mind.

"Very well," D said, a genuine smile sneaking across his lips.

Lilyth's eyes, mischievous and guarded, glimmered in the half-light as she pulled on my hand. "Come," she murmured in a tone both playful and conspiratorial, "I want to show you something… special."

Normally, I would stiffen at her touch, a conditioned reflex to memories of her earlier, more brutal caresses, but my hatred of the Hyena had overridden this response. She had just helped me further injure Grygor's pride, helped me to exact some small vengeance by amplifying the beast's suffering. Something else lingered as well. A long-neglected part of me, craving affection, found solace in her attention, regardless of what she had done before.

She led me down narrow, ancient corridors where the noise of the Dining Hall became a distant memory. The air grew cooler and thicker with the scent of old magic, as if the very walls whispered secrets of ages past. Eventually, we reached a heavy door with intricate carvings. It creaked open to reveal a chamber bathed in a soft, ethereal glow. Inside, three elegant coffins were arranged on the floor to face each other, as if caught in an eternal conversation. A macabre fountain flowing with blood was centered between them.

"Welcome to our tomb," she said, her voice soft and flirtatious, though a trace of reluctance laced each syllable. "No one other than the Master has ever seen where my sisters and I rest."

Hesitantly stepping forward, my gaze lingered on the cold, polished wood and the ornate carvings that seemed to hum with ancient magic. "I don't understand. I have seen your room before, been in your bed…" The words brought back memories that caused me to shudder.

Lilyth, feeling the reaction, squeezed my hand and pulled me closer to her.

"Yes, I have a bed, we all do. But this is different. Our private chambers are for rest and entertainment." She bit her lip before continuing. "The coffins you see here are our sanctuaries."

I watched her, my eyes narrowing in guarded curiosity. "Sanctuaries? Where I come from, such things are the final resting places of the *dead*." The term felt alien, having lost much of its meaning in the months since my arrival in D's realm.

Lilyth released my hand, then began circling a coffin, her fingers brushing against the cold, carved wood. She flashed me the same mischievous smile that had preceded so many torturous moments in the past.

"Immortality comes with certain strings attached to it. For us, one of those ties is a coffin. It heals us should we become injured and helps us reverse the effects of the passing ages."

"What effects?" I asked while circling the coffin to keep it between us.

My ignorance amused her. She laughed, not with her typical giggle, but with honest laughter that caught me off guard. She leaned across the casket, pressing her breasts together with her arms to accentuate her cleavage.

"We are immortal, but not invincible. Without the deep sleep offered by our coffins, we age as any mortal does, though at a much slower rate. Once a year, we retreat here to sleep, letting the magic reset the aging process. It's how we reclaim our youth, how we stave off the slow decay of immortality."

I folded my arms to mask my confusion. "So, you're saying that without these… rituals… you would grow old?"

Lilyth's eyes softened, and for a moment, the flirtatious veneer wavered, revealing a glimpse of the conflicted soul beneath. "Without these periods of true rest, time would ravage us. Immortality isn't a blessing when the weight of centuries shows on your skin, though some of our kind choose to age as a display of power and status. But for us Brides, rejuvenation is essential. It keeps us… alive, in more ways than one."

Her words hung between us, delicate yet potent. I searched her face for deceit or mockery, finding only the tumult of emotions she struggled to contain. Every word she spoke chipped away, just a little, at the walls I'd built to defend myself from her. I took a measured breath.

"Why share this with me?"

A slow, enigmatic smile played upon her lips as she rolled over to lie across the coffin's surface. "Because secrets bind us in ways that simple words cannot. Our little games hurt you, but such things are in my nature. Perhaps sharing this might help mend what was broken."

"You have been inside my head; I suppose I no longer possess any secrets that you do not already know." A shiver ran down my spine at the thought of her clawing through my memories, using them against me in the ways she did.

Her smile faltered as my words stretched into silence. "I know you harbor intense sorrow. Yet, it is heavier now than it was before you left. I can feel it radiating from you, even if your mind is sealed from me now. Something happened when the master sent you away with his pet."

Memories of the previous night flashed unbidden through my mind, forcing me to swallow hard. For the briefest of moments, the raw emotion shattered the barrier Hojo had taught me to create, which guarded my thoughts from unwanted observers.

When she spoke again, her words were but a whisper, betraying a vulnerability I hadn't dared imagine the woman could possess. "The beast claimed the last of your people... as he did mine."

Thin, bloody tears trickled from her eyes as the horrors of her past rose. She tried to wipe them away, leaving crimson streaks across her cheeks. "Being near you brings back feelings I thought were long dead."

She tried to turn, to hide the shame of her emotions, but I held her fast. As I cupped her face in my hand, I brushed a tear away.

Lilyth had always been a mystery, a tempest of cruelty and mischievousness. Here, though, as she revealed her secrets, I suspected that her invitation was a gesture laden with hope. It was as if she yearned for this sacred space to cleanse the dark stains of our past, to wash away the memories of torment and betrayal, just as the deep sleep in these resting places wiped the relentless marks of time from her flesh. In that moment of realization, something inside me broke, and all the barriers I had built to keep her at bay came crashing down.

I pulled her close, pressing her lips to mine, releasing my pain as I sought some sort of comfort in her arms. Lilyth let out a soft, breathless sound as she returned my embrace. In one fluid motion, she guided me down to her coffin, slipping on top of me like moonlight over water. What followed was not the standard, violent fare of previous encounters, but two lost souls looking for comfort and connection in a land where none could be found.

When we finished, our bodies were coiled together inside the cramped confines of her coffin. "I was afraid you would never forgive me," she whispered, running her fingers along the muscles of my chest. "I will not apologize for what I did; it was necessary to prepare you for this new life... but I will spend eternity licking those wounds until they heal if you will allow it."

Her words hung in the cool, sacred air of the tomb, a tentative vow in a place where immortality and decay intertwined. I wanted to believe it, to have some hope that my life would have meaning beyond violence and death, but a dark part of my soul refused.

Sensing my unease, Lilyth closed the lid of the coffin and slid atop me. "You belong here, Vision. You belong with me." She kissed me so passionately that I almost believed her. Almost.

Chapter 31
Embrace of Darkness

Eventually, Lilyth succumbed to the death-like stillness of vampiric sleep, her body rigid and cold. At first, being with her eased the churning abyss in my soul, but that peace was short-lived. While at rest, she was no more comforting than the stone walls that surrounded us. She became an exquisite corpse, a beautiful mockery of life.

Once I was sure she had succumbed to sleep, I opened the casket and slipped out to retrieve my clothes. As I glanced back at her breathless form, I couldn't help but acknowledge the paradox gnawing at me. Her presence alleviated, in many small ways, some of my deepest woes, a silent balm to my tortured psyche. Yet, lying so close in that intimate space with her stiff body was unnerving. Also, I did not completely trust that her sudden tenderness was anything but another twisted game. If her vulnerability was a clever ruse to further grind me beneath her heel, I did not intend to fall headlong into the trap.

Tired, anxious, and confused, I longed for a moment alone with my emotions, where the ghosts of trauma might finally be allowed to settle. I doubted there were many places in the Castle that I could accomplish such a feat.

I closed the lid of the casket, then pondered where I could hide — a refuge where Dracula and his cronies would never think to search. Through remote viewing, I pinpointed the current position of the room I was seeking and void-walked into it. The familiar, drip, drip, drip assaulted my ears as I entered the bleak space, with its damp, echoing corridors. What once had been my prison cell, deep beneath the Castle and just above the Doctor's laboratories, was to become a brief refuge. In its isolation, I found a perverse comfort, a place where I could reconcile with the scars of my past and finally allow myself to face the full weight of my new reality.

For starters, I found that I enjoyed being underground. The feeling of being hidden away from the waking world was comforting. The energy of the expansive caverns contrasted with the Castle's oppressive gloom. Here, there were no damnable Hyenas, Death Knights, or vampires to stalk my every move.

Overwhelmed by the crushing exhaustion of mind, body, and soul, I stumbled toward the damp straw, my knees buckling. I collapsed onto the bedding, the tension in my body sinking deep into the prickling fibers. My vision blurred at the edges as the glow receded from my eyes, swirling me into darkness. In a matter of moments, I surrendered to sleep as the maddening drip of water sang its relentless lullaby.

My rest was disturbed by dreams that twisted into feverish visions. I saw Dracula, his face contorted in a mad mixture of rage and desperation, tearing through his Castle in search of something unseen. Shadows stretched unnaturally in his wake, his fury warping the very air around him. Then came the Hyena, sniffing frantically, his movements jerky and distraught, before D's hand struck him down like a divine punishment. I felt no pity watching the beast suffer. Only when Lilyth wept blood before him, her terror palpable, did some sense of concern tug at the edges of my mind, but still I couldn't bring myself to care.

When I finally awoke, I felt as though I had joined the red-haired vampiress in the rest of the dead. My entire body hurt from sleeping on the stone floor for much longer than intended. Muscles, tendons, and bones cried out in unison as I tried to sit up, having lain dormant for much too long. I pushed myself up and, leaning against the wall, rested my head on the cold, unforgiving stone.

"I was unaware that you could teleport." D's voice shattered the air, cold and controlled, much different from the feral tone he had in my dream.

"It's a recent development," I stated with a grunt, not bothering to open my eyes just yet. When I finally parted them, releasing the green glow that allowed me to see in the dark, I saw D towering over me.

"You chose your hiding spot well. This was the last place I expected to find you."

I smiled at his response, finding some small joy in surprising the ancient vampire. "I wanted to be alone."

"Indeed," D practically spat out, not at all pleased. "I feared you had left our family. You've been missing for many nights."

Standing, I raised my hands and braced them against the ceiling, allowing me to stretch my entire body. "I was tired," I stated simply, doing my best to conceal my surprise.

The shock of how long I had slept in the cell lingered in every aching joint. Despite the dull pain, a strange lightness settled behind my ribs, as though the iron vise that had pressed against my chest for so long had loosened. The ache of despair was still there, but it had withdrawn to the recesses of my mind, dulled into something more distant — no longer an open wound but a fresh scar sensitive to the touch. Perhaps it was the rest, or perhaps I had simply grown numb to the weight of my suffering.

D studied me, unsure of what to make of the situation. "Are you ready to return to the Castle? Lilyth is beside herself with worry." He paused, his expression narrowing as he stepped closer. Then he wrinkled his nose, the faintest hint of distaste curling his lips. "You smell of stale sex and sweat. Perhaps you should bathe before seeing her."

I nodded in agreement as the unpleasant aroma found its way to my nostrils. Without hesitation, I relieved myself in the waste bucket, then transported myself to the bathing room where my first encounter with the Brides had taken place. The chamber was massive, constructed of gray and white marble, with a large pool of bubbling hot water in the center. Large columns lined the walls on either side of the artificial lagoon, stretching up to the roof high above. A magical sphere, floating below the high-arched ceiling above the bath, illuminated the space with brilliant light that danced in the steam, a stark contrast to the rest of the shadowed castle.

Moments later, D arrived. His veneer cracked, confusion etched into his features for but a moment, perplexed by my new ability to move from one place to another without a portal.

Eager to feel the healing embrace of the steaming waters, I ignored his shock and discarded my clothes with little concern for propriety, then hastened to the pool. The heat washed over my weary muscles like a soothing caress, and I allowed myself to be enveloped in its depths. When I finally emerged, I found the Brides assembled around D.

"Look, sisters, our champion has returned to us!" Ryvina said with enthusiasm when she saw me. Her tone struck me as unusual, considering she was the oldest and most reserved of Dracula's Brides.

I laughed at her, cocking a mischievous half-smile. "Champion?"

Mayna stepped forward, eyes alight with wonder. "You are the slayer of lycans. Our hero." She crouched down as she said the words, perching on the edge of the pool like a cat ready to pounce. "Even the Hand pales in comparison to your might."

I blushed at the compliments, which had caught me off guard, even though the undertones of manipulation were undeniable. Such praise was not something anyone had ever used to describe me. In the village, the labels given to me were far less flattering, usually some whispered variation of *"freak"* or *"outsider."* Even here, the only label gifted to me thus far had been *"pathetic"* by the Death Knight.

Before I had enough time to discern the thinly veiled plot, Lilyth stepped out from behind Dracula and began walking to the pool. "You've returned to me," she whispered, her voice more restrained and serious than I had ever heard before.

With a single fang pulling at her lower lip, she eased the straps of her gown from her shoulders, letting it fall to the floor. With painstaking grace, she slid into the water, gliding through it until she was once again straddling me.

"Never leave me again, Vision. Ever. You are mine."

The other Brides entered the water, encircling me with songs of praise and lament, yet they seemed to vanish. The sum of my attention was focused upon Lilyth, her yellow eyes drawing me to her until our lips met. I should have recoiled in the moment, should have pushed her away as the memory of our last encounter in the pool tried to force its way into my mind. But the memory was distant, slipping from my thoughts like water cupped in an open hand. Part of me hated how easily I succumbed to her embrace, but another hungered for her touch.

A satisfied smile pulled at the corners of Dracula's lips as he watched his plot unfold.

He was deploying a new tactic to entrench me into his world, and this one worked far better than he had hoped. The months of torment had pushed me away. The attempt to destroy my humanity using the Hyena only made it stronger. Having learned from these failures, D was leaning into his first victory over me: the praise he had showered after my first encounter with a werewolf. He altered his method, employing his Brides to cultivate within me a sense of pride in my accomplishments, to make me believe I was not just a part of the Castle but an essential and indispensable piece. He was giving me the sense of belonging that I had desired all my life.

I took the bait like a starving fish, ignoring the hook hiding in the worm. I doubt I would have even cared at that point had I known the true motives behind the Brides' plaudits.

When the sisters were finally done with me, they scrubbed me clean, showering me with compliments as they did. The three of them stayed by my side as I dried off and dressed in fresh, hooded robes of the same silken black that D had provided for me on countless occasions now. When I was once again presentable, they ushered me to a new area of the Castle where their Master sat waiting.

In a well-appointed chamber that reeked of ancient lore and whispered promises of power, D greeted me with an unexpected warmth. Spread before him lay a grand table, scattered with timeworn tomes.

"The Hand has informed me you wish to learn the language of lycans," he declared, his tone both proud and measured. "A wise pursuit. It pleases me to see you thinking like a true tactician."

My throat tightened, and for a heartbeat, pride bloomed in my chest as his words found their mark. I nodded, trying hard to mask my excitement. "Mastering their tongue would allow me to turn their secrets back against them. To that end, I would like to learn the languages of all our enemies."

D's expression barely changed, but I saw the flicker of triumph in his eyes. He had me, and he knew it. The word "our" escaped my lips without thought, but the vampire lord seized upon it like a shark sensing blood in the water.

Dracula pulled out a seat beside him and gestured for me to join. As the Brides turned to leave, I reached for Lilyth and held her near. She cast me a questioning glance but said nothing as I sat, drawing her close while I listened as D began his lesson. If she had once been merely smitten with me, now the vampiress was enamored.

The other Brides looked on in dumbfounded disbelief as D, oblivious to Lilyth's presence, launched into the basics of werewolf linguistics.

Chapter 32
Beneath the Frozen Moon

The Lycan language was complex and therefore difficult to master, consisting of barks, growls, whimpers, snarls, and even facial movements that relayed messages an outsider would never notice. D patiently worked with me as I learned, seeming to enjoy having a pupil worthy of his time. After the first few weeks of tutoring, the Death Knight delivered us a captive werewolf to practice speaking with. The beast was enchanted, removing any threat of it attacking, lying, or otherwise interfering with our work.

The Brides were less than thrilled with the creature being in their wing of the Castle, and Lilyth opted not to join these sessions. Instead, she would wait for Dracula to finish my nightly instructions so she could rattle off endless questions about what I learned. While D viewed this as an annoyance, I welcomed it. Repeating the information helped to cement it into my mind, and in short order, I was able to understand a great deal of what the beast said. Much like the Hyena, the werewolf could speak the common language while in its half-animal form, allowing it to communicate with me in both dialects.

As time passed, D was forced to leave me alone for days at a time; his prolonged absences had drawn suspicion from his court. To prevent the vampire nobles from discovering my existence too soon, he spent more time in his throne room, entangled in the ceaseless political machinations of the undead. Fortunately, Grygor remained at his side during these sessions, sparing me from the agony of facing him. My time in the cell dulled the ache in my heart, but the sight of Grygor rekindled it into a searing and blinding fury.

The Death Knight was often present at D's meetings, though his absence rarely raised an eyebrow. Unlike the Hyena, who never strayed far from his master, the Hand of Vengeance was the kingdom's sword. He was expected to be absent while dealing with the Lycan threat, rival vampire clans, or the countless horrors that lurked beyond the borders. His perceived duties provided the perfect cover, allowing him to continue my training in secret whenever D was unavailable.

During the rare nights when both D and the Death Knight were at court, I spent my time with Lilyth. She joined in on my education when she wasn't busy using me to fulfill her carnal desires. As weeks turned to months, the sting of her torments faded to a distant memory. I barely recalled the horrors she inflicted upon me, so consumed was I with the intoxicating comfort of having someone to call my own. I had even given up my private quarters, preferring to spend my days wrapped in her frigid flesh as we slept in her room.

Lilyth took it upon herself to teach me the intricacies of Vampiric script, adding yet another layer to my growing education. We frequented the room where D first began instructing me in the Lycan tongue, as it was lined with towering bookshelves. Each was filled with ancient tomes detailing the vast lineage of Dracula's dark dynasty.

I devoured everything the combined knowledge of my tutors offered, a relentless seeker of truth. Every spare moment alone was spent buried in texts, absorbing their secrets like a parched soul drinking deep from an endless well.

When the time came that D obtained a reprieve from the lower court, winter had set in outside the Castle walls. Most of the nobles had returned to their various manors and minor castles that dotted D's lands, adjourning the court for the next few months until the arrival of Spring. Dracula's mood, which had grown irritable from having to deal with his squabbling highborn underlings, was much more favorable as the nights grew longer and snow blanketed his lands.

Winter wrapped the Castle in an embrace of silence, the kind that only the dead and the eternal could appreciate. The cold did not affect Dracula, but he reveled in the season as one might a beloved symphony. The moonlight on the ice, the brittle stillness of the air, the way his land lay frozen beneath his gaze — it all pleased him in ways he never admitted aloud.

To indulge his love of these frigid nights, we began to hold our classes outdoors on a balcony overlooking the valley below the mountaintop where the Castle was perched. The vantage point offered breathtaking views of his lands, stretching for miles, and was even more awe-inspiring when the moon was full. The remote location of the balcony also helped ensure prying eyes wouldn't be able to discern my presence, though D also cloaked the area in magic just to be sure.

Why he kept my existence a secret from his people continued to puzzle me. However, I accepted his explanations and moved on. If he believed there were enemies out there who would hunt me, then I was inclined to believe him. My discovery of an assassin in the Castle and my subsequent saving of his life validated D's suspicions. Regardless of any threats, I finally felt a sense of belonging in my new home, a happiness I hadn't felt since long before my guardian's passing. I didn't much care if the rest of the world knew of me anymore.

On this particular night, D, the Brides, and I were all out on the balcony watching the moon rise, a giant yellow orb casting an eerie glow upon the land below. I had learned the intricate dialects of most of the higher-echelon Lycan clans by this point, enough to interpret what they were saying in any event. Speaking the language was a different story, but D didn't see any point in my wasting time on that aspect. Instead of teaching me to speak Lycan, he had begun to instruct me in his native Vampiric tongue, the official language of the Castle.

Until now, everyone I had encountered since being abducted had been speaking the language of my lands, which, unbeknownst to me, was quite alien to them. D had meticulously studied the vernacular of my old home to communicate with me, absent spellwork.

The Brides were forced to rely on magical means to speak and understand my words, as was the Hyena (though I doubt he realized it) and the captive werewolf. The Death Knight's curse enabled him to speak and comprehend nearly any language he encountered, though the reason for this was never disclosed to me.

Having put that much effort into learning my language was a testament to how important Dracula thought I was, as he was rarely moved to such extreme lengths for anyone.

I had picked up on Lycan with speed, but Vampiric was a hurdle I was struggling to overcome. The going was slow and had tested D's patience when he first began my instructions on it. He'd been a coiled spring while dealing with his court, but now, considerably calmer, he was far more understanding of my struggles to follow his words.

Once the moon was nearing its peak, D settled down and began going over the basic pronunciations with me for the thousandth time. Each time I would get a word wrong, the Brides would giggle madly, which would cause D a great deal of irritation. However, the four of them had been drinking Elven blood wine this night while we stared in wonder at the moonrise, so they were more than a little inebriated. This made D's lesson all the more entertaining to his wives and frustrating for me, as he was ever so slightly slurring his own words, which were hard enough for me to grasp already. To compound my issue, I, too, had consumed a hefty amount of alcohol.

I had drunk liquor with Dracula on many occasions, but I had only seen him affected by it once or twice. Yet, as the night deepened, he was showing the effects more, and it was not at all what I would have expected from him. He was laughing at my blunders alongside his wives, which in turn had me chuckling.

The levity would prove short-lived.

The night shattered. One moment, Lilyth's laughter mixed with mine — boozy, indulgent, alive. The next, a whisper of air sliced through the revelry.

A wet, sickening sound followed by a thump and a gasp.

Lilyth staggered. Her eyes, wide and disbelieving, lowered to the black shaft lodged in her chest. Her fingers twitched toward it, as if to pluck it free, but no strength remained. The wineglass in her hand tumbled first, shattering against the stone. Then, she followed, crumpling like a marionette with severed strings

For a heartbeat, the world held its breath.

An assassin had infiltrated our little gathering; D's intoxication had let the intruder slip past the vampire's senses undetected, as mine had dulled my precognitive abilities. There, standing on the edge of the balcony wall, was a vampire cloaked in black garb in the same style as the one I had seen in my vision months before.

Dracula moved before Lilyth's blood had even touched the stone. His snarl was thunder, his wrath a tempest. With a single, violent gesture, fire roared from his fingertips, turning the night into an inferno aimed at the assassin's perch.

As the intruder dodged D's magical onslaught, more arrows rained down on us from above. There was more than one assassin. My tendrils convulsed into life of their own accord, erupting from the pink flesh of my back and lashing out with a predatory instinct as they intercepted the incoming projectiles. In a burst of brutal precision, they smashed the missiles midair, shattering them into splintered fragments before any could close in to threaten us.

A second volley of arrows cut through the night, but before they could strike, the air split apart. A portal yawned open, vomiting forth the Death Knight and his skeletal warriors. Grygor followed in a blur of motion, his bestial form bristling with anticipation.

"Vision…" Lilyth said weakly before slipping beyond the realm of consciousness. The vampiress lay sprawled on the frozen stone, her pale skin losing color by the second.

Something deep inside me snapped in that moment. Fury, cold and unrelenting, coiled in my gut like a vast maw opening. The Void stirred, delighted, and my body obeyed its call.

Shadows slithered from me like living things, curling around my limbs, stretching hungrily toward the attackers. My bones twisted and lengthened with agonizing force; my skin darkened, thickening like blackened tar. In excruciating agony, my eyes ruptured, replaced by a single, bulbous orb that pulsed with an eldritch light. The world around me bled into a haze, but the sensations that followed cut through the fog like jagged glass, each pulse of my hatred sharper than the last.

I felt the assassin's fear before I saw it. A delicious, trembling hesitation. He was already dead. He just didn't know it yet.

"Get her someplace safe," I ordered, my voice cutting through the stunned silence of the Brides. Their wide eyes traced the remnants of my transformation, horror and awe warring in their expressions.

The assassin was likewise taken aback by my sudden change and paid dearly for it. Before he could recover, I impaled him with a tendril, lifting him off the ground and bringing him close enough that the glow from my eye illuminated his masked face. With a single twitch, the tendril arced, splitting the vampire in half from the groin up to his neck. When the remnants splattered on the tiles, I brought my massive, clawed foot down upon his head, sending a steaming spray of gore across the frozen stone.

The scene before me was one of total chaos. To my right, the Death Knight was engaged in swordplay with an assassin who was dual-wielding venomous black daggers. The contingent of skeletal warriors was likewise embroiled in melee combat with a troop of hitmen. Whoever sent the assassin was not playing any game; they intended to eliminate D and his rule. The sheer number of soldiers who had scaled the mighty walls of the Castle was proof of this.

Despite the flow of attackers swarming the terrace, there was still a unit of archers on the rooftops above our position, raining down poison-tipped arrows. As I turned my attention to them, ready to leap, the air in the courtyard crackled with gathering energy. D thrust his hand forward, letting loose a bolt of lightning that struck the closest archer in the chest and then arced through him to strike several more.

Dracula's voice boomed, drowning out the sounds of battle. "Let no one escape! *They've seen him!*"

Obeying his master's command, Grygor leaped onto the rooftop, transforming from human to hyena form midair. The werecreature then launched himself toward the remaining bowmen, as they pelted him with their projectiles. Even as the arrows struck home, the Hyena seemed unaffected. They either didn't hurt him, or he simply didn't care.

Deciding the Death Knight and his soldiers could handle the ground forces, I followed the Hyena, leaping up to the roof and sending my tendrils out to flay the invaders. Side by side, we tore through them — not as allies, never that, but instruments of carnage wielded by the same bloody hand. Grygor's claws sang through flesh, spraying the rooftop red. My tendrils lashed out like whips, rending armor and bone alike.

We fought as one, despite the loathing that curled like a living thing between us. The rooftop became a slaughterhouse, a silent, begrudging pact forming between us in the language of war. For one brutal, blood-drenched moment, we were not enemies.

We were death.

The Hyena, drenched in blood and bits of flesh, pointed to one of the sky bridges above us, connecting the castle proper to a floating tower. "Their commander is up there," he said, his voice lacking any of its usual taunting tones, "I can smell 'im." He was in kill mode, as was I, and we were both determined to satiate our need for vengeance.

"I will handle him," I said, void-walking to the bridge.

I materialized before the coward who was hiding behind a veil of magic. His illusion was worthless. My glowing, ovate eye pierced through the deception with ease. Clad in ebony armor, his form was nearly as dark as the void-forged skin that now encased me.

"The rumors are true," he whispered, "Dracula has found you…" Then, without hesitation, he hurled himself off the walkway, plummeting toward the distant forest valley far below the Castle's perch.

Blindly, I lunged after him, driven by a singular purpose — he would pay for daring to defile my home and for spilling Lilyth's blood.

As the ground rushed up to meet us, the armor-clad vampire morphed into a giant bat and changed direction, gliding away from the Castle. Being so single-mindedly focused on killing the man, I didn't even notice that I, too, had altered course, following the bat parallel to the ground and gaining speed. In a matter of moments, I was within striking range, unleashing a tendril through the air and slicing clean through the oversized rodent's wing, severing it at the shoulder.

The bat plummeted like a stone, hurtling toward the forest below before slamming into the frozen ground with bone-rattling impact. I descended beside the intruder, landing gently on my feet as his twisted form writhed and reshaped, the grotesque shift returning him to his humanoid state, minus an arm. Blood gushed from the wound, seeping through the snow and staining it red. Concussed, bones shattered from the brutal fall, he was little more than a broken husk at my feet. Incapacitated and helpless.

Standing over the mangled man, I allowed my tendrils to extend into the air, then shot them down, spearing the invader in multiple places, careful to avoid any vital organs. The tips of my tendrils drove through his armor with ease and burrowed deep into the ground to pin him down. The taste of his blood flowed up my tendrils, and they twitched with delight, compounding the assassin's agony. To his credit, the villain merely grunted, gritting his teeth and refusing to cry out in pain.

I poised a tendril above his heart, preparing to serve the man a true death.

"Do it!" he hissed, coughing up blood as he did.

Dracula landed beside me with an impact that shook the ground, rattling snow from the surrounding trees.

"Stop. Do not kill him," he commanded. "We shall give him to Hojo for interrogation. He will extract what we need, piece by piece if necessary."

The broken vampire flinched at the name, and deservedly so. While Dracula's rivals feared the Hyena and his particular style of violence, they were terrified of his mad scientist. Watching helplessly as their families were torn to shreds and otherwise despoiled by Grygor was one thing. The threat of being surgically altered over and over again for eternity was something else.

Reflections:

Even after more than a year with my new family, I had not learned to revel in cruelty. But this time was different.

The knowledge of what awaited the assassin filled me with a dark satisfaction, and I savored his terror like the finest wine. I wanted him to endure every torment the Doctor could devise and more. Given the horrors I had witnessed in the depths of that accursed laboratory,

I had no doubt Hojo would make my desires a reality in the most exquisite fashion.

Chapter 33
The Blood Price

The battle on the terrace hadn't lasted long following my leap of faith. The Hand's forces had swept through the invaders with ruthless precision, leaving no survivors in their wake. Once he had ensured no forces were waiting to launch a secondary attack, the Death Knight arrived to take possession of my captive. The attackers had placed all their bets on a single strike force and failed miserably.

"Who were they?" I asked D, my voice quivering with rage.

As his gaze rose to meet my glowing eye, he spoke with measured fury. "A rival family." He sneered, clenching his fist so hard that blood trickled from it. "They dare attack my home." Dracula's eyes were engorged with blood now, his fangs extended.

"No. They attacked our home," I said, words dripping with venom, "and we are going to make them pay dearly for it."

The vampire soaked in my words and smiled viciously. "Yes, we will."

I glanced back at the Castle, then stepped through the Void and reappeared beside Lilyth, who lay unconscious in her ornate coffin with the other Brides encircling her. They had removed the arrow, a lethal implement with a poisoned tip engineered specifically to kill Dracula, and administered a host of magical potions to neutralize the venom. The arrow had missed her heart, a single stroke of luck that spared her immediate demise. Yet, for Lilyth, a much younger and more vulnerable vampire, the lingering poison still coursed through her veins, threatening to bring about a true and irreversible death.

Ryvina and Mayna looked at me in stunned dismay, unsettled by my eldritch appearance.

"We couldn't wait to seal her coffin until you arrived. She needs to sleep," Ryvina stammered, her voice heavy with sorrow.

To help calm her, I shifted back into my human form.

"I understand. Thank you," I said with a faint smile that barely concealed my sorrow. Sliding my fingers across the intricately carved wood, I choked back the emotions that threatened to pour from my eyes. "How long will she remain asleep?"

"Until she is healed," Ryvina said. "It could take days, months, or even years. The wound was nearly fatal."

Ryvina rose and placed a reassuring hand on my chest. "She'll be alright; she just needs to rest."

I clasped her hand and squeezed, holding it against my chest. "For this, they will pay. I swear, I will make them pay."

In that moment, her face flickered with a green light; a telltale sign my eyes had betrayed the fury I tried so hard to hide.

The vampiress stepped onto her tiptoes, leaning in to kiss my cheek. "Make them suffer."

I nodded and stepped from the Brides into the laboratory, void-walking through the oppressive gloom. There, Hojo was already engrossed in his grim work on the new subject, the wretched figure strapped to an upright surgical table. The vampire's arm, severed by one of my tendrils, had yet to show any sign of regeneration, though that was merely a prelude to his suffering. His ebony armor had been torn away, exposing a tapestry of wounds that likewise refused to heal.

D, Grygor, and the Death Knight were all there watching the Doctor as he worked, slicing away thin strips of flesh. "Vision's tendrils have left quite the impact, have they not?" Hojo said, more to himself than to his audience.

Back in my avatar, I took my place behind Hojo as he worked. I stared a hole through the assassin. "Has he said anything?" I asked.

Hojo paused mid-incision and turned to me. "No, he has not, but he will." He returned to his work, taking samples from the wounds that refused to close and placing them in an assortment of vials.

"He is well-trained," D stated flatly, "but Hojo is quite talented at forcing his subjects to spill their guts."

The assassin had not so much as grunted in pain as the Doctor continued his dissection, his jaw clenched shut as he glared into my eye. Unfortunately for the captive, his struggle to remain silent was entirely in vain. D had gathered intel on the previous intruder after the Death Knight had split him in twain, but that wasn't the information that would damn his bloodline. As the vampire held my gaze, his eyes betrayed him.

I plunged into his mind, tearing through his memories like claws through parchment. Faces blurred past — elders in crimson robes, whispered orders in dark corridors, a map marked with our defenses. Then, a fortress in the north, its towers scraping against a sky choked with frost.

Once I had gathered enough details to identify the family and their home, I broke eye contact and relayed what I had seen to D. As I spoke, the helpless whelp wailed, his spirit breaking as I revealed his guarded secrets.

Time and space bent to my will as I cast my mind into the castle from which the assassin originated. Satisfied with what I saw, I withdrew my gaze and smiled at D, giving him an experience few entities in existence would ever get from my eldritch form and live to speak of.

"They haven't learned of their failure yet. If we move quickly, we can strike before they have time to prepare."

"The Sanglant family," D spat, "a rising brood of vampires who recently aligned themselves with the Alvah." Dracula turned to the Hyena, whose coarse fur was still matted with blood from the archers he had ravaged. "Go see them to their well-deserved fate."

"I'm going with him," I declared, leaving no room for debate.

Dracula's eyes narrowed. "I made it clear that your existence must remain secret. You stay here; Grygor will carry out our vengeance." He turned back to his pet, preparing to open a portal for the beast, but I was not about to let the bastard go alone.

My resolve hardened as I stepped forward. "I am aware of your decree. However, it makes no difference if they learn of my existence if none survive to speak of it."

The Hyena, smiling like a lunatic, reached up and slapped my shoulder with a chuckle. "Tha's the spirit. Le's go have sum fun."

Unaccustomed to having his authority challenged so brazenly, D bore holes through us with his eyes. I was perhaps the first person in a thousand years to openly question an order from the ancient vampire.

Aware that I had overstepped, I posed a question that Dracula likewise hadn't been asked in centuries: "Do you trust me?"

For a split second, D looked as though I had slapped him in the face, completely taken aback. Dracula was known for many things; trusting others was not among them.

"Allow me to do this. Let me avenge Lilyth and the insult to our home. Let me kill them all."

He stood in silence for many moments, fighting his desire to keep me hidden away like some secret, coveted treasure. Finally, he nodded. "No survivors. *None.*"

With the permission granted, I grabbed the Hyena by the scruff of his mane and void-walked us to our target: a fortification deep in a snow-covered evergreen forest far to the north of D's realm. The moon was still high in the sky, casting shadows through the woods to conceal our sudden arrival.

I set the Hyena down in the snow with a crunch and slapped his back hard enough to send him careening forward. "We're going to play a game, you and I."

Grygor's lycanthropic features betrayed his

sudden fear as I echoed the very words he had spoken before escorting me back to my former home, a place marred by atrocities that had driven a deep wedge between us.

"Wha's that?" His voice was a low, cautious growl, betraying his wariness of a potential attack.

I smiled, revealing long, needle-like teeth. "Who's the better killer?"

"Tha's my favorite game," Grygor said, then laughed, the relief readily noticeable in his tone. Without another word, he ran to the edge of the fortification and leapt up onto the battlements with a single bound, landing on a guard and spilling his entrails onto the icy stone.

The serene sounds of the night erupted in chaos as the watchtowers rang out in alarm, soldiers rushing out to meet the threat. It became apparent that Grygor had done this before, leaping from one soldier to another and killing them with little effort. His antics were impressive to watch, but they weren't the reason I was here. I found my target and void-walked to it, materializing in the castle's throne room.

The nobles gathered there gasped in unison at my sudden arrival, instantly aware that the victory celebrations they were engaged in were premature at best. Dozens of vampires were in attendance, standing or sitting around the grand room, celebrating the supposed death of Dracula until the moment I appeared. An elder vampire, the head of the Sanglant clan, sat on an elevated platform, his throne towering over the gathering below him.

A small throng of knights stood guard at the throne and sprang into action before their master could even utter a command. The efforts proved futile as my tendrils flayed their armor and flesh, exploring the soft, squishy meat beneath while releasing clouds of gore into the air. A blood-curdling shriek pierced the chamber, a high-born vampiress screaming in terror as what was left of the troop fell with a splatter to the floor.

I fixed my gaze on the vampire lord, a cold sneer twisting my lips to reveal my nightmarish teeth. "Lilyth sends her regards," I said, each syllable a harbinger of doom.

In one fluid, lethal spin, my tendrils lashed out in a deadly spiral, a pinwheel of retribution. The crowd went silent, a frozen tableau of horror. Then, a wet sound, soft and obscene. A noble reached for his throat, but his hands met only air as his head tumbled free, landing with a sopping slap against the marble. One by one, they collapsed, pieces peeling away like rotted fruit.

The vampire primus alone remained unharmed. I wanted him to see his family's downfall and understand that I was going to strip away all traces of their existence from this world. From his lofty position, he stared down at me in disbelief, watching as his throne room filled with the blood of his court. I allowed him a handful of moments to absorb the scene, letting him wallow in the carnage. It didn't take long for the shock in his eyes to transform into a blind rage, his features morphing into a half-bat monstrosity as it did.

He attacked me from his perch, launching a bevy of spells designed to disintegrate the most powerful foes an ancient vampire might ever face. The first wave of magic hit me with the force of a hurricane, slamming into my body with a thunderous crash so powerful it shook the walls of the castle and dislodged more than a few stones. My glistening black skin hardened against the onslaught, but the spell was potent enough to ravage my senses, the first outside stimulus to do so since I had learned to summon it.

Agony lanced through me. The magic coiled around my ribs, burrowing deep, trying to unmake me from the inside. For a moment, the fire in my veins warred with the eldritch hunger that made up my flesh, but I was unlike any foe the lord had faced before. I did not break; I consumed.

My void-born flesh absorbed most of the impact, drinking up the released energy as my vampiric family supped on blood. Ultimately, the vampire's attack had only fed my form, but the process was not a pleasant one. My flesh screamed where the spells had struck, as though thousands of needles were being forced into my skin. However, visibly, no damage was evident.

The room behind me was not so lucky. It ignited into a raging inferno, as much of the vampire's fury-driven blitz of casting had missed, instead striking the tables and tapestries around me.

The Sanglant progenitor, his magic proving useless, swooped down, deciding to use his fangs and claws in a last attempt to kill me.

I met his charge with a single tendril, impaling it through the soft flesh under his jaw, up through his brain, and out the top of his skull. The vampire lord twitched as his blood trickled down my tendril, dripping from it and mixing with the ocean of crimson pooled at my feet. In less time than it took to undress Lilyth, I had slain every entity in the throne room, including an ancient vampire who could have razed an entire city with the magic he had cast at me.

I looked on in wonder as the vampire's body shriveled, sinking in upon itself as death claimed the monster. In a matter of moments, the man's form was reduced to a skeleton, which liquefied before my eye, leaving behind a black pool of ichor amongst the garments he had been wearing. The throne room was aflame, and a shimmer from within the gloop caught my attention: the vampire lord's signet ring.

Down into the bubbling muck, I claimed my first trophy. The ridiculously oversized, solid gold ring, encrusted with rubies and bearing his fallen house's emblem. Seeing this trinket, still dripping with its former owner, made me smile. To prevent my prize from melting in the intense heat and flames, I clasped the ring tightly in my hand.

Content, knowing that the lord of the manor was now nothing more than a memory soon to be forgotten, I stepped out of the throne room, allowing the flames to caress my skin as I walked through them. The vampire's magic had been potent enough to hurt, but the inferno wasn't enough to even give me a sensation of warmth.

My desire for retribution was far from satiated, so I carved a path through the castle, slaying everything in my wake. None could hide from me, no matter where they ran to seek shelter. My paranormal perception highlighted every living and nonliving entity there, regardless of its concealment. Tendrils slashed through stone walls and into secret passages, turning the vampires hiding there into a puree of meat and blood.

As I ascended into the upper levels of the castle, my relentless tide of vengeance had long swept away any trace of humanity. Every act of brutal retribution had numbed my emotions until I operated on pure, instinctive wrath. Each savage strike against the vampire bloodline was executed without remorse. It wasn't until I stepped into a room filled with pureblood younglings, their faces smeared with streaks of crimson, that I was forced to pause. In that instant, the remnants of my humanity surged back.

The room was packed with toys, among them everything from porcelain dolls to wooden swords, and seemed out of place compared to the rest of the castle. The only sign this room was connected to the horrors outside was a slave gasping for air on the floor, her lungs ravenously searching for air to enrich the blood that no longer flowed through her veins. She was covered in bite marks from the clutch of vampirlings who were now huddled in the far corner. With one last gasp, the light in the poor girl's eyes flickered out.

My gaze drifted from the innocent girl who lay dead at my feet to the ravenous pack of monsters who had begun crying, the blood they had drained from her now streaming down their cheeks. I knew they had to die, told myself they deserved to die for killing the youth growing cold on the stone tiles. But I couldn't get myself to move forward.

Lost in my moral battle, I did not notice Grygor coming up behind me until he slapped my shoulder, snapping me back to reality.

"Blimey, you made a bloody mess down there!" He laughed as he said it, quite pleased with my trail of carnage. "Oh, what 'ave we 'ere? Young uns." The Hyena licked his massive, gore-soaked chops, salivating. He elbowed me in the ribs before stepping forward, "Mas'r's orders. No survivors."

"I will not kill them," I said, refusing to take

part in what was to come, even knowing each one was hundreds of years older than I.

Looking over his shoulder as he continued to move closer to the ball of terrified fledglings, he shot me a sadistic grin. "I will."

I turned and walked out of the room, unwilling to stay and see what the Hyena was about to do. As I stepped into the Void, eager to escape the burning castle, I heard a scream.

Chapter 34
Specters of the Fallen

Portions of the castle had begun to collapse thanks to the fire started by the elder Sanglant during our brief exchange before the Hyena emerged from the chaos. I scanned the wreckage using my enhanced vision, searching for the telltale glows of life and undeath. The stench of charred flesh and bitter smoke mingled with the metallic tang of spilled blood as corpses lay scattered across the battlements and courtyard, each a silent testament to the night's brutal reckoning. Every inch of the fortress, from the basement to the highest tower, was a grisly monument to D's wrath. True to our word, there were no survivors.

We stood there watching the castle burn as if it were nothing more than a candle until the sun rose.

Once the ruins were reduced to smoldering ashes, Grygor finally broke the silence.

"Good job 'n there," the Hyena said as he slowly licked away the evidence of his atrocities from his body. "You're a real *killer*."

His praise sent a shiver racing along my spine, the hairs on my arms prickling as revulsion mingled with a bitter pride. Of all the monsters I had met since joining the ranks of D's household, Grygor was undoubtedly the worst. The Death Knight was a seemingly emotionless, cold-as-ice slayer, but he didn't relish in cruelty, so far as I could tell anyway. He simply killed without thought or feeling in the most efficient manner possible. The Brides were twisted, as evidenced in the weeks of torment I suffered at their hands, but even they had limits on how far they would go. The Hyena had no such restraints; he not only delighted in the suffering of others but was excited by it in ways too vile to name.

As uncomfortable as his praise made me feel, Grygor's assessment of my performance was correct. I had walked into the stronghold fully intent on murdering everything within its walls and had nearly succeeded in doing so. I may not have tortured my victims as the Hyena was so fond of doing, but I did take a great deal of joy in sending them to the afterlife. They had attacked my home, hurt Lilyth, and, in the process, threatened my new life. In turn, I had become the very killer that Dracula had wanted all along.

It wasn't until I reached the room of vampire sucklings that I paused in my mission, my moral code making a grand, triumphant return. It would likely have been better for them had I finished the job rather than leaving them to the damn beast beside me, considering what he had done at my previous home.

I didn't want to think about that, what he had done, or why it had taken him so long to leave the ruins. Better to let the truth of it burn away with the castle and be forgotten altogether. Unfortunately, my mind was not ready to release me from the guilt over what I knew had transpired.

Haunted by the memories of what I had done, I couldn't bear another moment amid the ruins. With a heavy heart, I grasped the Hyena's arm and transported us home, leaving the smoldering tomb to its lonely vigil.

We arrived back in the laboratory where Hojo had stripped the would-be assassin of his flesh, revealing the muscle beneath. He hadn't snipped the vampire's vocal cords as he had with the previous experiment I had seen, yet the man was still barely making a sound, having already screamed himself to the point of being unable to continue doing so.

D stood at the Doctor's side, watching as he inserted a tube into a lacerated intestine, siphoning the juices from within out into a container. The subject's lidless eyes were completely crimson, and his fangs fully extended and ready to strike were it not for the straps holding him in place. Hojo was draining the vamp of every drop of blood, one of the worst forms of torture that could be inflicted upon such a creature of the night.

A vampire's need for blood extends far beyond mere sustenance; it is an addiction beyond compare. No drug in any world could match the rush a vampire would get when feeding. However, this need was a double-edged sword. Without the blood of the living coursing through its veins, a vampire would suffer withdrawals that words simply cannot describe. Eventually, this would cause it to devolve into a feral creature no better than a common ghoul. By flaying the assassin, Hojo had ensured all of the blood it had stored would seep out. To complete the process, he was draining the vampire's digestive system.

If that weren't enough, he was pumping a thick, noxious liquid into the captive's veins, which seemed to counteract most of the vampire's regenerative abilities. He would not heal, nor would he die, stuck in a bloodless, fleshless state until Hojo deemed otherwise.

D sensed our arrival and, without turning from the diabolical scene, which was spread out across multiple tables before him, began to speak. "I take it you were successful?"

My voice came out even as my stomach

churned with revulsion. "The Sanglant family is no more." Yet as I spoke, each deliberate slice and guttural sound from Hojo's work stirred a bitter cocktail of satisfaction and dread within me — reminders of the monster I was becoming. I had assumed Hojo would inflict unspeakable horrors upon the assassin and was even pleased with the idea, but I did not know just how maddeningly awful they would be.

Dracula was likewise enthralled with Hojo as he meticulously carved away bit after bit, inserting tubes into random organs to ensure his subject remained undead and not actually dead.

"And there were no survivors?" D asked, his voice low and detached.

"None. Everyone was eliminated, and the fortress was destroyed." The corner of my eye twitched ever so slightly as I said this, betraying the conflict within I was struggling to overcome.

"What became of Lord Sanglant? I trust he met his deserved end?" Dracula once again refrained from turning to face me as he spoke, his voice eerily distant and devoid of any emotion.

The Hyena, who somehow looked even more menacing in the sickly orange light radiating from flameless glass orbs attached to the cavern ceiling, spoke up. "Vision 'ere killed him nice 'n proper... 'e made quite a mess of his court, too. Blood 'n guts for miles." A venomous sneer spread across Grygor's face as he slapped my shoulder once again. "I told ya 'e was a *killer*. 'e just needed the proper motivation."

D's eyes were intently fixed upon the wounds I had inflicted upon the assassin, still readily evident despite all the Doctor had done to him.

"You killed an elder vampire *and* his entire court? Single-handedly?" Finally, Dracula turned from the mutilated remnants of the assassin to look at me. His jaw hung open, fangs revealed, almost as if he were salivating over the events transpiring in the room.

I told him what had happened in the rival lord's throne room, how I had killed the entire gathered court with a single spin, how the Sanglant patriarch had tried to attack me and failed miserably. D's eyebrows raised as I explained that the magical assault did not affect me at all. I withheld the fact that the attack had actually hurt, not wanting to diminish my victory.

As I spoke, Hojo set his utensils down, listening intently as my story unfolded. "Fascinating," he whispered, awestruck by my ability to take the full brunt of an elder vampire's wrath and come out completely unscathed mere days after accessing my avatar.

D simply nodded in agreement, studying my ebony flesh as if it were some grand prize whose true value far exceeded the initial estimates.

"Well done, my friend," D said, still lost in a trance. "Go get some rest; you have earned it." With that, he slowly twisted back around to stare at the assassin once again.

I was thankful to be dismissed, as Dracula's strange behavior was unsettling. Besides, I wanted to speak with the Brides and let them know their sister had been avenged in full. But first, I wanted more than anything to wash away the troubles of the night, so I slipped through the Void and into the bathing room.

Reverting to my human form, I slid into the water, eager to feel its steaming embrace once again. I leaned my head back against the marble and closed my eyes, only to feel hands suddenly upon my chest.

"Did you avenge us?" Mayna asked, her form gliding through the steam parallel to the water.

Ryvina was beside her sister, hanging upside down from some unseen perch. "Did you kill them all?"

"They are dead," I responded, closing my eyes once again.

"Our hero," they said in almost perfect unison before slipping into the water next to me, bringing their heads to rest on my chest. Neither made any move to initiate a sexual encounter; they were after more human comforts that they knew would not come from their husband. They simply wanted to be held. So did I.

Together, we sat in the massive pool for hours, lamenting our losses in the comfort of each other's arms.

***

After secreting the signet ring away in my quarters, I slept beside Lilyth's coffin in the hopes of being by her side when she awoke. Unfortunately, there were no signs of life from within the healing tomb. The vampiress's sleep was that of the dead, and she would not stir from it for much longer than I had hoped. The assassin's poison had done its work well.

My sleep brought me little in the way of rest, disturbed by a torrent of nightmarish visions of the Hyena indulging his dark desires. My guilt for leaving the vampirlings to such a hellish fate was thick and deep, which eventually manifested itself in another image, one in which I would wade hip-deep in a churning ocean of blood. I found myself standing in the endless glistening sea of crimson, Sight hovering just above the waves, staring at me through a thousand shifting eyes.

"So, you are my father."

"I did not seed you with mortal procreation, for such feeble notions are lost amid the cosmic gulfs. Rather, I unfurled the labyrinthine tapestry of the cosmos, threading a portal through the maddening fabric of existence. I am the ineffable catalyst that rent asunder the veil between realms — a key that unlatched the cyclopean door within the conjoined void of your mothers' womb." The words slithered through the

darkness, each syllable a maddening whisper of cosmic despair, as if the very stars trembled at the utterance. ***"Through that gaping maw of eldritch chaos, your form was exhaled into this wretched physical plane."***

I sat in uncomfortable silence, attempting to unravel the cryptic riddle as the countless orbs shifted in and out of Sight's gray flesh, studying me. The longer I pondered the being's words, the more frustrated I became. "I don't understand. How can I have multiple mothers?

"No mortal woman, not even a deity, could endure the unspeakable burden of birthing your form. To wrench you from the silent void and cast you into this realm, it required a triad of forces beyond mortal knowledge, the dread Fates themselves, ancient arbiters of destiny and decay."

The Fates. When I was a child, my guardian told me stories of these entities, of how they would sew the destinies of men, empires, and even the Gods themselves. She spoke of them with great reverence, demanding they be held with the highest of honors. Now I knew why.

"Why don't they visit me in my visions like you do?" I asked, the aching pit of loneliness in my stomach widening to an unbearable girth.

Sight's voice resounded, drenched in unfathomable indifference. ***They lie in eternal*** *silence. Your coming into being was the death knell that wrenched them from the fragile confines of the physical realm."*

The knowledge hit me like a war hammer. I had always suspected my parents were dead, but I did not dare to think it was my doing. Not only had I killed my mothers, but I was somehow created through magic that I couldn't even begin to understand. The revelations only served to deepen the expanse of sorrow in which I was struggling to stay afloat.

"This bothers you?" Sight said, slightly perplexed. *"The Fates were, they are, and they shall be again. Such is the cycle of existence. You know this."* His voice seemed to bypass my ears, speaking directly into my soul as he said these final words, imparting some ancient truth that was just beyond my grasp.

"Why am I here?" I whispered, looking up to peer into Sight's fathomless eye, desperate for an answer about my place in this maddening cosmos, only to find the eldritch presence had dissipated into nothingness.

In an instant, the sanguine echoes of my past deeds faded, replaced by an eerie silence. No longer was I wading through the carnage of my victims; instead, I found myself drawn into a realm of transcendent stillness.

I was lying upon an ice-cold marble floor

beneath the watchful gaze of the marble queen; a regal effigy whose stoic expression offered no solace, only an unyielding reminder of what was lost. The transition was disconcerting: one moment, the writhing chaos of cosmic visions, and the next, the pristine sanctuary of Dracula's missing lover's cathedral enveloped me in its solemn embrace.

This, however, was no phantom or dream; I was physically present, my body inexplicably transported from the stark, haunting vigil beside Lilyth's coffin to this hallowed hall of stone and silence.

I recognized the cathedral from my fevered visions, a place of solemn beauty and unspeakable secrets. Now, lying here, its pristine marble and regal artistry felt like a profane intrusion into a sanctuary meant only for the divine. Every breath echoed with both wonder and a creeping terror; I was trespassing on sacred ground, and the thought of what Dracula might do if he learned of my intrusion gnawed at me like a living thing.

Previously, everything in the room had been an unrecognizable blur save for the statue of the Queen. Now, being physically present here, the sheer magnificence of the room was mine to behold. The statue itself was made of white marble, as were the majority of the walls, ceiling, and floor. However, a stone pathway led up to the effigy, carved from an unrecognizable purple stone. The same material was also present in the walls, alongside ornate silver trimmings that gave the room majesty.

Behind the statue was a scene reminiscent of the one chiseled into the massive door leading to the chamber, an homage to a place not of this world but on a much grander scale. Sprawling, alien plants crossed the relief, sculpted in the same marble that graced the rest of the temple. Strange entities were hidden among the curving vines and massive vegetation as well, each bearing an immaculate set of wings. Crystal-clear water flowed from the wall in a few places, cascading down artificial hillsides and into a pool below.

Much like the idol of the Queen, there was something intoxicatingly familiar about the terrain carved into the wall, as if I intimately knew this place despite having never been there. I stood there, mesmerized by it, until my feelings of unease grew too great to be ignored. I was not supposed to be here, and I was not ready to find out what D would do should he learn of my trespassing.

With one final look at the Queen's statue, I stepped into the Void and out into my chambers.

Chapter 35
The Flawed Prince

In the days that followed my uncanny visit to the Queen's sanctuary, a nagging feeling haunted me. I felt a missing detail, a truth, just beyond my grasp. I tried to shove it aside, burying my unease by reading the musty tomes of Dracula's bloodline within the Brides' coffin chamber, where Lilyth was still recovering from her near-mortal wound. Yet, as I read aloud in the silence, I couldn't help but feel that every word was a pale echo of the mystery I'd left behind, and every line of history whispered of a fate I could not yet understand.

D had once again left the Castle along with Grygor and his Hand of Vengeance to handle the political fallout of the assault on his life, taking the issue directly to the Alvah clan. They were the only vampire bloodline on the continent that rivaled Dracula's and had made a very public alliance with the Sanglant family just months before the ill-fated attack. From what Ryvina had told me, Dracula was on the verge of declaring an all-out war against the Alvah family once again over the incident.

According to the historical records D had given me access to, the rival vampire nations had battled before in a bloody war that stretched for centuries. The details surrounding the onset of the conflict were vague. Still, they seemed to revolve around Dracula taking the now missing Queen as his original bride, somehow stealing her away from the current Alvah patriarch. This was a sore subject among his current wives, who refused even to acknowledge the existence of the previous Queen, who still held their husband's heart in a stranglehold, making my efforts to glean additional information fruitless.

Concerned with the prospect of being thrust into my first war, I began using my gifts to spy on the proceedings between Dracula and the opposing vampire lord. For such a tense situation, the pair appeared to be relaxed in one another's company, neither willing to show any form of weakness during their negotiations. Their discussions were tedious and rife with formalities, so I eventually gave up on watching them altogether.

The only point of interest I had seen was the

very noticeable tension between the Death Knight and the Alvah High-General, who seemed ready to draw swords at any moment despite their respective leaders' nonchalant demeanors. Even Grygor appeared to be well-behaved, sitting beside his master in his complete hyena form. Dracula had a small army of nobles with him as well, but I didn't recognize a single one of them. D's decree that my presence was to remain veiled from the world ensured I hadn't become acquainted with his lower court.

Back in the Castle, Ryvina and Mayna had become bored in D's absence and retreated to their coffins to partake in regenerative sleep, leaving me alone in the small portion of our home that I was permitted to explore. Aside from the skeletal servant who prepared my daily meals, there was no one else in the upper chambers with me. Within days of being left in solitude, I became stir-crazy.

I spent a great deal of time hovering beside Lilyth's casket, reading aloud the same books she had used to teach me. Doing this gave me the illusion of being with her, which helped to diminish the growing ache her absence had created in my chest. However, without her mischievous giggling and fingers running through my hair, the gesture lost its appeal, serving only to deepen my desire to see her again. It didn't help that the dusty tomes were also dull, focusing on the rise and fall of rival bloodlines, which became tiresome in short order. The thought of the Sanglant clan being added to the list of fallen bloodlines imparted the slightest of smiles upon my lips, though.

I had no inkling of how long Mayna and Ryvina would sleep. For days, I paced the corridors of my home until every hall had been walked and every shadow stretched thin. Even the Castle itself seemed to slumber, as the rooms and halls ceased to move around me.

My thoughts drifted in circles, restless and dull, until the dead silence of my new home hummed in my ears. Unable to bear the isolation, I stepped into the Void, emerging in the laboratory which reeked of chemicals and rot. The hiss of pressure valves and the clink of glass filled the air in a broken rhythm, but at least it was noise.

Hojo did not bother looking up as I approached. He was perched over a table, intent on teasing something black and pulpy from the remains of a creature that no longer shared a resemblance with anything natural.

"I take it you are bored," he announced categorically, still fixed on the pile of viscera beneath his scalpel.

"The Brides are buried in sleep, and D is gone. This cursed Castle is a mausoleum that offers nothing but silence," I replied.

At last, he paused. Slowly, mechanically, he looked up, regarding me from behind his mask as if dissecting my words like tissue. "Then train. Hone your abilities. The absence of sound is not an affliction; it is a gift. Use it."

"I have been watching D, but his negotiations are no better than staring at a wall."

The Doctor froze mid-incision. His gaze turned hard from behind the mask, staring at me in utter contempt. "You watch the most consequential political maneuvering in centuries, and you find this to be *boring*?" His words cut as though I were a specimen under the knife. "You could study them, learn statecraft, manipulation, and *patience*, but instead, you seek refuge in my laboratory like a stray drawn to firelight."

Hojo returned to his work, the wet sounds of dissection resuming. "Knowledge is the ultimate weapon, Vision. You have the innate ability to reach across space and time to pluck it from any corner of reality. *I suggest you use it.*"

Above all things, Hojo covets knowledge. His entire existence is dedicated to learning, to such a degree that he never sleeps or rests. The necessity of food infuriates him, something he considers a biological flaw, a thief of minutes. He spent decades calculating how to ingest the barest sustenance without breaking stride in his work. Thus, my misuse of time was not only an insult to the man who never stopped his quest to learn, it was an affront to everything he had mutilated himself to become.

The Doctor's scolding lingered in my thoughts long after I left the lab, festering like a wound I couldn't stop prodding. *Knowledge is the ultimate weapon.* The words gripped my mind like a vise. He was right, and thus far, I had done nothing but wield it like a bored child waving a wooden sword. I resolved to change that.

I did not want to return to the gloom of the Castle, its oppressive silence would only amplify the weight of my own wasted time. Instead, I allowed my mind to drift, my consciousness reaching for a place I could call my own in the caverns. I found it in a cave tucked away above the laboratory, sealed from sound and prying eyes, wide enough to stretch in my full avatar and still feel small.

There, I created a space where I could practice my gifts in the comforting pulse of the earth. No decadence was necessary, just the bare essentials required for extended stays: cushions, blankets, and food.

Once settled, I closed my eyes and cast my mind outward, across the lands and into the Alvah stronghold. This time, I did not merely watch; I studied. Every glance, every pause, every chosen word, I absorbed meaning from them all. Slowly, I understood what this kind of power looked like and how it moved the world.

Dracula sat in a lavish throne opposite Lord Alvah, the rival vampire family's patriarch, a grand negotiation table stretching between them. They were not alone. Nobles and soldiers from both houses surrounded them, forced to stand or sit on stools which denoted their lower ranks. Servants weaved through the crowd, pouring thick crimson wine crafted of exotic types of blood, but had to remain facing the leaders. Even as they exited the room, the servants walked backward, unwilling to turn their backs on the vampire lords.

The entire affair struck me as absurd, an endless parade of pomp that explained why Dracula vanished for weeks at a time. Each evening began with hours of ceremony, heralds reciting titles and accomplishments as the leaders stood smirking. Once seated at the long table, flanked by nobles and guards, they spoke in an archaic vampiric dialect that made their conversations hard to follow, though not impossible.

As the days drug on, it became apparent they were engaged in a duel of delay, addressing everything but the assassination attempt. Over a week had passed, yet neither man had dared name the true reason for their meeting. It was as if they were playing a game to see who would speak of it first and, in doing so, concede.

Still, I learned much from watching them; how to navigate court politics, how to manipulate your enemies through mental maneuvers and edged words. Even the formalities became etched into memory. I also learned of Lord Alvah's son, Guile, a natural-born vampire who appeared my age but was hundreds of years old. He attended every meeting, but his disinterest was plain.

Guile was a stark contrast to his father in both attitude and appearance. Lord Alvah had allowed himself to age with time, his skin a slight shade of blue. Creases of experience crossed his brow, matched by hard eyes that had seen war, loss, and the endless march of time. His shoulder-length hair was straight and black as obsidian. The man was controlled and confident, an imposing figure who demanded respect, much like Dracula himself.

His son, on the other hand, radiated arrogance. Unlike Lord Alvah, Guile had light pink flesh, similar to a human who had never seen the sun. He was manicured from head to toe, with each mahogany hair on his head meticulously combed into position. He struck me as the kind of man who would kill a servant over something so slight as a shirt that wasn't pressed to his satisfaction.

Every arrogant gesture and haughty word from Guile ignited a muted fury in me, a visceral disdain that promised retribution in due time. When he finally interjected, well within the third week of the negotiations, the simmering contempt within me solidified into cold, unyielding hatred. The cocksure bloodsucker had been sitting beside his father, listening to him discuss the state of their lands with D, when he finally had had enough of the cat-and-mouse game.

"Can we please just get on with this?" He droned, interrupting his father. "We all know why you are here, Lord Dracula. Your castle was attacked. A pissant bloodline tried to assassinate you and likely killed your wife. We had nothing to do with it."

Lord Alvah's head snapped toward his son, his eyes blood red with rage. "GUILE!"

Guile shrugged off his father's fury, unable to recognize the damage he had just inflicted upon his family. "What? We've wasted weeks on this pointless charade. Just get it over with."

Across the table, Dracula smiled ever so slightly, knowing the young vampire had just cost his father the game and given him a massive edge in the negotiations to come.

"You shall remain silent until I say otherwise," the Alvah patriarch snapped. "Lord Dracula is an honored guest at what is still *my* table." He gave his son a final, threatening look, then turned back to D and apologized.

D bowed his head in acceptance, then leaned forward, placing a hand palm-down on the table between him and his rival. "Guile is young and brash... but he is correct. My home was attacked, and my bride was grievously wounded. The Sanglant clan was behind the assault, a..." he glanced at Guile, "pissant clan you recently aligned with."

Dracula's tone dropped, cold as the aura that

seeped from the Death Knight like pus from an infected wound. "I trust you know the fate that befell them." He reached down and stroked the Hyena's neck to ensure the message was well received.

Kellan, the Alvah High-General, reacted immediately, placing his hand on the pommel of his sword, fingers flexing as if itching to draw. His gaze locked onto the towering Death Knight, unblinking. Across the room, the Hand tilted his head slightly, a motion slow and deliberate, as though sizing up a familiar adversary. No words passed between them, but the silence crackled with old, unfinished business.

Before the standoff erupted in violence, Lord Alvah raised his hand, motioning for his general to stand down. "The Sanglants received precisely what they deserved for such an act of treachery. I realize our recent alignment with the family looks implicating, but you know that a repeat of the Great War is not something I want. We had no part in the assassination attempt."

"I am pleased to hear that, *Alaric*. I would hate for old wounds to reopen." It was the first time I had heard either man use the other's forename. Guile had shattered the formality of the meeting, and D was driving home that fact like a thin blade through chain mail.

Alaric's eye twitched at the slight, but he kept his stoic composure. "What is done is done. *She* is gone now. We both lost."

"So we did." D sat in stony silence, glaring at the man he had fought tooth and nail for centuries. "Perhaps it is time we put the past behind us once and for all."

Lord Alvah leaned back in his massive chair with a resigned sigh. "We have been at each other's throats for long enough. What do you propose?"

D shrugged as if to imply the answer was obvious, then leaned back into his throne, leaving one hand cemented to the table while the other rested atop the Hyena. "You have a son. I have a daughter. Let us join our houses and move forward to a new future."

For a long moment, Alaric was silent as he considered the proposition, until his son burst out in incredulous protest. "What?! You can't seriously be considering this. No, I won't..." With a piercing glare, Alaric cut him off.

"I told you to remain silent. If I say you will marry this girl, then you will." His voice was low, a hiss dripping with venom.

"But what if she's hideous?! You can't expect me just to marry someone I've never met!" Guile said, his plummy voice suddenly little more than a murmur.

Alaric's eyes darkened, veins rising beneath the skin as his eyes fixed on his son. Without warning, he struck Guile across the face, the sharp crack echoing through the hall. The young vampire staggered, crimson blooming beneath his cheek.

"If she possesses even a fraction of her mother's strength," Alaric said, his fangs slipping past his lip, "then she is far beyond you." His gaze remained fixed on Guile, who dared not meet it. Only after many moments passed by in silence did he turn to face D.

"I accept your terms. When your daughter comes of age, our houses will join, and this feud will come to an end. In the meantime..." His voice dropped to a knife's edge. "My son will be *corrected*."

The corner of Dracula's mouth lifted as his nemesis accepted the offer, the kind of sly grin a spider offers to a fly trapped in its web. "Splendid."

With the matter settled, the vampire lords set about writing a contract to seal the arranged marriage. First, however, a massive celebration began marking the official end to the hostilities between the nations. The Great War may have ground to a bloody halt centuries ago, but the rival houses had never enjoyed genuine peace. Not only would this marriage mark the end of the rivalry, but it would lead to the creation of a new vampire nation, the likes of which would be unchallengeable by any outside clan.

Both parties migrated from the negotiation room to a Great Hall, where the festivities would stretch on for many nights. Everyone appeared to be happy with the conclusion. All save for Guile, who sat in a corner lamenting his fate. In my chamber, thousands of miles away, I smiled at the pompous prick's unhappiness and withdrew my gaze.

Reflections:

Though the reason for my overwhelming disdain for the vampire prince was unclear then, I felt an utter hatred for Guile rivaled only by my rancor toward Grygor and the Death Knight. As time would tell, my gut instincts toward Guile would prove spot on.

Chapter 36
Veins of the Pact

The days dragged, thick with ceremonial drudgery and political posturing. Each family guarded their legacy as if it were a jeweled crown, trading ancient grudges for written bargains. The negotiations appeared as though they would never end.

For me, this meant Dracula was away from the Castle for far longer than my initial estimates. To compound my isolation, Ryvina and Mayna had awoken during my time underground and hastened to the Alvah castle to join the celebrations. Lilyth, however, remained sealed away in her coffin, and I had all but given up hope for her return to the land of the unliving.

Hojo's prompting had paid off, as I had learned

much from observing Dracula and Alaric, but the negotiations had now fallen upon the shoulders of the nobles. Dowries and land titles became the focus, and my interest waned. I needed a new direction to aim my attention.

If only the damned assassin had missed, I thought. Then, instead of sitting in a musty cave, I would be with Lilyth. My heart raced at the memory of my time with her, but something lingered just on the edge of my mind, nibbling at me.

The assault on the Castle. The chase. I had *flown*, following the assassin from the sky tower after he dove into the darkness. The entire ordeal happened so quickly that I had not given it a second thought.

Just thinking about it made me shudder, my skin turning clammy. How had I done that? Moreover, *what else could I do?*

My visions had preceded my time in Dracula's lands. They were a curse that grew over time, gathering strength as I aged. However, since learning to access my avatar, many unsettling abilities had risen within the blink of an eye. The tendrils, void-walking, and an uncanny ability to heal my human body, to name a few. Each had awakened in times of duress, and each seemed equally impossible to my logical mind. Yet still, I accepted them as fact without much of a fight.

Flight, however, seemed different. There, the human in me drew a line in the sand between what was acceptable and what should not be. I chuckled at the thought as I contemplated the irony. I could summon ungodly tendrils and transform into a hulking monster with skin darker than the sky on a moonless night. That was fine. But *flying*? That was too fantastical to be real.

I must confess that part of me wanted to try again, despite the protest in my mind, but I could not get myself to do it. If I opened that door, I feared I would find more. More monstrous abilities. More horrors waiting to be unleashed. I did not want to face what might lurk in the shadows of my soul, not without some kind of forewarning at least.

So, I returned to the one person who might have answers.

The laboratory greeted me with the usual scents of chemicals, rot, and heated metal. Hojo stood hunched over an operating slab, stitching something abhorrent into coherence. A grotesque abomination, a chimeric mass of limbs and organs, stitched together with uncanny precision.

He did not look up. "Back so soon?" he asked with sardonic amusement, his fingers still working.

I ignored the question. "A failed experiment?"

Hojo chuckled, the shrill sound sending a shiver down to the base of my spine. "No. You have arrived just in time to witness the culmination of my work."

"But… it is dead, whatever it is," I muttered.

With deliberate precision, the Doctor retrieved a glass syringe from a hidden fold of his pristine white and purple robes. The vial pulsed with a strange green fluid, its hue reminiscent of the eerie glow in my eldritch eye, yet deeper. Sickly. After a flick of the needle, Hojo's gloved fingers probed the creature's patchwork flesh, searching for his target—a soft spot between the ribs. Slowly, he inserted the needle and depressed the plunger.

Almost immediately, the corpse convulsed in violent spasms. Its sewn-together eyes snapped open, burning with the same putrid green luminescence as the vial's contents. The mouth, *mouths*, opened as if gasping for air.

"Behold. I have conquered death," Hojo said, his voice echoing with boredom. "A trivial conquest in the realm of the undead." He placed the empty syringe into a polished metal dish before finally fixing his gaze upon me."

I sank onto the edge of a nearby desk and began a recounting of the distant negotiations and royal intrigues that I had watched from afar. From the social cues to the arranged marriage between the Alvah brat and D's daughter, I relayed everything I had learned.

"That is all very fascinating, but it does not answer my question." His eyes met mine before returning to his work, judging me as if my rambling were the idle chatter of a spoiled child desperate for attention.

"When the assassin fled, I leapt from the Castle

in pursuit, only to find myself soaring after him."

"Yes. *And?*" Hojo was utterly unimpressed with the revelation, causing my cheeks to turn a deep crimson.

"…And I don't know how I did it, or *what else I can do.* You seem to know more about me than I do. I thought you might help me understand what happened."

Hojo sighed. "Have you bothered to try again, or are you simply here looking for validation?" His tone was sharp, laced with impatience.

My silence conceded that I had not.

"Before you entered this realm once again, you commanded me to keep your secrets hidden. Self-discovery is the only path to growth. You already know you can fly. You simply refuse to accept it."

He paused, his golden eyes searching my face for a glimmer of understanding. With none found, he continued. "You were raised as a human, but you are not. Your mind clings to familiar limitations; it must let go. Embrace your true nature and silence the internal conflict that binds you."

I lowered my gaze, shame and longing mingling in the shadows of my thoughts. If only I could shed the weight of my past with such ease.

It was then that I witnessed something unheard of. A shard of the man Hojo had been before the Doctor was forged broke to the surface. "You are young; Your journey has barely begun. There is no shame in your struggle, only the boundless opportunity to learn. Look back at all you have accomplished thus far. It is astounding." His voice was soft, reverent, almost caring. The gold in his eyes flickered, and for a fleeting moment, a brilliant purple shone through.

My cheeks flushed at the compliment, a gesture I was certain he had never bestowed on anyone else. Hojo was many things, but being prone to offering praise was not among them.

"Thank you, Hojo," I murmured.

Without missing a beat, the Doctor inclined his head ever so slightly before returning to his grim work. "Will there be anything else?"

My eyes roved over the immaculate notes littering his desk, and inspiration sparked. "Where can I get some paper and a writing utensil?"

***

Back in my dimly lit sanctuary, I clutched the bounty Hojo had given me: a stack of pristine paper, an inkwell, and a quill. Unfortunately, spacious as the area was, there was little room where I could establish a suitable place to write. The space begged for transformation. With deliberate precision, I released my tendrils and set to work, carving through ancient stone to reveal an adjacent cavity.

For a full day, I sliced through rock and void-walked each hewn fragment away to the Doctor's waste pit. By dusk, my haven had blossomed into a sprawling chamber — a private sanctuary removed from the confines of the Castle. I then furnished the space with a battered desk Hojo wasn't using and a creaking chair.

The expanded chamber still yearned for a personal touch. From my private quarters above, I retrieved the ring from my grim conquest of Castle Sanglant and placed it on my desk as a stark reminder of my triumph. It found its resting place beside a candelabra, plucked from my bedchamber. As with all the candles in the castle, its flame burned eternally, untouched by the ravages of time or melting wax.

The last element was a recent addition to Dracula's collection: a tome filled with maps of his domain and its shadowed outskirts. Every chart was a masterful record of settlements, rivers, mountains, and hidden paths. This was a key component of my next plan.

Content with the state of my new chamber, I sat at the desk and began to work. My attention shifted from the endless wedding negotiations to a pursuit far more compelling: the lycans. With my gaze fixed on the distant Keep, I meticulously catalogued each nearby werewolf encampment, noting precise locations, the number of wolves at each, and their military strength. Thanks to D's painstaking instruction, I'd learned to eavesdrop on the wolves' conversations, extracting intelligence that would have otherwise remained shrouded in secrecy.

Remote viewing the wedding negotiations had been a graceful exercise, my mind gliding across distant halls with relative ease. The task at hand was another matter entirely. Keeping pace with the constant motion of the camps while trying to record every detail tore at the edges of my mind. I tried again and again to keep my focus, telling myself the process would get easier with time, but each attempt ended in skull-splitting agony. My sessions grew shorter instead of longer. At the peak of discomfort, when the weight of pain and exhaustion overwhelmed me, I could do little but collapse and allow sleep to overtake me.

Still, I refused to yield.

It was not until I pushed myself too far one night that something changed in the routine. Pressure built within until it felt as though my head might rupture. My vision pulsed black, my ears rang, and I felt myself unravelling.

Then it happened.

Without command, my higher form surged forth, tendrils unfurling, body stretching beyond human shape as the Void embraced me. The pain vanished, swept away in the cold clarity of my avatar. With it came focus. Precision. Endurance. From within that form, I could work for hours on end, capturing every nuance, absent fatigue. What had once seemed impossible now came with ease.

The only drawback came when I tried to write, my massive, clawed hands dwarfing the quill. This problem, like so many others, was quickly overcome with the tip of a tendril. I found myself to be uncannily adept at using the slick extension to grasp the quill and record my observations. It was as natural to me as writing with my hand in human form, perhaps even more natural.

I spied on the wolves for days on end, stacks of parchment growing to towers. I wrote every detail of my observations, but it was not until my eye beheld a meeting of Hollow Tooth alphas that a truly critical revelation unfolded before me. The leaders had gathered in a remote clearing under the cloak of night to discuss the next phases of their rebellion. Each alpha wore ornamental armor marked by the ancient sigil of their clan: a broken claw, a crescent moon, and a howling wolf, among others.

"The elders have lost their way," the first alpha spat, his voice a low growl. "Their betrayal stains the sanctity of the Citadel."

A second alpha, his armor bearing the stark image of a raven skull, nodded his head in agreement. "They bow in supplication to the dead," he hissed. "That sanctum, once a beacon of our wild spirit, now stands as a monument to submission. It is an insult that cannot go unanswered."

Before the assembled lycans could unleash their fury, they were silenced by the imposing presence of a massive werewolf in copper armor. A broken tooth was emblazoned on his chest plate, and his stature towered over the others, demanding a wary respect. When he finally spoke, his voice emerged as a bitter rasp.

"I was the first to stand against the treaty," he declared, his tone laden with old wounds. "The first to warn against the elders' folly. Now look at me, cast aside for a mere blood drinker. I would sooner die fighting the risen dead than submit as our elders have. They forged an alliance that mocks the very values our nation was built upon… for what? A hollow peace?"

A ripple of murmurs surged through the crowd, punctuated by low growls and fierce snorts. The leader raised a massive, clawed hand, and silence fell like a shroud.

"They've twisted our sacred bonds into chains, defiling the Citadel and the World Tree with their unholy pact," he thundered. "The so-called united clans have sold their souls for peace, but mark my words: they shall know no peace! We will bring war to both the blood drinker and the treacherous elders!"

As the chorus of howls swelled, a chill slithered down my spine. Their fervor was not merely rebellion against their own; it was a declaration to bring war to my home. I recalled the grim lessons imparted to me by Dracula during my time learning Lycan lore: the

Hollow Tooth would never accept this fragile peace, and the only cure to their threat, he warned, was their complete eradication. In that moment, his grim assessment rang with an almost prophetic certainty.

The hearts in my eldritch chest pounded as I realized the stakes were higher than ever. The embers of rebellion were being fanned into flames, and soon, the fragile borders between our realms would ignite.

Once I had cataloged all I could of the Hallow Tooth meeting, I directed my gaze toward the center of lycan power — the Citadel. Its architecture, spiraling like an inverted nautilus shell, was grown from a bizarre living ivory that pulsed in rhythm with the tribes' lifeblood. In stark contrast to the Castle, a brooding edifice of black stone and undeath, the Citadel radiated brightness and a fierce vitality. Here, every curve and crevice spoke of nature's embrace, a sanctuary where the clans found sacred unity. From the center of the structure, a tree of unparalleled size grew. The World Tree.

The wolves revered this towering, gnarled colossus whose roots burrowed into the bones of the planet and whose canopy pierced the heavens. It was ancient. So old that the outer bark had petrified in many places, giving it the appearance of stone. According to lycan lore, this was holy ground, the place souls born of the wild would return upon death until born anew in the flesh.

It was here that I found the allied elders locked in conversation. From what I overheard, it was clear that Dracula's assessment was shared by the werewolf hierarchy. The Hollow Tooths were causing a great deal of issues for their nation, bordering on a full-scale civil war. Were it not for a select few elders who held out hope that the dissenters would eventually see reason, it was quite likely the United Clans would have already rallied against the uprising with overwhelming force. Unfortunately, the misguided view of these ancients had given the rebellion a precious gift: time.

The Hollow Tooth exploited the complacency, bolstering their numbers with new recruits, drawing more packs into their rebellion. At that time, their ranks counted in the thousands, and each day that passed saw their numbers grow.

It would seem that while Dracula had prevented one war from erupting by offering his daughter to the Alvah family, another was about to burst through the door.

Chapter 37
Tendrils of Desperation

As the weeks passed in Dracula's absence, my command over the eldritch abilities I had unlocked grew by leaps and bounds. The constant use of my remote viewing had honed the skill, making it ever easier to perform while remaining functional in my physical, human form. At first, this bilocation of my consciousness had been agonizing. Now, after weeks of daily practice, I could go about my business while visualizing events unfolding in distant lands without the splitting headaches.

I kept an ever-watchful eye on the Keep, as a large contingent of Hollow Tooth forces had gathered in rough proximity to it. I knew from listening to the Alphas there that they were planning an attack. However, it didn't appear the Keep itself was the target for once. The fortress had passed back and forth between Dracula and the lycans so many times prior to my arrival that it was almost comical, and the Hollow Tooths were not interested in taking it back just to lose it again.

No, they were planning something big, a massive incursion that would see them invade deeper into D's lands, but their target was unknown to me. I was capable of understanding their language, but whatever location they intended to strike was being kept hidden through the use of codewords, and I had yet to listen in on any conversation that had identified them.

I might not have known where they planned to attack, but I had learned that they knew that the lord of the land and his top general were gone. As the rebels prepared for their attack, a growing urgency filled their camp; they knew time was running out. They were posed to strike at any moment, and I had no way of warning Dracula of the imminent threat.

Had the Brides been home with me, they could have sent a message to D informing him of the looming offensive, but they were busy mingling with the noblewomen of the Alvah court far away. I considered void-walking to Dracula when he was alone to warn him in person. However, doing so would risk discovery, as the Alvah patriarch undoubtedly had spies watching his every move, even in the supposed privacy of his guest quarters. To violate the one rule D had given me, to keep my existence secret from the vampire nations, seemed ill-advised. He had an army of loyal vampires guarding his lands, and they would rise in defense of his nation when the lycans struck. However, the scope of potential damage the small army could inflict before D's forces responded still had me worried.

Unable to contact Dracula and forced to watch helplessly as a pack of ravenous wolves lurked in the shadows, ready to strike, wasn't sitting well with me. I needed to do more than sit idly by writing numbers and locations, which I assumed would prove useless once the attack had begun. There were hundreds of werewolves gathered within marching distance of multiple targets in D's lands, and I felt an overwhelming urge to take action against them.

So I did.

In my underground chamber, watching a new unit of werewolves make their way through the thick woodlands to reinforce the Hollow Tooth battle camp, my desperation to do something, anything, to defend my home overtook my mind. These monsters were going to attack the only place I had ever found any sense of belonging, and I would not sit by and let them do so unchallenged.

Once I had decided on a course of action, my stomach promptly began to tie itself into knots. My heart pounded, blood surging through my veins with such force I could hear it. Was I making the right decision? What if I failed or made the situation worse?

With my doubts cast from my mind, I stepped into the Void, entombed in my ascended oily flesh.

The woods were pitch black, though the darkness did nothing to conceal my form from the lycans, who could see even better in the dark than they could in the daylight. Not that it mattered.

I materialized behind the last werewolf in the troop I had targeted. Silently, I thrust forward with a tendril, piercing the lycan's spine and severing his windpipe. Before the monstrosity fell to the forest floor, I void-walked to the next werewolf in line and repeated the process, killing it.

As the second wolf became a heap of dead flesh joining the detritus, the remaining wolves began to howl. The scent of their fallen comrades' blood flowing upon the wind had given them notice that something was hunting them. The entire pack turned on their heels and barreled toward me out of the darkness. I met them head-on, not bothering to void-walk again but choosing to stand my ground.

Tooth, claws, and tendrils clashed as a dozen werewolves erupted from the surrounding trees, slashing at my ebony flesh. After my encounter with the Sanglant lord, I was confident my skin would protect me from their attacks, and I didn't even bother trying to dodge their blows. This would prove to be a mistake.

At first, their claws scraped against my void-forged body, leaving only harmless streaks on my obsidian flesh. I struck back, cutting down another. More fell, bodies piling up. But then — pain. Genuine pain. A searing tear spread across my chest, something I had not experienced in this form since fighting the ancient vampire. I stumbled back. A mistake. Another blow came, then another, until I could no longer tell where my body ended and the pain began.

My tentacles went on the defensive, operating of their own accord and coiling around those lycans whose snapping jaws were biting into them. They squeezed, crushing the life from the werewolves they had ensnared, yet more assaulted me from all sides.

All at once, I felt trapped, and my mind raced. I knew this desperation well. It was the same gnawing panic that had gripped me when I first awoke in this new form, the same helplessness that had seized me when the Brides drowned me beneath their merciless grip. I swore I would never feel this way again, but as the weight of the wolves bore me down and the shadows pressed against my vision, it returned. The old fear. The old failure.

With a roar, I pulled the closest lycan to me and bit down on its head, crushing it. My mouth filled with viscera: brain matter and bits of skull exploding down my throat. As it did, my chest tightened, panic setting in.

My normally crystalline flesh had become rubbery, the shine matted, and the impossibly dark hue faded to an ashen gray. My gaze fell upon massive gashes in my chest, torn open by the claws of the largest of my opponents. An inky substance was bubbling out of the wounds, dripping onto the ground below.

"Look! The green-eyed demon can bleed!" a massive lycan exclaimed, rallying his brethren.

Before I could respond to the shock of seeing my eldritch form wounded, the wolves doubled their efforts, piling atop me. A dozen points of searing pain bloomed across my body, a fiery eruption of agony. The stench of their hot, feral breath filled my nostrils as their teeth tore into my flesh, their claws ripping and slashing with a sickening sound. Each bite felt like a red-hot brand, muscle screaming against bone. The weight of the monsters forced me to my knees, and the world became blurry. I recognized this sensation, sitting on the edge of the Void, about to lose consciousness. With one last roar, I unleashed my tendrils in full force at the beasts.

The moment before I vanished into the Void, something deeper than the fear and exhaustion, deeper than the pain ravaging my senses struck.

Hunger.

An aching, clawing emptiness that spread through me like wildfire. When my tendrils lashed out in that final, desperate moment, they did not just kill.

They devoured.

Each werewolf was gone in an instant, their massive forms replaced with explosions of gore, an ocean of blood raining down upon me. With my final reserves of energy, I void-walked from the forest, landing in a heap at Hojo's feet.

Before he could even register my arrival, nearly translucent tendrils shot out, piercing the nearest golems in his laboratory. Thick, glowing green energy seeped from the creatures and into my tentacles, flowing down their lengths and into my core.

"Help me…" I whispered before slipping out of consciousness.

***

Much to my surprise, when I awoke, my consciousness was untethered from my body. I hovered, a silent witness, as my avatar floated within one of Hojo's massive glass tubes used to house experiments. In the dim light of the laboratory, the Doctor and Dracula, who had returned while I was recovering from my injuries, were standing before me.

Dracula's measured, low voice broke the charged silence as he paced before the vat of pulsating green energy. "What happened here?" he demanded, each step deliberate as his gaze burned with controlled fury.

The Doctor's tone was icy and clinical when he spoke. "He arrived battered, his wounds unmistakably those of a lycan assault. It appears he overextended his eldritch form to the point it could be injured."

D spun around, glaring at Hojo with a contained rage. "You said he would be *invincible*. Instead, I see before me a dying beast." Dracula's long, pale finger jabbed toward my suspended form. "Does that pitiful figure appear invincible to you?"

The Doctor's reply was unyielding as he met D's accusing gaze with fierce dissension. "Yes, *he* does."

A cold, venomous edge laced Dracula's words. "You promised me a God. Instead, I have received a creature on the brink of collapse."

Hojo took a step toward the vampire. "You are an ancient, natural-born vampire of unfathomable might. Yet, I wonder, how capable were you at his age?" he asked, his tone laced with an almost casual arrogance.

Dracula's eyes flashed, his tone dropping to a low growl. "I was but an infant."

The smile on Hojo's mask deepened. "So is he. Invincibility is not bestowed overnight. In a thousand years, we shall all be eclipsed by the true potential of his might. Even you. Until that day, he must be nurtured like a child… and not in the ways you *nurtured* your daughter."

The insult did not go unnoticed as D's eyes flashed again, casting the Doctor's porcelain mask in crimson light. "I did what needed to be done to make her strong."

A sarcastic snort rose from behind the mask as the doctor turned away from Dracula. "Your pitiable attempt at parenting made her psychotic. Nothing else."

D's eye twitched, betraying some inner turmoil sparked by Hojo's barbed words. Dracula, ignoring the retort, returned his gaze to the wounds on my form. "How much longer will he be in this state?"

Hojo clasped his hands behind his back with a shrug. "Before losing consciousness, he completely drained every source of energy on this floor of the laboratory. Since then, he has consumed multiple vats of necrogen. At his current rate of regeneration, I would dare to suggest he will be fully healed within a few nights."

"Entire vats?" D said, his voice dripping with disbelief. "That is a costly setback. How long can this necrogen transfer continue?"

"His appetite is most impressive," Hojo said with a hint of reverence. "At the current rate, barely a week, with our stocks. I warned you of the dangers that bringing him here would present long before we set this plan into motion. He is an eater of worlds, and he must feed."

Stepping closer, Hojo added, "I've already set your mages in motion to replenish our tanks during your absence. Soon, we must expand our storage capacity; Our current reserves will not suffice for his demands."

Dracula inclined his head. "We must devise a more efficient method to sate his hunger. Condensed necrogen is painstakingly slow and costly to acquire. Until we secure a viable substitute, he must be deterred from invoking his avatar. Such power, uncontrolled, is a risk none of us can bear."

"All of this work to bring it out of him, and now you wish to suppress the very gift you so desperately wanted?" A fierce glimmer lit the Doctor's eyes as he countered, "Suppressing him now will stunt his evolution. We must instruct him in the art of consuming the life force from his victims, just as you drain blood from yours. His tendrils, with an instinctual hunger, reached out to every necrogen source in the laboratory, draining them to nourish his form. If he can harness this power with deliberate intent, he will become unstoppable."

Dracula's gaze shifted, laden with both doubt and resolve. "You would gamble with all our lives on this experiment?"

The Doctor's response was measured, almost dispassionate. "I remain living, unclaimed by his hunger. He *drained everything* on this level of the laboratory except for me, even the vials of necrogen in my robes. This leads me to conclude that, instinctively, he avoided claiming the energy coursing through me. In a controlled environment, I believe the risk of him harming anyone he values is minimal."

Dracula's eyes fixed on Hojo, skepticism etched on every line of his face. "So, what is your suggestion?"

A conspiratorial smile played on Hojo's mask as he leaned in. "Let the accursed *Quindulla* transport him to an alternate dimension — the very realm from which he was taken. There, should his eldritch form spiral out of control, he will ravage that reality while sparing ours. You may lose your precious Death Knight, but *it* can be replaced."

"I will consider it," D snarled, not at all pleased with the suggestion of sacrificing his prized general. "Alert me the moment he wakes."

Chapter 38
In the Wake of Ruin

When the sweet oblivion finally loosened its grip, I awoke suspended within the holding tank I had observed as D and the Doctor debated my fate. The viscous, neon-green fluid pulsed against my skin, sending electrifying shivers through every nerve. I reached out with a clawed hand, pressing it against the cool, slick glass.

Hojo, who had uncharacteristically halted his work so he could keep a keen eye on my recovery, approached the massive glowing tube and pulled a lever, causing the vat to drain. By the time the last of the liquid had flowed out of the tank, my skin had absorbed the remnants of the necrogen clinging to it.

A hiss of released pressure signaled the glass tank's unsealing. My tendrils, which had wrapped around me like a living shroud in my unconscious state, unraveled and extended, reaching into the dim air as the glass rose above me.

The Doctor stepped forward, his gaze examining the places my wounds had been. "Welcome back."

I answered in the ancient tongue, born before time itself, "Thank you, Hojo."

To my astonishment, the Doctor replied in kind. "You are quite welcome. I trust you are feeling better?"

"I feel like a *God*." The statement was far from an exaggeration. The energy coursing through me was palpable; I felt as though I had been reborn in pure adrenaline. Every cell vibrated with an almost divine power, my tendrils twitching, as if eager to reshape the fabric of creation. In that fleeting moment, I believed I might indeed be a God.

"What, pray tell, caused your injuries?" the Doctor inquired, his tone accusatory.

With reluctant honesty, I recounted the reckless assault on the approaching Hollow Tooth reinforcements, the overwhelming surge of lycans, their violent, gory disintegration around me. Bringing forth the memory of their power siphoning into me was both exhilarating and horrifying. The rush of heat, the taste of the energy as my tendrils lapped it up, then the scent of coppery blood as the wolves burst. All of it lingered on my senses as though they were stained by it.

Hojo's low grunt punctuated my confession. He walked toward me with hands clasped behind his back, his eyes scrutinizing the places where I had been wounded until he was satisfied I was healed.

"That was incredibly foolish; you could have perished in the attempt. Dracula's misguided instructions left you unprepared. You were taught to fight with mundane weapons, yet your ascended form, your true self, was never honed for battle. This failure, ultimately, is not yours."

"Lycans are powerful foes. I should have known better than to fight them alone," I insisted, trying to lessen the severity of my failure and defend D simultaneously.

Hojo, however, was not ready to accept my excuse. "Lycans are base creatures that should pose no more of a threat to you than an insect smashed beneath your heel. You *should* have torn them apart with ease, but your lack of experience left you vulnerable. This failure rests solely upon the shoulders of Dracula."

"Is he angry with me?" I asked, my alien voice a whisper.

Hojo shook his head slowly. "No, not angry. Concerned. He fears that the next time this happens, you will consume more than just our stores of necrogen. The lycans you killed burst as a result of you siphoning out their essence. Their life force. You did the same to the assassin on a smaller scale, which is why his wounds would not heal. Your tendrils absorb the very energies of creation, be it magical or natural. This is an ability you must learn to use on command to avert catastrophic consequences of using your eldritch form."

"You're saying I ate the Lycans?" I questioned. Nausea churned in my gut at the idea of swallowing those flea-infested creatures. The metallic tang of blood and the horrifying image of a werewolf's head bursting in my mouth still lingered, a sickeningly vivid memory.

"You consumed their *V'h'roth*, the soul-current that gives them life. Eating their flesh would do little, if anything, for your current body. While D and his kin drink the lifeblood of their victims, your tendrils drink the energies that hold the universe together. If left unchecked, you could end up draining the very land itself, threatening the planet and all life dwelling on it."

Hojo's words hit me like a tidal wave. The conversation I had overheard between him and D was no fevered dream from the vat of necrogen. It had been real. The realization was chilling. I wasn't merely inhuman, I was the embodiment of an ancient, ravenous force, capable of consuming worlds. In an instant, the intoxicating energy of necrogen was replaced by an icy dread.

Without warning, my form shifted. The

invigorating surge ebbed away, and I reverted to my human self, twitching tendrils retracting to be replaced with trembling hands and a racing heart. Visions of collapsing planets and anguished screams, memories from a time before I was born in this realm, flooded my mind. I did not imagine these horrors; they are imprinted on my soul.

"I... I have to go," I stammered out, void-walking to my underground chamber before the Doctor had a chance to respond.

Inside my sanctuary, I sank onto the makeshift bed. I muttered the word that extinguished the eternal candles, plunging me into utter darkness. In that silence, every regret and every loss, from the lonely torment of my youth to the final, heart-wrenching memory of Natka, rushed in unbidden. The walls of my past closed in: the fire that consumed my village, the Brides' brutal abuse, and the unbearable guilt for having ended a life so dear.

All at once, everything I had suffered since before the Hand had ever been dispatched to collect me came crashing down upon my senses. I had done my very best to ignore it all, to pretend it never happened, but in that moment, the full sum of my life hit me all at once, and I cried, screaming my anguish into the black abyss.

I wept — not just out of sorrow, but in a cathartic release of a lifetime of pain. My cries echoed into the Void as I pounded the cold stone wall, each fistful of shattered resolve a testament to the burdens I bore. If fate decreed that my existence be an endless litany of suffering, then I would at least claim one victory by choosing this pain on my own terms.

My hands battered, I collapsed back onto my bed, sobbing until sleep claimed me. When I awoke, my hands were healed, my higher form having mended the damage on its own. Defeated, I spoke the command to reignite the candles and found blood splattered all over the wall. I may have healed, but the evidence of my rage remained.

Turning from the dark spots in disgust, I found something entirely unexpected resting on the desk, and my heart stopped. Upon a fresh sheet of parchment was a wooden doll, the words "Thank you" scrawled in childlike script at its feet.

I ransacked my chamber, looking for some sign that an intruder had placed Natka's toy there, but I found nothing. Once again, the doll had appeared out of nowhere, somehow moving from its secret hiding space in my old hut to where it sat now. I gazed at the doll for minutes on end, my hands stubbornly refusing to move forward and grab it. I had fought lycans, faced down a death knight, and approached death multiple times, but somehow this fragment of carved wood scared me more than anything I had encountered in my new life.

When I finally gathered up the nerve to touch

it, the doll was the same as it had last time, radiating some strange energy that brought me comfort. Unfortunately, that comfort was marred by the memory of Natka's frail, lifeless body cradled in my arms. Still, somehow, the memory wasn't as world-ending as it was the night before. Perhaps the girl's spirit was watching over me, an undeserved blessing from a soul I had taken from the world.

Maybe Natka's ghost had delivered it while I slept. Maybe I void-walked it here in the night, scribbling the note in my sleep to offer my waking mind solace. With the doll in hand, I decided it didn't matter how it came to be there; I was just glad to have it in my possession once again.

Above my desk, I carved a small space in the wall using a tendril, just big enough for the doll and the parchment. I settled both gifts into the little nook, positioning them exactly as I had found them. No matter where I stood or sat in my cavern, the smiling figurine would look at me, a reminder of the mercy I had shown and what it had cost.

Once I was finally ready to face Dracula and his minions, I gathered the hefty pile of notes I had drafted regarding the werewolf clans — troop movements, encampments, numbers — and void-walked into the Castle proper. The family had just finished supping on a batch of human stock when I materialized before them. I marched up to Dracula and placed the pile of papers on the table in front of him.

"What is all this?" he asked, arching an eyebrow.

"Information on the lycans, both the Hollow Tooths and the United Clans," I replied, trying to sound as confident as possible. "I mapped their troop movements, noted encampments, and even updated your tome on lycan settlements to show new locations that were not listed. It is all written in my old language, though... I do not know enough of yours yet to accurately relay the information. I hope that will not be an issue."

Dracula thumbed through the papers and paused on a map showing several encampments near the Keep. "Impressive," he said, pointing to a marked war band. "Is this what drove you to leave the Castle and nearly get yourself killed?"

My pride evaporated, and I felt my cheeks burn. "Yes..." I responded meekly, looking at my feet. "They're planning a large-scale invasion, and the Keep isn't their target... I was trying to stop them from gaining reinforcements."

D frowned, his tone growing stern. "Why didn't you wait until I returned? The Hand could have assisted you."

"I was monitoring your negotiations," I explained. "Nothing looked like it was ending, and I feared you would return to a war. I had no way to contact you in the Alvah stronghold, so I acted on my own."

The corner of D's lip curled upward in the characteristic half-smile I had seen so often. "You were watching our negotiations, *and* you still gathered this much information on our enemies? I am *most impressed*."

"You were gone a long time," I said with a shrug.

He chuckled. "Humble to a fault. We will deal with the lycan menace in due time. But first, you must learn to fight properly in your true form. We cannot have a repeated failure the likes of which you suffered."

D waved to the Death Knight, who was standing motionless in the corner of the room as he often did while the family fed. "Have these translated, then deliver them to the generals. Inform them to prepare for an invasion, then return to me. You have more important tasks to attend to."

The Death Knight nodded, collected my notes, and vanished through a portal.

After a moment of silence, Dracula leaned forward. "Tell me, what did you learn from watching my meeting with the Alvah family?"

Without thinking, I blurted, "Their heir is a pompous prick."

Dracula laughed, a deep, genuine sound that eased some of my tension.

"Indeed, he is. His arrogance is matched only by his stupidity. It makes him the perfect puppet for my Vesputa. She will have him dancing on a string before long."

I frowned, trying to understand the meaning of his words. "So that is why you would give your daughter to him?"

D grinned fiendishly. "It provides a double victory. I turn an enemy into an ally and gain control over their bloodline through a pawn who never knows he is being played."

I mulled over his words like warm wine, ensuring I had grasped the full body of them before responding. "He'll be a ruler in name only, with your daughter holding the actual power and answering directly to you."

"Precisely," he nodded in approval. "If only half of my court were as quick to learn as you, this marriage wouldn't be necessary." He stood from his chair with a sigh, reaching out to place a hand on my shoulder. "I must make preparations to depart once more to the Alvah stronghold. Their *pompous prick* of a child wishes to meet mine, and I have no choice but to comply with his demands. I am not sure how long we shall be gone. In my absence, you will train with the Hand once more, but this time, you shall do so in your higher form until failure, such as you recently experienced, becomes an impossibility."

I nodded, looking into D's eyes. "I will not disappoint you again."

He smiled and gave my shoulder a powerful squeeze. "I am just glad you are alright. You are my champion; I know you will rise to the occasion."

Chapter 39
The Devouring Field

By the time the Death Knight returned to begin my training, D had already left the Castle with his daughter. They were traveling in the traditional manner, which, as I had learned, was customary between noble houses.

It is considered an insult to portal from one's homeland to the capital of another, having something to do with the host not being respected enough for the guest to take the time necessary to travel the roads and experience their lands firsthand. At the time, I didn't understand the intricacies of this tradition and thought it to be utterly absurd at best and downright dangerous at worst, but D was adamant that it was a necessary evil.

With age, my understanding of this tradition has grown. It was less about insulting another ruler for D, and more about breaking up the endless redundancy of immortal life.

The Hand had agreed to allow Dracula to leave without him but forced the vampire lord to take his best soldiers along. The Death Knight had no choice but to obey D's commands, yet still spoke up when it was his duty to do so.

To my detriment, the cursed one was displeased with his orders. Not being at his master's side as he travelled to a rival nation enraged the dead man. As my training was the sole reason for his absence, the Death Knight was in a foul mood when we finally arrived at the location he had chosen for the task.

We arrived at a barren valley at the foot of a grim mountain range. Where a lush forest once thrived, now only a wasteland of dead stumps and sunbaked red earth remained. Even the valley floor appeared as though it had been ravaged for decades by unseen hands. What vegetation remained was sparse and struggling to survive in the oppressive heat. A meandering river, its water a sickly, unpalatable green, cut through the desolation. On those muddy banks, the Death Knight tested me.

"Transform, now," he commanded once he had encircled me with a battalion of his skeletal archers.

I hesitated, haunted by the Doctor's warning and my own memories. Yet the Death Knight's impatience left no room for argument. His command was absolute.

"Defend yourself or die. I care not which you choose," he growled, waving a hand at his archers.

The archers responded with uncanny speed. They loosed a volley of arrows at me before their lord had finished speaking. Within a fraction of a second, the whistling sound of the projectiles filled the valley, reverberating off the stone walls above. Before the first of the flaming shafts struck home, I was encased in a glistening black shell. I deflected most of the arrows with my tendrils, but an uncomfortable number of them still hit, bouncing away to hiss in the mud.

"*Pathetic.* This is why the wolves bested you. Again!"

Another round of arrows tore into the air, raining down upon me. This time, I intercepted most of them, but a few got through the whirlwind of tentacles.

"Again!"

More arrows, more broken shafts split in twain by my tendrils, which were moving with such speed that they were little more than a blur to the naked eye.

"Again!"

Another volley came pouring out of the sky, followed by the Hand's command for more. This time, I had two consecutive rounds fired at me. As the arrows arced downward, the Death Knight launched a fireball into the fray. I caught the brunt of it while being pelted by the annoying, flaming missiles.

"AGAIN!" His voice was a roar, booming through the valley with such force that it shook loose small rocks high above, which tumbled down the slope.

While neither the fireball nor the arrows had done any damage, the situation drew my ire and rage seeped into my veins.

I braced myself in the mud, lips pulling back to reveal needle-like teeth in a sneer, all four nostrils flared below my single eye. As the anger swept through my mind, time seemed to slow to a crawl, and my awareness of the surrounding environment expanded like a massive balloon. I could see each arrow moving in slow motion through the air without looking at them, and my tendrils whipped them down with blinding speed. I watched as the Death Knight moved in slow motion, preparing to cast another spell at me, but this time I was ready.

As the flaming orb manifested in his hand, a single crack split the air as one of my tendrils lanced the flaming orb, draining its magic before he could finish. My countermeasure caught the dead man off guard, and he stumbled backward as his magic was siphoned out mid-casting.

He regained his balance, stopping himself from plunging into the soupy red mud sucking at his boots. Still, his shock was apparent as his eyes had grown to a blaze twice their normal size. Not only had I disarmed his spell, but I had blocked every arrow his archers had fired while doing it.

Before he could recover, a deep, primal bellow roared down the mountainside in thunderous waves. It rolled through the valley like a gathering storm. Each echo rebounded off the cliffs, multiplying until it seemed the ground itself held its breath. In unison, both the Death Knight and I turned toward the sound. The sight that awaited us was not at all what I expected.

High upon a hill overlooking us was a tiny figure, no taller than Natka had been when I first left the village. Its skin was a putrid garnet color, splotched with black blemishes. The bizarre creature was clad in torn strips of cloth and would have appeared comical were it not for the gleaming red eyes and a wide, razor-toothed grin.

"What is that?" I murmured, more to myself than to my undead tutor.

Without breaking his gaze, the Death Knight replied, "It does not matter. Kill it."

As we moved toward the malevolent little monster, another appeared beside it. Then another, and another. Before we had made it clear of the muddy riverbank, hundreds of the tiny brutes were swarming the valley, screaming in some unknown language. More surged from dozens of caves spotting the sides of the mountains. A second horn blew from far above, and the creatures started cascading down the mountainsides toward us.

"Hold your ground. Protect the archers!" the Death Knight ordered. His skeletal troops formed ranks behind him and fired enchanted arrows into the surging horde. Yet for every creature felled, dozens more rushed forward.

The sheer number of fiends running down the mountain was staggering. It was as if we had kicked a massive anthill and the entire colony erupted forth to exact revenge. Countless creatures blotted out the mountains, the view transforming into an ocean of moving limbs, pointed ears, and rudimentary weapons.

The archers fired round after round, each salvo cutting a swath through the mass of beasts. As each arrow struck home, the impaled creatures would fall, only to be trampled by their brethren until their strange, orange blood was pounded dry into the red dirt below.

Once the first wave crested the hillside before us, the Death Knight unleashed a torrent of fireballs into the mob. Each blazing orb exploded on impact, incinerating the savages nearby and blasting apart those on the fringes of the detonation. The resulting shockwaves and immense heat extended outward, sending bodies and limbs flying into the air and cooking the nasty little cretins. The noxious fumes emanating from the charred carcasses, mixed with the contaminated mire of the river, were so strong I opted not to breathe at all.

The valley erupted in chaos, a cacophony of death screams, arrow whistles, and the relentless roar of magical fireballs. My mind raced as they bore down on me, thoughts of being battered by the troop of lycans fresh on my mind. There had only been a handful of werewolves there when they took me down, and now I was facing hundreds, likely thousands, of adversaries. How was I supposed to fight against numbers like these?

It didn't take long to find out.

Tendrils poised to strike, I met the first creature to come into range with a swift jab that pierced its skull, killing it. The second was impaled and thrown into the churning mob cresting the hillside. More poured into range, outnumbering my tendrils and forcing me to sweep them away with long, arcing strikes. Each swipe of a tendril sent extremities flying, neatly cleaved with surgical precision.

No matter how many I put down or how many the Death Knight incinerated, the horde kept coming. Their thirst for violence had overcome any sense of self-preservation.

Soon, I was wading through sickly orange mud as I fought. The blood of those I killed was mixing with the hundreds slain by the archers, creating a vile stew of the red dirt. Bodies piled up in a circle around me to the point I could no longer see the Death Knight, just the flashes of light when one of his magical attacks would go off. Wave after wave crawled over the corpses of the fallen, only to be met with slashing tendrils of death.

The endless attacks took a toll. My movements became less crisp, and my tendrils felt as though they were cutting through the muck sloshing at my feet instead of the air. I was running out of energy, a realization that sent a chill through my mind. Hojo's warning rang through my head even as I trudged forward, slashing through bodies with far less vigor than I had minutes before. *"He is an eater of worlds, and he must feed."*

The thought occurred to me I may need to void-walk out of the valley, but I pushed the idea away as quickly as it came. I would not retreat. I would not fail D again. Damn these little bastards, I was going to kill them all, or die trying.

Resolute in my decision to fight, I began marching forward, carving a path through the mountain of corpses encircling me. The move proved futile as more bodies fell to my tendrils and filled the hole, leaving me with a fresh problem: the ground around me was rapidly shrinking. Each kill saw the space close in more until I was wading through a knee-deep ocean of severed limbs and apricot-hued blood.

I attempted to climb the growing wall of bodies before me, but the task proved impossible. The piles of remains collapsed beneath my weight, and I sank further into the medley of mangled flesh. To further complicate matters, the tide of fighters pouring over the ledge was causing the corpses to cascade down upon me. Each fresh kill filled the pit I was in a little more, burying me alive.

Before I knew it, I waded hip-deep in a marmalade of death that made the very act of staying on my feet a constant battle. My body was tired, exhausted to the point my tendrils were drooping in the air, and it took everything I had just to keep them moving. It was then that the first of the tiny creatures reached me.

A mouthful of sickly yellow fangs clamped down on my arm. Upon looking down, I noticed my flesh had reverted to its previous grey hue from when Hojo saved me. I was weak and, therefore, vulnerable. Black ink flowed around the creature's teeth, which were planted into my skin. It took a moment for the pain to register in my senses, a rush of molten lava flowing up my arm and into my mind.

Then, all at once, my world went black. In that critical moment between consciousness and oblivion, the battlefield transformed.

I saw, as if through a veil, golden strands crisscrossing the chaos, a vast, shimmering spiderweb connecting every creature, even the very mountain. I'd seen these threads before, in my cell, when Sight first visited me. They pulsed with an otherworldly glow, and as I watched, an insatiable hunger surged within me.

My tendrils lashed out, impaling a dozen of the

tiny brutes at the points where the golden strands converged. The strands snapped, transforming into vivid green energy that coursed up my writhing limbs.

V'h'roth.

A wave of ecstasy flooded me, an almost primal satisfaction that eclipsed the pain and terror. It felt as though I had dove into a lake in the dead of winter, forcing my entire being to quiver.

My senses sharpened as I drank up the stolen life-force. My vision returned to the waking world, but the golden strands remained as shadows as if my perception of reality had flipped on itself once again.

The initial victims of my feeding shriveled and exploded in bursts of gore as I drained their V'h'roth with the force of a black hole. The next flood of assailants was struck with a nightmarish shrapnel of shattered bones and teeth, cutting them to ribbons.

Then, for the first time since the battle had begun the creatures stopped pouring into the new valley I had created from slain foes. Collectively, their eyes widened and their snapping jaws fell slack, hanging low in disbelief as they all looked up in unison. It was then that I realized I was no longer looking up at the top of a macabre hill of bodies to identify targets, but was instead staring down at them from somewhere above.

I was hovering in the air. Flying. The latent ability, last surfaced during the assassination attempt on Dracula, had returned. As with so many of my other innate abilities, the heat of the moment had brought forth a hidden aspect of myself out of the Void and into the light.

A shriek emanated from somewhere beneath me as one beast turned to flee in terror. Before it could take a step, I lanced the screaming savage with a tendril, impaling its golden zone and siphoning out its vitality. The brute burst like a ripe fruit struck by a hammer, showering his allies with viscera.

All at once, the tide turned, and the horde retreated with haste. The blind aggression they had displayed moments ago was now pure panic, and the mob was clawing, biting, and cleaving through itself in desperation to escape the monster soaring overhead.

Unfortunately for them, I had gotten a taste of the essence which gave them life. Beyond the reach of their crude spears and swords, I rained down tentacles upon the squirming masses, bursting bodies with glee as I drained their V'h'roth with impossible speed.

I moved from creature to creature, impaling them with tendrils and snipping their golden cords until the entire mountainside was cleared, creating a flood of sanguine fluids and pulpy flesh. The river below, once a sickly green, ran brown with spilled lifeblood and shredded flesh.

My tendrils, engorged, blazed with an unearthly nuclear green, matching my eye. The energy of thousands was coursing through my body.

The feeling was indescribable, sending shivers of delight through my entire being. In the sky above the battlefield, basking in my gluttonous glory, I closed my eye and roared into the heavens.

Chapter 40
Anatomy of Loneliness

I hovered above the tranquil sea of carnage I had created, lost in the ecstasy of my accomplishment, savoring the energy rippling through my form. In moments, my eldritch power had turned the tide, siphoning the life force from thousands of enraged foes and reducing their army to a pulpy sea of reddish-orange ruin.

Every living being in the valley had fallen victim to my wrath, even the wounded, leaving the battlefield eerily silent. The blessed silence only furthered my satisfaction, allowing me to embrace the dying light of the setting sun absent distraction. I floated in the air, eye closed, and willed my body to feel the fading warmth until twilight swallowed the valley.

Once the blazing orb had disappeared behind

the mountains, I twisted midair to stare down at the Death Knight and his archers. The cursed one hadn't so much as twitched since I unleashed my devastation upon the horde. His flaming eyes were mere embers glowing within his helmet, staring up at me in disbelief.

The dead man had no doubt witnessed many strange and unbelievable events transpire during the course of his unnatural life, but watching me single-handedly lay waste to legions in the blink of an eye had him rattled.

For the first time, he was seeing me as the weapon of mass destruction D had promised.

Slowly, I descended from the sky to hover before the knight, stopping just above the muck. After many long moments, I finally shattered the silence. "What now?" My voice echoed off the valley walls, repeating my words with increasing menace.

The Death Knight turned, having come to some unspoken decision, and walked into a portal, taking his archers with him. My training, it would seem, was done for the day.

I half expected the dead man to be waiting in the Keep for me when I materialized there, but he was nowhere to be found. The only signs of life in the fortress were the statuesque skeletal soldiers manning the battlements, and they didn't even turn to acknowledge my arrival.

I focused my attention on the knight and soon

my consciousness found him in D's guest room at the Alvah stronghold. He had portaled in to find his master in the throes of passion with the Brides. Although Dracula was furious at the Death Knight for both interrupting his private moment and disobeying a direct order to train me, his anger melted into a broad grin as the Death Knight reported my victory.

"The matter is settled. My assignment is complete."

"That quickly?" D asked, amused.

The Death Knight, his eyes smoldering like tiny embers, murmured, "*You cannot imagine.*"

Dracula's smirk took a vicious edge as he sensed the awe emanating from his general. His Hand of Vengeance had not known fear since the curse was unleashed upon him, but he was closer to it now than ever before. This seemed to please the vampire more than anything I had seen since meeting him.

Mayna and Ryvina, catching their husband's exhilaration, exchanged knowing smiles and pulled him back into their grasp. As D resumed his intimacy with renewed vigor, the Death Knight slipped silently to the doorway to stand guard, his back turned to the proceedings.

To avoid voyeuristically watching them, I shifted my focus to the Castle. Seeing the Brides had caused a strange longing within me. I was not jealous of D and his fornication with them, but was missing Lilyth. My time with her had been volatile from the start, to say the very least, but I had grown fond of her presence. Of feeling wanted. She had manipulated my emotions and tortured me, yet here I was, lamenting her absence.

I peered through the shifting veil of time and space, straining to see the slightest indication that Lilyth had awakened. I encountered nothing save a haunting silence.

I admit, I was tempted to peer inside the casket, to confirm her state, but the very thought repulsed me. It felt like a violation, an intrusion into a sacred privacy I wasn't sure I had the right to breach. Not that she had ever shown such qualms about invading mine, mostly, I was terrified of what I might see.

I did not know what form a vampire would take while regenerating in such a manner, nor did I want to find myself staring at the rotting corpse of the red-haired vixen. I gazed at her tomb and waited.

Whatever it was I felt for Lilyth, it was entirely different from the bond I had with Katri, and I couldn't quantify exactly what had me missing her so. She was beautiful, and there was a shared attraction between us, but my ties extended beyond mere lust.

She was the first person who, to my knowledge, had ever opened their soul to me. She had allowed me to see her vulnerabilities and, in doing so, forged a bond I didn't realize could exist. For all I knew, it was all an act put on to manipulate me, as so much of my time with the Brides had been. Regardless, the gesture had moved something deep inside me and my heart ached in her absence.

***

With my entire family now at Alvah Castle, and Lilyth still lost to oblivion, I returned to the battlefield. I did not know what the creatures were and thought it possible that Hojo might identify them. With my newfound ability, I scoured the carnage until I discovered an undamaged corpse, save for a solitary wound where a tendril had struck.

Remains in hand, I void-walked to the Doctor's laboratory where I found him combing through records of a previous experiment. Turning from his work, Hojo shot me a quizzical look from behind his mask.

"What is this?" he asked, his measured tone unable to conceal his excitement.

In response, I held the carcass before him with one hand. "I was hoping you could tell me. We killed thousands of the damned things."

Hojo's eyes widened as he studied the creature, examining it as a child would adore a new toy. "I have never seen a creature such as this," he said, motioning me to follow him to an empty surgery table. "Lay it down here."

The Doctor's excitement over obtaining a new

specimen was palpable, and he was all but shaking with glee. He dashed to gather a gamut of tools I didn't recognize, along with a fresh stack of parchment, and began to scribble his initial observations of the little monster.

"You killed *thousands* of these? Are there more specimens available, perhaps some that are still living?" He spoke as rapidly as he worked, taking measurements of each individual body part and cataloging them with shocking speed.

"Most of the bodies were destroyed. I didn't leave any survivors."

"Destroyed how, precisely?" the Doctor asked as he began prodding the corpse with a variety of tools.

"I'm not sure. I lanced them with my tendrils and they burst into clouds of blood."

Hojo paused just long enough to look at me, then hurried back to what he was doing. "Rigor mortis is setting in. The body is decaying. Every second that goes by is one less I have to study the creature. Would you be so kind as to collect more specimens? The more I have to work with, the better."

Without saying a word, I traveled back to the site and procured as many bodies as I could carry, coiling them up in my tendrils once my arms were full. Upon returning, Hojo instructed me to place them in a cold storage area of his laboratory designed to keep corpses fresh for as long as possible. The location was a separate cavern from the lab where he was working and was enchanted with numerous spells which kept the remains stored there from decomposing.

When I returned to Hojo's side, he was busy placing samples of the creature's flesh into small glass cylinders filled with fluids of every color and viscosity imaginable. Some vials bubbled and hissed as they interacted with the tissue, while others lay inert. The Doctor moved with feverish meticulousness, his hands a blur as he dissected, cataloged, and recorded every reaction.

I observed his work for some time, watching him peel away layers of flesh and muscle with surgical precision until every component of the creature had been sorted, labeled, and preserved. The speed at which his hands moved was a marvel but was eclipsed by the pile of notes he had written while he carved away. One hand would work the scalpel while the other recorded his progress, somehow drawing impossibly detailed renditions of the beast without ever looking at the parchment.

When the last of the specimen was dissected, Hojo set down his scalpel and looked up at me. "Are you certain there were no living samples left to be gathered?"

"Nothing in that valley was alive when I left," I said flatly. "You are lucky there were any bodies to collect. Between the Death Knight's flames and my tendrils, most of the creatures were completely destroyed."

Hojo released a sigh of frustration, then began poring over his notes. "I will be forced to reconstruct a living specimen then. In the meantime, I will need you to recount every detail of your encounter with the new species."

I spent the next few hours recalling the battle, all while watching Hojo piece together undamaged bits of the bodies I had recovered until he had a complete specimen on the table before us. The creature was assembled from a mix of male and female parts, Hojo selecting the most intact pieces to use, with the lower half and head both sourced from the same female body.

I handed him a vial of necrogen sitting on a nearby table, only to have the Doctor reject my offerings.

"I said I was going to reconstruct a *living specimen*. Necrogen would only create an undead minion." With that, he wheeled the table down a ramp to a lower level of his laboratory, one that smelled of burnt ozone.

Hojo, having moved the body to a new table beneath an ominous cage, proceeded to inject a strange pink fluid. He then attached several wires to the stitched-together amalgamation, each connected to a thin needle that was pushed into the skin. Once finished, he lowered the cage and fastened it down, imprisoning the corpse.

Hojo stepped away from the body and began turning knobs and flicking switches on strange machinery next to the table, causing a hum to reverberate through the laboratory. With a final pull of a lever, the air began to crackle and pop as currents of raw energy zipped across wires on the ceiling and then down into the cadaver.

The body shook violently as the electricity flowed through it. To my astonishment, the stitched-together wounds on the beast sealed shut, where I thought for sure they would tear apart from the convulsions.

Hojo raised the lever, and the convulsing stopped, the hum in the air going with it. For many moments, nothing happened. The corpse lay still and silent as the air in the laboratory. Then, the stillness was broken by a single twitch of clawed toe and the flaring of nostrils as the pitiful little monster took the first breath of its new life. This was followed by groggy head movements and then the slow peeling apart of sealed eyelids. The creature's eyes appeared glazed over and glossy, as if it were drugged.

All at once, the creature saw me and shot up, banging its head on the cage and crying out in pain. It scurried away, pressing itself against the bars to get as far away from me as possible.

"It seems the specimen remembers you," Hojo said without emotion.

Realizing my eldritch form was likely terrifying, I reverted to my human body. This seemed to calm it down ever so slightly, though it still shivered and stared at me unblinkingly with its massive red eyes.

A swell of sorrow washed over me as I watched the creature's desperate attempts to break free from its confinement. Yes, mere hours before it and thousands of its kind had tried to kill me, but now it was alone and trapped in an alien environment. Worse, it wasn't the same as it had been when it died, and the Gods only knew what kind of hell being brought back to life would be like.

When the realization she couldn't break free of the prison set it, the little beast looked down at itself, then chirped in its strange language, tears streaming down its grubby cheeks. My stomach sank at the sight, my heart heavy with guilt. I had been in the same situation not so long before, trapped in an unfamiliar land surrounded by strange creatures.

I void-walked to the kitchen and collected some items I hoped would satisfy the poor cretin, then I brought them back to the lab, wanting to ease its suffering.

"What are you doing?" Hojo asked, his voice carrying a tone of irritation.

Not bothering to look at him, I tore pieces of meat off a roasted pheasant and placed them in the cage. "I'm trying to feed it. The poor thing is terrified."

"It is a *specimen*, Vision, not a pet. I resurrected it for study, nothing more."

"Then study how it eats," I said.

"I intend to, in a controlled environment," Hojo responded, then waved his hand which caused the creature to collapse into slumber. He unlocked the cage, flung the snoring beast back onto the surgery table, and pushed it past rows of tubes and machines toward another ramp leading further underground.

We descended multiple levels until we reached the Doctor's holding cells, each designed to replicate a unique environment. Each pod was encased in thick, fortified glass and contained a living ecosystem. We moved past a forest and a desert, then a massive aquarium with a bizarre man-fish staring at us from behind the glass.

The sheer scope of the observation level was mind-boggling, as each biome seemed to stretch out of sight. The tops of each container were also shielded in glass, ensuring the captive beings couldn't escape and allowing Hojo to watch his specimens from every angle.

We finally stopped at a mountainous environment, one with scattered trees and large boulders. Again, Hojo waved his hand, and a doorway appeared in the glass before us. He set the snoring beast down on the ground just inside the container and left, sealing the doorway with another gesture.

"Is there anything in there that can hurt it?" I

asked, suddenly stricken with worry for the freshly revived monster.

Hojo waved at the creature once more, and it woke from its slumber. "Not yet."

After a few moments of discombobulation, the creature darted off into the wilds of its new home, disappearing amongst the rocks.

"When a new specimen is first introduced to an observation platform, it typically requires a day or two to acclimate to its environment. The cell currently contains an adequate population of small herbivores for the specimen to hunt, but no predators. I shall introduce those once the initial behavioral data is collected. It is unfortunate there were no survivors. Your report suggests a reliance on communal living among these creatures. The isolation will certainly impact this specimen's behavior."

With that, the Doctor summoned a golem to return the surgery table to its proper level and walked away, his focus already shifting to other priorities.

I stood there for a long time, a swell of pity growing in my belly as I thought about what the creature must be going through. Taken from its home, reborn in a body pieced together from parts of its tribe, and placed into a fancy prison to await whatever horrors Hojo would inflict upon it.

The poor thing would have been better left dead.

Chapter 41
Bound by Sorrow

The next few days passed in a muted, relentless monotony. I spent most of my time observing the holding tank for the creature, *Monsius Goblynedea* as Hojo had labeled it, though I'd taken to calling her Chirp for the soft, wistful sounds she made in solitude. By day, she remained hidden within her artificial cave, emerging only under the cover of simulated night to hunt, drink, and relieve herself.

Chirp spent her remaining time weeping in the darkness for hours on end, running her clawed fingers across the scars crisscrossing her body. Much to my dismay, this led me to conclude the creature was sentient enough to realize she was in a body that was not wholly her own. That crushing weight of understanding compounded my guilt as a bitter taste filled my mouth, mirroring the gnawing remorse in my chest. Her plight, stark and painful, seared itself into my soul.

In a bid for atonement, I began slipping small offerings of raw meat to her when the Doctor wasn't looking, leaving them just outside her cave. Hojo insisted the creature remain undisturbed to preserve his data, but I cared little for his study. This wretched creature suffered unimaginably, and I was to blame.

On the seventh day, an unexpected wonder greeted me: outside the cave stood a crude effigy, constructed from stones and sticks that Chirp had gathered in the night. A single, massive green eye crafted from leaves bound with mud gazed over a dead rabbit placed at its base. I paused, transfixed by the silent monument, when Hojo's measured voice broke through.

"It appears you have gained a new worshiper," he remarked, a hint of amusement in his tone.

I didn't reply. Instead, I void-walked into the enclosure, emerging in my eldritch form to reach down and pick up the rabbit. As I rose, I could see Chirp's head peeking out from the darkness of her cave. I smiled at her, which in retrospect was likely not the smartest idea, as it revealed a mouthful of needle-like teeth. She did not move, though. She did nothing more than fix her puffy eyes upon me.

I lifted the rabbit up to my maw, then swallowed it down whole, hoping that seeing her offering accepted might somehow offer the creature a moment of solace. The gesture seemed to work as Chirp inched her way out of the cave. I stood as still as I could, afraid that any movement might be enough to cause her to flee.

After many agonizing minutes, she clutched my leg with both fragile arms and began to whimper, her head resting near my knee. As my enormous hand settled on her fragile back, an avalanche of sorrow cascaded into my mind. Every tear, every heartbroken lament from Chirp became mine, a torrent of grief that dredged up the haunting memories of my own losses.

I experienced the horror of her memories as she watched her tribe torn apart by my tendrils, reminding me of my terror when the Death Knight burned through my people. Her current isolation and loneliness compounded my suffering in Lilyth's absence. Even her revulsion at the form forced upon her echoed my own silent loathing for the eldritch body I had been thrust into.

In that moment, we became bound to one another in ways I still cannot fathom all these centuries later.

In that raw, vulnerable moment, I understood the crude effigy she had constructed. Chirp had created it hoping I, the very monster who had brought ruin to her people, might return to end her suffering.

She wanted me to kill her.

I lifted her into my arms and cradled her as if

she were a newborn babe, slowly rocking her until her sobs quieted and she drifted into a fitful sleep, her body convulsing with the weight of her grief.

"I'm sorry little one," I murmured, "I am so, so sorry."

I stood there, holding Chirp and seeing nothing but myself reflected in her broken form until night fell upon the enclosure and the little being stirred, stretching with a yawn in my arms. Sleepy eyes opened to stare up at me, and I smiled back down, careful not to expose my teeth this time.

Chirp was a monstrous aberration. Hojo's procedure had left her an unnatural patchwork of flesh: thick, mismatched scars binding body parts that seemed never meant to converge. Her arms sported different shades of red, as did her torso, while only her legs and head kept any semblance of harmony. Yet none of this repulsed me as I gazed down at her, locking my eye onto her large red orbs. Likewise, she didn't seem offended by my monstrous appearance. In fact, she seemed to be relaxed for the first time since she had been resurrected.

I carried the little one to an artificial stream and plunged a tendril into the chilly waters. Moments later, the tip reemerged with a fat, juicy fish impaled upon it. I raised the flopping creature to Chirp, who reluctantly grabbed it and tore into the flesh with a ferocious hunger.

Hojo observed from his elevated perch, his

irritation palpable. But his disapproval mattered little, as the only being in the world who mattered at that moment was my newfound friend.

Once the little beast had finished gnawing on the fish, she unleashed a surprisingly powerful belch for her meager size, then climbed down from my arms excitedly, pointing and chirping in her strange language. She began running as fast as her little legs could carry her toward the cave where she had spent her days since being imprisoned within the gallery. With a smile, I followed behind as a father would chase a child eager to show him something of earth-shattering importance.

Chirp disappeared into the small crevice only to return with a sharpened stick she had crafted. With a puffed chest, she pointed the crude spear at the ground and began to make her strange vocalizations softer than before. Unsure what to make of the display, I remained still as she marched into the forest with purpose. When I began to follow her, Chirp turned to me, pointed her little stick at the ground again, and spoke in her hushed tones.

The little one slipped into the foliage after one last look over her shoulder, checking to be certain I wasn't following. As her tiny form disappeared into the shadows of the trees, I was stricken with worry, despite the fact Hojo had assured me there was nothing in the environment that could harm her. Still, my stomach, or whatever is the equivalent in my eldritch form, sank as I lost sight of Chirp.

Minutes passed by until I finally grew bored and sat, leaning against the mountain face next to Chirp's cave. While waiting, a distant sensation tugged at my mind, hinting that something was amiss in the universe, even though I couldn't pinpoint it.

At first, I thought Chirp might be in trouble, but a quick scan with my senses showed me she was still in the forest, hunting some small animal. I watched her for a while, which seemed to ease my feelings of unease for a time. The reprieve didn't last long.

The sense of looming doom continued to grow within me, as though some colossal monster lurked in the shadows, ready to pounce. I turned my gaze to the area around Chirp, using my vision to peer behind every tree, stone, and blade of grass within her habitat. I found no threats. Nothing save for birds, rabbits, and insects. Eventually, I became certain Hojo hadn't released some predatory animal to harm the little one to spite my newly forged attachment, but the feeling was still growing stronger, bordering on panic.

As the minutes stretched by, the feeling became oppressive, like a weight pressing against my consciousness until I felt trapped by it. Something was very wrong. Then a thought came to me: Dracula. He was gone from the Castle in what I considered hostile territory.

I turned my gaze to the Alvah stronghold only

to find D and his Brides chatting with random nobles, both the Death Knight and Grygor by their sides. Rapidly, I looked from person to person searching for something, anything, that would suggest danger. Again, I found nothing.

Frustrated, I checked the Castle for intruders only to find it devoid of threats. After two full sweeps of the structure, I shot my consciousness to Lilyth's chamber like an arrow, and again, nothing. No assassins crawling the walls or red-haired vixens roaming the halls. Yet my senses were screaming at me, urging me to take action against some shadowy threat hiding in the mists.

Finally, I focused on the feeling itself. The moment I did, my consciousness was ripped from my body and plunged into the chaos of battle.

Lycans.

An army of wolves, far deeper into D's lands than they should be. One of the lesser castles was under siege. The vampire regent's army had been surprised by the filthy beasts and they were suffering heavy losses.

Without warning, my vision moved to a second location where another, much larger, army of Hollow Tooths were splitting off into smaller groups for a multi-pronged strike against Dracula. In the pandemonium of the moment, I heard a Hollow Tooth commander calling out orders to his troops, ordering them to leave no survivors. On his command, the wolves started running through the forest toward a large settlement in the distance.

I recognized the place from my initial travel to the Keep with the Death Knight. It wasn't the manor of a noble, nor one of the castles built to protect the duchies. No, the lycans were targeting a human farm, one of the multiple settlements that provided D's empire with fresh blood. Nearby, I observed lycan forces preparing to assault three more villages, preparing to wipe out the very lifeline that supplied sustenance to the vampire nation.

Without hesitation, I void-walked to Hojo's perch outside the glass wall.

"Are you bored with your..." he began, but I interjected before he could finish.

"The lycans are invading! You must alert our forces!"

The Doctor instantly vanished into one of his purple portals, and I hoped it was to fulfill my command. Moments later, he reappeared.

"The local duchies are being alerted to the threat as we speak, but the armies are amassed near the Castle, and far from full strength. How many lycans are coming?" Hojo asked.

"Too damned many, and they are already here." I said, not sure what to do next.

Hojo stepped toward me, his hands clasped behind his back. "You cannot aid our forces. Your presence must remain veiled, and we can ill afford a repeat of your last encounter with their kind."

The word stung, even though they were not meant to. "They are targeting the *farms*. By the time the armies arrive, the humans will be wiped out. I won't just sit idly by as these damn beasts try to starve my family!"

"To target the lifeblood of the kingdom is a bold strategy, one that could cost us dearly," Hojo reluctantly admitted, his tone annoyingly clinical. He paused, then turned his back on me. "The army will seek to defeat the lycans closest to the Castle first. *If* you were to interject yourself into this situation, you might strike the forces furthest away from the heart of the land. I am not condoning such actions, of course, but this would be the best way to ensure no vampire would see you…"

The Doctor's hint was all the permission I needed.

As I void-walked out of the laboratory, I saw Chirp walking out of the woods with a bird lanced upon her makeshift spear.

Her shoulders slumped when she found I was no longer there. I vowed to make it up to her when I returned.

Chapter 42
The Howl and the Hymn

With Hojo's warning in mind, I chose my target with care and emerged in the center of the settlement furthest removed from the Castle. Unfortunately, the lycans had already begun their assault on the town, and the misty night air was thick with the wails of the dying.

The blood farm was being torn to shreds, overrun by lycans who were pulling people out of their homes to ravage and murder them in the streets. Flames painted buildings in flickering orange, and unspeakable atrocities unfolded in the streets. The sight of bodies, of unspeakable violence, dragged my mind back to that cursed cabin and the horrors wrought by Grygor — echoes of a past I'd tried to forget.

In the town square, the carnage was absolute. The bodies of villagers littered the ground where the lycans had discarded them like broken toys. Those who were still among the living had banded together there in desperate resistance, but the odds were far from in their favor. The sight of them illuminated by the flames and the sounds of screams from those inside burning structures evoked painful memories of my village and the devastation it endured. Aside from the feeders, these were the first humans I had seen since that day, which seemed so very long ago.

Among the crowd, I spotted a little boy; tiny, frail, and clutching a worn wooden horse as if it could shield him from the horrors of the night. Tears streamed down his face as he stood motionless next to a corpse that I assumed had been his mother. An older boy, roughly my age when the Death Knight had visited my village, scooped the child up and ran with him into the night. Guilt and rage erupted within me like a geyser, rippling through my body and up the tendrils slashing at the air behind me.

Enraged beyond measure, I unleashed a roar that shattered windows throughout the town, an alien screech that split the night open and drowned out the sounds of screaming and death that seemed to come from every direction. The noise emanating from my body shocked even me, the unnatural cacophony of bone-rattling sounds clawing into the ears and minds of every living entity for miles. The lycans closest to me all dropped to their knees, clawing at their ears to dig the sound out of their heads.

"You filthy beasts deserve worse than death," I snarled, my voice uttering words in a language born long before the stars above burst into flame. *"Tonight, your souls will be cast into the Void. Come, meet your undoing."*

I rose above the smoke and chaos, stretching out my arms and drawing the Void down to join my wrath. Lips curled back into a vicious sneer, I rained down tendrils upon my foes, siphoning out their souls and feasting upon them. Lost in the ecstasy of satiating my eldritch hunger, I nearly missed the shift in the air.

Gone were the cries of death and destruction that had plagued the town moments before. In their place was a new, unsettling noise — laughter. It started slowly, a gurgling chuckle from a man whose lungs were filling with blood. Then, more voices joined the chorus, growing louder and more erratic with each passing moment until the noise was teetering on the very boundaries of reason.

As I turned to the town square, my eye was greeted by something that nothing could have ever prepared me for. Hundreds of villagers had amassed, laughing with hysteria that rose to a fevered pitch. Each face was twisted, their blank eyes reflecting the surrounding flames. Even those who suffered horrendous wounds from the lycans were dragging themselves forward, hands grasping at the air in feeble attempts to reach me. Whatever sanity had once dwelled in these people had fled.

From the mob, a lone figure pushed his way through, an elderly man whose cheeks were glazed with blood, which flowed down to stain his gray beard. With his hands held up to the sky, offering the eyes he had clawed from his face in tribute, the man chanted in the language of the Void: *"Iàh! Iàh! Y'uh Shog'hyg Ny'gvzà!"*

The entire crowd joined the self-anointed priest, incanting the same words with frantic fervor over and over with increasing madness. I knew their meaning, recognized the litany, despite these pitiful beings' inability to utter them properly. It translated to, *"Hail! Hail! Our savior has come."* As the townspeople chanted, they mutilated themselves, clawing and biting at their flesh to offer their pain up to me.

The macabre energy washed over me like a warm bath, comforting me even as the human part of my consciousness recoiled with terror. My mind struggled to accept the fact that the praise they offered to me was intoxicating, making all of my senses glow with ecstasy, despite the atrocities I was witnessing. As I grappled with the implications of the scene playing out before me, a series of howls pulled me from the prayer-induced stupor. In unison, the crowd stopped chanting and snapped to face the lycans, who had recovered from my bellow and were moving to encircle them.

Across the courtyard, an enormous werewolf stood, half of his face a nightmarish pulp of scars where it had been thrust into a fire many moons ago. His undamaged eye burned with a feral rage, while the other was milky white, blinded when I forced it into a magical pyre atop the Keep's battlements. With a sneer, the werewolf raised his hand to point past the eerily silent, deathly still mob directly at me. "Ignore the livestock, kill the demon," he said in Lycan.

The cult sprang into action with unorthodox uniformity, rushing the werewolves while chanting, *"Kill the beasts, protect the savior,"* in broken Eldritch.

The wolves were caught off guard, startled by the sudden offensive from the villagers. Pitchforks stabbed into thick hide, and torches bashed against fur, burning the beasts. The momentary change in tide did not last long.

The wolves tore through their ranks with ease. Blood and severed limbs flew as the humans were ripped to shreds.

As my fledgling cult was decimated, I launched myself into the thick of the battle. Tooth, claw, and tendril met in a swirling dance of death as I fell upon the invaders. The sound of whimpering wolves mixed with the otherworldly chants of the dying humans, who refused to stop screaming *"Kill the beasts, protect the savior"* even as they were butchered.

The first two lycans fell at my feet after being

lanced by tendrils, which siphoned their spirits out, claiming the sweet life force as my own. The closest humans dove at the corpses, biting, scratching, and hacking away at them with knives, all while laughing and shrieking their insane incantation. A third werewolf leapt into the air above the chaos, only to be met with my tendrils, which tore the golden thread of fate from its chest, exploding it in a shower of gore.

Another wolf jumped at me, then another, and another, each meeting a similar fate: tentacles and death. The feeling of their life forces slithering up my tendrils and into my core was euphoric, orgasmic on a level my mortal form could never hope to experience. As I basked in ecstasy, a fourth lycan flanked me, swinging an enchanted war hammer at my side. The weapon found its mark with the unnatural force of a tectonic shift. The blow sent me smashing through the wall of a nearby shop.

The humans gasped in disbelief and attacked the werecreature, their madness-induced rage making them abandon any sense of self-preservation. The beast hit one with the hammer before going down, causing the peasant's torso to explode on impact. They mob dragged him down and tore him apart with their bare fingers, some shoving handfuls of pulpy flesh into their mouths with sadistic glee.

In a flash, the group of villagers was sent to the afterlife by an enraged female lycanthrope, who beheaded two of them with a single swipe of her claws. The remaining few met similar ends, as the wolf shredded their skin and bones with blinding speed. She knelt next to the fallen werewolf, howling as he began the painstaking process of regenerating.

I pushed the scorching pain out of my mind and shot a tendril out of the wreckage to impale the wifewolf through the heart, killing her instantly. Her fallen mate erupted in a geyser of blood as I plucked his golden strand, healing the wound in my side.

After moving the rubble of the collapsed structure, I looked down at utter, unrestrained chaos. Lycans and humans were strewn about in twisted heaps of limbs, blood, and steaming piles of entrails. The villagers incapacitated a handful of werecreatures but they had paid a heavy price for such an insignificant victory. Of the hundreds of peasants that had turned savage at my call, only a dozen remained. Despite their grotesque wounds, they still moved forward toward the invaders, reciting their mantra.

To my surprise, the elderly man was among the survivors, though his jaw was now missing, along with his eyes. Even without it, his severed tongue moved, and blood foamed from his mouth as he chanted. Somehow, his gurgling and absent tongue made the chant clearer, closer to true Eldritch.

The remaining lycans, having witnessed horrors beyond their comprehension, retreated to their leader's side. Despite their supernatural strength and endurance, the pack was worn out. The wholesale slaughter and the adrenaline that came with it had run dry. Panting and dripping with sweat, the heat from the burning building sapping their vitality, the wolves were leery of moving against the crazed villagers.

I stepped into the square, now entirely surrounded by fire, and returned to human form. The lead lycan's one good eye widened in disbelief as recognition flooded his mind.

"So, you remember me," I said, a sneer pulling at my lips.

The wolf touched the contracture scars that ran from what was once his ear down to the bottom of his jaw. "Impossible…" he whispered in Lycan, unable to fathom how I could have survived our first encounter.

A lesson imparted by D resurfaced as I watched my foe, and I resolved to twist the beast's code of honor and wounded pride against him.

"I challenge you," I snarled, my voice echoing across the chaos. "If you prevail, let my death be your due, and your forces may claim the village." I turned to the remaining lycans and continued, "If I win, the rest of you shall retreat, and you will carry word to your kin of the green-eyed demon and his wrath."

The villagers stopped their forward progression as I spoke. Turning to face me, they chanted once more. "*Iäh! Iäh! Y'uh Shog'hyg Ny'gvza!*"

With outstretched arms, I began absorbing the

praise from my newfound followers while inviting the werewolf to accept my deal.

"Do you accept my challenge, or will you cower and disgrace your clan?" I said, goading the chieftain to fight.

Slowly, the lycans stepped behind their leader, their gaze fixed unwaveringly upon me. They had watched me slaughter their comrades in ways that should be impossible, watched me take the full force of the enchanted war hammer and walk away unscathed. None among them were eager to face me now, none save for their leader, whose eye was burning with the desire for revenge.

"I accept your terms. Tonight, I feast on your bones."

I smiled, eyes glowing bright green as I released my tendrils into the air. "No. Tonight, I take your hide for a trophy."

With a bellow, the beast shot across the courtyard, swiping its hand at a villager as he passed. In a single, brutal motion, the man's torso was cleaved in two with a sickening squelch, his entrails spattering across the cobblestones as his upper body crashed into a burning structure. Even in the throes of such agony, his frenzied chant persisted, drowned out only by the roaring flames that devoured him.

Before the villager's legs had fallen to the ground, the wolf was upon me. The beast lunged forward, slashing his claws and snapping his jaws, only to find the space empty as I void-walked behind him.

The lycan spun on his heels and swiped at me again. This time, I caught his wrist with a single hand, halting the blow mere inches from my face. The shapeshifter's jaw dropped in disbelief, his functional eye widening as though I'd struck him in the groin. Still in my human guise, I offered the beast a mocking smile.

"You truly are a demon," the lycan whispered, his rancid breath assaulting my nostrils. "No man could do that."

"I may be a demon, but you are nothing. A meaningless speck of life, soon to be forgotten. The only thing your tribe will remember is how you fell before me, as all of your kind eventually will."

As the words left my lips, the beast snapped forward, jaws spread and ready to crush my skull. He would never have the chance. With a swift dodge, I launched myself, slamming my forehead into his blinded eye. A sickening crunch reverberated as his orbital bone shattered, scarred flesh rupturing and spraying warm blood across my face.

As the werecreature recoiled, my tendrils pierced the beast's wrists and ankles, lifting him into the air as he screamed. I looked over my shoulder at the remaining Hollow Tooth soldiers, eyes aglow with eldritch light, then ripped their leader into pieces.

I let the severed hunks of meat fall to the

ground, and began walking toward the last of the assault force.\

"Leave now. Tell every lycan you see what happened here. Should any of your kind breach our lands again, I will be here to meet them."

A massive gray werewolf strode forward, assuming command. To my surprise, the creature bowed its head in respectful acknowledgment of my victory. "Our pact stands, and it shall be honored. Every clan will hear of Dracula's new demon," it declared. The great alpha lowered his head further and asked, "May we reclaim the bodies of our fallen? They deserve a proper burial on our soil — not here, not among the blood drinkers."

I gave a slight nod, and the lycans gathered their dead then disappeared into the night.

With the battle over and the lycans gone, the courtyard fell into an eerie silence — the only sounds coming from the flames hungrily consuming the last of the buildings. Then I heard, or rather felt, it: a voice straining to speak despite grievous wounds.

I moved toward the sound and found the youth I'd glimpsed in the crowd, the one who saved the young boy, kneeling by a charred plank of wood. In his tiny hand, he clutched a splintered bone — one torn from his own leg — which he used to carve the burnt timber. There, emerging in rough strokes, was the image of an eye.

Through choked sobs, he chanted, *"Iäh.. Iäh...*

Y'uh Shog'hyg Ny'gvza…" all while scraping away. Above the eye, he etched a crude V, then delicate tendrils rising behind it.

When the final tendril was complete, he collapsed, releasing his final breath. As the life force fled his ravaged body, the symbol burst to life, glowing the same eldritch green as my eye. Some unspeakable part of my soul knew this symbol, down in the depths where whatever I once was dwelt, waiting to be awoken.

What remained of my human side recoiled from the Elder Sign, begging me to run from it. The eldritch part of me, however, was enthralled by the symbol and refused to allow my body to move. Transfixed by the sigil, I stared into the fathomless eye, my soul at war with itself. Silently screaming not to, I slowly reached down and brushed the young man aside to claim the very reason for his existence.

As I touched his lifeless shoulder, the strands of Fate stretched out before me, showing me a truth I was unwilling to accept. For countless lifetimes, his family had lived, bred, and died, all so he could carve a symbol no mortal mind should know. My symbol. Overwhelmed, unable or unwilling to understand the full implications of what I was seeing, I grasped the board.

Power surged from the symbol. Pure, unequaled, unparalleled power.

My body convulsed as if it were struck by a thousand bolts of lightning, forcing me to cry out in a garbled mixture of human scream and eldritch screech as my body began transforming against my will. My skin, black as the darkest corners of the Void, soaked up the energy radiating from the symbol with the force of a star exploding to life.

All of my senses overloaded and every fiber of my existence shrieked with excruciating agony as my body struggled to absorb the sheer volume of eldritch essence. Unable to release the board from my grasp, I began to float into the air, which boiled and hissed around me.

Just as the pain became unbearable, searing magma racing across every nerve in my body, the energy exploded outward in a nova. The corpses of the villagers evaporated in an instant, along with their flaming homes.

Nothing was left standing in the town: not a single building, tree, flame, or blade of grass.

Chapter 43
Weight of Oblivion

I stood within the crater created by the mass ejection of eldritch essence for what may have been hours before the distant sounds of marching pulled me from my stunned stupor. The charred, sigil-bearing wood was still clutched in my hands, but the otherworldly green glow had faded away.

The sound of horse hooves pounding dirt and bat wings beating against the night air was drawing ever near, so I gathered my resolve enough to void-walk from the cataclysmic scene back to Hojo's laboratory. The Doctor wasn't at his observation perch where I had left him, nor was he anywhere on that level. When I finally tracked him down, I found him again on the upper experimentation floor, dissecting a gargantuan spider.

"I trust you saved the helpless villagers?" he said, his tone aloof.

"Not quite," I replied.

Hojo, setting down his utensils and looking up from his work, froze at the sight of the wood in my hand.

"What is that?" he demanded, a rare tremor of unease threading his words.

As I turned the board to face him, his eyes grew wide as they beheld the Elder Sign carved there. Hojo stepped back, never looking away from the sigil, and trembled. The Doctor, who was known to have no emotion, was terrified.

"This… this isn't meant for you. Not yet…" Looking up from the board to me, pupils fully dilated, Hojo's hands began shaking violently as he reached for a table to steady himself. "Where did you get *that*?"

I recounted the events at the village, the way my presence twisted minds, how the desperate cries and frantic prayers took shape beneath my power. With each detail, Hojo's fear deepened until he finally slumped onto a stool, his usual impassivity shattered.

"This is all wrong… Did you observe anything… unusual?" he pressed.

"What do you mean? The people were crazed and praying to me. Everything about what just happened was unusual!"

The fear in Hojo's eyes shifted, transforming into anger. "Were there other *eldritch* forces present?"

Until that moment, I hadn't entertained the idea that other entities from the Void might come to this plane of existence. Sight was the only other one I had met, and he was entirely disinterested in this realm. "No. Just me."

"Good." Hojo seemed to relax ever so slightly at the news, though his eyes darted around the lab nervously. "The energy released tonight will attract unwanted attention. You must not summon your avatar again until we are sure no other entity is searching for you. You are not yet ready to face an Old One... or worse."

"An Old One?" My voice wavered, and for a moment, I felt a chill as Hojo's terror seeped into my mind.

"Ancient beings as far above Gods as Gods are beyond men. They possess power beyond imagining, the likes of which you have only sampled. Until you have evolved to higher standing, any confrontation with one would be *worse* than fatal."

"If they are so omnipotent, why would they search for me?" I asked, my thoughts a jumbled mess.

Hojo rose, regaining his composure as he stepped uncomfortably close to me. "You already know too much. Your elder sign was never meant to be revealed until the stars were right — centuries from now. This changes everything and I cannot risk telling you more. *Do not* use your Avatar unless absolutely necessary. There are fates worse than death, and there are entities who will visit them upon you if they can. Do you understand?"

I nodded, even though I did not understand at all. After a few uncomfortable minutes of watching Hojo calculate the ramifications of the night's events in silence, I asked if my void-walking abilities were also off limits. Much to my relief, he explained it was such a basic skill that using it should be fine, so long as I refrained from traveling beyond our current plane of existence.

Before I could leave, Hojo grabbed my arm, careful not to touch the burnt wood. "One final note, Vision. By no chance can Dracula be allowed to see this symbol. Ever. Should he happen upon it, our plans will all be for naught." Hojo's tone was no longer clinical or controlled, but dark and conspiratorial. Whatever this symbol was, it had shaken the very foundations of the man.

Eager to escape the weight of the night's events, I void-walked to my hidden lair and hid the sigil beneath my cot, which I collapsed on, exhausted from everything that had transpired. My eyes drifted to Natka's wooden doll, a grim reminder of the price paid for my existence.

I drifted off to a fitful sleep where visions of her last moments played out again and again. The tormenting dreams continued until somewhere beyond the black canvass of sleep, a voice shimmered into being. Faint at first, like a silver thread drawn taut against the Void, the melody pulled at my consciousness with haunting familiarity. I recognized it. Knew it, as though it had once rocked me to sleep in a cradle of stars.

The voice flowed like crystalline waters over marble hills in a language as old as the Eldritch I spoke, but it came to me warped, refracted through the distance between realms. Notes bent like light through broken glass. Try as I might, I could not understand the words. Still, the emotion, the longing behind them, reverberated through me. I reached out to it, to *her*, but the more I tried, the more it receded. She remained just beyond the veil, like a name on the tip of the tongue or the warmth of a hand long removed from the chest.

When I woke, all I wanted was to return to her. Instead, I found myself once again looking up at a wooden doll whose lifeless eyes stared back at me. The weight of my reality crashed down once more, crushing the fleeting peace of the woman I couldn't quite see or remember had given me.

Hunger gnawed at me despite the knots in my stomach, so I rummaged through the remnants of the supplies I had brought into my little sanctum and settled on some stale bread and cheese. The quaint meal did little to ease my suffering mind or the pit of despair I was sinking into.

Desperate for distraction, I resolved to check

on Chirp, hoping my little friend might ease the crushing loneliness. But when I emerged outside the cave where I'd once waited for her, I found only a broken spear and a dead bird impaled on its tip. Ochre droplets stained the ground in a silent testament to recent violence.

In a panic, I stuck my head into the cave and cried out for my miniature companion, only to be greeted by the hollow echo of my voice. Quickly, I dashed to the stream where I had speared a fish for her. Not finding her there, I broke out into a full run to the forest where Chirp had been hunting. Again, all I found was disappointment and worry. The entire closure was barren of life.

The glacial dread, icy fingers tracing my veins, melted away and transformed into a searing inferno of understanding. Hojo.

I teleported to his side in the laboratory, intent on beating answers from him if I had to. "Where is she?"

The Doctor was once again himself, an emotionless creature, unimpressed by my anger. Without looking up from his work, he said, "She, who?"

Hands balled into fists at my side, I stormed up to him, leaning down until I was nose to nose with his porcelain mask. "You damn well know who. *Where is she?*"

"The goblyn? You corrupted the environment

and thus ruined the study. Therefore, the specimen was euthanized prematurely."

Rage ignited in my eyes, the familiar green glow reflecting on Hojo's mask. "Bring her back."

"I cannot. The reanimation process can only be completed once." Hojo's eyes narrowed as he looked at me quizzically, unable to comprehend my attachment to what he viewed as nothing more than another tool to be used and discarded.

"Then use necrogen," I demanded, unwilling to accept that my friend was truly gone.

"There is nothing left to inject; the remains have been incinerated. Even if I could, the results would not bring about the effect you desire. The specimen would have returned as a mindless zombie, not whatever it was you seem to have grown an attachment to."

The world swirled around me in a dizzying blur of muted colors and disorienting sounds. My skin prickled with a cold sweat, a stark contrast to the trembling in my limbs. Jaw clenched to the point I feared my teeth might shatter, I void-walked to the only other source of comfort I could think of: Lilyth's coffin. Upon discovering it sealed shut and unchanged, I engaged in the only pastime available to me, one that many men have lost themselves to when their will to survive has been ground to dust.

I returned to the room where Grygor had first

taken me, found the sickly yellow bottle, and drank the noxious liquid to drown my sorrow. Chirp was gone, and, like Natka and the youth from the village, I was to blame. Everything I had ever cared for had become a poison, tainting my veins and killing me from the inside.

I leaned the bottle back and swallowed as much as I could, which led to a coughing fit as the fumes burnt my lungs and the fluid seared my throat. It didn't take long for the alcohol to cauterize my emotional wounds, as I blacked out in a puddle of vomit.

Upon returning to the waking world, my head felt as though the dwarves responsible for crafting the spirits had been busy mining away at my skull while I slept. The meager light from the torches in the room served only as daggers piercing my eye sockets when I finally peeled my face from the dried muck. Squeezing my eyes shut, I attempted to sit up, only to discover the world was still very much swimming around me.

The churning in my stomach made me heave until my ribs felt as though a werewolf had smashed them yet again and I collapsed into the mess, drifting off into the bliss of unconsciousness once more. For how many days on end this continued, I cannot say. Each time I would sober up enough to think about my lot in this new life, I would drink again until I blacked out.

By the collection of empty bottles I had amassed around myself by the time Grygor shook me awake with his boot, I can only assume I had spent the better part of a month drunk and hiding from my self-pity. My mood didn't improve after being jolted awake from the Void to find a towering Hyena above me.

"Looks like I missed out 'n all the fun. Wha' a shame."

Unable to do so much as lift my head, I mumbled out a slurry of obscenities and attempted to ignore him.

"This won' do. Ya gotta be presen'able for yer bride boy. Up 'n at em." With a grunt, Grygor lifted me from the cesspool of bodily waste I had created and flung me over his shoulder.

Too weak and drunk to fight back, I allowed him to haul me off to whatever fate he had in mind. Preferably, I thought, one with a violent end. Instead, I found myself dunked head-first into freezing water, which shocked me into a semi-sober state.

I shot up from the frigid water, eyes wide and bloodshot, and gasped for air before glaring at the Hyena with seething hatred. "What is wrong with you?"

"Wha? You want L'yth to see ya like this af'er she's been 'sleep all this time?" he retorted with a cocky grin.

That grin, stretching ear to ear, showed he was enjoying the moment far more than his excuse let on and I was ready to fight him over it until the fog in my mind cleared enough for his words to sink in.

"Lilyth is awake?" I sputtered through chattering teeth.

"Mhm. 'N'ya better clean off 'fore ya go see her. Though' the servants' bath would be better for ya, 'sidering yer sorry state." His smile grew impossibly wider, revealing his unnaturally pointed teeth, as he reached down to slap me on the back. "Mus' admit though, I'm impressed by 'ow much ya drank."

Submerged again in the frigid water, I stripped off the soured clothes and scrubbed the filth from my body. Then, a tsunami of guilt rose in my chest as I realized Lilyth had awoken and I had been too lost in oblivion to be there. Yet another failure to add to my growing list of reasons to loathe myself, I thought.

Grygor, catching the anguish in my eyes, softened his tone unexpectedly. "Don' bus' your balls o'er na bein' there when she woke. It woulda ended bad for both of ya, I reckon. Mas'er 'as her feedin' on livestock, 'n she's already drained a damn village worth," he said before slapping me on the back again. "Tha' coulda been you."

During all the times I had visited her casket while she slept, I hadn't once considered the fact that a vampiress who had suffered a near-fatal wound would require substantial quantities of blood upon waking, or that such a ravenous appetite would cause her to attack any living being within sight to satiate it. Suddenly, I was quite happy I hadn't been there when her crimson eyes opened. Had she attacked me, I could have stopped her, but as Grygor said, it wouldn't have ended well for either of us.

"When she's ready to see ya, the Mas'er will find ya. 'In the meantime, I'll get ya some clothes. Then, we dine. Ya look like a 'alf-staved peasant."

As he walked toward the door, I called out his name, causing him to look back at me over his shoulder. "Ya?"

"Thank you."

He paused for a moment in the doorway before nodding his head with a grunt and leaving me to bathe.

Once the foulness was washed away and I was once again garbed in the black, hooded garment I favored, Grygor led me to the Dining Hall, where a fresh batch of servants brought us food and wine. To my overwhelming disappointment, D and the Brides were nowhere to be seen.

However, for the first time since I had met the beast, I almost enjoyed the company of the Hyena. I had been alone and miserable for so long that any sort of camaraderie was most welcome, even his. That, mixed with the lightning buzzing beneath my skin over the thought of seeing Lilyth again, had put me in a most agreeable disposition.

As we ate, Grygor recounted his time with the family in the Alvah stronghold, focusing on his debauchery. Tales of pleasure slaves and salacious encounters with a shocking number of partners initially entertained me but soon grew tiresome.

Desperate for a diversion, I broached another subject. "So, what of the wedding? Is everything set?"

With a single gulp, he emptied his flagon of wine, then signaled a servant girl to refill it. "Ya, I s'ppose i's gonna 'appen. Why the Mas'er would give 'is princess to that wretched lil' cunt is beyond me."

I laughed at his distaste for the Alvah boy, realizing we shared a common ground there. In all of my time watching Guile, the arrogant little prick had created quite the impression, and not a good one.

"Wa's so funny?" Grygor asked, his gruff face twisted in a state of confusion that was comically unusual for him, causing me to laugh even harder.

"I think we finally have something in common, that's all."

The Hyena's face twisted into its all-too-familiar smile, though this time it lacked the diabolical undertone usually present. "We're gonna be friends, you 'n I. Gah a rough start, t' be sure, but not'in we can't look past. Yer family now, an' we take care o' our own." He reached over and squeezed my shoulder. "B'sides, yer far better company than the Hand Mas'er wipes his arse with."

I laughed at the insult to the Death Knight and nodded. I wasn't sure I could ever count Grygor as a friend, much less family, after the atrocities he had inflicted upon me, but he was a far sight better than the cursed one so far as conversation was concerned.

"So, when does the big wedding happen?" I asked, curious.

With strings of flesh dangling from his mouth as he looked up from a massive hunk of meat, Grygor shrugged. "Not fer a long time. Princess is too young fer the ritual. The 'ouses 'ave a lot to sort out first too; big deal bringin'em together like this."

I wanted to know more about the event itself, especially this ritual, as I suspected D intended for me to take Lilyth off of his hands as a bride of my own. Vampiric weddings, I presumed, had to be every bit as alien to me as the rest of their society had been to this point, and I wanted some insight into what I would be getting myself into. Unfortunately, Grygor didn't seem the least bit interested in speaking on the subject any more than he already had.

Just as I was about to press the matter further, a portal tore open. The Hand stepped forth, scanning the room until his fiery gaze fell upon me.

"The Master wishes to speak with you. Follow me."

Excitedly, I set down my cup and dashed to the dead man. If D wanted my presence, it could only mean Lilyth was ready to see me. Despite everything the vampiress had put me through, all the torment and anguish, the thought of seeing her once more sent a wave of heat down my spine. So much had gone wrong in my life since being brought to this place. At last I finally had some good coming to even the scales.

For old times' sake, I followed the Death Knight through his portal which opened up into the private chamber where I had first sat with D. He was in the same chair where we shared our first drink, another round already poured and waiting for me. To my dismay, Lilyth was not with him, nor were his other Brides.

Dracula, motioning to the chair opposite, invited me to sit. "It has been much too long since we last spoke. I hear you have once again saved my lands from the lycan traitors, though there were... complications... that cost me a village."

I nodded, then sat as instructed. The smell of the liquor D had poured made my stomach churn, threatening to revisit the meal I had just consumed to the world outside my stomach, but I took a sip anyway.

"My avatar has adverse effects upon humans," I admitted, still unsure what had actually happened. "Unfortunately, the madness that overtook their minds led to the destruction of the entire village. I am sorry for that."

D waved his hand to dismiss the issue. "Your warning allowed my forces to rout the invasion and save the other farms. Losing one is a slight matter when weighed against what could have been lost had you not taken action. Besides, the village was burned to the ground. My troops assumed the lycans did it out of spite. No one suspects a thing. Once again, I owe you a debt of gratitude."

I decided to play a little game with D, inspired by my observations of his meeting with Alaric. "And the negotiations with the Alvah family? Are they progressing?" I asked, skirting the subject we both knew I wanted to speak on.

"As well as expected. Soon their family shall grace our home with their presence, at which time you will, unfortunately, be forced to stay underground in the cave you fashioned. We don't want our guests to learn of your existence prematurely." A sly smile pulled at the corners of D's lips when he spoke.

He had caught on to my little game and played along. Moreover, he had revealed he knew about my sanctuary beneath the Castle, something I had told no one but Hojo about.

"Of course. It is comfortable enough for an extended stay. I will, however, require a steady supply of mortal food. We don't want me to become hungry. There's no telling what I might decide to consume if I do."

D flashed me a wicked smile, one shining with the pride of a father. "You are a quick study, Vision. Bravo. I cannot wait to watch you decimate my Court with your mind."

"Speaking of the Court, at what point do you

intend to announce my presence to them?" I asked, genuinely curious about how long I must remain a closely guarded secret.

D sat back in his chair, swirling the liquor in his glass. "Not until the stars are right. That is customary for creatures of the Void, is it not?"

"So I've been told," I said with a sigh, realizing this meant I would likely remain D's secret for a very, very long time.

Dracula, realizing his words had lessened my spirits, leaned forward to refill my glass. "You have not been here long. Soon, you will discover that the years pass by more like days as time marches on. But for now, I believe you will be happy to learn that Lilyth is awake and asking for you."

Try as I might to conceal it, the joy of the moment broke through my facade of stoicism. "She is okay? Fully healed?"

"She is. No trace of the wound remains, not even so much as a scar. Once her appetite has been fully satiated, I will allow her to see you. I will not risk her trying to feed on you until after a marriage ritual has been completed, should such a thing be written in the stars for you."

I will admit that I was inexplicably smitten with the temptress at this time, despite a thousand reasons to hate her. Still, marriage wasn't something I was sure I wanted then, especially if it would include being turned into a blood slave for the woman. I had seen how such a fate played out for the humans in the Castle, and it wasn't an admirable end by any means.

I hid my misgivings about a potential marriage, or so I thought anyhow, and grinned as I imagined a love-sick idiot would. I was overjoyed to know she was safe and still among the so-called living, even if I wasn't yet convinced I wanted her to be my wife.

"Thank the Gods she is safe," I said, hoping that I could avoid raising D's suspicions that I may not be entirely sold on taking his wife as my own.

D sat in silence for many moments studying me, and I did what I could to remain calm, focusing on my breathing to steady my heartbeat, which I knew he could hear.

"Very good Vision. You are indeed a quick learner." Dracula clicked his pointed fingernail on the rim of his glass, smirking at me. "You've already begun to hide your emotions and control your body to keep your true feelings hidden. I am quite impressed. Half of the nobles in my court haven't learned to control themselves like this, and they've been alive for thousands of years."

"I apologize," I stammered out. "I am fond of Lilyth, but… I am not so sure I am ready to be married just yet. Besides, I cannot imagine what a wedding in this place is like."

Dracula laughed at my words, fangs extending as he did. "No, I don't imagine you can. It differs greatly from the simple affairs in your previous home, though the result stands the same. You become tethered to a woman who delights in spending the rest of eternity making your life difficult."

This time, I laughed. "You aren't selling me on the idea," I said with a smile.

"Some marriages are more rewarding than others, I will admit," he sighed, pushing away dark thoughts of his own. "You are still young. There is no need to rush into such things, though Lilyth may disagree with that sentiment."

"For argument's sake, tell me what a marriage ceremony is like for your kind?" I asked, taking another sip of my drink despite the protest from my gut.

"It depends on the couple and their status, but they all include a binding ceremony of some sort, and they all include blood. Some choose for their ritual to be a private affair. Others make a spectacle of the ordeal. The binding of my house to the Alvah shall be the latter. Days of celebration followed by a ritual with thousands in attendance to watch the union of our lands."

"What is the ritual?"

He sighed once again and peered into the depths of his glass. "For my family, it includes the exchange of a sacred rose. Both the bride and groom will pierce their flesh with a thorn. As their blood conjoins, so to do their destinies become as one, binding their souls together forever. The ritual is performed for each marriage a vampire has, though the magic only works the first time."

"That is a commitment of considerable magnitude," I said, suddenly understanding why D was so distraught over the loss of his first wife. "You must miss her very much."

"I wake each night feeling as though a part of my soul is missing... because it is." Tearing his gaze from the swirling liquor in his glass to look into my eyes, D forced a smile. "Enough of this. Tonight is a celebration, not the time to dredge up old wounds." Dracula offered a toast, raising his glass into the air. "To the beginning of a new forever, may the stars align for us all."

Chapter 44
Written in the Stars

I spent the following handful of nights in the den with Dracula, discussing the union of his family with the Alvah bloodline and what it would entail. Mostly, I was simply happy to have someone to talk with, following months in solitude while he was gone. I also relished learning about the politics of his court. As ever, I was a sponge soaking up all the information D could provide.

During this time, D explained that once the Alvah contingent arrived, I would be forced to stay underground. He was adamant that their family not learn of my presence. While having humans in the Castle wasn't unusual by any means, having one in particular that was off limits for feeding would raise questions D didn't want to answer.

The nights lingered until the Alvah family's arrival was close at hand, and I remained without even a glimpse of Lilyth. Knowing that her presence would be expected when the guests arrived, my heart sank. Would I even have the chance to see her before they arrived?

After my early evening meal, I went to the balcony where the assassins struck and sent Lilyth into a vampiric coma. There, under a moonless night sky, I gazed upward, absentmindedly counting the stars.

The imposing darkness eased my mind, each speck of light a beacon calling me back to a home I couldn't remember, where such light was exceptionally rare. Still, counting the flickering dots brought a strange peace. With my eyes relaxed, faint golden strands crisscrossed the sky, connecting each dot and the countless planets and stars beyond. It was a beauty unmatched, something no other mortal or immortal could ever hope to witness in their lives.

So lost was I among the stars that I failed to notice a new presence on the balcony. It wasn't until an unseen hand slid across my chest that my consciousness was thrust back into my body.

Startled, I looked down to find my shirt moving as invisible fingers danced upon the muscles beneath.

"I dreamed of you," a voice said, shattering the silence of the night. Lilyth's hand ran down my chest and over my abdomen, then across my side and up my back. "Each time you visited my coffin, I could sense you. Smell you. Oh, how I longed to feel you against me once more…"

I shut my eyes, surrendering my senses to bask in her presence, my skin shivering at her touch. Though I couldn't see her, the scent of her pheromones filled my nostrils. She ran her fingers playfully back down my back, then up my arms, dragging the points of her nails across my skin.

"My sisters told me what you did, how you killed those who hurt me. Slaughtered their whole family…" She moaned as she said this, a sound that warmed my blood and sent my heart racing. Though my eyes were closed, I knew she was biting her lip as she did when making such sounds.

"They told me what you are, what you became… a living… breathing… God…" she whispered in my ear, before placing the lobe in her mouth and sucking on it. Slowly, she pulled away, holding the bit of flesh between her lips until it slipped free of her grasp. "I intend to spend the rest of eternity worshipping you."

With the unnatural strength of the undead, Lilyth spun me around, lifting me into the air as she did. She flew us against the castle wall, slamming my back into the cold stone, but it wasn't the impact or the chilly night air that made my flesh quake.

I had let my guard down, allowing myself to

drown in the vampiress's intoxicating power. All of her charms were in full effect, the pheromones designed to overpower a man's will, the innate magical glamour possessed by all of her kind that bends the minds of their victims washing away all the sorrows I had wallowed in for so long. In that moment, I belonged to her, and there was nothing else in the whole of the multiverse.

The fiery woman I had feared, hated, and inexplicably loved pressing her body against mine then kissed me with such passion that I nearly missed the fact that something was wrong. Very wrong.

My eyes shot open, and I saw the Lilyth I had known reflected in the yellow orbs I had waited so long to see once again. The rest of the woman, however, was no longer familiar to me.

My heart, which had beat only for her moments before, stopped dead in my chest and fell like a stone into the pit of my stomach. The voluptuous body that had ravaged me time and again was now barren, a pale shadow of what once was. As I stared at her, my face contorting in an unsettling mixture of confusion and horror, Lilyth unleashed the full might of her powers upon me. But it was too late.

I pushed her away, my mind grappling with the shock of what my eyes were seeing. I wanted it to be a lie, some illusion the vampiress had crafted to play with my head, as she was so fond of doing. Unfortunately, what I was seeing was the unforgiving truth. Her body had reverted to her youth as it healed from the assassin's poison.

"Vision… I have waited so long to have you back… *do not reject me*," she said in a voice so much smaller than it once was, yet still carrying the same terrifying power. "*You are mine.*"

I stepped backward, my head swimming as though I was drunk once again, trying to distance myself from the abomination before me.

Her lips quivered, eyes beginning to pool with blood. She pleaded with me to stay, to ignore her form and remember who she was. She promised it was only temporary, that in time she would grow back into the body I had known, but my mind was numb and her words were lost to my ears.

"I…I can't do this…" I said, as I took another step away.

Crimson rivers cascaded down her cheeks as she watched me retreat. "You are m-mine…" she whimpered. Then, her slight frame shook with rage as her eyes sunk inward and her features became sharp and bat-like. "YOU ARE MINE!" she screamed as I disappeared into the Void.

The darkness swallowed me, returning me to my underground sanctuary, whose stone walls closed around me like a tomb. Neither it nor the Void could silence the voice ringing in my mind. *You are mine.* The words followed me like a curse.

Cold realization set in as I collapsed on my cot, curling up like a wounded animal. The woman I had longed for, the one I had imagined reuniting with in so many dreams, was gone. What remained was a cruel echo. A child's mask stretched across the face of someone I loved, twisted by powers I did not yet understand.

I did not weep or cry out. Instead, I lie motionless, disoriented as if the axis of the world had shifted, leaving me adrift. The damp, chill air pressed down, sinking into my bones, mirroring the heart frozen in my chest.

The next many moons were spent in total darkness, alone in my underground quarters. There was no will in me to move, no desire to train or spy or even to eat. I simply existed, breathing, blinking, and remembering.

I knew Dracula was aware of my little den now, and I admit some small, stupid part of me hoped he would come. However, that was not to be. The days passed in silence. He had a kingdom to tend to, alliances to forge, and guests to entertain. My collapse was a private affair, irrelevant to the immediate concerns of his immortal court.

True to his word, D had food delivered to me each day, but it sat untouched and rotting. No matter how appetizing the meals appeared, they turned to ash when I attempted to eat them. Even my tongue turned against me. I had become so lost that nothing held any joy, not even the exotic fruits D had acquired to lift my spirits.

The odd trinkets I had collected failed to shimmer, the pride I once held for them gone. Even the Natka's doll had seemed to lose its meaning, no longer bringing me any comfort. Instead, the hollow eyes peered down at me with judgement, multiplying the guilt I wallowed in. Memories of all that had gone so terribly wrong replayed in my mind over and over again while I stared blankly at the wooden effigy. Grandmother, Katri, Natka, Chirp, and now Lilyth. The sum of these sorrows was too great a burden for me to bear, and their combined weight was dragging me to my demise.

Sleep, which came rarely, wasn't any better on my mind than my waking thoughts. The dreams that plagued my unconscious hours were consumed with anguish.

Upon waking from one such bout of tortuous rest, I found that D had visited me while I slept. He left behind a curious package of gifts: a book, a note, and a hearty meal fashioned in the closest thing his coffers could get to the food prepared in the mountain village whence he had rescued me.

My desk held a bowl of steaming venison stew; its warmth suggested either enchantment or his recent exit. Either way, curiosity took hold of my senses and beat back the gloom which clouded my every moment long enough for me to drag my famished body up and into the chair. The earthy smells wafting up from the stew made my stomach ache with hunger, but the thought of eating anything after so many days of fasting made me sick. I pushed the bowl away and grabbed the note that had been penned with the very ink I had used while spying upon the lycan hordes.

"My friend - I have anxiously awaited a moment when I could escape my duties with our guests and speak to you in person, but it is evident you need rest more than my company. Once again, I have done you harm, this time by failing to prepare you for the state in which you would find my Bride. I apologize for the shock you must feel to find her as such. I will speak to her on your behalf and explain that it may take some time for you to accept how she has changed, as it will take her some time to return to what you once knew. Please accept my most humble apologies and this tome. I believe you shall find that we share a deeper bond than you currently understand after reading through its pages. I shall return to speak with you the very next chance I get. In the meantime, try to eat. You appear haggard. - Your Friend, D."

Something about the letter lifted the heaviness pressing down upon my shoulders just enough to allow my body to remember its needs. The dull ache in my stomach twisted, piercing my senses like a blade. I set the note back down atop the book with unusual care, as if disturbing it might break whatever fragile spell it cast upon me. Then I turned to the stew and ate with ravenous urgency, each bite grounding my senses back in the present. When the bowl was empty, I sank back onto the cot. Tension bled from my limbs and I slept without resistance.

When I woke, the cavern seemed less oppressive than before and the food in my stomach cried out for company. I ventured out to find my daily allotment of provisions, then appeased my stomach's desires and returned to my desk to reread the note from D. This time, however, when I picked up the piece of parchment, I saw the cover of the book beneath it and the air rushed from my lungs.

Carved into the finest of bleached leather was a perfect depiction of the statue I had seen hidden away in the forbidden marble room.

Hands trembling, I set the letter aside and reached for the book.

As my fingertips brushed the cover, the cavern violently shook, rattling my desk and sending my collection of baubles flying. The inkwell D had used the previous night spilled, sending its contents cascading toward the stark white tome. The fluid, however, stopped just short of the cover, instead flowing around the book as though some invisible force was holding it at bay.

The convulsions continued to increase in magnitude until I feared the very ceiling might collapse upon me, the roar of quaking earth pounding on my eardrums until an all too familiar voice stilled the chaos. Her voice. As the melodic sound washed over me, the rumbling ceased. The room fell still, leaving behind two words echoing through my mind.

"Find me."

About the Author

A. T. Hansen is a lifelong fan of all things gothic and cosmic horror – if it has fangs or tentacles, he loves it. Born and raised in Colorado where he obtained a bachelor's degree in small business management, he eventually made his way to the great state of Texas where he currently resides.

When he isn't reading or writing, Mr. Hansen enjoys delving into dungeons and fighting dragons (or painting miniatures and terrain to do so). His other hobbies include crafting dioramas to display his extensive collection of action figures, drawing indescribable abominations, and cosplay.

www.facebook.com/chroniclesofvision
www.tiktok.com/@a.t.hansen_author
For updates on future novels, projects, and public appearances:
the-chronicles-of-vision.mailerpage.io/